GW00455997

THE SHADOW WAR

THE SECOND MORTARAN NOVEL

MADELAINE TAYLOR

www.madelainetaylor.com

CONTENTS

INTRODUCTION

A long time ago, in a bedroom far far away, a story haunted my dreams. Night after night for years and years the world of Mortara invaded my sleep. So one day I sat down and began to write the story that just wouldn't leave me alone. A single book that I would write and self publish. A daunting task, perhaps, as I'd never written much of anything before, but one I was sure I could achieve or, you know, have a go at.

But then that book, and the characters within, conspired to become two books and that now has conspired to be three... I hope three... And so what you hold in your hands now is the second book of Mortara. A book that I thought would just be the final act of the Elemental Stone. And there is still yet more to come.

Anyway, it seems that some of the wonderful people that have read The Elemental Stone are not people that would normally pick up a fantasy book. And while that makes me happy, it presents a challenge that I hadn't taken into consideration. People unfamiliar with the genre may not understand certain things in my books. So here is a very brief guide and a secret.

Firstly, there are fae in my book, some writers call them "Elven races" some "Elementals" and some "Fairies" though fairies tend to be a lot shorter than the fae in my book. In this case that refers to the first children of the eight gods. Each race of fae have different abilities and strengths, which I explain as I go, but all are fairly close to humans in appearance. Think Legolas in the Lord of the Rings films.

Most of the fae come from our own mythologies. The Dryad you may recognise as spirits of the trees. The Nymph their freshwater cousins and the Mer their saltwater equivalent. The Sylph aren't as well known, but they too come from much older mythologies than my own, and are spirits of the air. The Noam, well, the noam are spirits of the earth, the stones, rocks and dirt beneath our feet. And finally the Sgàil are the spirits of the shadows that surround us. I say "finally" but if you go back to the second paragraph you'll know this tale is not yet complete! I have secrets!!!

Talking of secrets... The language of the fae, when they aren't speaking english, is Scots Gàidhlig (or close to it, I do tend to make stuff up). And as the Fae are the first born and got to naming things long before the humans that means the seasons, days and months are all in gàidhlig too. Some other "human words" use the language of the fae as well. So, if you don't recognise a word and you just have to know, google translate may help.

Now, it's been a while between books so would you like a little refresher? Not the sweet... Put that down! I meant would you like to know who the main cast are and what they're up to? Well, if the answer is yes read on. If not you can skip the rest of the intro and get stuck right into the story!

If you haven't read The Elemental Stone (tsk) then these are very quick and vague spoilers...

Lana – Our main character. A farm girl that got caught up in some horrendous things and had to leave home in a hurry. She entered the woodlands at the heart of Mortara and was changed. Discovering that she had some of the abilities of the Dryad and Sylph – shaping wood, travelling by tree and surviving great falls unharmed – she helped spoil the plot of foreign kidnappers and got to meet the queen... two queens, in fact, one dryad and one human. Now she is trusted by both and is on the way to start a new life in the human queen's palace.

Selene – A young sylph who loves history and learning. She met Lana on the road to Southport and became embroiled in her adventures. Now she works at the Great Library with the Lore Keepers and Lore Masters of Mortara. She's very clever.

Tinnion – A human hunter who also met Lana on the road. After the adventures of TES she was named steward of the stead that Lana grew up in and now resides there alongside Lana's family.

Brighid – A human warrior. Skilled with the sword she won a tournament in Southport and became a member of a secret order of warriors. She travelled north with Wren (a sylph warrior) part way through TES and discovered the plot that now plays out in this book. Though she barely survived that discovery due to an attack by the sgàil. She too initially met Lana on the road to Southport.

Cat (Caitlin) – A young thief in the city of Southport and the person who discovered the fiendish plot of the kidnappers in TES. She eventually destroyed the den of thieves that had been her family and now runs it as an orphanage.

Laywyn – A retired soldier that met all of the above, except Cat and Wren, on the road to Southport. He fell for Brighid and is currently looking after her stately home in the city. He also helped Cat to overthrow the den of thieves.

Yorane – The brother of Wren and a sylph warrior that helped Lana defeat the evil kidnappers. He was made a royal guard at the end of TES.

Daowiel – A dryad princess and warrior that watched over Lana as she grew up and saved her life in the Heartwood. Now a dear friend, she is travelling with Lana to the human queen's palace.

So, there you go. Now you're more or less all caught up and can jump right on into The Shadow War. I hope you enjoy it!

Falcon
Isles
Mortara

Lochmead
Northfort
Glamithren

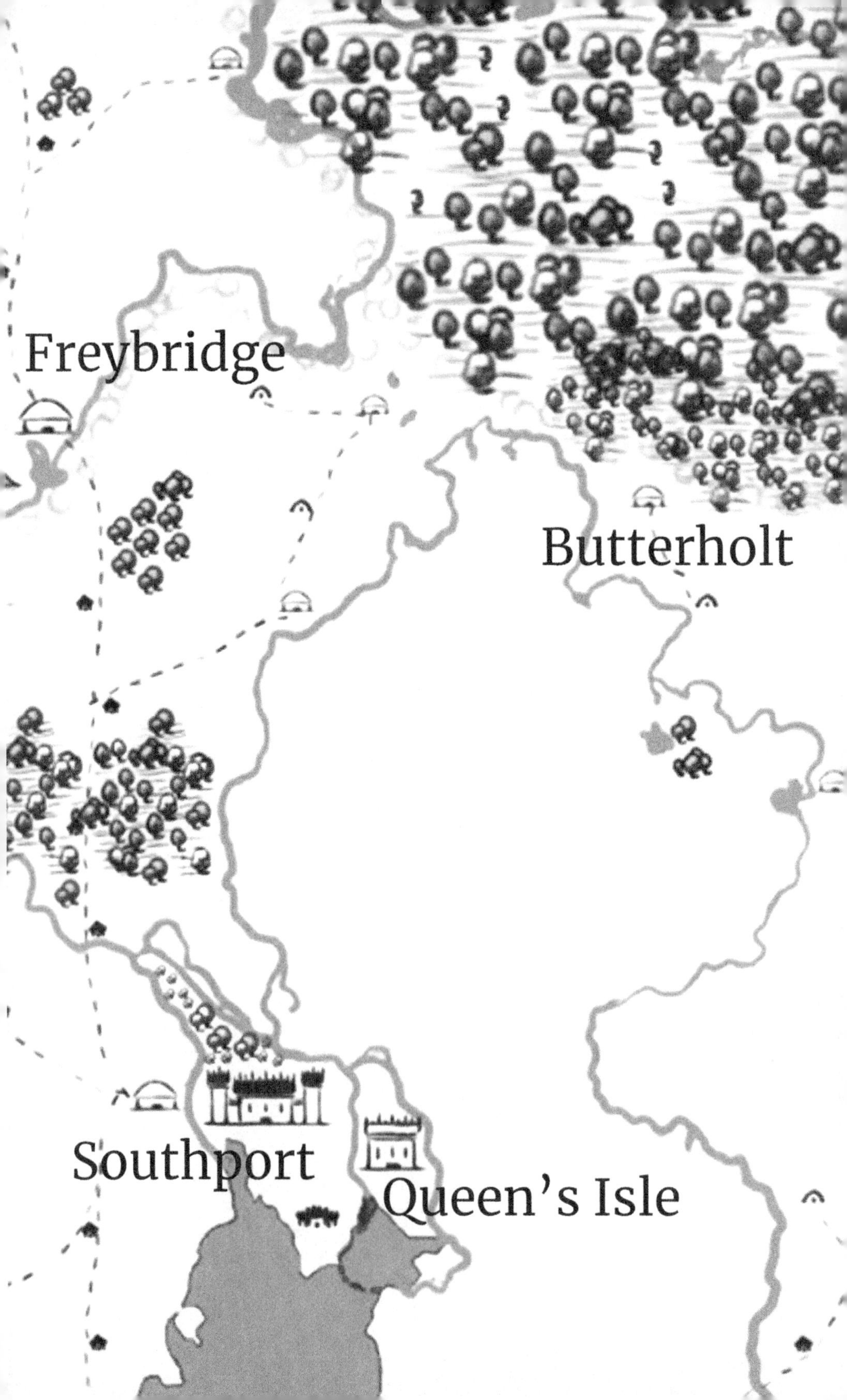
Freybridge
Butterholt
Southport
Queen's Isle

PROLOGUE

The Battle of Sgailburgh

It was cold and dark. The winter sun, shrouded in grey cloud, was pale and failed to warm the earth. There were fires burning in the village square, surrounded by people trying to warm their bodies before getting back to their work. The long shadow cast by the fortress temple of Sgailburgh stretched across the village and chilled the hearts of those living there.

They would leave if they could, those terrified villagers. Flee to Northfort and the tuath lord's protection. Indeed, some hundreds had tried down the decades. Though none had ever escaped the plains at the feet of the Sgàil mountains. For the shadows watched them, never seen, never heard until it was too late, until they were on top of them; tearing their flesh and spilling their blood.

The shadows would leave what remained of the villagers' bodies, the bloodied husks of those that ran, on posts around the village edges. A stomach churning warning to all within.

No, they don't run now; they don't speak of running; not if they want to stay alive. They try to find some sense of joy in the hardship and exhaustion in which they live. Tiny moments of joy at the scent of a flower or the sight of migrating birds. The warm touch of a lover, the smile of a friend. Small things, fleeting moments. Not that their lives are ever long.

As night fell and the tiny sliver of the silver moon hung in the skies above the village, the vilagers went to their beds in fear. Hoping and pleading with unseen forces to escape the priest's eyes in the morning. Sadly, it was the grasp of a god that they plead to evade and the gods of the humans, if they ever existed, were elusive; they never listened, nor did they ever act on behalf of their children.

Chaint, goddess of the shadows, knew the power of belief. It was the belief of her children, their devotion to her, that gave her strength. It was the fear of the humans and their fireside tales that gave her power. Chaint knew she could not allow belief in other forces to grow. She knew that belief must only be in her, whether in love, hate, or fear.

Chaint herself hated the humans. They had become a blight on her world. On her creation. Humans destroyed everything they touched, cutting down the forests, burning the trees. They damned the rivers and dug up the land. They mined the stone of the mountains and killed the animals that should have fed the fae. She objected strongly to their creation. She objected further to giving them will and intelligence. Her children had not needed the humans, her children had not grown apart. Her children would continue to live in this world, that she had helped to create, long after she had destroyed the invasive men and women that plagued it.

And so the goddess herded them. She broke them, and used them for her entertainment. She had them build her temple, her fortress, and the surrounding villages. Then she used them to grow food and look after her animals. She used them to better the lives of her children and be the subject of their games. When the moon was dark, she allowed her priests to select a dozen of the human adults and take them for sport.

The dark priests would bring the cowering villagers inside the fortress walls and lock the heavy gates. Then they would play with them, as a cat plays with her prey. They hunted, teased and terrorised the humans while the moon was dark and when the first sliver of light appeared in the night, they sacrificed them to their goddess. Feeding her power, making her strong. In the morning, they would release the bones of those taken. Those bones would roll through the stone channels carved from the mountain rock back into the villages under the temple's shadow. And as those bones rolled the human's fear would grow and, with that fear, Chaint's power grew.

Three days to the west of Sgailburgh, on a range of high ground, burned hundreds of campfires. Around each camp fire sat a dozen tuath warriors, cold and tired but determined. They were marching east to face the shadows and rid the world of the dark fae and their goddess. The fight would be hard but they would free the people of the north, and then they would march south through the haunted trees of the Heartwood to join their cousins and take the fortress at Loch Heart.

Three thousand men and women, all highly skilled warriors, all determined to succeed or die in the attempt. They would fall upon the shadows like a wave of light, overwhelming the dreaded fae with their numbers and their ferocity. Those that would fall, and there would doubtless be many, would fall in honour and join their ancestors in the halls of the dead to feast in eternity, free of the hardships of life.

At the head of the Tuath army stood Eoghan MacFaern. A man in his prime, a warrior that had fought many battles and a leader with the respect, not only of his clan but of all those around him. When he spoke, the other clan chiefs fell silent. When he marched, the others followed and when he called the banners to war, the whole of Fearann an Tuath rose in answer.

The MacFaern clan was the largest of those in the tuath army. Their warriors were the most fearsome, many were blessed with the ability to transcend the battle field and draw upon the power of the ancestors to fuel their fight. It had been the MacFaerns that brought the clans together to build Northfort. It had been the MacFaern clan that first gained a victory over the shadows in the east, and all in the tuath force looked to the MacFaern clan to lead them through the coming war.

Bones, stained and muddied, rolled into the village from the fortress above and the families of those taken mourned their lost.

Niall Huran, a child of nine winters, now orphaned, picked up his blanket and his father's blade and he ran. He ran as hard and as fast as he could. He sensed the shadows behind him. Niall knew they were stalking him, waiting for their moment to take his life as they had his parents. But he didn't stop. He didn't cry; he gripped his father's blade tight, and he ran; ran for his life and he swore that the shadow who stopped him would know the sting of the blade before he died.

The path beneath his feet turned to a muddy trail and then faded away completely as it touched the base of a hill. He stumbled as the land rose before him, falling to his knees, his left hand stretched out to touch the earth and soften his landing. When he touched the ground, he spun over, his blade biting into the shadow that took advantage of his prey's fall and leapt at him. The fae backed away, its hand tracing the cut across its chest and it smiled.

"I will enjoy this all the more for your fight, child." The fae's voice was a hiss, its dark eyes glaring.

Niall scrambled to his feet, the blade held high. A tear came into his eye as he shouted at the shadow and his throat became a knot of fire.

"I'll die with your blood on me, fae." His voice broke as he screamed and the tears broke their dam, turning his eyes red and staining his face.

"But you will die, child." The shadow drew its dark blade from the sheath on its belt and started forward, its vicious smile revealing teeth that had been filed to points and a blood red tongue.

Niall swung the blade wildly, half blinded by his tears. The shadow brushed his blade aside with its own and kicked him to the ground. He landed heavily, pain shooting up his spine in an instant, and he closed his eyes, waiting for his death to come.

There was a gurgled cry from the fae above him and he opened his eyes once more. An arrow was embedded in the shadow's chest, an arrow with red brown fletching dotted with the dark blood of the fae. The shadow's dark eyes were wide, and it coughed as it struggled for breath. It lifted its head to the crest of the hill and a second arrow pierced the flesh of its stomach. A curse left its lips as it fell backwards, rolling the short distance to the flat earth at the foot of the hill.

Niall turned onto his side and lifted his head up, looking up the hill to see just who it was that had saved his life. Eoghan MacFaern stood there, bow in hand, a stern look on his face. Niall let himself fall gently back to the dirt, took a deep breath, and wiped his face on his blanket. Then he stood and greeted the tuath army, a smile pushing through the tears.

The battle of Sgailburgh was hard fought. Though the tuath outnumbered the fae by a thousand or more, they lost half of their host before they entered the temple fortress. In the end, though, the shadows fell or merged with the night and disappeared. With the city now in the hands of the humans, they renamed it as Norhill and those whose ancestors had helped build it led Eoghan through the darkness of its alleyways. MacFaern called out to the goddess, his blade in his right hand and a torch in his left, challenging her to face him. But no answer came. And so they searched the fortress for a week, sealing tunnels as they were cleared, but there was no sight of Chaint.

The tuath had won their battle and taken the north from the fae, but they had paid a heavy price and Chaint was still free. A dozen or more of her children were still at her side. And to the north, on the icy shores of Mortara's coast, the goddess met with her brother Solumus. Together they set sail to the west. There they would establish a new home on the islands beyond Mortara, beyond the reach of the humans. Their siblings, all but Ulios god of the sea, were in the Heartwood. They were preparing to leave the world, to abandon their children and leave Mortara in the hands of the human plague.

The goddess was wary when Solumus insisted she take a second ship with her children, rather than share the journey with him. But, with her mind still reeling from her defeat, she boarded the ship, and they set sail, following her brother's vessel through the rocky straits of the northern sea.

ACT ONE

The Calm

Chapter One

ESCAPING LOCHMEAD

The skies to the east were tinged with the red light of dawn as the last of the wagons left the town. Brighid and her father, Cohade, sat in the back of the last wagon in the line, looking out at the now empty stronghold. They each had bows to hand and their swords, but after the fight in the tower of Shadowatch, neither was in much of a position to fight.

In the west, beyond Lochmead, the campfires of the rebel army scorched the ridges of Ben Goath. Smoke billowed into the cloudless skies and hot ash blew down the icy, sloping face toward the farmlands that fed Clan MacFaern.

"I don't like running, Brighid. Never have, never will. It pains me tae be leaving Lochmead tae those traitors."

Brighid's hand tightened on the grip of the bow, her knuckles white.

"We'll be back here, Father. When it's over, we'll be back and we'll build a castle that no-one, nae matter their force, could take. We will not run again, not once this is done."

She watched as her father's face turned red, and tears welled in his eyes. And she held a hand out to him. A smile momentarily touched her lips as he took it.

"We'll make our stand at Northfort with the Tay, Da. I'll be better ready tae fight by the time we reach it and we'll make them pay. I'll put my blade through that traitor's stomach. He'll pay for what he's done. I swear it."

"There's a lot of ground between us and Northfort, Brighid. If MacTiern rode on ahead, he'll come upon us on the other side of the Diawood. We could yet have tae fight our way through."

"It's not MacTiern that worries me, Da. I've beaten the best warriors he has more times than enough, and by the time we get through the woods, we'll both be better ready for a fight if it's needed. I'm a hell of a lot more worried about the shadows MacKenna has with him. I thought them long dead. Thought we'd never see them again, and I fear them, Da. I've fought no one that fast, that vicious. No one's ever beaten me like that. I'm not going tae let them beat me so easy again, I'll be ready for them next time. But, I'm scared. What if they're too fast, even when I'm ready for them?"

"Yer right to be feared, Brighid. There were few warriors that stood against shadows and come away alive. We were lucky to escape as we did." The clan chief sighed. "I can't understand the man. Making a deal with the very enemy his family swore tae guard against fer hundreds o' years. 'When a Tuath lord breaks his oath, the North fails.' It was Morag Ni Huran said that when she held Callum MacFaern tae his promise of marriage. Those words brought Fearann a Tuath and Fearann an Liath together. Now we see the truth in them. And I'm feared too. It's over Brighid. Fearann a Tuath, it'll never be the same and it's all because that worm wants tae wear a crown that'll never fit his head. "

The wagon trundled on over the dirt path on the southern side of of the loch, the creaking of its wheels and the thudding of the horses' shorn hooves were the only sounds in a moment that seemed to last an age.

"Anndra!" Cohade's voice split the silence as he called out for his son.

"Aye, Father?" Brighid's brother rode a lively chestnut mare, the scales of his mail reflecting the orange light of the hour.

"Take a half-dozen men and set the fields ablaze. Those houses not made of stone too. We'll leave nothing behind tae aid or entertain the traitors."

"Aye, Father. What of the bridge tae the keep?" There was a sadness in her brother's voice, a resignation that was reflected on his face.

"If it'll light, son, aye. But don't take too long over it. We've no idea if they've sent men ahead."

"We'll manage, father." Anndra turned his horse away and called for his men to join him as he galloped back toward the town.

For a moment, a fleeting instant in time, Brighid saw before her a man. Not her father, not the mythical tower of strength that she had always seen, but a man in his waning years. A man whose shoulders had rounded, whose eyes were red and whose voice cracked as he fought to hold back tears. Her stomach fell as her heart filled with pity and love. She felt a heat fill her cheeks and tears fill her eyes. Brighid leapt, as if rushing into battle, across the space between them and sat beside her father. She wrapped her arms around his waist and placed her head against his chest, listening to the beating of his heart as she had as a child. A smile came to her lips as she felt his arm, still full of strength, though trembling, wrap around her shoulder and hold her close.

They sat this way in silence as the people of Lochmead marched along the dirt road, across the boundary of their town. Leaving their homes behind, never to see them again.

The wagons rattled along the dirt roads around the southern edges of Lochmead. Brighid felt every bump and dip in her bandaged stomach, her stitches threatening to tear as the wagons rocking threatened to tumble her over.

The smoke from the burning fields filled the air behind them, a blessing and a curse. It would hide their progress from the forces on the ridges above them, but it also prevented Brighid and her father from seeing what might be chasing them. Warriors flanked them. Half the fighting folk of the stead rode at the back of the line and half at the front beside her mother.

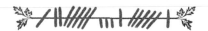

As the day drew to a close, Anndra and his men rode out the smoke. Their faces blackened, their mouths and noses covered with strips of material torn from a bright spring cloak. Brighid's bow was raised and aimed at her brother, the lead rider. As recognition reached her, she smiled and lowered it, keeping the arrow nocked in case he wasn't alone.

"You're lucky we didn't hit a bump, brother! You'd have been skewered. Why didn't you blow your horn and let us know you were approaching?" Brighid teased her brother almost gleefully.

"It's hard tae see more than a metre ahead in the smoke and the noise from the wagons is echoing through the valley. I had no idea we were so close. Though I might have smelled you if it weren't for this mask." He flashed Brighid a challenging look, but it was fleeting.

"Were there any difficulties, son?" Cohade ignored his children's games and pressed on.

"None, father. We managed to set flame to the keep bridge. It took a wee while, but we made sure it held before we left. We watched the camp on the ridge being struck as we waited. They were preparing to march, but as the smoke rose, they pitched back up again. I reckon the fire we've raised should give us an extra day or two on them. Then it'll take 'em a day tae come down from the ridge when they come, so we've likely got three days on them. Maybe more if they take their time sacking what's left of the town."

"That is a blessing at least, son. You've done well. Join your mother up ahead, tell her to keep us going a while yet. We can make camp around the Mill. We'll pick up supplies and gather the folk there before we move on in the morning."

Anndra nodded and pushed his horse forward, his men at his back.

For three days, the caravan rumbled along the loch's shore, growing larger as they passed through settlements and farmsteads. The dark smoke of their burning homes and fields billowed behind them, keeping them hidden from the force that they suspected was in pursuit.

By the time the caravan reached the edges of the Diawood, it had grown to over four hundred people and their livestock. There were three herds of cattle and each of the families had goats and chickens. The ground they moved along became churned and muddied, no longer a road and difficult for wagons to pass along.

It was the fate of the animals that caused Cohade to call the clan's elders together as they camped.

"We can't take the cattle into the woods. They'll be impossible to drive forward. I'm open tae ideas, but I think we need tae consider a cull."

"Why slaughter them? We can leave them, scatter them and herd them again on our return." A young man raised his head and spoke.

Cohade shook his head slowly, his face serious, an almost unnoticeable quiver of his lip. "We will not be back, not for some time at least. Fearann a Tuath is no more, my friends. Lochmead Hold is no more. Whatever the outcome of this will be, one thing is certain. The North will need remaking. At best, we'll be victorious, but with that we'll stand as the only Tuath Clan. I'm sure there'll be folk who'd join us, but they'd be leaving their clan chief behind tae do it. At worse we fail, MacKenna will hold up in Northfort, declare himself king of the north and gather his strength tae march on Fearann an Liath. It's worse than that, though. If he wins, if we fail, the shadows will roam free in the north again. We have had to set flame to our homes and to our lives as we've travelled. It's caused pain to us all." The clan chief took a deep breath. "It's been the most difficult thing I have ever had to order done, but it has been necessary. We have tae take that same tough decision now and cull this herd. I really can't see any other option."

"The herd has already been thinned, Lord. Our people have eaten more meat in these last three days than in the last year. Can we not spare them this slaughter?" The young man persisted, unmoved by the clan chiefs argument.

"Lord, I believe that some of this herd could be driven through the woods. It's my feeling we should try, at least. Even if it is just to sustain our people through the rest of the journey. Let the herders try. We can butcher those that cannot be driven. The meat can be salted, or the corpses burned." It was the newest addition to the caravan that spoke, a cousin of Cohade that had set up home on the south-eastern edge of the loch and his words caused Cohade to smile.

"If you feel it's possible, then we can try. Have the herders drive what they can into the forest this evening. We should butcher or burn those that remain in the morning. We don't have the luxury of time and need tae be deep in the forest's shelter by sunset tomorrow."

The forest was dark, there was no road, there were no paths, only the tracks of those wild animals that lived within. The cattle did not want to leave the open air and fresh earrach grass. They were wary of the forest and they resisted the attempts to drive them into it.

The stubborn cattle weren't the only problem facing the caravan, however. There was no way the wagons they were using to transport their belongings and their food could pass through the forest. Small bubbles of protest rose as the order to re-pack only those things that were vital passed through the camp. Many of those who had not seen the threat whispered their dissent. As the wagons were being broken up and the wood piled, those protests grew stronger. Many called for the wagons to be saved and for the caravan to turn North, avoiding the forest and the many problems it was already throwing up.

"Turning north is what they'll expect us to do. It'll take us a week or more out of our way, all told, and it will take us into the arms of our enemy. There's none of us ready for a battle. We're outnumbered. We'd have no protection and no shelter. They'll not be expecting us tae travel through the forest, they'd never travel through it, so we've more chance of getting tae Northfort unhindered by taking this route. I know it'll not be easy. Nothing about what we're doing is, but it needs tae be done." Cohade looked around the faces of those that stood in opposition to his plan. He saw fear and anger. Red faces with dark, heavy eyes, looked back at him and he paused. When he spoke again, his voice was quiet, not the booming, certain voice he had used at the beginning of his address.

"I'll not order you tae follow me. I'll not force you. If ye all want tae turn north, I'll not stop you. But I'm pleading with you. My warriors will be with me. You'd have no protection from what lay ahead. Stay with us and we'll do all we can tae protect you, to see that you get tae Northfort and safety. We can't do that if you turn north."

Not one wagon, not one person, went north as they set off. Progress into the forest was slow as each person took the time to sort through their belongings and make packs that could they could easily carry. Horses and the cattle that could be driven became pack animals, and the clan folk piled everything that they couldn't carry alongside the broken up wagons.

A dozen mounted warriors stayed behind on the edge of the forest to protect those tasked with butchering the herd. A sombre task made worse by the unknown location of the rebel army. Tension was high and the careful, methodical practices of the farmers and butchers were discarded in favour of speed. The cattle suffered and many of the men picked up injuries. Blood from the cattle soaked the ground, puddles of viscous red liquid forming on the surface of the still cold dirt. Haunting cries of the animals filled the air. Those carrying out the slaughter emptied barrels of salt, treating and preserving as much of the meat as was possible. Then, once all that could be done was done, they piled the remaining corpses high with the wood from the broken up wagons and cremated them.

The moon was high in the sky by the time the flames caught and those tasked with the slaughter were exhausted, the horror of their task echoing through their minds. They moved into the forest with as much haste as they could muster, pushing through their exhaustion to catch up quickly with their families and friends. No matter how tired, no matter how much pain they felt, no matter their feelings about the dense, unexplored forest, none could stomach the thought of spending the night in that place.

Chapter Two

The Queen's Isle

There were no roads to Queen's isle, no bridges or causeways. The only way to get there was by boat and then, there was only one place to come ashore and climb the road that wound its way up the high cliffs to the plateau. Gatehouses, guarded by the elite guard of The Silver, spanned the road at the port and at the point where the path reached the flat ground.

Daowiel clung tight to Lana; she had struggled to ride solo throughout the journey so when they arrived at the small dock of the island she climbed up on the chestnut mare and sat behind her friend.

"Say nothing, Ògan." The Princess whispered as she wrapped her arms around her friend's waist. Lana laughed happily. She had heard Daowiel giggle at her awkwardness many times and now she had the chance for revenge.

As they passed through the gatehouse to the plateau Lana's laughter stopped. The walls of the palace rose from the ground to form a formidable fortress, capable of holding against the most determined force. To the north of the palace there were acres of farmland and to the south, some distance from the walls, a large lake surrounded by woodland.

Within the walls their horses were taken to the stables and they walked through the grounds. Tall spires and large buildings surrounded pristine gardens; filled with colourful, beautiful flowers with scents that mingled to form a heavenly perfume which made both Lana and Daowiel close their eyes and smile.

"Welcome home, Lady Aelwynne." A young lady approached them from the main hall. "The queen was delayed and remains in Southport, though she has sent instructions and her apologies. She expects to return within days."

"Thank you, Hild. Please see the Princess Daowiel and Lady Lana to their rooms, have baths prepared and provide them with fresh clothing. It has been a long day and a long journey, it will be good to take a moment to refresh ourselves before dinner."

"Yes, M'lady." The woman turned to address Lana and Daowiel. "Please follow me."

Lana smiled at her friend and, arm in arm, they followed the lady into the residencies of the palace.

"Let us go to the woods on the Southside of the lake, Lana. Three days stuck inside the palace has me stinking of stone. It is worse than a noam's armpit in here. I do not know how you humans can stand it. Wet stone, eurgh." Lana chuckled at her friend as Daowiel stuck her tongue out and crossed her eyes.

"Oh yes, let's. We could explore the woods a bit and maybe have a swim?" Lana looked pleadingly at the princess. She knew the dryad wasn't particularly fond of swimming, especially in the cool air of early earrach.

"You confuse me, Lana. We have spent three days in the palace sheltering from the rain, so as not to get wet, and now you want to go and deliberately throw yourself into a large puddle."

"Well, you don't have to if you don't want, but I'm gonna have a bit of plodge. You can just watch from the shore if you don't wanna join me." A smile grew on Lana's lips. "I'll race you to the garden."

"Again?" The princess sighed. "It really isn't a very fair race, Lana. I have to walk down three flights of stairs, along two corridors and through a kitchen full of curious staff in order to get to the garden. You go up two flights, climb a ladder and jump off the roof. Falling a distance is quite a lot faster than walking it, you know."

Lana's smile disappeared as she screwed her lips tight and off to the side. "Yes... I... Well, yes I know... But going up stairs is harder than going down too. So it's really all the same, isn't it? Besides, I have to make sure I jump properly and keep my arms right and catch the right breeze. It's not as easy as just falling. Any fool can fall off of a building."

"And on to an unsuspecting maid." Daowiel laughed.

"That was just once! And I didn't fall on her. I was at least half an arm's length away from her." Lana pouted.

"You knocked the basket from her hands, though, and sent her eggs all over the path. The poor old girl was three days in bed from the shock."

"Well, I said sorry, and I took her warm milk every day 'til she was better."

"Anyway, I won't be racing you today. If you want to practise your gliding I understand. I would want to as well, but running through the corridors is not nearly as much fun. Besides, if we're heading to the copse of trees today, I will stop in the kitchens and pick up some food for us. That will take some time. I shall meet you at the birch."

Climbing the tower stairs was not half as strenuous as Lana had suggested to her friend. Not now, anyway. Now she could leap up six stairs at a time easily. The race, for a person can still consider themselves in a race, even without an opponent, up the tower's stairs went by quickly. They used the room below the crenellated roof for storage. It held barrels and chests filled with unknown odds and ends covered in dust. There had never been a need to defend the palace since its construction, so the warlike tower had been filled and forgotten; no one ever went up there. Lana jumped and caught the top rung of the ladder to the roof. She pushed open the trapdoor and pulled herself up into the open air.

The wind seemed to swirl around the tower top as if guided by the circular architecture and Lana smiled as it caught her hair. She kicked the trapdoor closed and spread her arms, twirling in union with the wind. That moment took away the disappointment of her friend refusing to race, and she danced for a moment, free of all care. Remembering the moment she had leapt down the stairs of the harbour, the exhilaration as she had realised what she had done, and the thrill of each leap since.

Stepping up onto the lower part of the wall, she looked down into the garden below, checking for people taking a stroll or going about their work. When she saw the area was clear, she spread her arms and leapt.

Her stomach filled with butterflies and she giggled as the wind rushed past her. With the ground speeding toward her, she twisted and rolled, playing acrobatic games with a glee that reminded her of chasing calves in the field. A final roll in the air and she landed gently on her feet on the freshly mown lawn.

"Lana Ni Hayal!" She recognised the voice of her mentor and the tone in which the lady had spoken her name. She was about to be told off and she sighed before turning to face the lady Aelwynne. "Yes, m'lady?" She said through an innocent smile.

"You have been told about your acrobatics, Lana. If you insist on throwing yourself from high places, please do it outside the palace. You scare the people half to death when they see you rushing toward the ground like that. You must remember, most people could not possibly survive such a leap."

"Yes, m'lady. I'm sorry, I won't do it again." Lana tilted her head to one side and bit her lip in an attempt to look suitably sorry for her actions. The lady Aelwynne raised a knowing brow and nodded slightly.

"Your tutor arrives later today, and your lessons will begin tomorrow. Perhaps you should take the opportunity to wander the island a little and enjoy the freedom. You will spend most of your time in the library from now on."

"Dao... The Princess and I are planning a trip to the trees on the western shore of the lake, m'lady." She smiled again, forgetting her telling off. "We're taking a picnic and we're going to have a plodge."

"A plodge?" Aelwynne looked confused.

"Errr, it's when you splash about in the water but don't go so deep as you'd need to swim." Lana explained.

"I see. Well then, enjoy your plodge, Lana. I look forward to seeing you at breakfast tomorrow."

"Yes, m'lady. Me too!"

The day passed quickly in games and laughter. Lana even managed to convince Daowiel to enter the lake for a moment. Though it only lasted as long as it took for the cold water to touch the dryad's knees before the princess protested and ran out of the water, sending spray and great splashes through the air as she went.

One thing did pique Daowiel's interest that afternoon. A tree grew on the banks of the lake that she had never seen before. Its branches bowed over the lake and long trails of leaves reached down to touch the water. The dryad spent some time with the tree, touching it, speaking gently with it and showing the strange tree her desire to know it.

"She was unsure at first, Lana. She did not know about us at all, she had not seen or heard of a dryad before. Do you know how strange that is? Can you imagine? It was only when the other trees assured her, she opened up and allow me to touch her mind. I think she comes from a foreign land, a place far away from Mortara. Perhaps one of the islands. I really must return here soon so we can talk some more."

“I hope we get to come back soon.” Lana nodded. “My classes start tomorrow and I don’t want to be stuck inside every day. I’d miss this too much.”

“Ah, our little, Ògan. Finally, learning formalities and diplomacy. I wonder if you will ever be the same again.” Daowiel teased her friend with a wicked smile.

“Will you come with me? At least for a while? I’d feel less awkward if you were there with me and I had someone friendly in the room.”

“I shall think about it, Lana. I have been through this before and joined the laoch rather than continue it. Books and scrolls and dusty old tutors... It is something my sister was far more suited to. Still, it would be mean of me to abandon you when you have provided me with so many moments of laughter. Perhaps I will suffer it once more to support you.” Lana reached out and held her friend’s hand, swinging it slightly with a grin.

“I’m sure we could find a moment or two of laughter even with all the books and dusty tutors.”

Chapter Three

A New Line of Work

Blood flooded the priest's mouth, washing the broken teeth to the back of his tongue and causing him to choke. The viscous liquid from his shredded gums and cheeks spotted the leathers of the large man stood before him.

"Who gave you your orders? Tell me and this pain will stop."

The priest spat at his torturer with a sneer. "I feel no pain. My god protects me from your violence."

"You may say you don't feel the pain, priest, but your body will shut down just the same if I continue to damage it. Save yourself that. Tell me what I need to know. You have nothing to lose now. But can keep your life."

"My life is worzless if my soul is condemned. You cannot take what I have given to my god."

"Enough of this, Tyrell. Take his hand, then take him back to his cell to consider his fate." The voice came from the shadows in the room's corner, a deep voice with an authority that dwarfed the presence of the torturer.

"Aye, commander. I'll take my time with it an' all." The face of the bald man twisted into an evil smirk as he picked a small saw from the short bench at his side.

"What news do you have for me, Crurith?" Tay Gathwyn sat in his garden, the scent of the early blooming flowers filled the air.

"Nothing good I'm afraid, my Tay. The man is a zealot, more interested in the fate of his soul than anything we can do to his body." The commander shook his head as he spoke. "I don't know that I will ever understand the mind of a religious man. Even the fae aren't this fanatic and their gods were real. The god of the circle is nothing more than a story, cobbled together from tales of old heroes."

"Yet we know the men of the circle to be relentless in their dedication." The tay slipped into a few moments silence, seemingly wrapped in thought. "I want our sheriffs vigilant. Anyone associated with the circle should be watched closely, none should be allowed in the city, nor the waters of the straight. Until we know who ordered the princesses kidnapping and the ambassadors assassination we should assume that the circle are our enemy." He shook his head with a sigh. "I wish I knew why they killed their man, we had who we thought was the leader and dropped the investigation. What message are they sending? Who were they sending it too? Was it meant for us or as a warning against failure for other agents?"

"I wish I could give you an answer, lord. My feeling is that they wanted us to know they could get to a man, even one in our prison. It certainly wouldn't harm them with any other agents though. It would most definitely keep them in line. We'll keep at the priest. Perhaps his last breath will be a confession."

"Leave him, for now. Let him think we're done. We'll try a different approach in a few moons. Just keep the circle out of city in the meantime."

"Yes, my Tay." Crurith saluted and turned to leave.

"Oh... I'd like to have a little conversation with the leader of the orphanage. Have our favourite retired thief brought to my office, will you?"

"Aye, lord. I'll have her brought to you by weeks end."

Commander Crurith was not a man you could ignore. The tallest of his guards stood no higher than his shoulders and his arms were as large as most soldiers legs. Were it not for the roundness of his ears you could easily mistake him for a Noam warrior.

His fist pounded against the heavy wooden door like a blacksmiths hammer.

"Don't make me break this down, Cat. I know that you're in there." His deep voice boomed through the narrow alleyway and a number of shutters closed at the sound of it. He was not well liked in this part of the city.

A breathless child, no more than eight years old, face red from running, opened the door with a scowl.

"What do you want, tin 'ead? We aint doin noffin' wrong and you've no call to be hammering on our door as though we are."

"I'm here to talk with Cat is all. Now, are you gonna step aside or do I have to let myself in?"

"'Ere, there's no need to be like that." The young boy's voice rose to the pitch of a soprano and he slammed the door shut, barring it against the commander's advance. "I'll go see if she wants to have anyfing to do wif you." He shouted through the thick oak.

Cat was sitting in her favourite chair by the fire, warming her feet as the boy stumbled into the room.

"Sorry, boss. It's that commanda. the big 'un. 'E says 'e'll not go 'way 'til he's seen ya."

Cat picked up her cup of warm cider and wrapped her hands around it, smiling at its warmth. "That's okay, Sammi, let him in. There's nothing for us to hide anymore, so he can't do us no harm."

"Yes, boss. If ye say so." Sammi, bent at the waist, put his hands on his knees and puffed for a moment before taking a deep breath and turning to run back to the doorway some way through the tunnels.

"What do you want, Commander? We ain't breaking any laws here, I makes sure of that." Cat didn't bother to look up as the guard entered the room. There had always been a rivalry between the two of them though, if she were honest, it was always one tinged with respect.

Crurith laughed. "Of course you aren't. Cat the thief is gone now, replaced by Cat the mother of the lost. You're as pure, these days, as the water in the palace fountain." The commander paused, the smile leaving his face with a sigh. "Quite frankly, Cat, I don't care about your games. The Tay wants to see you and I'm here to escort you to him."

"The Tay? What does he want from me? Is this some kind of trick Crurith?" Cat pulled her feet from the table and sat upright, alert, ready to bolt from the room in an instant.

"I've got better things to do than rounding up the likes of you, Cat. I'm not a city guard anymore. As for what he wants? I think he has a job for you." The commander took a step forward and Cat stood.

"A job is it? Alright, give me a minute then. I'll meet you back up in the street. Wouldn't wanna go to the palace in these dirty ol' rags now would I?" There was a moment of silence in which the two old adversaries tried to come to terms with this new twist in their relationship and then the commander turned and left the room, stopping only briefly at the door.

"Don't be long, Cat. He doesn't like to be kept waiting."

Gathwyn was sitting behind his desk, his face was pale, his eyes puffy and dark. The new level of threat from the circle of light was taking its toll on the Tay. He had suffered sleepless nights trying to understand why the circle would assassinate a man who, it seemed, was protecting their secret despite the hardships they had put him through.

"Come in, Cat, please. "

Cat walked into the room, her eyes darting from side to side, taking in her surroundings; noting any items of value around her and looking for anything that stood out as important. The Tay raised his brow.

"Old habits?"

"Hmm? What? Oh, yes... Sorry. I swear I won't try to help myself to anything."

"That would be best, Cat. Have a seat." The Tay had a wry smile on his face as he gestured to the chair in front of him.

"I understand that you have become a rather useful source of information since you took control of the... What are you calling it? Orphanage? I have even had reports you're prepared to help the city guard, if the price is right."

"I stole to live, Lord. That isn't a way of life I want any other child to be forced into, but we do need to eat so we have to beg. We've no choice in that. Sometimes we hear stuff on the streets, stuff that might be interesting to others. So we sell the information. It gets us food and clothes and that."

"I understand, Cat, that is sadly the way the city works and I prefer you selling information than leading my guards a merry chase. There is some rather important information that I need to have, but it is proving rather elusive at the moment. I hoped you might help get it."

Cat leaned back in her chair and raised a brow.

"Of course, Lord. I am happy to help you, if I can. And of course, if the compensation matches the difficulty of the task."

"You will find the compensation generous if you can discover what we need, Cat. But it will not be easy. There was a man in the city prison, Yirema. I believe you were acquainted with him?"

"The ambassador from the falcon islands?"

"Yes. We were certain after interrogating him that the plot to kidnap the princess was one which he lead. That with his capture and the princesses rescue meant that the threat was over. Several days ago, however, he was killed and a circle of golden thread was placed on his body. A message, no doubt. But of what?" Gathwyn took a deep breath and closed his eyes for a moment before continuing. "We have the priest your friend rescued from the bay and have been questioning him. But, he has been very reluctant to tell us anything more about the plot that you helped to foil. I find it difficult to believe this murder was not carried out by the circle, but he is keeping his secrets well. He refuses to talk to any of my men and has been extremely good at recognising those I send into the prison as spies. It has made me wonder if you would have more success."

"I think he'd know me, Lord. But I reckon I could get someone close to him. It might mean making promises of freedom and pardons."

Gathwyn nodded and slid a small box over the desk toward Cat. She opened it to find an engraved disc, the size of a city coin, on a chain. The Tay's seal on a pendant.

"Taking that will make you my agent, acting on my behalf in this matter. It is no small thing. You will be given some authority and leeway in your actions, but you must stay within the law. I will provide you with a letter of pardon and a few coins to help you get what we need. Your reward will be based on the information you get."

Cat picked up the seal and examined it. "I've seen one of these before, Lord." She looked over to the steward that had shown her in and then back to the Tay, her brow raised in a motion that suggested she had more to say.

"You may leave us, Gillan." The Tay gestured to his steward, who nodded his understanding and left the room. Cat waited a moment, ensuring they were alone, before leaning forward and breaking the silence.

"You'll probably not want to tell me this, but I have to ask. Do you know where every one o' these is? Seems like that'd be an important thing for you. Right?"

The Tay leaned back in his chair, looked into Cat's eyes and held his gaze for a moment in silence.

"What do you know, Cat?"

"I've seen one of these afore, and the man what had it certainly isn't stayin' within the law. What do you know about Khasric?"

The Tay's brow furrowed at the name, and his gaze intensified. "What do you know of Khasric, Cat?"

"I know he aint doin' anything you want him doin' and I know he's got one o these hanging round his neck. Almost had it in my pocket once, 'cept some clumsy waster tripped over his own feet and woke the lump of a man up with his clatter." Cat sat back in her seat, spinning the token on its chain. "If that ones one o' yer men, you've been betrayed. If he ain't, he's killed one o yer men and stolen yer token."

The Tay leaned forward in his chair and placed his elbows on the desk, resting his chin upon his clenched hands.

"Khasric watches the port for me. There are people there involved in the worst kind of crime."

"Khasric is bringing women. Women what've been kidnapped around the coast, through the port. He sells 'em to a noam who puts collars on 'em and gets 'em bound to his less honest friends in the noam district. If you reckon he's helpin' you, you're makin' a mistake... I reckon he's likely had you cleanin' up his own problems for him. Wasn't all that long ago you had one o' Keikon's spies down there arrested in time to stop us taking a bundle of the fat oafs cash. Bet he had you thinking Bowden was one of his bosses and not one of ours." The Tay nodded, turning his thumbs as he thought. "That is... Interesting news, Cat. If it turns out to be true, I'll see you well rewarded."

Sensing that she had a momentary advantage, Cat smirked. "You might need me a lot more than you know. My Tay."

Gathwyn laughed a short, breathy laugh. "Is this your way of asking for a more permanent role, Cat? I didn't think you were the type."

"I'd be interested in knowing if one existed. And what it would mean for the orphanage?"

Intrigued, the Tay coughed, ending his laughter, before taking a more formal tone. "You would swear an oath to me and I would be your priority as far as information goes. You would come to me before you went to sell it anywhere else. Anywhere else... You would be given a living wage and a bonus if the information you provided was useful. You would also have the right to ask for things you needed in order to pursue something important, like the coins and pardons I'm prepared to give you for this assignment. As for the orphanage, well, if you were serious and loyal, we might find a way for the city to help with funds and food to keep the children safe and fed. We would insist that we have someone we trust helping you to manage those funds, however."

"Would I have a say in who that person was? I would want someone I trusted with the children as much as you trusted them with the money."

"We could certainly discuss the appointee."

"And the 'living wage'? You'd remember that I was impossible for your guards to catch when I didn't want to be caught? That it was me that had the information on the kidnapping plot, that I tried to tell your men and that when that failed, I spoke to people I knew could help? You'd remember that when we discussed what a 'living wage' is?"

"Why don't you tell me what you want, Cat? And then I will tell you what I'm prepared to give."

"Well, there's risk. Your agents prolly die quite regular. What's Crurith getting? I bet he gets a silver each moon, don't he? So how's about that? A silver every moon?"

"A country silver, every moon? You place yourself amongst the elite, Cat. A member of my own guard takes a city copper every week, a city guard takes slightly less. Yet you want more than twice that?"

"None of your guards could ever catch me. None of 'em listened to the information I brought 'em. I'm clearly worth more, just for having the brains to know what I'm doin'"

"Six city copper each moon. More than my own guard by half and twice a city guards pay."

"Two city copper each week. And then the bonus. It will be the best coin you spend this year."

"Very well, once you have sworn yourself to me and this employment. I will instruct that you are paid each week."

Cat smiled and put the Tay's seal in her pocket. "I'll expect to hear from ye about the orphanage soon as well, then?"

"Indeed. You are forgetting something though, Cat."

"What's that then?"

"Your oath. Swear it now, before you leave here."

Cat chuckled and spoke in an accent she used to mock the rich. "Alright then. I, Lady Caitlin of house Feline, do swear my loyalty to you, Tay Gathwyn. I shall bring to you every tittle and tattle I hear, every rumour shall be whispered into your ear. I shall impart upon you the wisdom of the street. And all of this you will have in return for your shiny coins."

Tay Gathwyn rolled his eyes, barely able to conceal the smirk on his face.

"How eloquent, Cat. I look forward to working with you." He watched her turn and approach the heavy oak door of his study. "Before you go, Lady Caitlin of house Feline." Cat turned, a smile on her face. "I hope you are able to prove your skill. I'd be disappointed if I had to drag you in here and renegotiate." Cat's mouth fell open and her brow wrinkled tight. She looked at the smiling Tay and let out a sigh. Then she reached into her pocket and took out a small pouch. Made from soft leather and monogrammed. The steward's purse wasn't as heavy as she had hoped it would be when she took it, but it would have been a loss to him. She threw the purse across the room to the Tay, who caught it with one hand.

"I usually get what I set my mind to, Lord Tay. That's my skill, and it's never failed me so far. Keikon woulda had me dead if I'd failed, so I learned not to. Tell yer man he should use a different knot on his purse, it was far too easy to take." She saluted and laughed, then turned back to the door and left.

Chapter Four

DUSTY BOOKS

Lana yawned. Her day had started with the rising sun and it had not been easy getting out of her bed. The soft mattress and warm blankets made her the most comfortable she remembered ever being, and the early earrach air around her bed was still a little chilly. She had washed quickly and changed from her nightgown into a newly sewn blue and silver court dress before rushing out into the corridor and knocking on the door to Daowiel's chamber.

"Come on, Daowiel! Get out of bed, it's time. Breakfast is waiting and I don't wanna be late for the queen or go face my tutor alone."

There was a rustling behind the door, the dull thud of a closing chest and the whistling sound of the Dryad's song. Lana knocked again, tapping her foot in unison. "Daowiel! We'll be late."

The door opened, and Daowiel sighed. "I am a princess, Lana. I have breakfast with a queen almost every morning. It's not really all that special for me anymore. Your queen surely knows you cannot rush a visiting princess in the mornings."

"I know, but it's the first time we're having breakfast with this queen and her full court. I love your mother and having breakfast in the dryad palace is amazing, but it's always just us four and it's not formal and there aren't people watching and judging."

"They are actually supposed to be formal, Lana. We just learned early that you were a little flighty and not likely to get used to the formalities." The princesses smile was wide as she teased her friend. Lana stomped and tugged at Daowiel's sleeve. "Come on. Or I'll tell everyone about the first time you left the Heartwood." She took the princesses hand and half skipped with her down the corridor, making their way to the great hall.

Breakfast was a sweet mix of honeyed porridge and berries. It was nice, nicer than anything she had eaten in the stead, though Lana had to admit that her breakfast at the Dryad palace had been nicer. She had thought, before coming to the palace, that as the Queen of all Mortara, Rhiannon would undoubtedly have the best food in the country available to her. She was a little disappointed to discover it wasn't true.

"Did you sleep well, Lana? Is your chamber comfortable?"

"It's so nice." Lana nodded a spoonful of porridge half in her mouth. "And the bed is so soft and warm, I almost didn't get up this morning. It's enormous too, bigger than the room I use at Brighid's manor even. And it's so quiet, I guess because it's high up and away from the courtyard and the kitchens and everything. I really like it and I slept so well, I had really nice dreams. Is your bed as cosy? I bet it is. I bet it's cosier even. I can't imagine how you ever leave it. Oh! It must be like sleeping on clouds." Lana smiled warmly at the Queen as the room fell into silence. Lady Aelwynne, the queen's voice, and Lana's new mentor coughed gently into a napkin and raised her eyebrow as she caught Lana's eye. "Oh... Your Majesty. Sorry, your majesty... "

Princess Eleassa giggled, and Lana's cheeks flushed red. She lowered her head, biting her cheek.

"It's not polite to laugh, Eleassa." The Queen gently chided her daughter. "Lana is not used to court life. You should remember that and help her adapt." Lana noticed the queen's voice was soft but had an air of authority that suggested there could be no dissent.

"And I thought it was only Dryad that found you amusing, Ògan. It seems, though, that it is all princesses!" Daowiel laughed as she gently poked her friend's side. Lana squirmed and pushed the Dryad's hand aside, a smile growing on her own face.

"I can't help it if I'm fun to be around, Daowiel. And even if I am silly and clumsy, I still beat you at Hide'n'Hunt every time we play now!"

Daowiel cleared her throat and looked around the table before addressing the Queen. "I am afraid my friend's informality is my fault, your majesty. As you can see, I have been far too friendly with her, even letting her believe she could best me!" The princesses smile was wide and infectious, spreading around the table in a moment.

"Pfft." Lana let out a rush of air and looked around the table. Everyone from Queen Rhiannon to Lord Reynard was laughing softly at the interaction between her and her friend.

The queen lowered her spoon, letting it sound off the side of her bowl. "I am pleased you are so excited by your life here, Lana. And it is good to see you at last. I would have liked this moment to have come sooner, but being queen means putting aside one's own hopes, from time to time, in order to help the country grow. I'm afraid that the more mundane aspects of palace life have kept me from spending time with you. They may also become rather dull to you in time. Lord Reynard, for example, barely finds anything to smile over." The queen turned to her most trusted guard with a smirk that the soldier greeted with an exaggerated roll of his eyes and a sigh.

Lana laughed with the teasing Queen and tucked into her porridge with renewed delight.

The study was bright. Not a speck of dust covered the books or the large oak table that filled the centre of the room, surrounded by a dozen chairs. Aelwynne sat at its head, signalling her status for the upcoming activities. Lana and Daowiel sat to her right facing the door, their backs to the large, decorative window that flooded the room with coloured light.

"Your actions in the city last year were impressive, Lana. You showed yourself capable of decisive action and, though I would have done things differently, I believe you did that which was right for you to do. I wonder, though, would you do the same today as you did then?" Aelwynne had slipped into her more formal way of speaking, a sign that it was time to be serious.

"No!" The exclamation lasted as long as it took to shake her head a half dozen times. "If it happened today, I would tell Lord Reynard. I'd still help, of course, but I think Lord Reynard could have stopped it from happening at all. He'd listen to me now, though. I couldn't even get to talk to him back then."

Aelwynne smiled. "And if you had been in Lord Reynard's position, what would you have done?"

"Oh, I'd have had the men brought in, and I'd have questioned them and found out what they were planning, and I'd have arrested the ambassador before the feast. And I'd have made sure there were soldiers at the port so that the priests could be arrested if they weren't before. Course..." Lana paused and drew a deep breath. "If I was in charge of the palace guard, Cat would never have told me. She'd have been too scared that I'd lock her up."

Aelwynne nodded slightly, the fingers of her hands touching her lips. "Do you think she would trust you now? Even though you are here in the Queen's court and my apprentice?"

"Oh, yes! I think so. At least, I hope so." Lana's brow furrowed. "She is a good person, even if she did some things that were against the law, and I think that we're friends. I'd never deliberately hurt her or put her in a dangerous place. I think she knows that."

"You believe she is a good person, despite breaking the law?"

"Oh Yes!" There was a slight pause as Lana considered her next words. "I think sometimes the people that make the law don't understand what people's lives are really like and they make mistakes. I don't think people in big houses that wear nice clothes and have people to cook and clean for them know what it's like to have no food, no money, no home of their own. They don't know what it's really like to be hungry and scared and cold."

Aelwynne's eyes narrowed as she leant forward, grabbing Lana's gaze and holding it as she spoke. "You are one of those people now. Living in the palace, no less. Wearing fine clothes, your food cooked, your chambers cleaned. Will you forget what it is like to be hungry, cold, or scared?"

Lana shook her head rigorously. "No, I... I mean, I don't really like to remember the bad moments. Some of the days we were on the road were really difficult. But I don't want to forget either. I don't want to be like that."

"Like me?" Aelwynne's eyes never drifted from Lana's, her gaze was hard. Lana felt her cheeks warming. She wanted to look away, to break the eye contact that her mentor so skilfully held.

"No... I mean, yes, kind of. You're not a bad person. I don't mean to say that you are. You're really nice. I like you. But... But we're different. I don't want to be the same as you. I don't think I ever could be. Even if we had the same things and did the same work, we wouldn't ever be the same."

Aelwynne smiled and sat back in her chair, breaking the tension that had grown in an instant. "That is good, Lana. I want to teach you what I know. I want you to understand what I do and why I do it. But I don't want you to be like me. I want you to make decisions because you believe them to be right, not because you believe I would make them."

"There will be times we disagree, and I want you to be able to tell me why. There will be times we do the same thing for different reasons, and I want you to be able to explain those as well. I want you to be able to see my view and to explain yours in everything we do. And I want you to understand the reasons others do as they do."

"That is our role within the Queen's court. To understand and to advise her, to negotiate and to make decisions on her behalf. To do this, we must know ourselves, we must know the queen, we must know the laws and traditions of our land and we must know the person we sit opposite. Do you understand?"

Lana nodded silently.

"You showed me in Butterholt that you are capable of that. Your work with the dryad was wonderful. Sometimes, however, you let your tongue race ahead of your thoughts. I need to be sure that you can be thoughtful and sure all the time. And so, you will learn. This is why I have arranged a tutor to help you understand the history and traditions of Mortara. That will be a start."

Aelwynne turned to Daowiel with a warm smile. "I fear this may prove dull for you, your highness. I can arrange other activities for you if you would prefer to pass the time elsewhere?"

"No need, Aelwynne. I am certain there will be moments of amusement as we go, there usually are when my dear Ògan is learning. Besides, I may be a help. I imagine I am rather more qualified on some issues than your tutor."

Lore Keeper Coccus was an elderly man whose long grey beard seemed to drain the colour from his deeply lined face. He took the seat opposite Lana and placed a large, leather bound book before her, opening it to reveal a page of beautifully illuminated script.

"The history of Mortara is a long and complex one. To understand it, one must understand the gods and their decisions. We will begin by learning from our greatest scholar. Lore Master Guilenn. You will read aloud." The old man's voice was dry to the point of making Lana want to cough. His outstretched finger, pointing now to the first word on the page, was long and fragile looking.

Lana looked around her at the expectant faces of her mentor, the lore keeper, and her friend.

"I can't read. We never learned how to do that in the stead."

The lore keeper turned his head toward Aelwynne and raised a brow. "How am I to teach this child about our world when she cannot even read?"

Lana's face reddened, and she screwed up her mouth, lips tight for a moment, before muttering quietly. "I learned lotsa things at home and I didn't need no books to do it."

"Perhaps, rather than making her feel bad about her background, you could support and teach her? Is that not why you are here?" Daowiel placed a comforting hand on Lana's arm as she challenged the lore keeper.

There was a moment of silence as the dryad and the old man held each other's stares. Then Daowiel placed a finger on the text.

"Each of these figures makes a sound, Lana. To hear what word they make you speak the sounds together. See this one..." She pointed to the first letter on the page. "This one makes an 'ih' sound and the one to its right is a 'n' sound. So we put the sounds together, and it makes the word 'in'. Do you see?"

Lana nodded at her friend and leant over the large book, pointing at the word. "These shapes are like the ones painted on the sign outside the 'old king's dog inn', but with another one of those." She pointed to the 'N'.

"Yes, when it has one of those, it means 'in' like 'in the woods' or 'she was in bed'. When it has two, it means an inn where you stay and eat." The princes pointed to the next letter. "Now this one is a 'th' sound and the one to its right is an 'eh' so the word is 'the'."

"In the." Lana recited, smiling at her friend. "This isn't so hard! What's this sound?"

The lesson continued in the same manner throughout the morning, with Lana reading the text of the book slowly out loud as she learned each letter. Absent-mindedly rubbing her forehead as she went. When she came across a word she didn't know, she turned to Daowiel for an explanation and they discussed it together, ignoring the lore keeper and his sighs.

"The deity most worshipped on the island of Gaoth, now the location of Southport, was Qura." Lana read slowly, breaking each new word into its individual sounds. "Daowiel?" Lana looked at her friend with her brow furrowed. "Why do they sometimes write god and sometimes write deity? It doesn't make sense. The god wasn't called deity, she was called Qura, so it isn't a name."

"Humans like to make things complicated, Lana. It makes them feel better about themselves if they can make simple things difficult and only they can understand them."

"Oh. That's a silly thing to do."

"That may often be true, Princess. But not in this case." Aelwynne had watched the friends silently as the morning progressed, impressed by the ease with which Lana seemed to learn. "Our language is as complicated as our history. You see, Lana. Some of our words are the same as the words the fae use: our names for the seasons, for example. Others are words that the human tribes created when they named things. But, because the tribes were separated, they sometimes called the same thing by different names. Then, when the tribes united, the words became mixed together."

"Like, when Brighid calls a lake a loch and says tae instead of to?" Lana's eyes seemed to light up as she asked.

"Exactly." Aelwynne nodded with a smile.

"Well, that makes more sense. So... This says that Southport is on the island that used to be called Gaoth. When me and Tinnion and Laywyn found that old ruin... That must have been the temple of Qura they're talking about?"

"We believe so, yes. The lore master has a group looking at all the things you found there and examining the chambers. There seems little doubt now, though, that Qura was worshipped, and likely lived there."

Lana's grin was wide, and she clasped Daowiel's hand in hers. "We found the goddesses home! Isn't that fantastic?"

"You have been in the home of Kaoris too, Lana. That is the palace tree."

"Really? I didn't know that! No wonder it's so beautiful."

The lore keeper coughed, a loud, unnatural cough, and pointed to the newly turned page of the book. "Yes, all very impressive. Well done. Now. Continue."

"I don't think the lore keeper likes me."

The friends sat on Lana's bed after their day of study. The sun was low in the sky and they had candles burning to light the room.

"You shouldn't worry too much about that, Lana. You were doing something he didn't believe you were capable of, and that made him question himself. It happens a lot with males." The princess winked as she finished her point, and Lana laughed.

"Not all men are bad, Daowiel!"

"Hmm. Perhaps. But it's easier to assume they are and be surprised when you find a good one than to assume they aren't and be disappointed when they let you down."

Lana nuzzled up to her friend with a smirk growing on her face. “Maybe you’ll find a man you like and be the first ever dryad to marry one!”

The princess feigned a deadly blow to her heart and collapsed upon the bed in laughter. “I have to confess, though. I’m a little surprised at how easily and quickly you learned to read. That was not normal. The gods seem to have given you more than the ability to work with flora.”

“It’s this circlet, I’m sure. I’ve been able to remember so much more since I was in Qura’s temple. Except putting it on... I don’t remember doing that. Tinnion says I was doing all kinds of strange things then though. Maybe one day I’ll remember.”

“Maybe one day you’ll meet Qura herself and she’ll tell you! Of course, you’d probably trip over your own feet trying to curtsey.”

Lana smirked. “You marrying a man would definitely be a reason for the gods to come back!”

As the two friends broke into laughter, the palace bell rang, calling them to the great hall for dinner.

Chapter Five

THE GROWTH OF A STEAD

The Butterholt Pact, that deal that had been struck between the stead folk and the dryad upon the death of Gesith Heriloth, was working out well. The dryad had planted a line of trees along the existing border, a line that took up very little of the hold's land but gave two hundred or more trees the chance to grow; and in return, the stead had been given access to just as many trees within the Heartwood itself.

One of those trees planted was visited every day by a dryad and fed a small amount of the thick dryad draught. As it grew into a small sapling, it was marked with a ribbon and a message was sent to Tinnion to ensure that it wasn't disturbed. No reason was given, but Tinnion had heard many tales of dryads and believed that this was a dryad birth tree. No human had witnessed the birth of a dryad and none truly knew how they were born, but there were tales, stories as old as anyone living, and they all started with a special seed, planted within the body of a man. The rumours of a kidnapped and murdered man feeding the growth of a dryad started to spread around the stead, though no man had been reported missing. It didn't take Tinnion long to quell the rumours in Butterholt, but she didn't object particularly strongly to word spreading in neighbouring holds.

Because of the success of the new pact and the large amount of timber being brought into the stead, Tinnion insisted that the first new building to be erected should be a sawmill. She sent four of the steads more experienced men a half day's walk from the steads centre to that place along the holds border where the Heartwood met the Swimmingwillow Beck, and they set about their work. Building a large water wheel and smithing a large, strong saw. Those men were watched, at every hour, by one curious dryad or another.

Meanwhile, in the stead itself, Tinnion, with the help of Hayal and Ellie, had come to know most of the steads folk and had ensured that all were housed in comfortable lodgings as their homes were rebuilt. Sera was tasked every day to make sure that all the folk of the stead were fed and she had a small army of women working with her to make that happen. The trestle tables and benches that had been used on special occasions were now a permanent fixture in the manor courtyard and everybody gathered at the end of each day to eat together and share their news.

The stead was, for the first time, a place in which everybody was given an equal share and all worked toward a common goal. There was not one person who did not smile as they ate, though there was not one person who was not tired by the time the food was served. Everybody slept well, and the stead was at peace.

The skies were dark, and the foxes that lived on the edge of the forest were active. Tinnion sat with her back to a young tree, her bow drawn with an arrow nocked. A flash of yellow caught her attention as the eyes of a fox reflected what little light there was. There was no hesitation, no thought, just instinct and muscle memory acting in unison. The arrow struck the fox just behind its shoulder, killing it almost instantly. She nocked another arrow and walked slowly toward her kill, constantly scanning the trees around her for other predators.

"An excellent shot."

Tinnion spun, her bow aimed directly at the dryad's heart. Then breathed a sigh of relief as she recognised Cinerea, one of those dryad that had accompanied Princess Erinia on the day of their talks.

"You should give a woman a warning before you step out of the trees behind her. I almost shot you."

The dryad smiled at her. "I shall greet you from behind the tree next time, Lady Tinnion. Your aim is remarkable, particularly in this light."

"I feel it as much as see it, Cinerea. Do you hunt?"

"All dryad hunt, Lady Tinnion. Sometimes just for the sport of it, if we can find the right prey." She laughed, a light, melodic laugh as she spoke.

"So the stories are true? You really do hunt men?"

"It is rare, but it happens, yes. Only those that threaten our trees though, and of them only those that catch our eye. " The laughter was gone, but a smile remained on Cinerea's face.

"I don't know that I've ever met a man that needed hunting. A few have tried to catch me. They tend to be really eager, but they usually found me too elusive." Tinnion leant on her bow, her eyes fixed on the dryad's smile.

"Usually?" The dryad raised a brow.

"There was one." Tinnion's hand moved to the necklace she wore.

"A bear?"

Tinnion shook her head slowly. "He died just as he was becoming interesting..." Her smile faded. "He was a good man and deserved better than the end he got."

Cinerea stepped forward and placed her hand on Tinnion's shoulder.

"Perhaps you are destined to be caught by a fae, Lady Tinnion. Somebody less fragile than a human male." She squeezed Tinnion's shoulder gently and raised the corner of her mouth in a half smile. "I wonder how you would do in a game of hunting? You would be at a disadvantage, of course, being unable to use the trees as we do; but perhaps I should take you into the forest and show you how our children play some day. I think you may enjoy it. Though we would need to make your arrows dull, you're far too effective with that bow, and I'd rather not end the game full of holes."

"Provided you brought me out again. I think that would be a fun way to pass an afternoon."

"Of course! We aren't half as devilish as you humans insist we are." The playful look in the dryad's eyes did little to assure Tinnion that her words were true. "I shall let you get on with your evening, Lady Tinnion. You should get your prize out of the wood before the smell attracts something bigger." With that, the dryad turned and melted back into the forest. Tinnion stood a while, looking after her, before finding the felled fox and starting her walk back to the manor.

"Another fox, M'Lady? You're gathering quite a collection of furs now." Sera sat in front of the kitchen fire, taking a cup of hot cider before retiring for the night.

"It seems a shame that there is nowhere to trade them, Sera. I'd have made a decent purse if I could have taken these to the market in Southport. Still, the meats good enough and it's good to keep their numbers down a bit. They might not be a threat to the cattle, but they bother the smaller animals and the birds."

"Aye, there is that, m'Lady. May be's you could send a wagon over to Frey-bridge to sell 'em once you've added a few more. It'd take a couple of weeks, but it'd get you a bit of coin." Sera poured a cup of cider out for Tinnion as she spoke.

"It's a possibility, Sera. Did Heriloth do much trade in the bigger towns?" Tinnion smiled and blew across the hot drink, sending steam toward the fire.

"Not at all, m'lady. He was a lazy one was Heriloth. Content to sit on his backside and be pampered by the pretty stead girls. He had us work to keep him fat, but had no ambitions beyond that. Well, none that I could see anyways."

"There're lots of cheese wheels and leathers here, more than seems possible to use. What happens to it all?"

"We makes what we can with the leathers but it's right enough some gets scrapped before it's treated or gets worked but sits in the tanners workshop waiting for a use. The cheeses we make are alright; though we do let a fair bit of milk n cream go to waste, even now that we're all allowed a share."

"Then perhaps it is time we sent a wagon to Freybridge. There're bound to be things we could buy there that the stead could use. Do you think we could use up the spare dairy to make extra cheeses?" Tinnion sipped at her cider, careful not to burn her tongue.

"Oh, aye. No doubt we could. There's just never been much of a need." Sera's nod and her smile gave Tinnion confidence that they had come across another way to improve life in the stead. It would mean that two of the stead folk would spend a bit of time on the road every few months but it would open up a bit of trade that would make it worthwhile.

Tinnion had called for Hayal, Ellie, Andel and Ara to join her for breakfast as she did most mornings. Sera always took a seat too, once the breakfast bowls had been filled.

"Is Ara joining us, Andel?" Tinnion looked at the empty seat at the young man's side.

"No, m'lady. She's sleeping. I think she might be coming down with something. She's been so tired and I didn't want to disturb her."

Tinnion smiled. "That's okay. Best to let her sleep if she's not well. I hope she's feeling better soon. If there's anything I can do, just let me know."

"Thank you, m'lady I will." Andel nodded.

"There was a bird this morning with news from the palace. Lana is back there, happy and well. She's had a few new dresses made and is learning to read! It says that she's doing well, and she sends her love."

"That's good to hear, m'lady. She's missed terribly, but I'm happy to know she's doing well and happy with life. She'll get more chances there than here that's for sure." Ellie smiled as she spoke, but there was a heavy look in her eyes that showed how much she missed her daughter.

"There was confirmation that I'm to be named Gesith of Butterholt too and instruction to go ahead and make some official appointments. So I guess I'm going to have to get used to the whole m'lady'ing and you're all going to need to put up with me for a lot longer than I guessed."

"That's good news, m'lady. I'm pleased. You've gotten the stead moving in the right direction and the stead folks are all happy to have you here." Hayal barely looked up from his bowl but Tinnion recognised a sincerity in his statement that made her heart swell a little. Lana's family had welcomed her as one of their own from her first day in the stead and they had only grown closer in the moons since then. She saw in Hayal a steady man, always honest and true to his word, gentle but strong and full of love for his family. Lana had always spoken so highly of him, but Tinnion had thought it little more than the blind love of a daughter, until she had spent time with them all.

"I was hoping you'd be my steward, Hayal? And that you'd run my house, Ellie? Would you be willing to take on those roles? It's more or less what you've been doing, but now I can make it official and pay you properly."

"Aye, I'd be happy to, m'lady." This time Hayal did look up from his bowl and he gave Tinnion a smile and a wink.

"It'd be an honour for me too, m'lady." Ellie placed her hand on her husband's and gave it a squeeze.

"You know the younger men and women, Andel. There's not been any trouble since we cleared things up in the stead, but I think we've been too long without sheriffs. There are predators to look out for and an entire hold beyond the stead that we've no real connection to at the moment. I was hoping you'd take some folk you know and trust and head them up for me?"

"You want me to be head sheriff?" Andel's eyes grew wide and his jaw dropped. "You shot the last sheriff I spent any time with! I mean, I'd have done the same given the chance, but still!"

"I promise I'll try not to put an arrow in you, Andel." Tinnion laughed. "I like Ara too much to make her a widow!"

Andel joined in with the laughter, looking to the seat at his left for a moment, forgetting that it was empty.

"Can I count on you to keep the kitchens running, Sera? Once we've got a wagon going back and forth to Freybridge you'll be able to bring in more ingredients and sell anything you don't need."

"Oh yes, I'd be happy to. I hadn't thought I'd be able to buy things from the big town. That'll make things exciting. I'll be able to make things I've not got the fixings for now."

When breakfast was over, Andel returned to the room he shared with Ara and her daughter, Ranya. He sat on the edge of the bed and gently kissed his wife's forehead.

"How are you feeling?"

Ara smiled and nodded, waving her fingers to say that she was fine.

"I've news." Andel paused a moment before going on. "Lady Tinnion has been officially made Gesith. She's asked dad to be her steward and mam to run the manor. Sera's going to keep running the kitchens, of course. But she wants me to be head sheriff! Me!" Ara smiled and threw her arms around his neck, kissing him full on the lips. "She says we'll get paid well and we'll get our own house in the manor grounds when everyone's got somewhere to live. It'll be nice."

Ara's fingers moved quickly, making shapes in the air that Andel tried to follow.

"Slow down, Ara. Please... you're talking too fast for me to keep up." He reached out his hand and cradled hers, forcing her to stop for a moment. Her face dropped into a frown and her eyes rolled back into her head. Then she leant over and took his other hand, placing it on her stomach before placing a gentle kiss on his lips.

He let her hand go and caressed her cheek, looking deep into her eyes, his mouth dropping open. “You... You’re pregnant? We’re going to have another baby?” A tear welled up in his eye as Ara nodded slowly, confirming his guess.

“I’m asked to be sheriff and my wife gives me a baby all on the same morning! I don’t remember ever being this happy! We’re going to need a bigger house than I thought. I love you so much Ara, but.. Are you alright? You’ve been ever so tired, is it because you’re pregnant or... Is there something else?”

Ara shook her head. She brushed the hair from his face and she rubbed her nose on his. “I’m fine.” Her fingers made simple shapes that Andel knew well, not wanting to confuse him while his mind was racing.

Chapter Six

A Lesson Learnt

Lana sat, her head hovering over the large leather book, her fingers tracing lines under each word read. "The Sylph accounts show that the fae existed for millennia before humans were created, living in harmony with each other, with the gods and with the earth. It is known that the Sylph were created by Qura and Zeor and they lived in the high places of Mortara. The sylph were always one people. They never separated and remain to this day, the only fae that maintained one society and one culture." Lana paused and looked at Daowiel, her brow furrowed. "What's a millennia, Daowiel?"

The Dryad princess smiled. "It's a very long time, Lana. A thousand years is a millennium and millennia is more than one of those. The dryad and the noam separated after six millennia, maybe a little more. We did not keep records in the way the sylph do. It was after that, the gods created humans, there was no need for you before then."

"And Kaoris created the dryad, didn't she?"

"Kaoris and Khyione, Lana. They worked together to create us, but they grew apart over time. In the beginning the dryad and noam were one people, like the sylph are. Khyione felt his noam were better than us, however, and the noam agreed, their god taught them to enslave the dryad. That is why we split, and why your kind were created."

"So Kaoris and Khyione created the dryad and the noam, and Qura and Zeor created the sylph. Did the other gods work in pairs too?"

Daowiel nodded. "They did. Each pairing of god and goddess are brother and sister, and in turn they are cousins to the other gods. The others stayed together in pairs for a while longer than Kaoris and Khyione, too. After the Dryad and Noam split, Khyione took his noam to the mountains of the north and Kaoris hid us away in the place where her palace tree grows. The noam could not enslave us anymore; but that caused problems for us all, because we needed each other. After a hundred years or more having no young, things became difficult. Our people aged, and the elders died and the gods became concerned. It was then that Khyione created the first humans, he only made females at first, to serve his noam. But it soon became clear that they only had noam babies. There were no females being born. That is when he reached out to the other gods."

"Wait." Lana was frowning as she listened. "You mean Khyione made us just so that we could have noam babies?"

"Not just to have their babies." Daowiel shook her head. "You were their slaves. And not just theirs. Khyione, Ulios and Solumus all kept human females in their temples, to serve them and to entertain them."

"That's..." Lana struggled to find a word that summed up how she felt. She stuttered for a moment.

"It's how gods are, Lana." Daowiel interjected. "In time, they created human males, and they kept all the humans together, like you keep cattle on your stead. They stayed like that for a hundred years or more, but they still were not having many babies. Khyione had created the females to serve the noam and had not given them the desire to mate with human males. So the eight gods came together, and they gave the humans thought, and free will, and that is how your species became what you are today."

There was a dry cough from the other side of the table. "That is what the fae insist occurred. Of course, they would, as it suggests they are superior." The old lore keeper made it clear that he did not believe what Daowiel had said. "Lore Master Guilenn, however, states things differently. He believes that when Kaoris ran from Khyione and their people split, the gods realised that their 'firstborn' were flawed and so they combined their skills and their energies to create us. A more advanced species and society."

Daowiel rolled her eyes and sighed. "Of course, a man whose race was not even sentient at the time would have a better understanding than the elders of the races that were."

"This brings us nicely to one of the most complex issues we have today." Aelwynne's voice was calm and ended the small tiff that was growing between the dryad princess and the lore keeper. "Some time after the war, when we humans had settled as rulers of Mortara, the noam reappeared. They helped us to build and rebuild our cities, they helped to create our harbours and fortresses, and they began to live alongside us. In time we discovered these noam were a small faction that had split from their families in Stonemount. They had moved away from what they call the 'old lore of Khyione' so that they could live alongside us. Those in Stonemount shunned them, and, even now, consider them weak. When Queen Rhiannon ascended the throne, that group of noam signed the Eastmarch accord and now live in Southport and other large cities around Mortara. They still believe, however, that which Daowiel has explained and, though they no longer treat women as possessions and slaves, they still use the traditional collar and leash when they are joined. And of course, the curse of Khyione still has its effect. That, at least, cannot be denied, and lends credence to Daowiel's version of what passed so many millennia ago." Aelwynne reached out to touch Lana's arm as she continued. "You have to understand, when you sit opposite the noam, that the way they behave with us, particularly with us women, has been passed down from their god for as long as humans existed. It goes against everything they have ever known to accept us as equals. It is abhorrent to us and it makes talking with the noam extremely difficult, but it is something that we need to accept and try to overcome. Each of the fae and each different society of humans have things that will be difficult for us. Our skill, our job, is to look beyond those things and search for common ground and ways to work together."

Lana smiled, a slight, uncertain smile. "When I first met Daowiel, I was sure she was going to kidnap me and put me in a cage and hunt me for fun. That turned out okay, though." Her smile grew as she spoke. "I think if I can get Daowiel to like me, I can manage with others too. Though noams might be harder."

Daowiel laughed. "There is time and there are plenty of empty cages yet, Ògan!" Lana gently pushed her friend away from her and joined in her laughter until a dry cough turned their attention back to teh lore keeper.

"This is why we cannot truly trust the Dryad, nor the Noam. For they will always seek to capture us and cage us, in order to continue their lines." Daowiel's face twisted as the old man spoke, and she started to stand, but Lana placed her hand on her arm and held her.

"I know the dryad aren't like that at all. I know that they do use the men that enter the heartwood. They have to. Princess Daowiel has told me all about that. But they don't hunt us and capture us or trick us the way you're saying, and it isn't their fault that the men die. I'm sure it's not the noam's fault that the curse changes us, either."

The Lore keeper stood, his face burning red. "I think I am done with this one, Aelwynne. She is stubborn and refuses to learn."

"You're asking me to believe the things I've seen are wrong and the things you've read about in dusty old books from hundreds of years ago are right. You don't like me because I know more than you think I should, and it makes you feel less. You're just like the noam were with the dryad all that time ago. And you're behaving like a child instead of a lore keeper. Getting all angry and threatening to storm off. I won't miss you if you go, you know. I can read all the stuffy old books too now and I can go to the dryad's home and I can talk to the sylph and the noam too if I want, but you can't. You refuse to leave your study, you refuse to believe what isn't written down, and that's why you're angry really, cos *you* made a cage for yourself and you can see that I'm free while you're caught."

The lore keeper's jaw dropped, and he gaped at Lana for a moment before slumping back down in his chair with a huff.

"Perhaps you are right, child." His voice was soft, the authority he had tried to maintain before gone. "I will continue."

Lana smiled at the man. "I didn't mean to be so harsh, but you weren't being very nice. I want to learn from you, but I want to know that you'll listen too when I know things that you don't, or when Daowiel tells you about her people. If you refuse to learn, you can't be a very good teacher, that's what I think, anyway."

The old man nodded silently, his eyes narrow.

When the lore keeper was gone and the three women were alone in the study Aelwynne turned to Lana, her hands forming a triangle that she rested her chin upon. "Now I understand you more, Lana. Perhaps I've seen this afternoon what the Princess Daowiel has always seen. You look and play just like a pup, but you bite like a wolf, strong and targeted. Exposing your prey's weakness to bring them low. That is something you can use to your advantage if you can learn a little more control. Perhaps even more effective if we can work together as the wolf works with her pack. You should be more gentle with Coccus, however, he is quite influential. "

Lana turned red and bowed her head low. "I didn't mean to be so hurtful with him, Lady Aelwynne. Really, I didn't. But he was being stubborn and childish and very disrespectful to Daowiel. He needed to be told he wasn't behaving very well."

"He is lucky it was you and your words that cut him, Ògan. It could have been much worse for him." Daowiel's voice was calm but distant and Lana recognised the danger that the lore keeper had almost faced. Her friend was loving, kind and playful, but she was also a fierce warrior and a princess. She was more than capable of strong and deadly action when she felt the need.

"I think, perhaps, you should take tomorrow to explore the island some more, enjoy the day a little, and bask in the sun. I will talk with the lore keeper and see if he can carry on in a more appropriate manner." Aelwynne paused over the word appropriate, suggesting she had another in mind.

A smile broke out on Lana's face and she turned to her friend, clasping her hand. "Oh, Daowiel! We could go back down to the lake and explore the woods on the Southern side. You can get to know those strange trees even better and we could see how deep it goes. I really enjoyed it in the small copse and the woods are even more exciting, and it looks ever so pretty. I can just about see it from my window and I've wanted to go there for weeks now!" Lana had shrugged off the sombre mood in an instant and the smile that she gave the princess was infectious. The dryad relaxed and smiled back at her friend.

"That sounds nice, Lana. We'll do that."

"Good morning, m'lady. Did you sleep well?"

Lana jumped. She was comfortable in her bed, slowly waking up as the sun's cool, early morning light slid across her face.

"What? Yes. Yes, I did. Who are you? Why are you in my room?"

"I'm sorry, m'lady. I thought you were expecting me. My name is Brendwynne. I'm to serve as your personal maid."

Lana crossed her arms in front of her face as she yawned and then clasped her shoulders, hugging herself and closing her eyes again for a moment.

"Why? I mean, why are you my personal maid? I'm sure I don't really need a maid, certainly not a personal one. That sounds like you're only here for me, and I don't think I've got so much for you to do."

"I'm sure I'll have plenty to keep me going, m'lady. I reckon it's normal to not know you need a maid 'til you've got one. Bit like a nice feather pillow, m'lady. You go your whole life without one and it's fine, but then you lie down on a nice comfy bed and your head sinks into one as if you're lying in the clouds and then you thinks to yourself. 'How did I ever do without?' And you never want to go without again."

Lana smiled. Brendwynne seemed nice. She was young and had a friendly face and a big friendly grin. "You might be right, Brendwynne. I definitely love my pillow. So, emm, what is it you do then?"

"Whatever you need, m'lady. I've laid out your clothes and filled your wash basin. I'll help you dress once you've washed and when you leave to start your day, I'll straighten your chamber. In the evening I'll arrange a bed warmer and warm your night dress too. Then in between I can do anything else you need. I'll liaise with the kitchens, the housekeeper and the seamstress for you, so's you just need to tell me the things you need or want to do. The lady Aelwynne mentioned you were planning on exploring the island today so I've asked the kitchen to pack you a light lunch. They'll have it ready for you once you've had your breakfast." Brendwynne was brushing down Lana's walking boots as she spoke.

"That's, well, that is really helpful. Thank you, Brendwynne."

"I can come with you, if you'd like, m'lady. Lay out your lunch as you and the princess explore. I've never been out of the palace walls since I came here. It might be nice to see a bit myself."

"Oh, yes, of course you can come. It is nice there, the calm of the lake and the birds singing in the trees. I think everyone should take a walk out in the fields and the woods from time to time." Lana smiled, her eyes gently gazed as she thought back to wandering the tree line in Butterholt stead.

The southern shore of the lake was dotted with trees, grown wild and untouched for hundreds of years. The weeping willows that so fascinated Daowiel grew close to the water itself, their leaves trailing in the gently lapping waves. A woodland grew beyond the shore, stretching southward. The dryad princess and her friend explored those woods as their maid sat by the lakeside, enjoying the sun.

Daowiel and Lana had wandered through the trees, introducing themselves happily. They ran through the woodland, touching each with a smile and an occasional hug. But their exploration of the woodland came to a sudden end around noon, interrupted by jutting stone and what appeared to be a small mountain. No vegetation grew on that massive rock, but it did not rise any higher than the walls of the palace. Dark and ancient, it seemed cold to the touch.

"I don't like this, Lana. I would rather go back closer to the lake. These trees are all like those willows on the western shore. They have never known a dryad, it is sad. They are nervous, some are scared. And this stone, rising from the ground it... It seems to reject all life. They do not like it and nor do I." The princess seemed angry, her eyes narrowed as she mentioned the towering rock formation before them.

Lana felt concern for her friend. She had not seen the princess so troubled over anything before. "Brendwynne will have laid out our lunch by now. Let's head back to the shore and eat. I want to plodge for a bit anyway" Lana smiled and took Daowiel's hand, gently pulling her away from the rocks and back toward the shore.

"Oh, m'lady! You startled me! I didn't hear you coming." Brendwynne was sitting on the bank, her boots at her side and her feet in the water. She started to get up.

"Stay where you are, Brendwynne. There's no need for you to get up." Lana smiled sweetly. "I'll be sitting there beside you soon. Just need to fill my belly a bit first. Did you eat already?"

"No, m'lady, I wouldn't eat first. I was just trying to cool my feet off. I'm not used to walking so far over rough ground." The maid puffed a little, as if to show how her feet felt about their morning hike.

"Do not let your skin get too soft." Daowiel took the authoritative tone she often used when teaching Lana something new. "That will just make the walk back to the palace worse for you."

"It's not that I'm not used to being on ma feet, your highness, not that I mind that. But I like the ground beneath them, flat and firm. Walking over the uneven grass and the mud, it just isn't what I'm used to."

Daowiel shook her head and rolled her eyes back. "You humans... You live in a world of beauty and life and cover it over everywhere you go."

Chapter Seven

Visiting Old Friends

Cat sat at Keikon's old desk, bent double over a battered old book.

"You've had your nose stuck in that book every time I've seen you of late, Cat. I didn't know you were a reader." Laywyn had been visiting the new leader of the orphanage every dozen days since her struggle against the head of thieves and her old life ended.

"Yeah, no, not really all that bothered about books, but..." She paused. Laywyn had proven himself to be a good friend, and he had taken the time these last few moons to see that she was getting on alright. But she was sure he wouldn't approve of her having the book. "I thought this might be the thing that got me away from Keikon. Thought it'd be what gave me a new life. Course, that was before he tried to have me killed."

Laywyn raised a brow and tilted his head, trying to get a peek at the contents of the book. "I've never known a book that powerful, Cat. I've heard of spell books, but they're the stuff of children's tales. What's so great about this one?"

"I... I aint gonna use it, Laywyn. I'm gonna turn it over to the Tay. There's no need fer you to go thinkin' I'm goin' back on ma word and back into bad stuff."

"I wasn't thinking that, Cat. I trust you. I saw past all that street thief stuff long ago. But you've made me even more curious now than I was a moment ago. What's in it? And why would the Tay want it?"

Cat slid the open book across the desk to her friend.

"It's a list of lords, ladies 'n' officials, of debts they owe and rumours they'd rather no one ever heard. It made an old woman rich once, and I figured it'd do the same for me. I found it hid in her chamber one day when she wasn't at home and... It was before I really knew you all. You and Lana and Tinnion. I wasn't thinking I could ever get out of Keikon's family in those days." Cat's voice faltered as she spoke, and her eyes swelled. "I swear to ye, Laywyn, I swear I won't use it." Laywyn reached across the table and lay his hand on hers.

"You've grown up so quick, Cat. And we're proud of you, all of us are. And more than that, Cat. You know, leastways I hope you know, that if you need help, you can come to us. You never need to get yourself into trouble."

Cat nodded, a smile growing on her lips. "I know Laywyn. Thank you. And I... I don't need this anyway now. I've got something much better. Something that'll keep me well fed and keep the orphanage going. Mebbes keep the kids off the streets all together. And it's legit Laywyn, it aint dodgy at all."

The old soldier smiled. "As long as you're safe, Cat. Is it something I can help you with?"

"No, at least not at the minute, Laywyn. I'm gonna be helping the Tay with something is all. I doubt I'll really need to be doing much beyond convincing some people to do stuff they'd more than likely enjoy anyway."

"It sounds interesting, Cat. And it's good to know you're working with the city and the Tay rather than against 'em now. It's a whole new life for you!"

The Southport city prison was more populated than the Tay was comfortable with. Cages surrounded a large open area where the prisoners mixed, exercised, and ate. Each cage could hold ten people and were, mostly, segregated, though not by the guard or because of prison rules. The women of the prison stayed in those cages on the north side of the courtyard. They were warmer and less prone to damp and mould. They did, however, often mingle with the men throughout the day, and some went so far as to share their beds through the night.

Guards patrolled the walls above the square, each armed with a crossbow and a quiver of bolts. They often made a show of aiming them, though they only ever used them when a prisoner tried to escape through the heavy iron gate on the eastern wall or threatened a fellow guard. The prisoners were, for the most part, allowed to do whatever they wanted to do.

The outer walls of the prison contained barracks, the officers' area, storerooms, the mess and a couple of processing cells. Those cells were dark and cold. Though today, in one, a single torch burned. A hard wooden bench stretched across the back wall of that cell.

Cat sat with her back in the corner, her legs up on the bench. A figure lay upon the floor before her, blood flowing from her brow. The figure struggled for breath, coughing and spitting up the excess flem that usually precedes a fit of vomiting. The guards had been very physical when they dragged the prisoner into the cell, throwing her violently to the floor, where she hit her head off the stone slabs.

"You look weak, Adney, and ever so thin. Is it not so easy to steal the food from the mouths of your new family?"

"Cat? Dahlin' Cat. Is that you?" The woman looked up, wiping the blood from her eyes. "Have they finally caught ye? Have you come te join yer mother in her misery?"

"You aint my mother, Adney. We aint related, and you never cared one bit for me. Don't bother trying to pretend you did." Cat's voice was calm and cold.

"Oh, now, Cat. That aint fair. You was always my favourite, I always had a soft spot for ye, right up until the end."

Cat snarled in the darkness of the cell. "Shut up, Adney. Shut up and listen to me, cos I'm gonna give you a chance to do something good for once. Do it right and I might even help you out a bit. You hear?"

The woman turned herself over and struggled to a sitting position. "Now I see ye, Cat. And lookit that, no chains on you at all. What do ye want?" She growled her question at Cat, her face twisted into a picture of hate.

"You know the man, Yirema, the former ambassador of the Falcon Isles. Your husband had a very special relationship with him. He's gone and got himself killed and the man what might know who did it has decided he doesn't want to speak to us no more. Decided that he's said enough. But there's stuff we need to know and you're gonna get him to tell."

"I din't know the man, Cat. Never met him. And I know noffin of what him and Keikon had planned. I don't know this other one yer talkin' about either, so yer outta luck and aint that a shame?" The woman laughed, almost a cackle as she taunted Cat.

"Oh, you're going to meet my silent friend, Adney. You're going to get to know him very well, gonna be very close to him, you are. You're going to find out what I need to know and you're gonna tell me everything. "

"Yeah? What makes you think that then, dahlin'?"

"Cos if you do what I tell you, if you find out what we need to know. And... If I'm feeling kind enough. You might just get out of this prison alive. If you don't, though, you definitely won't."

"And 'ow do I know I can trust yer to keep yer word, Cat? What you gonna give me to prove you mean it." Adney sniffed deep as she talked and ran her sleeve across her nose.

"You don't know, Adney. And I've nothing to show you or give you. 'Cept, you know I always did what I said I would. Never once did I make a promise, nor a threat I didn't make good on." Cat threw a handkerchief down to the floor by Adney's hand. "Best clean yerself up, Adney. You wanna look your best for the reluctant priest."

"A priest? Are ye kiddin' me, Cat? You want me to get close to a religious man? Yer mad. There aint no religious man allowed to be doin' what you want me to do with 'im."

"I don't know that you ever met a religious man, Adney. They're not as full of light and innocence as they say. Trust me on that."

Chapter Eight

Hunting Games

The earrach sun was at its highest above the canopy of the forest trees. The air, heavy with pollen and the scents of a forest in bloom, made Tinnion feel drowsy. She stood still and silent. An arrow notched to her bow. The dryad had taken the tips from her arrows and replaced them with leaf wrapped cones, dipped in a colourful, thick liquid that would leave a mark to show her aim but not hurt her target beyond a sting.

She heard the gentle sound of laughter behind her and spun, letting the arrow fly. Her aim was true and would have marked her prey had the dryad not vanished as quickly as she had appeared.

"How many arrows does the sealgair have left?" The words seem to echo around her, not coming from one place, but from many. Tinnion turned cautiously, another arrow ready.

"Enough, Cinerea, enough." She smirked, her eyes sparkling in the dappled light of the midday sun.

She stepped to one side quickly as a cone tipped spear flew past her ear and sprang forward toward the area from which it was thrown. She hadn't seen the dryad; she hadn't heard her, but the spear was evidence that she was there. Or had been. Dropping her shoulder, she fell to the ground and rolled as another spear flew through the air above her. She let her arrow fly as she rose and sighed as it struck the trunk of the tree less than a second after the dryad had merged with it.

"If this were a field in my stead, I'd have tagged you by now and the game would be over." Tinnion called out to the surrounding trees, not knowing where the dryad might emerge.

In a flash, the dryad's arms were round her legs, their shoulder in the small of her back. She let her bow fall as she reached out to soften her own landing. As she hit the ground, she spun and kicked, trying to break the dryad's hold. The dryad was strong, much stronger than Tinnion, and used her strength to keep Tinnion pinned. In a moment she was face to face with her assailant, her right wrist pinned to the forest floor, her left hand beneath the dryad.

"I believe I win, Sealgair," Cinerea said playfully, a mischievous smile dancing on her lips. Her breath, unlike Tinnion's was calm.

"I think you rigged the game, Cinerea. If we weren't in a forest, I'm sure I would have won." Tinnion relaxed, letting her muscles rest. She took a deep breath and sighed.

"I'm sure you would, Sealgair, and if I were other than dryad too. You are skilled and quick, but today you are my quarry. And now... I'll take my prize."

"Your prize?" Tinnion's brows rose with her voice. "There was never talk of a prize. I didn't bring my purse."

"A coin would be a poor prize, Sealgair." The dryad grinned. "It was hard work to catch you. No, I will not settle for a coin." Cinerea moved her hand from Tinnion's wrist and gently stroked the huntresses cheek. She lowered her head and pressed her lips to Tinnion's.

It lasted no longer than a breath might take, but Tinnion felt it as though it lasted a morn. She took a sharp breath in, her chest rising as their lips touched. Her eyes widened and then closed and her stomach tightened, knotting in an instant. As the dryad drew slowly away, she found her own lips follow, lingering for a moment in the kiss. And then her head dropped gently back to the ground.

Her jaw tightened, and she swallowed hard. Her hand, now free, moved to cover her face, her burning cheeks and quivering lips. She lowered her eyes, not daring to look at the dryad that still lay atop her.

Cinerea giggled. "You're redder than a toadstool, Sealgair!" Her words were soft, her eyes never leaving Tinnion's. "That cannot have been your first kiss?"

Tinnion shook her head slowly, not saying a word. She raised her eyes and looked into Cinerea's. A moment passed and then the silence broke.

"I didn't mean to shock you, Tinnion." Cinerea spoke her true name softly, dropping the name she had given her for the first time that day. "I am sorry if I have caused you distress."

Tinnion shook her head once more. "Surprise, that's all. I... I should get back to the stead, though. I've much to do." She spoke in little more than a whisper, her cheeks still red. Cinerea nodded and let her up.

As they stood, she reached out and placed her hand on Tinnion's arm. "Will I see you again this moon?" The dryad's eyes looked heavy, her own face red.

Tinnion moved her arm slowly, drawing the dryad's hand down and let their fingers touch, interlacing gently. She nodded. "I need to draw even." She raised the corner of her mouth into a half smile. With that, she reached and pressed a finger lightly to the dryad's nose, then turned and walked back through the trees to the stead beyond.

Tinnion met with Sera and Andel just outside the manor walls as the morning sun warmed the stead. A wagon, loaded with skins and cheeses, was being covered with a tarpaulin by a couple of stead folk.

"What is this sigil?" Tinnion examined the painted sign on the side of the cart. The ancient fae rune for cow nestled inside an acorn.

"The dryad, Lothalilia, said we should paint it, m'lady. She said it'd mark the wagon out from any others what might follow the tree line, and show that we're friends." Andel traced the rune with his fingers as he explained. "I like how it mixes the steads cattle with the acorn. It kinda suggests we might grow together."

Tinnion nodded with a smile. "Yes, it does, doesn't it? Is everything aboard?"

"Yes, m'lady. There's the cheese what we'll not need and all the furs you and the new sheriffs've been bringing. We aught to get a pretty trade from it all I'd say." Sera rocked gently on her heels as she spoke, a grin on her face.

"Well, it all seems good to go. Well done. You know where you are heading?"

"Aye, m'lady. We've to keep the trees to our right and the beck to our left and when they split, we've to keep on heading west. Never been west before, it'll be an experience, so it will. Been south to the other farms in the hold, and me old dad went east once, but no one's ever been west, far as I recollect." Thom was in his twenties, a friendly lad with a broad smile. He had asked to be the one to drive the first wagon from the stead as he wasn't so good with the cattle or felling trees and hoped it might give him a chance to be more useful. Sera had been quick to agree. She felt his friendliness would be an asset when talking with strangers, and he was quick-witted enough not to be taken as a fool when agreeing on a trade.

Garen, one of Andel's new sheriffs; a tall, strong young man, was travelling too. He carried a bow and a blade in case they happened across any trouble, and Andel assured Tinnion that he was capable with both, if not up to her level.

"Well then, don't let me keep you from the road. Good luck to you both!" Tinnion's smile was wide, and she slapped each man on the shoulder in a friendly fashion as they climbed aboard the wagon.

"Come back rich or not at all!" Sera laughed as the wagon pulled away and started on its journey.

The day was going well. Another house had been finished in the stead, Andel and Ara had moved out of the Manor House into their own home in the manor square and Hayal had returned to the manor, with good news. He had been in the hold's south, visiting the farms and smaller steads with invitations to the elders to form a council; a council that would be invited to the manor on every third moon to discuss the holds issues. Every farm and stead had agreed, and that gave Tinnion hope. She believed Butterholt could become a hold of riches and equality. There were plenty of resources and skilled workers, they just needed a gesith that didn't hoard and waste it all. Allowing every farm and stead the chance to have their say would make sure she was making the most of the holds people, keeping them happy and healthy.

"There's a dryad wants to see you, m'lady. She's out in the square, didn't want to come inside." The maid was red in the cheek and gasping for air.

Tinnion furrowed her brow. "Did she say what she wants?"

The maid was fanning herself. "Said something 'bout drawing even, m'lady. I didn't really understand if I'm honest, but I reckoned you'd know what she meant."

Tinnion stood and walked to the door, straightening her tunic as she walked. "Thank you, and... Take a seat, take some time and have something to drink. There's no need for you to be running yourself into the ground."

"Yes, m'lady. Thank you, m'lady." She plonked herself down onto a chair with a puff and poured herself a cup of wine.

"Cinerea. Is there a problem? It must be something important for you to leave the forest." Tinnion smirked, showing her words to be an act.

"My Queen prepares to travel. She will soon meet with your Queen on her island and I have been asked to join her guard. It is a great honour for me, however, it means that I will not be here to defeat you again for sometime."

"So you've come to surrender now?" Tinnion caught the dryad's eye and smiled.

The dryad's eyes sparkled, and she gave a gentle laugh. "Perhaps next time we meet, Sealgair. Sadly for you, not today. No, I need advice. I've never been out of the forest. You are the only human I have talked to." She lowered her eyes and her voice "I'm feeling... nervous, Sealgair."

Tinnion stepped forward and placed a hand gently on the dryad's shoulder, looking up into the heavy eyes of her friend. "Let's go sit on the tree line, Cinerea. We can talk, sit, whatever you need."

The two walked, barely a hand's width between them, from the manor to the northern pasture. There they climbed the gate and walked the tree line. Coming to a cherry tree, they sat in its shade.

Cinerea placed her hand against the bark of the tree and smiled. "Princess Daowiel used to watch the Ògan climb this tree and ask for its fruit. She knew then that there was something different about the child. Now we sit together under its branches. Only two humans have sat beneath the trees with a dryad since the war. This is not normal for me, it is not normal for our people. I feel the world changing and I'm not sure what my place will be."

Tinnion sat, crossed legged, across from her friend, picking at the grass. She leant forward a little and, putting a long green blade between her lips, chewed thoughtfully.. "You're going to the Queens island. You're going to be there when the two queens sign an accord that will make that change happen. Your place is right there at the moment of change, being part of that, helping the world move forward."

"I will only be there to stand behind my queen, nothing more." The dryad lowered her eyes and bit her lip.

"The queen would not travel without someone she trusted at her back. She chose you. Out of all those that could travel with her, she chose you. You'll be there, in a room with two queens, a princess... At least one princess... and the queen's voice. That is an honoured place, Cinerea."

"The Ògan too. She will be there. I did not think I would meet the Ògan properly. I may even have the chance to talk with her. What an honour that would be." The dryad's eyes lit up and Tinnion let out a laugh.

"I'm sorry, Cinerea. I didn't mean to laugh... It's just that... well, I know Lana. She'll be sat wondering why on earth she's been asked to sit in that room as well and is probably a lot more confused about it all than you are."

The dryad shook her head. "How can that be? She is the cause of this change. Without her, this would not be happening. She will bring our worlds together. Even the queens are little more than the tools for her destiny, for our destiny."

"She's barely older than a child, Cinerea. I love her and respect her, she is growing so fast. But she's still a child in so many ways, she's like a little sister and she has a habit of getting into trouble and tying her tongue up in knots. It's impossible not to love her though. I doubt you'll meet her without feeling the same." Tinnion's smile grew wide. "If she's destined to bring our worlds together somehow, it'll be through us all wanting to take her under our wings and keep her safe. Not that she isn't capable of protecting herself. That girl can swing a staff as well as anyone I know."

Cinerea's shoulders dropped. She slumped over, her head bowed. "All my life, I have been told that humans are dangerous. That they want to destroy us and that I should be wary of them. Now you tell me I will feel love for another. I do not doubt your words, Sealgair, but it is difficult to understand."

"Another?" Tinnion looked up into the dryad's eyes, her own eyes wide.

Cinerea nodded slowly, not speaking a word.

Chapter Nine

Games and Cakes

The old lore keeper was back in the study the following day and he smirked as Lana entered alone to sit opposite him.

"The dryad will not be joining us today?" He raised a brow as he asked.

"Not today. Princess Daowiel is walking in the trees." Lana slowed in emphasis as she said the word Princess, a pointed response to the lore keeper's question. "There are trees on the western shore of the lake that she has never seen before, the ones that trail their leaves in the water. She says that they must have come from an unfamiliar land since the war and she wanted to get to know them."

Aelwynne smiled. "We call them weeping willows because they seem melancholy. Beautiful but a little sad, they're related to the willows of Mortara, but they come from the Falcon Isles. I do hope that the princess enjoys her day."

"Oh, I'm sure she will. She was very excited to go back there." Lana glanced at the old man across the table. "She doesn't really enjoy being stuck indoors with dusty old books."

The lore keeper coughed. "Yes. I'm sure the dryad would rather be out, dallying through trees, than learning." Aelwynne flashed Lana a warning look and shook her head slightly. Lana bit her cheek.

"Today we will look at the end of the Great War and the killing of the gods." The lore keeper announced as though unaware of the tension his words were causing.

"They didn't die." Lana mumbled under her breath and rolled her eyes.

"What?" The lore keeper's voice was sharp.

"The gods, they didn't die. They left, but they didn't die. Least ways Kaoris and Khyione and Zeor and Qura and Ophine left. Ulios stayed in the deep oceans. Of course, they say Solumus and Chaint died when their ships burned up in the northern seas, but I don't really know anything much about them. Well, except that other gods were angry at them for running away." Lana's voice became more certain as she spoke and she sat up, straight and sure.

"What you're saying, Lana. It can't be right. All the lore we have, every lore master since the war, they all agree that the gods died. What makes you believe they live?" Aelwynne interrupted the lore keeper, who was blowing air and shook visibly.

"I saw it." Lana turned to look directly at her mentor. "Sometimes I just see things. It's happened ever since I was in the Heartwood. I've been seeing things that happened in the war, and a little bit before it. Oh and then, when I was in the temple in the woods north of Southport, I ended up with this circlet attaching itself to me. Since then it's like I remember things that Qura did, and saw. They're kind of like dreams I have, only sometimes they happen when I'm doing other things. It happened at the tournament when I was watching Brighid and Wren fight. Qura made the circlet to do that from what I can tell, but the memories from before she made it aren't really very clear. I'm sure she made it to hold memories, though. I think that's why I remember the letters so well."

"Anyway, I saw them, the gods and goddesses. They were in the fortress at Lochheart and the war was almost over. They stood in the gardens and they cast some sort of spell. And then there was a great burst of light and they all disappeared." Lana was happy to be talking with Aelwynne. She didn't think the lore keeper would ever listen to the things she knew, the things she saw.

"Why would they do that?" Her mentor's voice was soft, her head tilted, her eyes focused on Lana's.

"They said that they had to go, to leave the world so that their children, the fae, could learn to stand on their own, to stop relying on them. They were talking about being somewhere outside of the world and that if they needed to, they would create a new place and begin again. I think they regretted a lot of things they did here. They all seemed very sad." Lana's eyes felt heavy, and she felt that fuzziness on her forehead that connected her to the visions.

"I'm not sure that these dreams are what you think they are, Lana." Her mentor looked concerned. "I think you should write the things you see down though. Perhaps you could ask your friend, Selene, to help you? I know she has been tasked with understanding Qura's temple. She may have more information on your circlet. And if you write these visions down, the lore keepers can investigate them." Aelwynne sat back in her chair again, her hand covering her mouth.

"You don't believe me, do you?" Lana's mouth scrunched up, and she sighed. "It's alright, I don't think I would believe it either."

"I believe that you're seeing these things, Lana. I'm just not sure what they are, what they mean. But this isn't my area of expertise. I learn what I need in order to do my job, to know the people I am talking with. I'm not a lore keeper, I prefer people to books." Aelwynne smiled, nodding her head quickly in the direction of the lore keeper. Lana put her hand up to her mouth to hide a giggle and turned away to look at the door.

"I see that my expertise is not appreciated here." The lore keeper huffed. "I have never heard so much nonsense being entertained. What is worse is that it is not only the child that cannot see the value of learning. I had expected better of you, Aelwynne. You have not grown as I thought. I shall return to my study at once and wait for an apology. Perhaps when the queen learns of your ignorance, you will stop this foolishness." There was an air of superiority throughout the old mans statement but he said the word 'queen' with a venom that shocked Lana. She glared at him and opened her mouth to speak, but stopped as Aelwynne grabbed her right hand with a strong squeeze.

"As you think best, Lore Keeper." The lady's voice was formal and stiff. She stood and bowed her head, then turned to Lana. "Why don't we take a walk and let the Lore Keeper gather his things in peace, Lana?" Lana nodded and stood, following her mentor from the room.

"It will take several days for Coccus to calm down. I doubt he will emerge from his study for a while and I think that might be a good thing. Queen Olerivia is due to be here on the full of the moon and she wants you to be involved in the talks. We can spend the next few days discussing what you know about the dryad so that we can be better prepared." Aelwynne held her hands clasped at her waist as they strolled through the gardens. She turned to Lana, her head tilted. "Do you know why she wants you there?"

"No!" Lana felt surprised by the question. Queen Rhiannon had asked her the same some moons before and she had been honest with her answer. "She never told me she had asked for that and hasn't told me why. I think, maybe, it's just because she knows me and if I'm there, she won't be surrounded by strangers. She's never left the Heartwood. It must feel odd for her to think about coming here." Lana paused and sucked on her bottom lip. "Do you really want to know more about them?"

Aelwynne's head tilted back a little, and she looked at Lana sideways. "What do you have in your mind, Lana?"

"I think we should go for a walk tomorrow. You, me and Daowiel. You should watch her in the woods, see how she is when she's more... at home. Be with us like a friend would be, not like a teacher or a diplomat." Lana was smiling, her eyes glistened as she spoke.

"Do you think she would accept me in that way?"

"Yes! But you have to relax and have fun. Daowiel is a princess and she can play that role, all formal and commanding. But she's really playful when you let her be. She just doesn't get the chance in the palace."

Aelwynne nodded with a smile. "Then I will try."

The water was chilly, despite the hot earrach sun, but that did not seem to put Lana off her play. She waded waist deep, splashing and laughing, occasionally diving under the water and popping up close to her friends with a shout and a fountain of frosty water. It had taken some time to convince Aelwynne of the fun they could have splashing around in the lake; she thought it a little childish, but as Lana and Daowiel played around her, she loosened up and enjoy herself.

When they tired, they waded back to the shore and lay out on a blanket to dry in the sun. Aelwynne sighed, the pleasant sigh of a person feeling relaxed. "Now I understand why you both look so sad sat in the study all day. It's nice spending time with the two of you. I'm not sure I understand the dryad much more than I did, though."

Lana chuckled. "That's cos we haven't finished playing yet, Aelwynne. You haven't ventured into woodland at all and that's where you'll see a bit more of Daowiel... or... well, maybe not see her. That depends on how good you are at the game."

"What are you planning on having me do, Lana?" Aelwynne shifted to lean on her side and look at her apprentice.

"Well, Daowiel will go into the woods and we'll play hide and seek a bit. 'Cept she'll be looking for us as we look for her and if she catches you first, you'll owe her a honey cake... That's what we play for now, anyway."

"You want me to have a honey cake sent to you?" Aelwynne raised a brow.

"No!" Lana chuckled again. "You have to bake it! It wouldn't be the same just having the kitchen send one."

Aelwynne's jaw dropped for a moment. "I don't know how to bake a honey cake, Lana. I've never baked anything before."

"See." Lana smiled broadly. "You'll be learning so much, spending time with us instead of stuck in that stuffy room."

Lana watched as Aelwynne tip toed through the woods, hiding behind trees and peeking through branches searching for the dryad princess. She giggled as Daowiel appeared through the trunk of the tree Aelwynne was crouching by and gently pulled on the ladi's braid. Aelwynne spun her head quickly, but the princess was gone in an instant.

Seeing the dryad princess and her mentor playing their game gave Lana confidence that the day would be a success. Encouraged by the sounds of laughter floating through the woodlands, she sank into the tree behind her, ready to join in the playful teasing.

As she reached out through the network of trees and flora to find the princess, she felt a presence that didn't match either of her friends. A darkness, a familiar presence to the woodland, yet stood apart from it, not fitting with the sense of life. A mysterious void that seemed to cause the trees to recoil.

Lana pulled herself to the bridge and ran to the tree nearest the presence, pulling the handle of her staff from her belt as she went. Reaching the far end of the bridge she paused, taking a deep breath and calming her mind, then she slid through the tree, silently, staff ready should she face attack.

The dark, smooth stone had the appearance of midnight ice and seemed to soak the warmth from the midday sun. At the base of the jutting formation stood a man. As tall as any man Lana had ever seen and lithe. His well-defined muscles rippled as he moved, climbing the rocks like a snake slithers across stones. The man was naked, his skin as black as a raven's feather and when he turned his head to look around, Lana gasped in shock. His eyes were as dark as the rock and seemed to soak up the light in the same way.

The sound of Lana's surprise caused the man to turn, hanging from the rocks by one hand and one leg. He twisted to stare right at her, his dark eyes showing no emotion. In a moment, the figure had leapt from the rocks and was walking toward her, his eyes fixed on hers, unblinking.

Lana's knuckles whitened as her fingers tightened around her staff. Slowly, legs trembling, she moved away, desperate to feel the trunk of the tree at her back again and sink back into safety.

The mans head tilted, and he stopped, becoming as still as one of the statues in the palace. Had she not seen him moving, she would have sworn that a statue is exactly what he was.

Lana felt her heart beating faster. She spun her head, checking on her distance from the tree, then back to the dark man in front of her. He was closer now and lower to the ground, his feet set behind him, his hands touching the ground in front. Lana spun her staff, pointing it to his face, her arm shaking.

"Stay back. Please, stay back." She stuttered as she spoke and stretched her left arm out behind her, her fingertips touching the rough bark of the tree.

The man showed no sign of understanding, and in a moment, he leapt. Springing forward across the gap between them. Lana pushed her hand into the tree and stumbled backward. She fell to her back on the bridge, dropping her staff with a clatter and bruising her behind.

Letting out a breath she hadn't realised she had been holding, she lay back on the bridge and tried to stop shaking.

The palace's head cook was not surprised to see Lana. She had become a frequent visitor to the kitchens, watching and chatting with the staff as they baked and cooked. Her jaw dropped though when Aelwynne joined them and asked to be shown how to bake a honey cake.

The Lady had never been below stairs, though she often had instructions for the staff. The cook was flustered and stammered as she talked. A far cry from her normal confident and very controlled self.

Lana helped, fetching ingredients and giving the Queen's Voice hints and suggestions. Though she also did her best to ensure that her mentor ended the evening with as much flour and batter in her hair and on her dress as was possible. The lady had complained with the first puff of flour but was soon laughing as much as her apprentice; and was thrilled when she took the sticky honey cake from the oven.

The cake looked a little sad, sunk in the middle and rather heavier than it ought to be with honey dripping across the platter. Once it was cool, it was put on the table with a pitcher of milk for the pair and the dryad princess, Daowiel, to eat.

"I'd like to thank you both for today." Aelwynne blew flour whitened hair from her face as she spoke. "I was sceptical at first, but I really have learned a lot from you, and had a lot of fun along the way." Lana smiled across the table at her mentor as she listened. "I have never quite felt the way I did when I was in the woods. A mixture of fear and determination, of pride and of humility. I would not have survived a moment if you had truly been hunting me." Aelwynne bowed her head to the dryad princess. "I did not know you could use the trees as you do. That is... I knew you could travel through them. Lana taught me that, but I did not know you could do it so smoothly, so precisely. "

"You made good prey, Lady Aelwynne, but I don't think you should volunteer to lead a hunt anytime soon." Daowiel laughed as she spoke.

"I'm hoping that I will never need to, Princess." Aelwynne smiled. "There are people so much better suited to that than I! I'm far more comfortable in a warm and dry room. I didn't see you much in the woods, Lana. Did you have fun watching me trying to hide?"

Lana looked up from her plate, honey covering her chin, and swallowed the spoonful of cake she had with a gulp. "I... I thought I saw something, but I'm not so sure now. Maybe I was just tired after playing in the lake."

Daowiel stopped eating and put a hand over Lana's. "What was it, Ògan?"

"It was... I really don't know. It looked like a man, at least at first it did, but he moved like a snake and his skin and his eyes were all black. Like a raven. But it might have been just shadows, I don't know."

"You went to the stones again, Ògan? I told you, there is something... something wrong with that place."

Lana nodded, twisting her mouth. "The trees could feel something... Something odd. I thought I should see what it was. I've never heard of anything like... well, like what I thought I saw. Have you?"

"A man that moves like a snake and is as black as a raven? I have not. Perhaps a sgàil, a shadow, as you call them, but their skin was pale or blue, not black. No, Ògan, I do not know what you have seen."

"I will have our lore keepers at the library search the texts, Lana. If there is a record of this man, or anything of those rocks, we will find it." Aelwynne's voice was soft and her smile warm.

Lana nodded and dug her spoon back into her cake. "Your cake is like the ones my friend Ara used to make. So sticky and thick. It looks sad, but I like it. You should definitely eat it while it's still warm, though. That's when they're nicest."

Chapter Ten

THE PLAINS OF SINDALE

The journey through the forest was long and hard, Brighid's wounds slowed her and caused her pain but she grew in strength as the days went on and by the time they reached the eastern edge of the forest she could exercise with her blades again. Her movement was stiff, but it was progress and it lifted her spirits.

Wren was not fairing so well. The forest was old and dense, the air thick and musty. It was difficult for a Sylph to breathe. She felt caged, entrapped in a prison of wood. Trees obscured the sky from sight, the light from the earrach sun barely finding its way through the dense dark needles of the pines that towered over her head. She had become withdrawn on their journey through the forest, barely speaking, often walking alone. Brighid worried about her, the sullen look in her eyes, the heaviness of her steps. She tried to coax her friend out of her misery with bawdy stories and songs that had won smiles and snickers from warriors across Mortara.

"The border of the forest is less than half a day's walk, Brighid. Why do we wait? You say it is night, but how can you tell? We have not seen the sun in days. If it is days. It could be weeks, moons for all I know."

"Be patient, friend. We'll be out in the open again tomorrow. The plains to the east are wide, flat and open. You'll see nothing but the sky for days. Come on, pick up that stick there and swing it at me. I need to practise again."

"You're better starting with one of your family, Brighid. You're far too slow for me right now. I'll wait until you can move more freely."

Brighid looked at her friend, her eyebrows raised in feigned shock. "Too slow, is it?" She hooked her foot under a thin fallen branch and lifted it, sending it flying toward the sylph. By the time it reached Wren she had her twin blades in her hands. "Come on, Wren! Gimme your best."

"There are camp fires on the plains, Brighid" Wren had run on ahead of the tuath clan as soon as the first light of the sun could be seen. She was sick of the trees and could travel much faster than her human friends. She had reached the edge of the forest mid morning and looked around the plains. Now, as the caravan was preparing to take lunch, she was back and the news she brought was not good.

"How far?" Brighid put her plate aside and grabbed her belt from from the ground.

"No less than two days. Distance is hard to judge over this terrain, it is deceiving, but they were far enough away that I can be sure we wouldn't meet them before that. Not unless they took to marching fast toward us." The sylph was calm, not allowing emotion to enter her voice.

Brighid settled a little at that news, putting her belt and the blades it held back to the ground at her side. "How many?"

"Three dozen fires, at least."

"A large force then, three hundred warriors or more. I'd hoped they'd be waiting in the north for us. They'll make this journey much harder for our caravan, that's for sure."

"Yer getting soft, Sister. It'll take more than three hundred o' MacTiern's men tae stop us. They've never come close tae us in the games." Anndra was smiling, almost laughing at the news. He was a good fighter, almost as good as his sister, and had a growing reputation in the tuath games.

"Aye, but these aint games, Anndra. It's a proper war, and most o' the people with us aint fighters. We've less than a hundred warriors. We'll need tae be cautious. We cannae just run in, swords flying. Where's father?"

"He's with the group at the rear. He'll be here soon enough." Anndra's smile was gone, his sister's words highlighting the potential danger.

Brighid stood and looked down at her brother with a smile. "I'll scout on ahead with Wren. Get the warriors here lined up and send someone back tae father with the news. I want ye tae be ready for him getting here. We'll need tae go forward in formation once we're out on the plains. There's nothing can come at us from our rear so we'll form our front line. That way, if they've scouts out, we'll be ready."

Anndra smirked again, and his eyes sparkled with mirth. "Aye, M'lady, as ye command!" Teasing his sister with mock formality was a familiar game and one that made him relax.

Three hundred and twenty-three warriors stood in the way of the MacFaern clan. Fifty sat on horseback, with long-handled axes resting across their saddles. The others lined up five deep, each carrying a round shield and a short sword.

The warriors of the MacFaern clan had travelled on ahead of the villagers to meet this threat. They knew they were outnumbered, with three warriors to each of them, but they had an air of confidence about them that belied the situation.

Cohade, Brighid, Anndra and Wren rode slowly forward, a makeshift flag of parlance held high. They were met on the ground halfway between the two forces by MacTiern and his three sons.

"Yer warriors look happy MacTiern. I assume you've told them you're joining us?" Cohade had a wide smile on his bearded face and he slapped his thigh joyfully.

MacTiern turned his head and spat upon the ground. "You're on my land MacFaern. Turn back or face yer death like a man."

"Ye know I cannae turn back. There's an army of rebels and shadows on my heels. I need to get my people tae Northfort and safety." Cohade tried to reason with his neighbour.

"Rebels? No, MacFaern, those warriors chasing ye are true to Fearann a Tuath. Yer a traitor to your lands."

"Aye, I knew ye were too dense tae see the right of the situation. Yer siding with shadows, MacTiern. Can ye no see how wrong that is?" Cohade shook his head sadly. "Ye know I'll have tae kill ye if you stand between my people and their safety."

MacTiern laughed. "Look behind you MacFaern, you've less than half the force than I have and half again the men." The mans laughter stopped and his face twisted in disdain as he looked over at Brighid and Wren.

"Start praying it's ma father you meet on the field, MacTiern. If ye fight at all, that is." Brighid rested her hand on her blade's hilt and gave the clan chief a glare that could freeze over a loch.

"I look forward tae a fight with the old man or any of you, girl. It's time clan MacFaern was taken down and I'm proud tae be the man tae do it." MacTiern scowled.

"Let's end this now then, MacTiern. Spare yer men and ours. Get down frae yer horse, all four o' you, and I'll end yer line here." Brighid handed the reins of her horse to her brother and climbed down, drawing her blades as she walked toward the men.

MacTiern looked to his sons, his face blanching, then tugged on his reins, turning his horse. The four men pushing their horses to a gallop back to their lines.

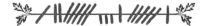

The mounted warriors of the MacTiern clan raced forward toward them, steam billowing from their horses' noses and waving their axes over head. Their voices raised in battle cries.

Clan MacFaern stood silent, a front line of twenty-five warriors, shields held high in a solid wall of wood. They stood four deep in a formation that was much narrower than their attackers.

As the horses approached, long spears emerged from behind the shields, their butts anchored into the ground at the warriors' feet. A unified grunt accompanied the movement, a loud expression of readiness from a hundred powerful warriors that visibly unsettled a few of the onrushing men.

"NOW!" Cohade, still mounted and patrolling the front line, bellowed before he rode his horse around the unit. The first line dropped to their knees and those in the second line swung rocks from slings. Then they too dropped and the line behind followed suit. By the time the last line loosed their rocks, half the onrushing warriors were unhorsed.

The front line stood once more and met the crash of the offence with their shields raised high. Their spears thrust upward into the flesh of man or horse. As more horses and their riders fell, Brighid, Anndra and Wren rode in to the flanks of the attackers and cut at the men down their weakest side.

The attacking horsemen that had not fallen turned aside and rode with speed back toward their kin and safety, many were wounded and some fell even as they rode.

Cohade called to his warriors to reform their lines. There had been casualties within their ranks too. Perhaps two dozen warriors had fallen and others had been injured in the attack. Still, seventy warriors formed up and stepped forward, their spears discarded in favour of their blades.

As they marched forward, several of the clan that weren't fighters ran forward with litters to carry the injured back to the tree line for treatment.

"That could have been worse." Anndra rode beside his father.

"Aye, son. Though it was bad enough. We've four men tae each of our warriors waiting tae cut us down. It'll no go well for either side if we cannae convince the damn fool MacTiern of what's right."

They marched and rode on across the plains between the forces. Each swearing a silent oath or whispering a prayer. Determination on their faces, the survival of their clan depended on this battle, the survival of the north might very well be on their shoulders.

Cohade called a momentary halt a hundred metres from his enemy's lines and his clan drew their swords, steadied their shields and prepared for the clash. Both Brighid and Wren gave up their horses in favour of marching the rest of the way with the clan and fighting on foot. Cohade and Anndra remained mounted and rode the lines, stirring their clan's spirits.

When the gap between the forces closed by half, Cohade gave his call. The shield wall formed once more on the front line and his clan's slings were once more set with stones.

Cohade rode his horse in front of his clan, addressing the men that would keep them from Northfort. "Your lord would have ye fight today, he would have ye turn upon your friends, yer neighbours, yer cousins. He would have ye side with the shadows, who have returned, and fight against Clan MacFaern." Cohade's face showed the strain of his shouting, reddening as he spoke to the men that faced him. "You all know us. Each of ye. Ye know we will not yield. Are ye prepared to die today? To die for a lord that has betrayed the north, that has betrayed yer families, that has betrayed yer honour? We will welcome all those that want tae join us. And we will not hunt those that turn away now. But we will kill each and all that stand against us. Make yer choice!"

Two dozen shields dropped. The men that held them fled the field, running back toward the hills on the horizon. Those that remained faced each other, the tension clear. One man stepped forth, a large man with a long red beard. He carried twin axes and stood a head above the rest.

"I am no shadow friend, MacFaern." The man made his way toward the horse of Cohade, his axes in hand. Brighid drew her blades and stepped forward, ready to meet the giant. "Hold, Brighid! We've fought before, you and I, in the tournaments and I've no a mind tae do it for real. I'll stand with you now if it's shadows we face. Give me the truth, shield sister."

"My father speaks true, MacAllister. A dozen shadows fought at the rebel's side. They killed most that defied them and tried tae kill us. Your lord saw danger and bowed to MacKenna. He surrendered tae the shadows. MacTiern has no courage, he has no honour, and he would betray yours to save his cowardly hide."

The giant man, now stood in the centre of the land between the two clans, turned to MacTiern, the lord still mounted on his horse behind his force.

"Ye told us MacFaern had turned, tried to claim Fearann a Tuath as his own. Ye told us ye stood strong against him and that we must as well. I know Brighid MacFaern. She does not fear us, she does not fear death. She does not lie and has nae reason to do so here. I will not fight for a coward. I will not fight for a traitor." The warrior turned back to Brighid. "Will ye have me at yer side, shield sister?"

"Aye, MacAllister, and gladly! And any other man that has courage and honour."

Two dozen more men pushed their way through the lines of MacTiern's force, causing skirmishes to break out along the ranks. Some didn't make it to the ground between the clans, but eighteen men did and they offered their swords to Brighid. Wren made her way to join the group and stood at Brighid's side.

"A gold coin says I kill more than you, Brighid." The Sylph gave a wicked smile to her friend and laughed as another half-dozen men threw their swords to the ground and ran.

"Aye, yer on, Wren. I'll take yer money!" Brighid smiled at her friend and together they ran toward those warriors that remained. They broke through the demoralised front line with little resistance. Men fell in great numbers as Brighid, Wren and those that had turned away from MacTiern cut through their ranks and double their number fled. The warriors pushed on and Cohade sent fifty of his clan warriors to join them.

The ghosts of the wounds to Brighid's stomach and leg ached, and her arms tired quickly as she moved her way through the crowd. But she never showed her pain. Her movement was not as fluid and she favoured her right side as a result, but her mind was as sharp as it had ever been. She struck and moved, never still.

No blade or spear found her but her swords drew blood with every slash and thrust.

In a moment MacAllister was fighting beside her, his axes crushing and cutting through those that stood before him, his strength and ferocity all the more obvious beside the precise dance of Brighid.

The space around the pair opened up, warriors moved away, keeping their distance from her blades and his axes. In no time at all, they stood alone with nothing but bodies and dropped weapons around them. Men ran from them, dropping any thought of glory or honour in battle. Wren stood ten feet away to their right, a smile on her face.

"I had expected they would put up some form of a fight, Brighid. Your cousins disappoint me!" The sylph leant on her staff, making a show of how relaxed she was.

"Few men would choose to stand against a MacFaern, sylph. Fewer still would succeed." MacAllister hung his axes from his belt as he shouted across the field. A smile that threatened to displace his jaw adorned his face.

A horn sounded, not too far from where they stood, MacTiern calling those men that remained his to his side. Thirty men, no more, rallied to his call and formed a circle around him and his sons. Cohade and Anndra rode slowly toward them, a force of twenty warriors marched behind them, still unchallenged in the battle and fresh.

"Lay down yer swords and yer lives will be spared. Yer lord has led ye in a lie and will face trial. Ye have been loyal, as ye should be. But yer loyalty now, must be tae the north, tae the Tay and tae the Queen. Ye need not share the fate of this traitor. But ye should show your side now."

Several warriors threw their weapons to the ground, though sixteen men held on to theirs. Those men turned to their lord and his sons and they dragged them from their horses to the dirt of the plains.

Cohade nodded and turned to a warrior at his side.

"Secure them. They will face their fate here." A half-dozen men went to meet those that held MacTiern, carrying ropes to bind the failed lord.

"Set camp!" Anndra turned his horse and commanded the warriors of his clan.

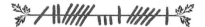

Once the camp was set, fires lit and food was eaten, Cohade called on a dozen men to stand judge against MacTiern. Each was the eldest present of their family and each held the respect of their clan. Wren was also asked to join the circle. As a warrior with no allegiances or connection to the north, her thoughts were greatly valued.

MacTiern and his sons were bound with rope and stood in the centre of the circle. Cohade stood to make the case against them and recounted what happened in the tower of Shadowatch. He spoke with the men that represented families in MacTiern's clan and exposed the gesith's lies.

All men know that a fae who breaks their word, once given, dooms their soul. So when Wren spoke up to support Cohade's account, all doubt was removed from those present.

Once Wren had finished her testimony, an elderly man of MacTiern's clan rose to his feet and addressed the crowd. "Tae judge a clan chief, a traitor is a terrible burden. It is not a judgement that can be made in haste. But we have all known Cohade MacFaern throughout our lives. We know him tae be honourable, we know him tae be loyal. With the word of the sylph added tae his there can be no doubt. MacTiern led our clan against a loyal and honourable man. He aligned himself with shadows and plotted tae overthrow the Tay. He is a traitor. All who agree say, aye."

The circle spoke as one, a single word of agreement that set the disgraced clan chief's fate.

"So it is then. Callum MacTiern, ye have been found a traitor tae the north and to the crown." The old man went on. "Yer head will be returned to yer wife. She will be given a purse and offered the chance to re-marry or serve. If she declines, she will be stripped of her name and banished. Yer sons will die with you for their part in this. The MacTiern line ends here." The old man's face was sullen as he spoke. "MacFaern, you and yer clan have been wronged more than I and my family, will ye swing the blade?"

"If that is the decision of the circle. Though I feel it would be better served by an elder of the clan he lead. Justice served restores the honour of the clan more than my blade could."

The old man nodded, a strained movement that seemed to show the weight of the act before him. "Aye, that is fair." He looked to the surrounding men. "MacAllister." He looked to the giant, bearded, warrior that had been first to stand with Brighid. "Will ye swing the blade and right the clan in this?"

"If it's the circle's choice, aye." MacAllister nodded.

The circle spoke again, this time the 'Aye's' were quieter, but they were spoken in agreement just the same.

Chapter Eleven

TWO QUEENS

Lana was sitting alongside her mentor on the grass under an old birch tree in the palace gardens. The skies to the east were a shade of soft purple as the rising sun pushed back the night. The stars still sparkled, and the moon was full and bright.

She hadn't slept long; she was far too excited and more than a little nervous.

Today four women that she knew well, four strong and incredibly important women that she respected, would come together to discuss the future of Mortara.

This would be the first time that these four women would meet, and Lana had some concerns.

Her new mentor, Aelwynne, was a gentle woman that had an expert knowledge of Mortara and a powerful belief in the queens values. She was patient and a wonderful teacher, allowing Lana to learn in her own time and encouraging her to speak her mind and decide on important matters. There were times though that Lana could see the granite like strength of the Queen's Voice. She was not somebody that suffered fools lightly, nor was she somebody that you would wish to cross. She had convinced the dryad princess Daowiel that she was a trustworthy person with an honest intent to carry out her queens promise to make Mortara a better place for all. But that had taken a moon to achieve and had looked doomed before Lana suggested they leave the palace for the woods on the south side of the lake.

Today Aelwynne would be sat opposite Daowiel's sister, Erinia. The heir to the dryad throne was more suspicious of humans, less trusting and more determined to expand the dryad's territory and reclaim the woodlands around Mortara. Lana loved Erinia, in the same way that you love a cousin but she felt, sometimes, that the princess deliberately pushed and pulled on that feeling and made it difficult to maintain. Lana wouldn't have the chance to take them to the woods to play, not that Erinia enjoyed playing the way Daowiel did, and she worried that the two women would clash.

She was less concerned about the two queens, both were strong and independent, both were determined and both could be strict, but they were also both eager to make these talks work and wise enough to know when to give and when to take.

As the Dryad had never left the Heartwood and could not travel the bridge to the Queen's Isle unaided Daowiel had left the island the day before and returned to the dryad palace so that she could guide her family to a giant redwood in the palace grounds. There, they would be greeted by the human royal party in a ceremony that would stretch into the evening.

"Are you looking forward to the party, Lady Aelwynne?" She looked to her mentor, who was humming happily to herself.

"It's a formal event, Lana. Everything will be proper and controlled." Aelwynne was talking like a teacher rather than a friend again which made Lana sigh.

"Well that sounds dull, Aelwynne. I reckon once you've had some Dryad wine you'll be singing songs and calling for dances like it's a Beltane feast."

A smile broke out on Aelwynne's face and the two had shared a moments laughter. If you caught The Queen's Voice at the right moment, you could see her sense of fun and humour shining through. Something she repressed in favour of seriousness when she was working, which made Lana sad.

The arrival of the dryad to the palace grounds was a festive occasion. A magnificent feast had been prepared, the gardens decorated and lit with lanterns and musicians had worked with Daowiel to learn some of the dryad tunes and dances. It was clear they were truly enjoying the opportunity to play for Queen Olerivia and Princess Erinia.

For their part, Daowiel's mother and sister were delighted at the festivities. Erinia seemed overwhelmed by the greeting they had received and the stern mask she usually wore when discussing the humans had melted away to a look of simple joy.

"My sister spoke of grey walls and cold stone in the human world. I see those, of course, but they are not as horrendous as I had imagined. There is even a little beauty in your home."

Queen Rhiannon nodded with a smile. "I am pleased you approve, princess. I hope that the rest of your stay exceeds your expectations as much."

"How have my children been, your majesty? I trust they have been respectful and well behaved?" Queen Olerivia smiled warmly at her counterpart.

Rhiannon's brow raised, and her reply was slightly hesitant, tinged with a questioning tone. "Princess Daowiel has been a most welcome guest, Olerivia. She is pleasant and thoughtful company."

"And Lana?" Olerivia pressed.

"Ah." Rhiannon nodded, setting her jaw but smiling through it. "She is doing well. She has shown a great deal of interest and ability in her learning. A curious and energetic addition to the palace. I hope that she will decide to stay long after these talks are done." The queens exchanged a look that made Lana uneasy. A fleeting competitive glance that few noticed. But Lana had seen it and held her breath til it passed.

Olerivia smiled warmly and returned the queens nod "The Ògan was in my care, in my home. She endeared herself to me and I feel a responsibility to her care. She may not have my blood, but I think of her as my kin."

The queen's faces softened, and honest smiles replaced the questions and competition in their eyes.

"I have noticed she has a similar effect on myself and my staff, Olerivia. There are times I feel she could take this kingdom from me with a smile and a whisper. Though I doubt it would ever cross her mind to try, for that I am grateful."

The women laughed then, and Lana felt Daowiel's elbow in her ribs.

"You've broken the royal demeanour of them both, Ògan!"

Lana nudged her friend away and scrunched her mouth and nose into a tight little ball, then she leant into the dryad and hugged her.

"I missed you this morning. Breakfast was so stiff and formal without you there."

"Excuse me, your highness. I was hoping I might speak with the Ògan?" The musicians struck a chord as Cinerea approached them and Lana's face lit up in recognition of the tune. She grabbed Daowiel with her left hand and Cinerea with her right.

"You can if you can speak while you dance!" Lana pulled the dryad to the dancing square, skipping and laughing merrily as she went.

The following day was a very different affair. The frivolity of the previous night was gone and a small party gathered in a chamber off the main hall. Rhiannon, Aelwynne, Lana, and Reynard sat on one side of a large oak table. Olerivia, Erinia, Daowiel and Cinerea sat on the other. The friendly chatter turned to serious talk of past deeds and future hopes.

Erinia laid out her thoughts of expansion for the Heartwood and demands for the dryad to be protected and free to travel around Mortara. Much of her demands made Rhiannon smile.

"My Mortara is not the one you know, princess. I made laws to give all fae their freedom when I inherited the crown. I would accept no more harm to befall a dryad than I would a human."

The princes scoffed, "Yet your people destroy our home, they hunt us and kill us on sight. The heartwood shrinks year on year and with it, my people."

Rhiannon sat back in her chair and raised her fingers to her lips, her hands forming a triangle that framed her chin.

"The same accusations of hunting and killing have been made against dryad hunters, Princess." Aelwynne's tone was cold, her eyes tight.

There was a moment of silence as the 'Queen's Voice' and the princess held each other's eyes in cold stares. A chilling tension filling the space between them.

"Are things in Butterholt going well?" Lana broke the silence and the tension with a soft-spoken question.

Olerivia turned to her, seemingly grateful for the question. "They are, Lana. We are very pleased with the way our people have been able to work together and help one another. Your idea has truly helped, with your stead and the forest." Olerivia smiled sweetly as she spoke, her deep green eyes sparkled.

"Perhaps we can talk about that a bit? It seems silly talking about things that we can't change when there are so many we can." Lana sat up straight, her own eyes sparkled at the dryad queen's praise.

"Silly?" Aelwynne's voice was soft, but her eyes were hard as she turned to face her apprentice.

Lana nodded slowly, the sparkle in her eyes gone as quickly as it came. "When I was a bairn in the stead, my dad told me stories about dryad coming onto the farmsteads to kidnap children. The stories said that they put them in cages and used them for sport. I was told that I had to stay well away from the woods, even though we lived right by them, cos all the stories said that if you went into the woods, even just a step, you would die. I was told the dryad were fearsome and couldn't be trusted and that they'd kill you soon as look at you. Then, one day, I went into the Heartwood to get at some berries."

Lana was settling into one of her long, storied, speeches. She took a deep breath and looked around the room as her intended audience sat back in their chairs to listen.

"When I first saw Daowiel I felt for sure she was going to kill me and instead she gave me the most beautiful flower I have ever seen, or smelled. It was so lovely. Then, when I first went to the palace tree, I thought I'd never leave, that I'd be caged and hunted 'til I couldn't run no more. But I was fed and given a bed and I talked with the people there. Queen Olerivia and Princess Erinia and Daowiel they were really kind, and they taught me things and listened when I was sad. And they told me their stories. I learnt that the people of Butterholt and other holds had been chopping down living trees. That dryad were dying because their home was being destroyed. I heard dryad children being told tales of humans invading the woods, hunting and kidnapping dryad and burning trees. They told the same stories of horror and fear to their children as I was told as a child and I realised that we're all just scared and that it was all just silly stories. The dryad don't hunt children and humans don't either, but all of our children are terrified. So of course they want to kill each other when they meet, they think they have to. Then they grow up and tell the same stories to their children. That's silly!"

A smile grew on Daowiel's face as Lana spoke and, as her friend finished, she chuckled.

"I thought about hunting you, Ògan. But you don't run well enough for it to be fun."

Lana laughed and rolled her eyes at her friend.

"Anyway..." She cleared her throat. "We've been telling the same stories forever, probably since the war, one parent to the next and it's keeping us stuck in the past and not looking at what's really happening." Lana looked around to see how her friends were reacting, pleased to see they were all still with her and listening, she went on. Her tone becoming sad. "Have dryad killed humans in the woods? Yes. Have humans cut down trees and killed dryad? Yes. When I was coming to Southport, I tried to stop two horrid men from burning a dryad in her tree. It was horrible. Can we bring the people that are dead back? No. Can we change what we have done? No. Mebbes, we can stop it from happening anymore, though. That's why we're here, isn't it? To try to stop it, and to talk about how. Not point fingers at each other and trade blame... That's just trying to score points against each other, like it's a nasty game. Besides, we're all to blame. We've all done things we shouldn't have. That's what I think, anyway."

"Lana. Enough." Aelwynne's voice rose barely above a whisper, and her words were clipped.

"Sorry, Aelwynne, but no." Lana shook her head. "I understand it isn't very 'diplomatic' of me." She mimicked her mentor's serious voice as she said the word. “and I swear this isn’t how I’d normally do this if you still let me. But this isn’t a normal situation. Every one at this table is a friend to me. More than half of you have become like my family and I won’t watch my family arguing when we should be getting along and making things better for everyone. I wouldn’t be doing my best if I didn’t say something.”

When she finished, she slumped back in her chair, holding her breath and chewing her cheek, waiting to see what reaction her comments would bring. There was a silence that lasted too long to be comfortable before the dryad queen spoke.

“Lana is right. There is no point in labouring on the past. We are here to make the future better.” She turned to her daughter. “Perhaps you could explain to Queen Rhiannon how our agreement at Butterholt works, Erinia?” She turned to Lana as she finished and smiled. Lana mouthed a silent ‘Thank you.’ to her.

Chapter Twelve

Hunting Angry

Tinnion sat at the foot of the tree, her dark cloak wrapped tight around her, her face hidden in shadow by the deep hood. The skies were clear, the full moon bright and the air still. A fox and a badger had fallen to her bow already, and the night was still very young.

She sat in silence, looking up to the stars, her surroundings lost to the moment.

She had been involved, over the last four years, with two men. Both hunters, neither a serious prospect for bonding. The attraction she had to them was physical, and they had kept one another entertained and warm during long hunting seasons.

She reached up to the bear tooth that hung around her neck, rubbing it between finger and thumb. Allric, the young soldier she had met on the road to Southport, had been different. She had ignored him at first, finding his flirtations irritating. Over time, what she had considered annoying became endearing. He had not been looking for a few moments of intimacy on the road as she first thought, and though he may have been naïve, he had started to win her over. His death had hurt more than she cared to admit, and she had often thought of him as she sat in her camp north of Southport. Tears welled in her eyes. It felt somehow wrong to be thinking of somebody else now. She wasn't even entirely sure what she felt now.

There was a feeling of emptiness in her chest, a cold void that had touched her when Cinerea had said goodbye. The dryad had only been gone one day, and yet Tinnion felt lost already. She had woken up knowing, absolutely, that she would not see Cinerea that day and, though they didn't always meet, there had always been the possibility. It felt as though a large portion of her life was gone.

A horn sounded. Pulling Tinnion back into the world around her, she leapt to her feet and started the run back to the manor.

"What is it, Hayal?" Tinnion walked into the main hall, handing her bow and her cloak to a servant as she approached her advisor.

"There's a farm on the eastern borders, m'lady. It's just a small farm, not much going on there, but there're a dozen people live there and work there. They don't have much, bless 'em. There was a problem there. They had their crop taken from 'em."

"They what?" Tinnion's eyes widened.

"It was sheriffs from Southwood hold, m'lady. They rode up with a cart and told them it was tax payments..." Hayal sighed. "They told 'em it was by order of the Gesith, m'lady."

"The Ge... Who in the void do they... Who is the Gesith?" Tinnion's face reddened and her jaw tightened.

"Lord Hubertus, m'lady. His daughter married Aeloth before... well, before things here went the way they did, m'lady." Hayal mumbled as he finished his sentence.

"How far away is this Gesith's manor?"

"Ten days ride perhaps, m'lady. It's five days to the farm on our border and another five, I reckons, to Lord Hubertus' manor from there."

"Andel?" Tinnion turned to her head sheriff, her look more serious than he had ever seen her.

"yes, m'lady?"

"I want you and six of your sheriffs ready to ride at first light. I won't have this." She undid her belt, throwing her quiver to her chair. "I won't have anyone taking food from my people."

"Yes, m'lady." Andel nodded, his face blanched.

Tinnion was a hunter, used to stalking and killing prey. She was good at, very good at it. She never grew emotional on a hunt, she never allowed herself to take an animal's life in anger or spite. On those occasions that she had taken a human life, it had been in defence of herself or another that needed it. It was considered, measured, important.

Tinnion was not a diplomat. She wasn't used to talking through her problems. She was only now getting used to having people she considered friends; since she met Brighid in the freezing north and Lana on the road. Now she felt she had people around her she could trust, that she could talk to a little. But Tinnion didn't know how to defend herself or her friends with words. She didn't have the skill that Lana, or her new mentor, the queen's voice, had. She didn't know what would happen when she came face to face with the Gesith that had stolen from her people. But she knew she was angry, and she knew that was not a good thing to be. The anger had only grown on the long journey to her neighbour's hold.

Today she rode through Southwood stead toward the manor, seven sheriffs at her back, her bow in her hand, her face like thunder. She would leave the stead with compensation for her people and a promise that they would never again be visited by sheriffs from Lord Hubertus' hold. If she didn't have those things by the end of the day, she would know what it was like to hunt angrily.

A dozen men rode out to meet them. "Halt! Who are you?" The lead rider was an elderly man, around forty-five. He wore chain armour and his hand rested on his sword hilt.

"I will speak with your lord. Now!" Tinnion spoke with as much authority as she could muster.

"You will answer me or you will leave here, peacefully or otherwise." The older man returned her tone.

Tinnion's eyes narrowed. "You dare threaten me? You ride into my hold, you steal from my people and now... Now you threaten me? You can take me to your lord or you can drag him out here to face me. But I will see him."

The man's face blanched. "You're from Butterholt?"

"Your lord. Now. And now it's clear you know who I am. You get to drag him out here to me!" Tinnion's voice was low but commanding.

"My daughter is the rightful heir to Heriloth and so is the rightful gesith of Butterholt. I will take what I need from my daughter's lands as I choose. You are nobody. And what is more, you are trespassing on my land." The lord sat uncomfortably astride a shire horse, an old broadsword lay across the saddle in front of him.

Tinnion glared at the gesith. Her right hand brushed across the fletching of the arrows at her side. "I am Gesith of Butterholt by order of Queen Rhiannon. Any claim you, or your daughter, had was denied by our Queen in that moment." Tinnion turned her head, watching as the lord's men loosened their swords at their belts. "I am prepared to forgive your trespass and your theft on this occasion. Once my people have been paid for their goods and the distress your men caused them."

The older sheriff pulled his horse forward, level with his lord, and whispered something Tinnion could not hear. The lord's face twisted into a grimace.

"It was your man's kin that killed my son-in-law." The lord pointed to Andel. "That murder has not yet been paid for and yet you dare bring him to my stead, claiming wrongs done to you?"

Tinnion's jaw clenched. If the man would just raise his sword, this would be easy. An arrow to the shoulder would end it and make him do whatever she asked. She pulled her hand away from her quiver, removing temptation. "His death was an accident and was tried by the Queen's Voice. Neither Andel nor his kin were to blame. As for your son-in-law, if I were you, I would distance myself as far from his behaviour as possible."

"So you say." The retort was half spat, and the lord raised his hand. "Take him." Two of the younger sheriffs rode forward toward Andel, a look of concern on their faces. The sheriffs Andel chose to join Tinnion on this journey closed around him, their hands on their weapons, ready to draw and fight at Tinnion's command.

"Raise your sword or the coins from your purse. I am done talking. Four silver or your sword arm, I'll have one or the other, now!" She didn't move. Her eye's never left Hubertus'. Her hand didn't reach for an arrow. There would be plenty of time for that if he chose the sword. She knew she could put an arrow through him before he could lift the heavy blade to attack. She had her mark.

The mans sheriffs halted, uncertain what to do. "What are you waiting for? I gave an order!" Hubertus yelled at them. His hands tightened around the hilt of his sword.

"Your sword or your coin. Choose now." Tinnion's voice was calm, the anger had passed. She sat straight in her saddle, ready but relaxed.

The lord's men paused again, looking between their gesith and Tinnion, their faces white. The lord screamed, his face red, his words unintelligible, accompanied by spittle. He lifted his sword.

The gesith of Southwood fell from his horse, dragged from his saddle by the sudden shifting weight of the heavy blade, now held only in his left hand. His right arm swung loosely, uselessly, an arrow deep in his shoulder.

A second arrow was nocked on Tinnion's bow string as soon as the first had flown and the lord's men raised their empty hands. They had no appetite to fight.

Tinnion and her sheriffs passed through the farmstead that had suffered the theft of their crops. They handed the four silver coins Lord Hubertus had volunteered after his fall to the family's head.

"I had food sent from one of our other farms, did you receive it?" Tinnion's voice was soft. Her hands cupped those of the elderly farmer's.

"Aye, m'lady. We got that and good food it is too, m'lady. We can't thank you enough, m'lady." The farmer bowed his head with every m'lady, and Tinnion giggled.

"There's no need for all that! I'm gesith of the hold. It's for me to make sure you're doing well. You have to let us know if you have troubles or needs. Hayal spoke with you about council?"

"Aye, m'lady. He did that. I'll be sending me daughter if that's alright by you, m'lady. I know as some prefer the men to be the ones speaking, but my daughters got a way with words and I thought as you're a lady yourself, m'lady."

Tinnion bit on her lips, trying not to giggle as the farmer m'lady'd her again.

"That's fine, really it is. I look forward to your visit." She smiled at the young woman at his side. "Well, the road is long. We must be off."

"Yes, m'lady." The man nodded. "Thank you, m'lady. My daughter'll be there, m'lady. No fear."

Chapter Thirteen

A Treaty Signed

The second day of the talks went ahead without either of the queens present and were a lot more relaxed. Lana was much more comfortable with the way things were going. She sat at the table with Aelwynne to her right and Daowiel and Erinia opposite her. Pitchers of water and soft cider sat amongst platters of fruit and nuts and the quartet picked at the food as they talked.

"So, the noam and the sylph have lived in peace with the humans for the twenty years Queen Rhiannon has been on the throne?" Erinia looked sceptical at Aelwynne's claims.

"There have been difficulties, of course. Our cultures are very different after hundreds of years apart. There are still things that aren't perfect, things we would like to change, to make better for all, but the process is slow. There has to be a willingness to compromise from both sides. Take the noam, for example.

They have helped us to expand our cities, to create roads and defences along the coast. In return, they have settlements outside of Stonemount. One of the largest being in the city of Southport, where they have an entire district that celebrates their culture."

"Their culture? Including their treatment of females?" Erinia's eyes narrowed.

"There are, of course, things that have been difficult. And only those that agree to follow the accord of Eastmarch can live alongside us. Those that follow what they call the 'old lore' remain in Stonemount and do not mix. However, we understand that to find a compromise which works for everyone is difficult when the survival of your species depends on..." Aelwynne paused, waving her hand as if to wave away the negative words that came to mind. "- certain things. The accord dictates that in order to bind the noam must make a 'claim' on the female they wish to be with. That female can refuse. If they accept, they will then live with the noam. Though they will not be enslaved, they wear the collar and they follow the traditions in every other way. It is as it would be for a man and a woman to marry and should the relationship fail beyond repair, the two may separate. Though we have never seen that occur. Some say the curse of Khyione prevents it, though it is impossible to know if the curse truly exists."

Erinia shook her head. "I cannot imagine that any female would ever agree to be bound."

"You would be surprised, Princess. Several couples are bound each year in Southport. It is not a life that suits everyone, that is true, but a number of women are more than happy to be bound with a noam."

The dryad princess sat back in her chair and paused, clasping her hands. "You understand that this isn't the kind of arrangement that would work for us?"

"I do." Aelwynne nodded solemnly. "Princess Daowiel has explained that particular need to me. It certainly poses a more complex problem. You will not find a man or woman that is willing to give up their lives. I have to be honest, this is an issue that I'm struggling to find a solution to." She bit her lip, turning the flesh white, and took a deep breath. "That doesn't mean that we can't find agreement on other things, however. An accord that will take us a step closer to living in harmony. We shouldn't allow one issue to destroy any chance that we have." Erinia nodded as Aelwynne finished speaking.

"Can I make a suggestion?" Lana leant forward, rubbing the table with the tip of a finger.

"Of course, Ògan." Erinia smiled.

"I don't think we can say for sure that no one would volunteer. I mean, I don't know that it would work. I don't know that anyone would, but perhaps... Some people die in a lot of pain. Sometimes they're given an option of a quick death so that their pain can end. If we gave them the choice, the chance to have their pain numbed, to live the last days of their lives in the haze of the dryad nectar, perhaps they would take it?"

"You're suggesting that those people in our hospices or those mortally injured in accidents or battle be given the option of taking the dryad seed?"

Lana nodded "umhmm. I think that if I knew I was gonna die, and I was in a lot of pain, I would do it."

"Would that work?" Aelwynne looked to Erinia for an answer. The dryad sat for a moment in silence, her chin resting on clasped hands.

"Yes. That would work for us, at least. Though we would need to transport those people to a place where a dryad tree could grow."

"There is the forest north of Southport city. Perhaps we could create a place there where some dryad could live, like the noam district in the city itself. I know the forest is full of hunters at the moment; but they stay away from the edges at the very top of the island; and it is large enough to do that... I think. And..."

"And?" It was Aelwynne that asked, but it was clear in the faces of everyone around the table.

"Well. The northern part of the island is close to the Northern Road as it goes through another forest. There are way stations on that bit of the road, but no large steads or anything. That's the kind of place that could be good for the sort of agreement we have at Butterholt. The dryad could live in those woods; they could help the sheriffs and villagers that live at the way points to get wood and it would definitely help keep the peace along that bit of the road 'cos no outlaw gang is going to want to live in a dryad forest." Lana tilted her head, her fingers pressing hard as they rubbed the varnished wood.

"How long have you been sitting on this little plan of yours?" Aelwynne turned to her protégé.

“A couple of days.” Lana shrugged. “I was looking at the maps in your study and it just kinda made sense.”

“Did you know about this?” The Queen’s Voice turned to Daowiel.

“No!” The princess shook her head with a smile. “I’m as surprised as you. Though neither of us should be, I suppose. The Ògan is growing up quickly.” The princess paused for a moment. “She is not an Ògan anymore, in fact. I am proud of you, Lana.” She turned to her friend and wrinkled her nose with a smile.

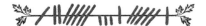

They spent the following few days hovering over maps and working out the details of the plan. Lana had been so happy at her idea being taken up and thrilled at the encouragement and praise she had received when it was announced. This, however, she found extremely boring. She sighed as Aelwynne pointed to another area of badly drawn trees and tried to describe why she thought it might make a good place for the dryad home.

“I’m sorry, Lana. Did you want to say something?” Aelwynne turned to her apprentice, her eyebrow raised and her jaw clenched.

“I’m sorry. I… Would it not be better for the dryad to visit the forest and see what it’s really like rather than looking at a map? We could spend days looking at this and then get there and find the trees chopped down. It seems a bit…”

“Silly?” Aelwynne’s voice was dry, her brow now furrowed.

Lana lowered her head and looked at her toes.

“I’m sorry.” She raised her eyes, looking to Daowiel for support. “I took you here one time, Daowiel…” She hesitantly pointed to a spot on the map that had so far been ignored. “Do you remember? It’s where I first travelled the bridge on my own. There’s a wonderful old oak and a little freshwater spring not too far from it.”

The dryad princess nodded with a smile. "I remember, Lana. There were some old trees there that had character and memories of dryad. I think it might be a suitable area, though it would be nice to revisit and be certain."

"I could take you." Lana said with a smile, hoping to avoid Aelwynne's glare.

"It would be better if you were to stay here, Lana. I would appreciate the time to talk with you. If the princess is able to find this place herself?" Aelwynne's words dashed Lana's hopes, and she slouched in her chair.

Daowiel nodded. "I can, of course. Go easy on her, Aelwynne. She might not have the hang of all this diplomacy, but she was right." She turned to Erinia and stood. "Shall we leave our friends to their talks, Sister?" Erinia nodded, and the pair left the room.

Within days, the treaty was signed. It was hailed as a great success by both parties and grand feasts were held on the Queen's Isle and in the city of Southport to allow the citizens a celebration. Once things settled down, the dryad said their farewells and returned to the Heartwood, promising that they would return to the Queen's Isle again, once their new settlements were founded.

Daowiel was chosen to lead the small group of dryad that would settle in the woodlands along the North Road. A second group with only a handful of dryad, lead by a more experienced dryad named Oa'lynn, would tend the grove and see to the birthing rites on the northern tip of Southport Island.

Daowiel's upcoming departure made Lana sad, and the two spent the morning together at their favourite spot by the lake. They talked about their time together at the palace, and all the things they had learned together. And they promised they would visit one another regularly.

"Are things well with you and Aelwynne?" Daowiel asked, her hand on Lana's comfortingly.

"They're alright, Daowiel. She wasn't happy at some of the things I said when we were all talking, but she says that my ideas were good."

The dryad nodded. "Diplomacy seems often to mean letting foolish things happen without challenge in order to maintain talks. It can be infuriating and tedious, Lana. But you must try to follow Aelwynne's example… If you are going to pursue it."

"You don't think I should?" Lana was surprised by her friend's suggestion.

"I do not know that it is right for you, Lana. You tend to speak with your heart rather than your head. It is endearing, most of the time, but not a great thing when negotiating treaties. I feel you will learn in time or… find something which suits you better."

Lana felt her heart sink. "Perhaps I should go home to the stead. I'm not sure I belong in a palace and with you gone, I'll be alone."

"No, Lana." Daowiel shook her head. "You should stay. Without you, none of what has been done here this moon could have been done. I am certain you will find your place. If that is in diplomacy, alongside Aelwynne, or as the queen's advisor perhaps, or something less formal, you belong here. At least for now."

Chapter Fourteen

A Motley Crew

"I want to go back with ye, Cat dahlin'. Whatever ye doin', I want to be part of it. There's noffin else for me to do here no more and I've burned me bridges to get ye information. Ah've no protection neither, not since you killed me man and threw me into the hands of the guards. I aint got a chance on me own"

Cat scowled at her former matriarch. "I don't need you getting in my way, Adney, and frankly, I don't want you. You're a snake and I don't trust you."

"Then I'll be keeping what I learned to myself then. Oh, and then you'll be for it, cos this is good stuff, Cat dahlin'. Someone'll pay me for it n pay me good."

The scowl became a growl aimed at the woman, and Cat drew a knife from her belt, placing it against Adney's chin.

"You cross me and I'll pay you alright. You'll get yourself a smile you can't get rid of, right across your mug."

"Now, come on Cat dahlin'. There's no need for that. I was just saying how much I wanted to be spending time wiff you is all."

"Tell me what you've got and I'll consider having you freed, but you aint coming back to the tunnels with me, you hear?"

"Alright then, alright." The old woman that had terrorised Cat throughout her life was fawning at her feet now. "Put that knife away and I'll tell ya."

Cat pulled the knife away from the woman's face and slid it back into her belt. Adney smiled.

"That's better, aint it?" Her voice trembled. "So, I did what you said I should do. I got close to that man." She chuckled nervously, "Very close, if you knows what I mean? And he talked a lot in his sleep. He talked about princesses and ships and how some dirty scrote got wind of his plans and got him sent to prison. And he mentioned a few names n all and how they might wanna punish all them what was caught. A few names of people not from 'ere. Least ways not originally."

"From where, then, Adney?" Cat's voice was hiss, her jaw clenched.

"Well, if I was to guess, I would say they was from a whole other country, dahlin'. Odd names they were. Not like any northern or eastern names."

Cat threw a hand in the air, coming close to the woman's cheek. "What were the names, Adney?"

"Well, you know, for the life of me, I can't quite remember. You know, they was difficult names, names you couldn't just say in the heat of the moment like. Hard to remember names you can't say, aint it? Course, if I heard them again... Like, if I was in the room when someone was talking bout them..." Adney breathed heavily as she spoke, her lips quivering behind a fake smile.

"Well, you won't be, Adney. And neither will I. So there's no point in you keeping them from me." Cat's tone was brisk.

"Yeah, I figured as much, you aint asking for yourself is you? You're asking for the guard, you wanna know whose plan it was so's the guard can go out and catch 'em. Well, you aint got no luck, have you? Cos these people are in the falcon isles not 'ere. So yer guards'll just have to forget their plans."

Cat cursed under her breath and signalled for the guard to take Adney back to the prison yard. As they were dragging the woman away, she held up her hand and spoke. "Wait, just a minute." The guards paused. "Listen up, Adney. I don't like you, I don't want nothing to do with you. But I need to go think about this. I'll be back in two days. I might come to get you out of here or I might bring a big bloke with lots of sharp knives, but one way or another, you're gonna tell me what you know. So think on it, Adney, think long n good."

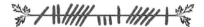

"I had assumed the trail would lead to the Falcon Isles eventually, it being where the damned circle come from, though I hoped there would be more to follow here." The Tay tapped his fingers on his desk, drumming an unheard tune, and looked directly at Cat, waiting for her to speak.

"No. No way. This was never part of our agreement. There is no way in the name of the eight that I'm leaving Southport, Let alone on a ship to the bloomin' Falcon Isles." Cat shook her head wildly as she spoke. "It aint happening. It just aint." She slumped back in her chair, still shaking her head, and put her feet up on the Tay's desk. "You can stare at me all you want, I aint going. It won't work. I hate ships, and I know less than nothing about the islands. So you can find someone else to finish this task. One of your captains or summick."

"This woman, Adney. Do you think she can be trusted?" The Tay's eyes never left Cat's face.

"No. Not on yer life. She's a sneaky one, manipulative, she'd have you thinking she was helping while she was robbing you blind." Cat relaxed a little, if the Tay knew how untrustworthy Adney was perhaps he wouldn't want her to follow up on the little she'd learned.

"It would take someone as sharp as she is to keep her in line, then." The Tay went on and Cat nodded her agreement. "I think, perhaps, you are right. You wouldn't be suited to that. I will have a captain follow up with her. Terrin, perhaps. He has, shall we say, an interest in the case and should have just enough wit to out think an old lady."

"Terrin?" Cat laughed as she spoke the name. "She'd have him wrapped around her finger before they left the harbour. Nah, you need someone that knows the game, knows how she plays, knows how to play her as much as she's trying to play you."

"Somebody who's bested her before." The Tay stopped drumming his fingers on the desk and crossed his hands in front of his chin, his fingers interlaced.

"Yeah, exactly." Cat nodded.

Gathwyn smiled. "Do you know of anybody?"

Cat twisted her mouth, her brow furrowed. "Oh, I see. Yeah. You're worse than she is, you are."

Cat walked into the smoke filled common room of the inn, her fingers fidgeting with the knife hidden in her tunic. Many of those thieves that had stayed loyal to Keikon had come to the Portlands after Cat took over the family. She had given them their freedom and some coins to see they could eat for a week or two, but they despised her. She was safe in the main city now. No one would challenge her there, but out here, no one would intervene if one of them decided to attack her.

The man she sought sat at a table in the back of the room. Surrounded by smoke and stale, spilled ale, yet she could smell his unwashed frame as easily as she could see him. His hair was unkempt, his face dirty. His clothes, ragged and filth ridden. She slid onto the bench opposite him and called for a cup.

The man looked up from his tankard and snarled.

"What the hell do ye want, Cat? Get out of here befores I skin ye!" His slurred words, along with his accent, made it difficult to understand the man.

"Charming as ever, Xentan. And there I was, thinking you'd be glad to see me."

"Why the hell'd I be glad fer yer company? You cost me my ship, my reputation, my livelihood!" He slammed his tankard down on the table, spilling more of his ale, and reached down to his belt.

In the blink of an eye, the knife that Cat had been fingering was embedded in the table between the fingers of his left hand. She smiled at him, as a tabby smiles at a mouse.

"Careful, Xentan. I came here to offer you a chance to get back what you lost, but I'll gladly take whatever's left of your life if you pull that blade on me."

The pirate growled an unintelligible curse and put his right hand on the table.

"What do ye want this time, then? What price am I gonna have te pay?"

"I need to get to the Falcon Isles. To Tanearam, to be exact. And as I can't fly and I can't swim that far, I got myself a ship. Now I need someone that knows how to sail it." Cat sat back, leaning against the half wall that separated the booth from the rest of the room.

"You got a ship? That seems unlikely. Why didn't you just pay someone for passage?"

Cat frowned. "Because I don't like the thought of being trapped out at sea with a bunch of strangers and no control. I don't much like the thought of being at sea at all. If it's my ship, then I'm in charge and that helps a little."

"And you came to me to captain it for yer? How thoughtful." The pirate's voice was thick with sarcasm, making Cat sigh. She took on the more matter-of-fact tone she had used when she spoke of having Adney punished.

"You lost your ship when the circle got you messed up in their scheme. I thought you'd like the chance to pay 'em back and get a new one into the bargain."

The pirate raised his eye browned tilted his head back, looking at Cat properly for the first time. "I dunno that I wanna go up against the circle in their own country, Cat. Why poke that bear?"

"I don't plan on being the one poking it, Xentan. I'm just hoping to find out how big it is."

"I see, fine." He took a big swig of his ale. "But don't tell me any more. I'll get you to the islands. I'll even wait to bring you back again, but I want nothing more to do with whatever it is you do there. I don't wanna know who's sending you there neither. I do want to keep the ship once it's all done, though."

Cat shrugged her shoulders. "That's fine by me, Xentan. I ain't gonna need or want a ship once I'm done. But you aint going nowhere near my ship til you're sober and you've cleaned yourself up. You reek worse than the sewer trough outside the Pig N Tackle."

It was only a short walk from the inn down to the back end of the port where the ship was moored, though it took longer than it should due to Xentan's state.

When they reached it, Xentan scowled. "This? This is what I get? I'm risking my neck fer ye again and this pile o' junk is all I get fer it?"

"You're not the only one taking risks, Xentan. And I can always find another captain to take the ship if you'd rather go back to drinking stale ale in your piss soaked clothes?" The walk had soured Cat's mood, and she was almost ready to give up on the man.

The pirate glared at Cat. He knew he had no choice, not if he ever wanted to get back to sea. He looked the ship over. It would be fast once the repairs had been done, maybe faster than his old ship, and there was plenty of space to carry goods in the hold.

"I'll need money te hire a crew. And more to get her seaworthy."

Cat nodded. "You'll have it. How long before it's ready to sail?"

"Half moon at least. You don't want to rush repairs to a ship you're hoping will take you out to the deeps. This aint just a trip along the coast yer talking about."

Cat handed the pirate a couple of country silvers. "I need to see what you spend every last bit on, Xentan. Cheat me and the only place you'll be going is the bottom of the harbour."

The pirate started to climb the plank up to the ship's deck. "I don't know what yer up to, Cat. Or where yer getting yer money. And fer what it's worth, I don't care neither. If I get the ship once yer safe on land, I'll not con ye."

With Xentan on board and Adney forcing her inclusion on the journey, Cat felt a need to have a friendly face with her. So she made her way through the city to Brighid's manor.

"I need you Laywyn. You're someone I know I can trust, someone I know aint gonna turn on me if things get tough. You're the only man I know in Mortara that's ever been there when I needed it. It aint just fer me either Laywyn, this is for the Tay, for Mortara."

"I dunno Cat, ye aint talking about a quick trip over to Eastwood or anything. You're asking me to go across an ocean, on an old ship that's seen much better days, with a drunk as its captain. You want to go to a country that're potentially preparing to start a war with us, with no backup, and try to steal secrets from them."

"Yeah. Don't it sound exciting?" Cat grinned and raised her eyebrows.

"Exciting? Cat, it's completely insane! Do you even know how long you're likely to be away?"

"'Bout three or four moons getting there, three or four getting back, and I reckon another three or four moons to get what we need."

"A year? Damn, Cat. I'm supposed to be here looking after Brighid's estate for her."

"Yer a soldier, Laywyn, not a housewife! 'Sides Kaorella is more n capable of taking care o' this place. Better 'n you can, I'd wager too."

Laywyn nodded with a sigh. "I'd feel a lot better about it if it wasn't just the two of us that could be trusted. Is there no one else that can come instead of that old thief's wife?"

Cat slumped in her seat. "Not like I want her either, but she has to come." She sighed. "She's the only one knows who we need to see and she aint sayin' til we get there. I wish we had Lana comin', or Tin. But I guess they aint never gonna get mixed up wi this kind o stuff no more. It's just the likes o us that's left to get their hands dirty."

"That's not really fair, Cat." Laywyn shook his head. "From what I hear, Lana's making a lot of big changes with the fae that're gonna be good for everyone long term. And I don't even know how to get to Tinnion without adding another three moons to that year away." He paused, sinking his head into his hands and rubbing his forehead. "I'll come with ya Cat, cos you need someone decent with you, but I need a couple of days to get myself sorted."

"That's great Laywyn, it's gonna take a while to get things ready to go anyway, according to Xentan."

"You're gonna owe me big after this though, Cat." Laywyn teased her with a smirk on his face and Cat rolled her eyes.

"Yeah, I know it. You ain't the only one gonna be owed."

Chapter Fifteen

The Southern Rise

The plains of Sindale were flat and wide, rain clouds rolled across the skies soaking the grasslands before settling on the hills of the rise. Mud made the journey difficult and progress was slow. The injured, those that could not walk or ride, were drawn on litters. Those that had fallen in the battle were buried, though little time had been given over for ceremony.

On the whole, the caravan had grown slightly after the battle, with those that thought it better to join clan MacFaern than fight against them. With MacTiern now dead, those men looked to the giant MacAllister to lead them, and he seemed to grow in the responsibility.

Sindale tower, the home of the MacTiern clan, nestled at the foot of the hills that formed the rise, looking out over the windswept plains. The tower itself was fortified, but there were no defences for the homes that surrounded it.

Cohade ordered a halt half a day from the stead that surrounded the tower and camp was set. There he sat with his children, Brighid and Anndra, and their new ally, MacAllister.

"Go on ahead, MacAllister. My clan'll camp here. I don't want to be seen as an invader to yer hold nor a threat tae those whose families fell. I'll be happy tae follow and stand for what was done once you've been reunited with yer families and assured them we're not looking for a fight."

MacAllister nodded. "Aye, I reckon it'd be best for ma self and ma men tae enter the town first. Calm their nerves and break the news of the fallen. I'll have the clan gather up and ready themselves tae march. We'll join ye, if ye'll have us. We're certainly not safe here with an army heading our way."

Cohade held out his hand to the warrior and smiled as the man shook it. "Yer welcome, of course, MacAllister. You and your kin. It's an honour tae stand with ye and I'm sure we'll be needing tae stand firm again afore too much longer."

The two men nodded at one another and MacAllister left the fire to ready his men.

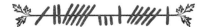

Look-outs were set in the tower at every hour, ensuring that any signs of an approaching army would be seen across the plains days before they arrived and the clans prepared. Wagons and horses were loaded with supplies. The injured took some time to heal, and those that had lost family or friends mourned.

Three days they stayed in the stead before they saw the smoke rising in the west. The traitorous tuath army was burning the Diawood. It was impossible to know if they were clearing the trees ahead of them or destroying the trees behind them. It could even be that the bulk of the army had gone north, skirting the woods, while a handful remained to burn it in spite. The clan had a week on the army chasing them. A week's lead they wanted to maintain, if not grow. And so the order was sent to ready for travel on the following morn and the stead became a hive of activity.

"I intend tae stay, me and mine. We'll not leave our home, MacFaern." The wives and children of MacTiern and his sons had been the only voices to speak out against the clans and their alliance. They would not believe that their husbands had betrayed the north, or that shadows rode with the rebel lords.

"Yer hoping for honour from those that come, and I fear for you. Shadows and men that would turn on their own, they cannot be trusted." Cohade shook his head and sighed. "We've no grudge tae hold against you or your weens and we'll protect ye as we'd protect our own. You've nothing tae fear from us. Don't stay here tae be killed. Come with us tae Northfort. We'll be safe there if there's any safety left tae have."

The eldest of the women shook her head. "No, MacFaern. We'll not go. If it is as ye say, we'll die here in our home, but I don't believe it's as ye say."

Cohade shrugged and turned to MacAllister. "Can ye no talk sense into them?" The giant man simply shook his head in silence.

The valley path meandered through the rise, winding its way around the feet of the hills. A river had run here in the days of the war but, aside from a seasonal stream, was now gone. Still, the way was muddy and the wind, funnelled along the passage, was strong.

The warriors split into three groups. MacAllister and his men, being more familiar with the road, lead the caravan with Cohade and a handful of his. Anndra rode at the caravan's rear with the largest share of warriors and Brighid and Wren took a dozen warriors up onto the hills to watch the land below.

Fifteen days they marched through the valleys, snaking around ever growing hills, then MacAllister called a halt. The path climbed from here. Up on the southern rise. It snaked up a hill, ragged and hard. To a bridge that crossed the raging Alawe.

"We'll have tae take the climbing path here, Cohade. The Rise Bridge is the only place a group this size'll cross safe." MacAllister pointed up the rise to the southeast and at the roaring waterfall of the Alawe.

Cohade shielded his eyes from the sun. "That's going tae be a tough climb for these wagons, MacAllister. Is there no way we can ford the river down here?"

"None. Save for a few weeks in samhradh there's no way tae ford it. Even then I would nae risk it with this many wagons. Once we're over the bridge, there's a waytown. We can pick up supplies and get some shelter. If we're in luck there'll be a troop of the queen's men there, an' all."

"We'll do what we can tae lighten the loads tonight and start the climb first thing." Cohade paused, tugging at his beard. "If this is the only way over..." He stopped his words, shaking his head.

"You want us to do what?" MacAllister was red faced and panting from the climb up the steep path of the rise. His jaw opened almost as wide as his eyes.

Cohade slapped the warriors back and walked him to the edge of the river. "We take the bridge down. It shouldn't be too hard tae do. If the river can't be forded and we destroy the bridge it'll buy us time tae call on the liath and the queen's own. Can yer men do it?"

"Aye, it'll be easy enough tae take down. If we weaken it, the force o the water will wash it right over the falls. But that isn't the point. That bridge took years and cost lives tae build. If we destroy it, we'll be throwing that away. And we'll not have a bridge tae use on the way back hame. By the gods! We'll no have a bridge for the queen's own tae use coming tae our aide neither."

"But we will, MacAllister. Or else we'll not need one. If they want tae cross and take Northfort, they'll have tae build a new crossing and that'll take time. Time we can use tae ready ourselves. And as they'll be certain of a win, they'll not destroy it once it's built." Cohade smiled broadly.

"You're a sly man, Cohade. I like it! I'll set ma men to it once we're all across and sure we've no need tae head back for anything." A smile broke out on the warriors face, soon followed by laughter. "Is that yer daughter there, Cohade, or a ghost! I've never seen her so peely wally!"

The view to Brighid's left as she crossed the bridge made her stomach turn. White waters rushing to a fall one hundred metres high. Her knuckles whitened as she gripped the reins of her horse and her face blanched. She felt Wren's hand lightly touch her shoulder.

"Are you well, Brighid?" Wren's voice was low, barely audible over the roar of the falling water. Brighid nodded, her mouth closed tight.

"I'm not a fan, Wren. I can feel the bridge shifting in the waters. I don't trust wood or stone this close tae a drop like that."

"You'll be fine, Brighid. Just look ahead, fix your eyes on the waytown and away from the edge. I'll not let you fall."

They walked their horses on together, Wren's hand on Brighid's shoulder until they were off the bridge and back on solid rock.

The waytown had grown from a small way point with an inn and a couple of market traders to a small town, covering the flat land halfway to the top of the rise. The only access to it from the west was over the bridge and down the steep hill they had climbed. To the north there was a winding road leading down to the Northfort plains. To the south the land rose again steeply, a sheer cliff face giving shelter to the town. They would be safe here for a time and they intended to make the most of it.

"Lady Brighid, Lady Wren. Lord Cohade is wanting yer presence. He's up at the 'Birds Nest Inn', m'ladies. Just up the street there." The warrior was one of MacAllister's. He was heading back toward the bridge with two others. Each carrying their war axes un-sheathed across their shoulders.

"Where are you heading? Are we sending out a watch?"

"No, m'lady." The warrior laughed. "We've been tasked with breaking up the bridge."

"You've been what?" Brighid's eyes were wide, her tone questioning.

"Perhaps Lord Cohade is best tae answer, m'lady. I'm just doing as I'm told."

Brighid nodded and made her way up the stone street, Wren at her side.

"Ah, Brighid! I was beginning tae think ye'd gone for a swim." Cohade chuckled and smiled at his daughter.

"Aye, ah thought I might on that rotten bridge too. Not sure I hate it enough tae have it broken up, though. What's with that?"

"Oh, that's yer father's brilliant idea." MacAllister grinned over his tankard of ale. "Not even the shadows'll be able tae cross the Alawe until they build a new one."

"Aye, none o the Tay's messengers south neither. Did that slip yer minds?" Brighid shook her head.

"Ach, I sent one o' mine off already, Brighid. If ye'd been riding with us, where ye belong, ye'd have known it." Cohade grinned.

"Aye, and our backs would only be protected by Anndra, if he could tear his eyes from Wren long enough to glance behind. Better I was there than not." Brighid pulled up a chair and poured herself a tankard of ale, handing the pitcher to the red faced sylph as she finished.

"I want ye tae ride ahead of us, Brighid. You and Wren. We'll camp down on the plain two or three days until we're sure yer at the fortress and then we'll follow. I don't want the Tay mistaken us for the army come tae trouble him. I'll have some of our men stay up here and watch for MacKenna. He'll not be able tae cross until he builds a new bridge either here, or downriver a way. That'll give us a bit o' time."

Brighid sipped at her ale and nodded. "Aye, that sounds like a decent plan. We'll leave once we've had the chance tae eat. Nae point hanging around up here."

"Still bothered by being up high, eh, Brighid?" Her father teased her. Wren smirked, ready to take the opportunity to avenge her red-faced moment.

"I'd feel secure facing an entire army with just Brighid by my side, but ask her to climb so much as a table and you'll turn her stomach!" The sylph chuckled.

The fortress was three day's ride across the plains, three days of rolling grasslands that rose and fell on gentle slopes. It would have been a pleasant ride were it not for the urgency and desperation of their mission. They had to get to the Tay long before the waytown and the clan were in any danger from the rebel lords.

"I have never seen Northfort, Brighid. It is impressive, even imposing. I wish I were seeing it in different times."

They pulled up on a small hill and paused for a moment, taking in the city fortress that loomed over the valley. Grey walls three metres thick and twenty high built around and within a mountain. Steep slopes, unassailable from the south, east or north, rose from the earth in sheer, sharp, solid peaks. A solitary road lead up to the city. A narrow road that climbed a winding path up the western face. Bordered by the mountain to one side and an unguarded deadly drop into the raging river on the other.

A market town spread out along the southern feet of the mountain. An area to trade without the need to climb that treacherous road. Wooden buildings mixed with stalls and marquees that reminded Wren of Shorebridge.

"This will all be gone within the moon. That makes me as angry as it does sad. All these lives destroyed, if not taken." Wren sighed.

"I fight, every day, I fight or I practice fighting. I never thought Ah'd have to use my skills in war. I'm not scared, not of being beaten, not of dying. But I'm everyday wishing for a way this all goes away." Brighid paused, taking a deep breath and fighting back tears. "I'm going tae kill MacKenna, mark my words, Wren. I'm going tae kill him and I'll be sure he knows I'll not be doing it for what he did tae me, for the wounds his shadows inflicted. I'll kill him for what he has done tae the people of the north. He needs tae die because he's destroyed it all."

Wren nodded solemnly. "I think I am done, Brighid, when this is over. I have fought for twenty years. In tournaments and skirmishes. I have killed when I had to. I became good at it. Almost the best." She flashed a melancholy smile at her friend. "Almost. But when this is done, I am done. I will give back my purse and my title if they ask, but I cannot go on. I need to know what life is like without a weapon in my hand."

They sat a moment more in silence, deep in their own thoughts. Then spurred their horses forward toward the rising path.

ACT TWO

SKIES DARKEN

Chapter Sixteen

SETTING SAIL

The ship had been patched and tarred and there were ten men aboard her, busy with maintenance or setting her riggings and sewing her sails. Xentan was stomping across the deck cursing the slow work rate of his sailors and his growing sobriety. "Is there not one damn drop of rum on this cursed ship? How's a man supposed to work with nought but blood and water in him? You there." He pointed a large wooden pin at a sailor that was hauling wooden crates up the loading planks. "You had better be loading some alcohol soon laddy or I'll be loading ye in one of them there barrels and throwing yer off the side. Ye hear?"

"What? Ye said not to be bringing no liquor on board. Ye said ye'd never touch another drop. Ye told me ye'd skewer me if I tempted ye wi booze." Xentan lobbed the heavy pin at the sailor with a grunt, hitting him square in the gut and sending him to the floor gasping for breath. "One o' you dirty lot had better get themselves to an inn and get me some booze before I get mad. Ye hear?"

"You aint getting no booze Xentan; you drink and you lose this ship. I aint sailing no ocean with you when you can't even stand." Cat stood at the top of the gangplank playing with a gold coin that glistened in the sun. "What'll it be Xentan? The ship and a coin or two or sitting in your filth in a two bit inn again?"

"Aargh, come on, Cat. I aint planning on being drunk when we sail, I just need a drop to see me through til then. I aint good company on dry land when I'm sober."

"You aint good company at all, Xentan. Get the ship ready and fast. I've a few things to arrange but I want to be away before three nights have passed."

"Three nights? Yer mad! There's still too much work to be done, Cat. Ye can't rush repairs on a ship for the ocean." The pirate snorted his response to the deadline.

"Yeah, you said that thirteen days ago and I've been patient. I've things to do, Xentan, and I want to get them done and get back here as soon as we can. Three nights and we set sail, if you aint ready I'm sure one of these men will be."

"Ye come on my ship all making demands..."

Cat cut the pirates words short, shouting over him as he spoke. "This is my ship, Xentan. It's mine til you've gotten me where I need to be and brought me back safe. When I'm back here in Southport, the ship will be yours, not a moment before then. Not a tiny bit of a moment. Can you be ready in three nights or not?"

Xentan grumbled and spat over the side of the ship. "Aye. She'll be ready. If I have to get the whip out, she'll be ready."

The three were attracting attention as they walked, arm in arm, through the city. Cat and Laywyn flanking Adney, keeping her upright and sometimes dragging her along when she refused to move or stumbled. The woman whined and complained incessantly about the injustice of being kept in chains. "You said I'd be free, Cat. This aint free, this is just chained someplace else." She forced a scream out as she stumbled as if dealt a heavy blow and the people of Southport stared and commented on her treatment.

They took the shackles from Adney's ankles after the third time she forced a stumble. Her screams and grunts attracting the attention of some city guards.

Though Cat knew the guard could not cause her any trouble, she was acting on the Tay's behalf after all; she did not want the attention or the hassle of explaining herself.

"What about me hands then, Cat? Undo me hands and we'll get by a lot better."

Cat grabbed the chain that bound the woman's wrists, pulling the old thief round to face her. "Once we're outta the harbour, Adney. You aint getting out of them 'til you can't go nowhere."

The woman scowled and pulled her arms away from her keeper.

"Why you gotta be so mean to me, dahlin'? I'm helpin' you aint I? You'd not be going nowhere if it weren't for me."

"Can we not gag her, Cat? I'm tired of hearing her whinging. It's bad enough she has to come along without her whining the whole time." Laywyn limped along beside them, his cloak wrapped around him, keeping his sword from sight. The thugs down in the port district were odd when it came to weapons. Some would step aside from a man carrying a sword, not wanting the trouble. Some, though, would see a sword at a man's side as a challenge and move against him.

"I don't think a gag'd be enough, Laywyn. She'd just whine with every out breath if we did that. Only thing that's gonna keep her quiet is a drink and someone to hang herself around. We'll put her in the boat's bottom once we're aboard and let her cuddle up with the rats."

Laywyn chuckled. "I'd hoped as our leader on this journey you'd know more about ships than me, Cat. I thought you'd been spending time down there. Didn't they show you round?"

"Not on your life, Laywyn. I'm gonna be stuck on that thing for the next three moons. That's plenty long enough. I don't need to be taking tours of it before we set sail an all."

The ship rocked gently in the harbour, the building wind blowing the rigging. Cat brushed her hair from her face again and called out for the captain of her ship. "Xentan! Where you at?"

The pirate captain staggered from his quarters at the stern of the ship and made his way toward her.

"The last of the supplies came aboard this morning and your gear's all down in your cabins... Are these two the only ones yer bringin' I thought there'd be more o' ye given all the stuff ye sent'?"

"You've been drinking, Xentan. I told you not to drink." Cat's hands clenched, her knuckles whitened.

"I've had a couple of cups, Cat. Nothin' more n that. I'm fine to sail... I know what I'm doin'."

"You." Cat pointed to a burly sailor coiling rope up on the deck. "I want any alcohol there is found and thrown off the boat. Get to it."

The sailor looked up to the captain and shrugged.

"Best do as she says, lad. She'll just throw us all off the ship if we don't."

"Aye capin." The sailor nodded and made his way below decks.

"I need her locked up 'til we're too far away from here to swim back. Is there somewhere you can put her?" Cat pointed to Adney and watched the grin grow on Xentan's bearded face.

"Oh, aye... I can find somewhere to keep 'er alright..."

She shook her head, curling her lip. "Do whatever you like with 'er. I don't care, just remember I'm in charge and when I tell you to do something, you've to do it."

"Aye. I'm aware of it. You keep bloody tellin' me enough."

Cat rolled her eyes. "How long afore we can get going?"

"Soon as you're ready. Ain't nothin' I wanna be doin' 'ere and the tides good right now. Or we can wait 'til night if ye prefer."

"No, I wanna get it over with as soon as we can. I'm going' down to my cabin. I want us goin' as soon as the booze is off the ship. If you're wanting her company, keep her in sight and more or less healthy. If she escapes or winds up dead, this is all for nothin' and this boat stays mine."

The ship rolled gently as it sailed out of the harbour and around the Suffham cliffs to the sea beyond. Cat stayed in her cabin, a large room with a bed and a table that equalled the captain's quarters for size and style. Cat sat on her bunk beside the window, looking over the stern of the ship. She had wedged it open with a knife and often stuck her green tinged face through it to vomit.

A knock came at the door and she heard Laywyn's voice over the lapping of the water. "You there, Cat? It's Laywyn... I wondered if you wanted to come up on deck a bit and watch the cliffs go by?"

Her stomach tightened and she retched, her cheeks bulging and her eyes crossing slightly.

"Cat? You alright, Cat?" The door creaked open and Laywyn stuck his head in the room to see her gripping the window's sill with one white knuckled hand while wiping her mouth with the sleeve around her other. The soldier chuckled and walked over to sit beside her on the bed.

"A nice cabin you've got here, Cat. Bigger than mine and a window, too." He smiled, putting his hand on her back and rubbing her shoulders gently. "They say it's easier if you watch the waves as you go. I guess it prepares your stomach for the rolling or something."

"I don't want people seein' me throwin' up."

"It's gonna be a long trip, Cat, and the waves are gonna get higher. You can't sit in your cabin alone the whole way. Come on, we'll go up on deck and I'll poke anyone that laughs at you with an auger."

Chapter Seventeen

Leaving the Palace

Lana was sitting in her favourite spot on the southern shore of the lake, her eyes closed. She listened to the sound of the water lapping at the soft clay of the banks and to the gulls flying overhead. Their cries were tales of waves and fish in the southern seas. The sun would warm as it reached the midpoint of its daily journey, but this early in the morning it had no time to heat the earth, and the water still carried the memory of an icy night. She found it far too cold to swim today.

It was quiet here. Nobody ever came to this side of the lake now that Daowiel had left. She felt it was a secret only she knew of, a place she could sit in peace, in silence, unseen, unbothered by the busy rush of life in the palace. Not even Aelwynne came here now. The lore keepers were researching the stones on the southern edge of the woods and the man she thought she had seen there, but they were doing it by looking through books in the comfort of their studies, not by coming here.

She dipped a toe in the water and flinched, sucking in the steam of her last breath with a sharp gasp. Then she watched as a young gull flew overhead, making its way from the peace of the lake to the ocean, and she wondered what it must be like to fly.

It was a question she had asked herself a few times since the night of the princess's rescue. Since the chase through the city and her tremendous leap down the steps of the harbour wall. It had been an instinctive leap and exhilarating. She had not fallen to her death as she should have; but floated gently to the carved rock platform below. She remembered how her arms had lifted as she descended, like a bird before it touches the ground. She remembered a feeling of controlling her descent. She had leapt from the palace tower a few times since then, wanting to feel that rush of air, wanting to see how far she could go and she had learned how to control her landings, though there had been a few accidents as she practiced. It made sense to her that if she could float down to the ground, then she should be able to glide some distance before touching it. The palace gardens, though, were too small for her to try it. There was a chance she'd end up in the fish pond or one of the thorny bushes if she tried.

She had hoped to talk to Yorane, or Selene about it, to ask them how the Sylph controlled their gliding through the air. To ask how she could have possibly done it, how it had happened at all. The stone of Lochheart had given her the abilities of the dryad. She could shape wood, she could travel the bridge between trees, and she could sense the life of the surrounding plants. She could feel their sense of the world as though they were thoughts in her own mind. Could the stone have done more? Could she have somehow gained the traits of the sylph, too? There was no one to talk to about that. No one knew the whole truth of the stone. The only clues came in those moments when memories of events long past came to her mind. Flashbacks of things she never saw, of times long before her birth.

A sudden sound distracted her, a cracking and the falling of small stones behind her. Her eyes opened and she span around, springing to her feet. Emerging from the darkness, in much the same way as a big cat stalks its prey, was the raven skinned man that she had seen by the strange rocks further south. She put her hand to her belt, pulling at the handle of her staff.

The man crouched, his hands resting on the ground in front of him. He twisted his head, looking Lana up and down silently.

"What do you want? Who are you? What are you doing here?" The words tripped and stumbled from her mouth and she shook as she spoke them. Lana had faced danger before and she had been scared. She would never claim to be a brave warrior like Brighid. There was something different about this, though. This fear was deeper, it was older, she felt it as much in her being as in her body. The man had her cornered. The freezing water of the lake was behind her, and she wasn't close enough to a tree to reach the bridge before he could reach her.

There was no expression on the man's face, there were no features to speak of. He had a nose, a mouth and eyes of course, but they were black, pitch black, no light reflected from his skin, no shadow touched him. It was as though he were made from the void itself. Lana swallowed hard. The man stood and pointed an outstretched finger at her.

"Piuthardia." His voice was a snakelike hiss that sent a shiver along Lana's spine. With a movement more fluid than Brighid's fighting dance, he leapt toward her.

The staff sprung into life in Lana's hand and she swung it as it extended, bringing it to rest a hand's width from the mans nose. He froze, glaring at her down the length of the staff, his lips curled into a scowl.

"Don't come any closer! I'll hurt you... I will... I'm not scared of you." She shook as she spoke, belying her words. "Who are you?"

The man struck at the tip of the staff, knocking it away from his face with a force that almost threw Lana off balance and stepped forward. Instead of stumbling, Lana moved with the force of his blow, bringing the staff around in an arc that connected with the man's knee. He grimaced and stepped away, favouring his right leg slightly.

"I'm... I'm sorry... I warned you... I did... I told you to stay away." Lana held out a hand, palm facing the man.

The man stood, silently glaring at her, and then raised his right arm. Slowly, a shape formed in his hand. Lana watched in disbelief as a staff, as dark as the man himself, grew from his fist. He sprung forward, swinging his newly formed staff in an arc. Lana raised her own to meet his, and they clashed with a sound like thunder. Again he swung, again Lana raised her staff to meet his. He was strong, so much stronger than Lana, but he was clumsy. Fighting with a staff was new to him and it showed. He over extended, using too much force and stumbled. Lana brought her staff down across the back of his leg once more and he fell to his knees. Taking advantage of the break, Lana ran toward the nearest tree and pulled herself close to its trunk.

"I don't want to fight. I don't want to hurt you. I just want to know who you are, what you want with me?" The man stood, and the staff in his hand shrank away. When it was gone, he raised his hand and pointed his finger.

"Piuthardia." With that single word, he turned and slinked back into the woodlands.

Lana let out a held breath and doubled over, crouching she held onto the tree for balance and threw up on the ground at her feet.

"There will be no lesson for you today." Aelwynne sat at the head of the old oak table in the study, her hands folded on her lap. "Nor for some time, in fact."

"Have I done something wrong?" Lana's face was pale, her eyes red. She had been crying as she ran across the bridge. The fear that had held her at the lakeside had twisted her stomach in knots that she felt might not unravel for days.

"The queen has a new task for you. I think you might enjoy it. You are to head to Southport and meet with your friend Selene. She has been working at the ruin you found and has confirmed that it is indeed the temple of Qura spoken of in the old texts. She believes there is more to discover, beyond the altar room you have seen, and also, she believes you can help to uncover what secrets may be hidden there." Aelwynne looked at her apprentice, as if seeing her for the first time, and stood, dashing to her side. "You've been crying, Lana? Are you alright?" Lana shook her head and bit her cheek. Her eyes welled with tears and she clung to Aelwynne, shaking.

When Lana finished telling of her encounter at the lakeside, they sat in silence, Aelwynne's hands clasped around hers.

"I… I think it's good then that you'll be heading to Southport, Lana. I'll need to speak to the queen about this. I think it is time she knew about this man and the strange rocks."

Lana nodded, sniffing back tears. "I don't know what he is. I don't know if he really means us harm, but he feels wrong. The trees pull back when he's there and they won't grow close to the rocks. He doesn't feel like any fae I've ever met before."

Aelwynne nodded slowly. "Perhaps it's time to send some of the silver to the woodlands? The queen will decide what's best, of course, but I don't like the thought of a man that scares you this much being so close." She reached out and placed her hand on Lana's shoulder, drawing her close again, their heads lightly touching. "Go get cleaned up, Lana. I'll meet you in the queen's study."

The sun was high in the southern skies as Lana emerged from the tree in the garden at Brighid's manor. She brushed her windswept hair behind her ear and called out to her friends. "Laywyn?! Kaorella?!" She wandered toward the house. "Laywyn? It's Lana, are you there?"

A door opened to the manor revealing a flour covered Kaorella, her lips wide with a smile as warm as a freshly baked bun.

"Lady Lana! Oh, how wonderful to see ya, M'lady. Come in… come in… I'll have a bun glazed in honey and a cup of sweet tea brought up to the lounge for you. Ser Laywyn would be ever so happy to see you." She sighed. "If only you'd come yesterday. Never mind, never mind. It's lovely you're here and I'm as pleased as he would be! But lookit you, you've grown! Like a proper lady now, you are."

Lana ran the rest of the way to the manor, up the few steps to the door. She threw her arms around Kaorella and hugged her tight. "Kaorella! I've missed you. It's nice up at the palace, but everyone's so formal. You know, they won't even lick their fingers after a sticky bun? It's like they don't even know that's the best bit!" She grinned. "But... Why should I have come yesterday? Is everything alright?"

"Oh, yes, of course it is. It's just that Ser Laywyn aint here. He went off yesterday with young Caitlin, took all his belongings too he did. Said he'd be gone a good long while, something about a ship and a pirate. He said to give Lady Brighid a letter when she's back. He left it up in the study. Left me his seal too, said I was to be in charge while he's gone. But I can give that to you now!"

Lana shook her head. "Oh, no! It's not for me, Kaorella! I'm not going to be here that long. I've got to meet Selene at the library and head off to the woods with her. There are things she wants me to help with at the old temple we found."

Kaorella sighed. "I guess I'd best get used to it then. But you'll stay the night, won't you? You can't go traipsing off to the woods at this time. It's far too late in the day for that."

Lana nodded and smiled. "Of course! But... About that bun..."

Lana asked if they could sit at the kitchen table rather than in the lounge, she enjoyed the smells and the warmth of a kitchen and after months of lessons with the old lore keeper she wanted to sit in a room where she wasn't surrounded by dusty old books. Kaorella was happy to oblige, and the pair sat chatting until the sun went down.

Lana yawned and smiled as Kaorella placed a small slice of cake in front of her with a steaming cup of thick brown liquid. "You must try this, Lana. It's something they calls cocoa. They brings it here on the ships from Karos and it goes so well with the cake. I do like to have a cup before bed."

Lana picked up the cup and sipped at the drink. Her smile shone as much in her eyes as on her lips. "This is lovely, Kaorella! It's like a nice warm hug but inside you." She brought the cup back up to her lips and sipped again.

"Well, I'm happy to make it for you whenever you're in the city, Lana. It's nice sitting here with you chatting about the world again without a worry beyond cake. Still, I'll not keep you up too late. I know you've an early start and a long day ahead. You enjoy your cocoa and I'll go pop this ol warming pan in your bed for you."

Chapter Eighteen

DRAWING EVEN

The dryad queen and her entourage had been back in the Heartwood three nights now, and Tinnion had spent each of those nights wandering through the southern edges of the forest. She had her bow in hand and a quiver of arrows ready at her side. She kicked at an errant stone at her feet, sending it rolling through the undergrowth. The moon was high now, and the air had a chill to it. Her breath formed small, short-lived plumes of steam.

She let out a disgruntled moan and sent an arrow into a nearby tree, then slumped against the trunk as she retrieved it and sighed.

"You really shouldn't do that. It is that kind of action that used to get your woodcutters killed."

Tinnion raised her head and looked at the dryad, her jaw clenched. Placing the arrow back into her quiver, she pushed herself away from the tree and walked past her, heading south.

Cinerea tilted her head, pursing her lips, her eyes wide. She turned and watched Tinnion walking away, then reached out and sunk into a tree.

"You are angry at me, Lady Tinnion?" Cinerea reappeared just in front of the hunter.

Tinnion stood and took a deep breath. "It's late, I'm tired." The dryad put her hand on Tinnion's chest. She didn't intend to push, but to keep Tinnion from walking away again.

"We have sat together and talked much later than this, sealgair. If you do not wish to speak with me, be honest and say so. I will not keep you where you do not wish to be kept."

Tinnion looked up into the dryad's eyes, her jaw set.

"I do not know many humans, sealgair, but I know when a woman is holding onto words they wish to scream out."

"I'm sure you do, Cinerea. I imagine you make everyone you know want to scream." Tinnion shifted her eyes, looking past the dryad as she spoke.

Cinerea shook her head. "Perhaps I should leave you to your night, sealgair. Perhaps I have made a mistake." The dryad turned and stepped toward a tree. She placed her hand against the trunk and began to push when a blunted arrow struck the bark between her fingers. She spun, ready to leap toward the shooter, but Tinnion was gone. Another arrow, blunted but stinging, struck her side below her ribs. She dropped to one knee and picked a fallen branch from the ground. As long and thick as a sword, it wasn't her preferred form, but it would do to swipe the arrows from the air. Standing, she turned to search for Tinnion, but the hunter was gone again. Cinerea raised a brow and smirked. "These woods are my home, sealgair. You cannot hide from me." She spun, swatting an arrow from the air from her makeshift weapon, then winced as another struck her breast. The dryad moved to the nearest tree and held her hand to it, reaching out to the network of life that flowed through the forest. Looking for the orange tinged green glow that belonged to the huntress. She felt her sisters, on patrol to the east of them and the animals that hunted through the night, as well as their prey. There was no human. Confused, she pulled her hand away from the tree and turned, looking through the branches, hoping her eyes would see what she could not sense in the trees. "Sealgair! Tinnion! You win. You marked me and you win. Show yourself that we might talk."

The surrounding forest grew silent, her cry causing hunter and prey to still. "Tinnion?" She called again.

"They're back! The wagon is back." The cries from the courtyard invaded the hall and Hayal looked up from his porridge.

"Do you want me to head down there, m'lady? See what they've come back with?"

"There's time, Hayal. Let's finish our food and we'll head down together. It seems too soon to be seeing them yet. I hope we haven't still got a wagon full of cheese and skins."

The wagon was full, and the pair that had driven it were standing with broad smiles. Surrounded by stead folk wanting to hear their tales and see what goods they had found in the big town to the west.

"You look well, Thom. Your journey seems to have been a short one, though. Were there problems?" The crowd parted as Tinnion approached and she clasped the wagon driver's arm in a friendly gesture that made his smile grow.

"No, m'lady. There were no problems. We didn't get to Freybridge, that's true, but we didn't need to. We came across another stead not long after the river turned away and they were eager to trade for our things. They haven't got cattle over there, would you believe it? Just fields full of flowers. So many flowers I've never seen fields so colourful. And bees." Thom chuckled. "You shoulda seen Garen, m'lady. He got stung so many times, I ended up the guard, keeping the bees away with a twig full of leaves."

"It's good to hear you found a stead to trade with, Thom. But how are you now, Garen?" She turned to the sheriff.

"Oh, I'm fine m'lady. Now the little stinging buggers've gone. I've never been so tormented. Give me a bow and a family of badgers any day over bloody bees."

Tinnion joined Thom in his chuckles and patted Garen on the back. "So... What did you bring us?"

"So much, m'lady. We've got so much. There're jars of honey and some herbs for Sera and a couple of barrels of mead." He smiled a broad smile and winked at the crowd around him. "There's medicines here as well, some in bottles what are ready mixed and some are dried leaves and things. They marked em all up so we can see what they're for... Well... Them what can read can... Oh and they gave us this stuff." He took a sack from the back of the wagon and pulled it open, pulling out bundles of yarn. "They makes it from plants that they grow there and it's really strong. Stronger n sheep's wool, they reckon. They make all their clothes and ropes and, well, sacks and everything from it."

Tinnion nodded with a smile. "You've done well. There's a use for all of these things. I'm pleased. Did they show any interest in trading again in the future?"

"Oh, aye. They did, m'lady. They said that if we were to pass by with more cheeses and mebbes, some butter and cream in two or three moons, they'd be happy to trade for them. They liked your skins too, of course, but they were thrilled to get the food."

"I think we can do that, and I'm sure Sera will get you a list of things she wants once she knows what she might get hold of. Why don't you take her things over to the kitchens? I'm sure she'll have a bit of hot breakfast for you when you do."

"Aye, m'lady, We'll do that."

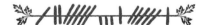

Cinerea leant her back against the cherry tree that once stood on the edge of the forest tempting Lana with its fruit. The sun was still filling the pasture with its light, but it wouldn't be long in the sky. She sat crossed leg with her bow across her lap, humming quietly to herself.

Tinnion climbed the fence and made her way across the pasture toward the dryad, watching her closely as she walked. The hunter hadn't been sure she would leave the manor this evening. After three nights of wanting to speak to the dryad, she couldn't find the words when they were face to face, and she wasn't sure she had found them since. Tinnion didn't carry her bow today. The desire to hunt wasn't with her, and she felt done with the games they had been playing. She wanted to know what was happening between them and that meant they would have to talk, honestly and frankly. Her stomach knotted at the thought and she considered turning back.

When she reached the tree, she sat at its base, her knee almost touching the dryad's. They sat together in silence, watching the sun on its journey to the horizon. It was some time before the huntress spoke.

"I was angry. It's stupid, I know. But I was angry. I knew you were back, and you didn't come here. After everything you did, the things you said. I thought you would want to see me, but you didn't come." She lowered her head and started picking at the grass by her feet.

"I am sorry, Tinnion. There were many things that needed to be done on our return. Many decisions to be made. The Princess Daowiel is leading a group of my sisters to a new woodland area the Ògan has chosen for us... a place that you did battle, as I understand. They are making a new home there and it was thought that I might be amongst that party. I had to be sure before I spoke with you."

"A new home?" Tinnion turned her head to look at the dryad, her eyes wide.

"Indeed. As part of the new treaty, we will create a home along your northern road and work with the people that live along it as we work with you here."

"But you're staying here? You aren't going?" She turned her face back to the ground as she asked her question.

"I have always been in Princess Erinia's circle. There was doubt, as Daowiel hoped to take Lothalilia, they know each other well. But Lothalilia is a leader in the laoch. It would be an enormous loss to the heartwood for her and the princess to leave. And so they considered having me go in her place. I am sealgair, not laoch, and would be easier to replace. In the end the princess made her case and Lothalilia is joining her."

A smile grew on Tinnion's lips as she heard the news. "So, you'll be staying here? And we can... hunt together?"

"We can. Though, may I be candid with you, Tinnion?"

Tinnion nodded, her brow furrowed.

"Hunting with you is a lot of fun. I enjoy it greatly and I am fascinated by your technique. You have none of the advantages that we dryad have and yet you would stand easily with our elite. But that is not why either of us are here. We are here because I kissed you and you want to know my intent? That is why you are here?"

Tinnion took a deep breath and opened her mouth to speak, then paused. She leaned back against the tree. "So that was dryad candour? I don't really know, Cinerea. What is happening between us? How am I supposed to feel after you kissed me? What am I supposed to think? I feel drawn to you. But I... You're dryad, dryad don't join with humans, you play games with them."

Cinerea brushed her hand against Tinnion's and smiled. "You were angry with me last night. You would not have been were this just a game, a short-lived fancy."

Tinnion's face flushed, and she stretched her little finger to prolong the contact with Cinerea's hand. The dryad mirrored her and their fingers interlaced. "I have never chased a relationship, Cinerea. Usually I do what I can to escape them. I don't know what this is but... But I want to see."

"Then we will see, Tinnion. Though I know the feelings I have and I believe I know what this is. I will wait until you have 'seen'."

"You know?" Tinnion raised her brow.

"I do, of course. I intend to bind with you." The dryad smiled.

Chapter Nineteen

Northfort

"We've tae speak with the Tay on a matter of great urgency. Where is he?" Brighid shouted her question as she handed her horse to a groom at the keep stables.

"And who, may I ask, are 'we'?" The steward that ran down the steps of the keep to confront them was a young man, his slight frame marked him as a person more suited to scholarly and administrative tasks than to physical work or fighting, and his manner showed no respect for the two muddy warriors that stood before him.

"I'm Brighid MacFaern, Queen's Thegn and daughter of the clan chief, Cohade MacFaern. My friend here is the Queen's Thegn Wren. Now." Brighid stepped toward the man. "The Tay? Where can we find him?"

"Forgive me, m'ladies." The steward's face flushed as he apologised. "Your appearance, well, it, err, hides, your station."

"The Tay?" Wren interrupted, her voice soft and kind.

"Yes m'lady. The Tay is bathing. He will be in the great hall as the sun begins its descent."

"I am afraid our business is most urgent. I am sure the tay will forgive the interruption once he hears our news. Where is the bathhouse?" Wren tilted her head, expecting the answer.

"Forgive me m'lady but you can't... It wouldn't be proper." The young man spluttered.

Brighid rolled her eyes then placed her hand gently on the stewards shoulder with a smile. "I don't want tae get ye in tae trouble, wee man. The problem is, the shadows are back and on their way tae kill us all, you see? So, we'd really like tae speak with the Tay before they get here and start skinning all these fine folk."

The man opened his mouth for a moment and then paused, as Brighid's words filtered through his mind. He shook and stuttered as his reply finally came. "The... They're back...? Yes... yes, of course, m'lady."

"Do you doubt ma word?" Brighid looked down on the steward, one eyebrow raised and moved her hand from the man's shoulder to wrap the loose cloth of his light scarf around her fingers.

The man's eyes widened and his cheeks blanched as he realised the shadows weren't the greatest threat he faced in that moment. "No, m'lady... It's just..."

"Do as yer here to do then. Show us to the Tay. Now, wee man."

The man slaked back from her, and turned, taking a few shaky steps back toward the keep then paused and changed direction.

"If you will follow me, m'ladies."

Wren turned to Brighid and laughed. "I don't think the poor boy knows where he is anymore, Brighid. You've scared him into a stupor."

The bath house was hot and thick with steam that clung to the women as they entered and caused the dirt on their faces to run in streaks of dark brown and black.

"What is this, Tarrick?" The Tay looked up from the pool of milky hot water that lapped at his chest. "How dare you bring these women into the bathhouse to disturb me?"

The steward bowed, still shaking. "Forgive me, my lord. Lady Brighid insisted that this matter is of the utmost urgency, lord."

"Lady who now?" The Tay gestured dismissively as he asked.

"Brighid MacFaern, Lord Jendawyn, Queens Thegn and daughter of Cohade MacFaern." The steward stuttered as he spoke the introduction.

The Tay's face turned in an instant from anger at being disturbed to delight at seeing Brighid and then to confusion. "Brighid? Is it really you? Little Brighid! Yes! You've grown into the picture of your mother, dear child. You're Queen's thegn now then are you? Well, of course you are. I shouldn't be surprised. I always thought you were a fighter, near bit my finger right off at your naming, you did. But... Why are you here, Brighid? And disturbing me on my bath day?"

Wren laughed at her friend. "Little Brighid..." The tuath gave her a sharp look, lessened in seriousness slightly by her smile, then approached the bathing pool.

"There are troubles in the west, Lord. MacKenna has betrayed us and fights side by side with shadows. He has his eye set on Northfort, Lord. And your head. My clan and those that were MacTiern's were forced to flee our homes. My father and clan are a day or two away, Lord, and seek shelter here. The shadows, sadly, no far behind."

The Tay held up his hand, a finger extended to touch the bridge of his nose. "There is a lot in your statement, Brighid. I have many questions. First you say MacKenna has sided with the shadows. How can that be? The shadows are gone."

Brighid sighed and bit her lip a moment before taking a calming breath and softening her voice. "I don't know how, m'lord. Only that I saw, and fought agin a dozen of them in the tower of Shadowatch. There was no mistaken what they were, lord. Even after so long."

"I can confirm their identity, Lord Tay." Wren spoke to support her friend.

The Tay of Northern Mortara sat bolt upright in his bath, no longer relaxed. His eyes moved between the young warrior he had known since her birth and the fae at her side. He took a handful of water and splashed his face, as though trying to remove the moment as much as any dirt that remained there.

"A sylph?" He wiped the soapy water from his eyes. "And who are you, my dear?"

"I am Wren, queens thegn, lord Tay." She bowed her head gently.

"Shadows and tuath then. And you said 'those that were MacTiern's'?" The Tay stressed the use of the word 'were' as he spoke, hoping that was enough to draw an explanation.

Brighid nodded slowly, leaving her head bowed as she began her explanation. "He sided with MacKenna, lord. As all but Clan MacFaern did. But he made the mistake of trying to waylay us on our journey."

The Tay nodded his understanding and sighed. "A costly mistake that. So... Of all the tuath only clan MacFaern stand with me?"

Brighid nodded again, slowly and silently, her face a mask of despair. A look quickly mirrored by the Tay. A few moments of silence followed as the Tay considered the news brought to him. When he broke the silence, his voice was surprisingly bright and strong.

"Then I am fortunate in that, at least. Your family represent the best of the Tuath, Brighid. They always have. Now... If you'll excuse me, I shall ready myself and meet you in the great hall to discuss this further. Tarrick!" The steward had not moved from the side of the pool and the shout made him jump. "Show these ladies to the hall and make sure they have what they need."

"Yes, my lord." Tarrick bowed and gestured for the warriors to follow him.

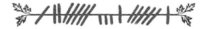

The Tay listened carefully as Brighid and Wren described what had happened since the betrayal in the tower of Shadowatch. He stopped them occasionally to ask questions and clear up confusions, though he tried to interrupt as little as possible. His face blanched as Brighid described the burning of Lochmead and he shook his head as he exclaimed his belief that this was the most certain sign of the seriousness of the situation.

The recounting of Clan MacTiern's end had his face red, a mixture of anger and sadness at the passing of a once great family. And he sighed deeply as he heard of the destruction of the bridge on the southern rise. "I suppose it was necessary... It will slow them. There is no doubt of that, and the time we gain from it may make the difference in what is coming. Your father sent a messenger south, you say?"

Brighid nodded. "He did, lord Tay. He thought it best to inform the Queen as soon as possible, though he asks your forgiveness for acting without command."

"There is no need to forgive your father, Brighid. He has done what was right and what I would have commanded were I there. We will send a call out to the Liath, as well. And I will have the beacon lit. I cannot give up hope that there are other Tuath that remain loyal to the north." The Tay's face was gaunt and his eyes heavy. Though he tried to hide his concern with a smile, it did not work.

"I pray that you're right, lord. I hate the thought of having tae fight my own. Not like this, at any rate." Brighid own attempt to hide her dismay turned into a sigh.

"Tell me though, Brighid. There is one thing that just makes little sense to me. Why were two of the queens newly appointed thegn in Shadowatch? Were you not expected in the queen's court?"

"It was coincidence, lord Tay." Wren spoke quickly, cutting Brighid off before secrets were inadvertently spilled. "Ser Reynard had asked us to look into rumours of ships from the falcon isles. We arrived in the town late and took rooms at an inn to rest before setting out to ask questions. It was a surprise to see Lord MacFaern and the other clan chiefs arrive the following morning. We had heard nothing of the intended meeting."

The tay nodded. "Ah, that makes sense. There have been several circle priests here in these last few months. Passing through, you understand. I'll not have the circle setting up temples here in the north. I have been wondering why myself. Did you discover anything?"

"No, Lord." Wren shook her head slowly. "Things took their turn at that point. Rather, we had found a secret temple of the circle than the dozen sgàil we faced. They'd have been a lot easier to deal with."

"Aye, there's nought but truth in that. Well, I've heard enough. We'll have our folk on the plain gather supplies and head on up to the fortress. Tarrick..."

"Yes, m'lord." The steward stepped forward with a nod.

"Get the word out to my knights and bring me a messenger. I want to get one out and riding to the Liath before dusk. And have someone light the beacon."

"Yes, m'lord." The young man turned and left the room at a trot.

With his steward gone the Tay turned back to the two women. "You've had a long and hard journey, the pair of you. I'll have my maid show you to a room and fetch you clean clothes. Take some time to rest before dinner. You'll sit at my table this evening."

They gave the tay a nod of gratitude in unison before Wren spoke again.

"Lord, do you have a healer within the fort?" Wren's voice was low, suggesting that the question was one she wished to keep between them.

"Of course, Wren. Are you unwell?"

"No, lord. But Brighid was injured in the fight with the shadows. I treated the wound as best as I could but I am a warrior, not a healer and she had little time to rest before leaving Lochmead. It would be good to have someone look at her. And the Gesith, when he arrives."

The Tay gave Brighid a look, his brows raised.

"I don't have full movement yet, Lord, but I can still fight." Brighid tried to reassure the Tay.

"Go on to your room and wash. I will have my own healer, Neve, join you there and examine you."

"Thank you, Lord." Brighid bowed her head slightly and Wren smiled.

The morning skies were clear and blue. The sun was bright but gave no warmth. Frost had formed on the stone of the courtyard overnight and was hanging on despite the sun's presence. Wren and Neve sat close to one another, watching

Brighid as she moved, working the stiffness from her leg. The movements were simple, flowing, and relaxed, but Neve, the nymph healer, watched intently.

"You move as a fish through water, Brighid."

Brighid stopped and looked at the fae who had spent part of the previous evening helping her old wounds heal. Her breath formed mist in the cold air as she spoke. "It's important for me tae see the flow of the battle. I like tae move through the space that is there. It's no good forcing yer way through a fight, pushing against folk doing the same, that just uses up all yer energy and ye tire too fast. Sometimes ye've to break through a line or stand strong against a push. That's true. But I prefer tae do that as little as possible."

"As the stream runs over the earth on its long, winding journey." Neve smiled.

"Aye, I guess so, in a way. I had nae really thought of it like that." Brighid nodded.

"Why then do other warriors not move in this way?" The healer seemed genuinely confused. As a nymph, she was used to moving with the river. It seemed beyond ridiculous to her that a warrior would fight against the flow of battle.

"We all have our styles, our ways." Brighid moved toward the healer and her friend with a smile. "Ye can't teach a warrior tae fight in a way that goes against their nature. Some are strong but can nae move so well, they'd not last long trying tae fight like me."

"Most do not last long when fighting against you either, friend." Wren chuckled as she spoke.

The nymph leaned forward, resting her chin on her hands. "I see that, I think. Wren uses her speed to react more quickly than her attacker. The Tay uses his strength when he fights, overpowering and beating his opponent. I think I find your way more appealing. If I were forced to join the battle, I would like to fight as you do."

"I hope that ye don't, Neve. I hope there's never a need for ye to take up a weapon. Yer skill lies in healing and that is a far better skill tae have than swinging a sword. Best you keep Wren and me well and let us do the fighting." Brighid smiled.

"How are your wounds now?" The healer stood and looked the warrior over.

Brighid touched her hand to the scar on her stomach. "They're not causing any pain now and they're not as tight. I hope tae start working with Wren again soon, get used tae sparring at speed again. The soldiers here are decent, but they're soldiers, not warriors, and I need tae get back in tae shape with a warrior as soon as I can. I can't imagine the rebels are far off now."

"Do you think there will be many, Brighid?" Wren broke her silence, her voice was low.

"I find ma self torn, Wren. On the one hand, I hope that there are. MacKenna'll kill any that stand against him and there are good families out there that I'd hate tae think dead. I'd hope that we can turn the tide, and they'd join us once they get here. On the other hand, I'd rather not face all the clans. They'll outnumber us greatly if they all stand with him."

Wren nodded, her sympathy for her friend clearly written on her face. "I wish we had more time. The market town below is moving up into the fortress and bringing their food, but we will still face a hard time. The fortress is strong, but there are no natural sources of food. It is an oversight of your people that surprises me."

Brighid sat next to her friend and looked over the fortress grounds. "You've tae understand, Wren. We weren't fighting each other. It was the cursed shadows we were defending against and they never took to the field in numbers. They'd never think o' using a siege tae break the battle. When we built this place, we designed it so they had no way of sending their assassins without us having the best chance tae stop them. Being atop a long narrow path does that for us. You're right though, we did nae think we'd ever be short of supplies. There's plenty of food out there and it was never a problem getting to it before." The tuath sighed deeply. "I can't believe they're back and that they've found weakness and greed in the clans. That pains me, it shouldn't be. MacKenna is a poor fighter and a coward. He'll camp his force at the bottom of the mountain and starve us out. All we can do is sit in hope we get some help, before we have tae force the fight."

"Perhaps your father and the Tay will make the clans see sense as you did with MacAllister." Wren placed a hand on Brighid's arm.

"Aye." Brighid tried a smile. "There's a chance they could settle it that way. It's one thing tae face Clan MacFaern and another tae come face tae face with the Queen's Tay and real treason. I worry the shadows have their claws deep into the others too, though. Fear is a mighty tool when it's used right and by all my learning, the shadows are masters at that."

"Tay Jendawyn has called on the eastern lords. We will have allies if we can only hold on." Neve's voice was strong and full of certainty as she interrupted the warrior's thoughts. But it was met with a snorted laugh from Brighid.

"MacHuran will come. I'm fairly sure of that. He's a warrior and our clans are close. I would nae be holding ma breath for the other lords tae jump into war, though."

Wren looked at her friend, her brow raised. "You don't trust in the eastern lords?"

"It's not that I distrust 'em, Wren. But they aren't tuath. They've always looked tae us for protection against the shadows. They'll not be quick to come and fight here when they hear the battles against the clans and the sgàil. MacHuran is different. He has clan blood and knows how tae fight. He'll not let fear get in his way, at least. Though he might ride here alone."

Chapter Twenty

The Temple of Qura

Lana hugged Selene as they met. They hadn't seen each other since their adventure with the princess and the priests of the circle.

Selene looked paler than she had when they first met, though healthier on the whole, and her wide smile was warm. "You look so different, Lana! I think you have grown since I last saw you."

"You have too, Selene. You look happier for sure." Lana smiled.

"Oh, I am. Life in the library is wonderful. I have access to every book and scroll I ever wanted to read and I get to talk with lots of brilliant people whenever I want."

Lana puffed. "You're smarter than the lore keepers I've met, by far. I bet they all come to you for help and advice."

"Oh, I'm not that smart, Lana. Though they often come to see the lore master and I help him. I believe that is why I was chosen to investigate the ruin further.

Some of the older men are not too fond of having a woman so close to the lore master's side and prefer me away from the library."

"See, you are smarter than them. I think some of the lore keepers spend so long looking at words in books they forget what it's like to be people and that us women are just as good as they are."

The sylph chuckled. "You may be right, Lana. I don't mind though, I enjoy discovering new things at the temple and the lore master is thrilled with the work I am doing." The sylph took her friend's hand and pulled gently. "We should make a start on our road. There is a camp along the way that we use as we go back and forth, and I'd like to get there before the sun is close to setting. Shayell will meet us there."

"Sure, I don't mind starting straight away." Lana smiled. "Who's Shayell?"

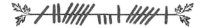

Shayell was a noam, a tall man, at almost two meters, with a muscular, bulky build. He kept his face shaven, which was odd for a city noam, and his smile was warm. Lana noted his smile grew a lot brighter when he talked directly to Selene.

"It is a pleasure to meet you, Lana. Selene has told me much about you." He held out a large hand, which Lana took and shook lightly.

"It's nice to meet you too, Shayell. I didn't know there were any noam in the lore council."

"Oh, there are not, Lana. No, I am my lord's advisor and so I have a knowledge of history and will help with the stonework."

"Shayell can tell us a lot about the building by the stones, Lana. He reads them as I might read a book. And he is very useful to have around when there are rocks in the way." Selene smiled at the noam and the three sat around the campfire. The formalities, such as they were, over.

"So, is it true? Did we really find Qura's home?" Lana's eyes sparkled as she questioned her friend.

The sylph's face lit up, and she took Lana's hand as she answered. "It is. It was immediately clear that what we found was a temple to Qura. But as we have revealed more of the building, our understanding grew and we believe she did indeed live there. At least part of the time. Though there is still a lot to explore."

"It's wonderful! To think all those..." Lana paused, putting her hand to her chin. "... Millenia..." she smiled. "All those millennia ago, the goddess was walking through the temple and living her life there. I wonder what she was like, really, I mean. Not what people wrote about her after she was gone."

Selene nodded with a wide grin. "We hope we can learn something about that, Lana. As we dig and reveal more. We hope to find things that help us understand what her life might have been."

"It's very exciting, Selene. Are there more people there helping?"

"No, sadly. There were two others, men that helped clear the rubble and examine the objects we found. But they are gone now, recalled by the council. So it will just be us three. I hope you don't mind getting your clothes dirty, now that you are used to wearing delicate dresses." Selene chuckled as she teased Lana.

"I've got my normal clothes in my bag! I'm not afraid of getting dirty, still."

The corridor was lit with torches, their flickering light sending shadows dancing across the grey stone of the walls. Shayell stood at a wall, tracing the images carved across it with his fingers. Rubble piled up against it as high as Lana's waist.

"I think Selene would appreciate this. This stone is older than those in the main temple, and the carvings seem to have been made around the time of the divide." The large man's voice was deep, though soft, and put Lana at ease, almost lulling her into a sleep.

"The divide?" Lana reached out to touch the carving.

"When Khyione and Kaoris divided the earthen fae. They built this wall before Khyione even created your kind, Lana. It is that old."

Lana looked up at the noam, her eyes wide. "I think it must be the oldest thing I've ever touched, then! What does it say?"

"I do not know, Lana. Though the fae all speak the same language, that is to say, our words are the same... or very close. The carvings and the letters we use differed greatly. The Sylph used these pictures to create their words in the time before the divide, whereas the noam and dryad have always used runes. I can tell that they were carved with pride. The stone still resonates with that, but I cannot tell you what it means. I am certain that Selene will have more understanding."

"Are you saying you can feel what the person who did this felt through the stone?" Lana's brow furrowed.

"Yes. The person who carved this felt powerful emotion and, through their carving, they channelled that into the stone itself. The stones hold echoes of these things. Memories can be held in stone eternally, if you know how."

Lana placed her hand flat to the stone and tilted her head. "Do you know how?"

"Yes." The noam turned to look at her. "Selene tells me that the dryad have shown you their ability to shape wood?"

Lana nodded quietly. It made her a little uneasy that Shayell knew this. Not that she didn't trust the friendly noam, but that she felt there were things she would rather keep amongst her close friends.

"There is one line of dryad only that can do that, in this age. The line that is descended directly from the first child of Kaoris. That line holds the royal crown within the dryad forests. Similarly, the descendants of Khyione's first son can shape stone. In shaping it, we communicate with it, we tell the stone what we want, though sometimes it is necessary to negotiate. Stones can be stubborn." The noam's laughter rumbled so deeply that Lana could feel it.

"Like oak." Lana smiled before pausing for a moment. "You said we. Does that mean you're a noam prince?"

Shayell shook his head. "No. No. My ancestors were, in fact, my great grandfather was heir to the noam throne before he left Stonemount. I have no title beyond advisor. My family gave those up. The noam of Southport elected a lord when we settled and I serve him now. I have no interest in the throne or in crowns."

"So... What else can you do?"

"What else?" Shayell repeated Lana's question as he thought it through.

"I mean." Lana interrupted his thought. "The dryad, they can all travel through the trees and talk with them. Can you travel through the stones?"

"Oh, I see. No. Not through the stones, not really. Though Khyione himself could. If there is a vein of metal or of crystal, then most noam can travel through that. I have never tried. I never found the idea useful... veins go from one rocky place to another. They rarely go anywhere you would want to be. Though it is useful that we can detect these veins. Especially when you are short of coin in a human city." Shayell laughed.

Lana's eyes widened, and her mouth dropped open as she realised what Shayell was suggesting.

"You must be very rich?"

The noam laughed again and shook his head. "I have what I need and I will never be poor, but there is little reason to hold purses or chests full of coin. It is, in itself, simply metal. Very few people even know I can do this. I would ask that it stays that way."

"Oh yes, of course. I won't say anything if you don't want me to."

Shayell nodded with a smile. "Let us go and tell Selene what we have found."

They lay around a campfire on the floor of the temple, happy with their day's discoveries and tired from their work. Selene was examining a rubbing she had taken of the carvings and Shayell was absentmindedly rubbing on a stone he carried in a pouch on his belt. The temple was silent, besides the sound of their breathing, and Lana found herself yawning. She wished her companions a good night and turned on her side; her back to the warmth of the fire. As her eyes closed, she thought she saw a shadow move just outside the temple archway. She rubbed her eyes and gazed into the darkness, but she saw nothing and heard nothing other than the breathing of her friends and her own heart beating. She lay her head back down and closed her eyes, drifting into sleep.

The sisterhood met in the temple of Qura on Gaoth Isle. Each goddess, accompanied by her chosen daughter, watched as the human female nursed her baby.

"We gave life to these humans in order that your children and your brothers could continue their existence, Kaoris. But our brothers use the females as their playthings, they abuse them and the children of Khyione enslave them, they overwhelm their fragile minds. Are we not as responsible for their safety as we are that of our own children?"

"They were created to carry the seeds of our children and to bare their children, Ophine. Nothing more."

"And had they remained as we created them, I would feel no obligation, Kaoris. However, we have given them thought and will so that they could breed amongst themselves and ensure your children's line by ensuring theirs. We have given them life only to condemn them to abuse and slavery. We owe them our protection." The goddess raised her voice as she addressed her sister.

"You would have us gift these creatures as we have gifted our chosen daughters. They would become more than our children, they would become stronger." The goddess Chaint was in dark mood and the air surrounding her grew as night as she spoke.

"Unlike our first children, these humans were born of us all, dear sister. It is right that they receive each of our gifts. They will never, however, become more than our first. Their lives are too short and their bodies too fragile." Ophine was prepared for dissent and for her sisters' questions and so answered quickly to assuage the goddesses' doubts.

"One line only. Beginning with this child, one line of humans that will carry our gifts from mother to daughter. That is all that we ask of you, my sisters. One line that may join us and live within our halls. One line that might be protected from the abuse of our brothers and be safe from Khyione's 'blessings'. Join with Qura and I in this and strengthen the sisterhood."

The chamber fell silent as the goddesses of earth and light considered their sister's plea. It was Kaoris that broke the silence. The mother of the dryad, moved by the sight of the helpless child in its mother's arms.

"I will join you, sisters. And I will give to this child the same gifts I bestowed upon my own. I will welcome this one and it's line into my halls."

"Very well." Chaint conceded. "I shall offer my gifts as you have. I have grown disappointed by the behaviour of our brothers, though I love them still. They should not be allowed dominion over all of these creatures." The air around the goddess Chaint was lighter, though her mood seemed just as sullen.

"Then it is settled. This child and her line shall be blessed. She will be welcomed in our halls and educated with our children. I believe we have made a positive change in the world today, sisters." Qura smiled as she approached the human female, and with great care, took the babe from its arms to be blessed.

Chapter Twenty-One

Voices

The dream had been so real, Lana felt she had been in the room with the goddesses and their first children. She had felt the dark mood of Chaint and the loving warmth of Ophine. But the events that she had seen made little sense to her. If the goddesses had granted their gifts to a human line, then many humans could do the things the fae do. They could shape wood and travel the bridge, they could see the movement of air and glide like the sylph, they could heal like the nymph and hide like a sgàil. But humans couldn't do that, none of them ever could, not that she knew of, anyway.

But you can do some of those things, Lana. The thought came to her as though from someone else's mind. Yes... yes I can but that's because of the stone, the stone changed me. And I can't do them all. Only the things the dryad can do, and only because they taught me. ***And the sylph, Lana, you glide as the sylph do and you feel a storm before it comes.*** But that's all, I can't hide in the shadows or heal people. And even if I could, even if I could do all those things, no one else can. So it doesn't make sense. If the dream was real, my mam would be able to do all these things too. ***Perhaps she could if she were taught.***

Taught as the dryad taught you. But she can't... And I can't do those other things. ***Yet, Lana. You cannot do them yet.***

Lana opened her eyes. The fire was low but still burning and the room was still dark. She stretched and rubbed the sleep from her eyes then got up and gave the fire a poke and added some wood to feed it. Then she lit a torch and walked to the temple door to stretch her legs and look at the sky.

The dark orange tint of dawn touched the blue of the night sky in the east, the air was cool and fresh, blowing lazily around her making the leaves dance in the trees. Lana smiled and took a deep breath, clearing her head of the dream and thoughts that it caused. A horn blew in the distance, a hunter's horn, no doubt calling their companions to a fresh kill. It hadn't been so long ago that this area was Tinnion's hunting ground. Now she was weeks away in Lana's stead and Lana was here on her land. She laughed to herself. Life was strange.

She heard the sounds of her friends stirring behind her, the soft shuffle of blankets being moved and Lana turned to greet them to the new day.

In the distance, another horn blew.

"There is a door!" Selene shouted down the corridor as she ran toward Lana and Shayell. "A hidden door to a secret chamber. You must find it, Shayell. Talk to the stone and find the way."

Shayell looked at his friend, uncertain. "A door? Are you certain, Selene? I have not sensed one."

"Yes, Shayell. It is clear in the carvings. It must be here, please, Shayell, you must find it." The sylph watched as Shayell put his hand to the stones and closed his eyes. She bounced on the balls of her feet, a wide grin on her face and the rubbing clasped tight in her hands. "Is it there? Can you feel it?"

The noam turned his head and sighed. "You need to give me time, Selene. And quiet. I cannot hear the stones if you are babbling in my ear."

Selene snapped her lips closed, biting her cheek, but her eyes remained wide and she continued to bounce.

Shayell shifted his hand, sliding it slowly across the face of the stone. A few moments passed in silence, and then he shook his head. "I am sorry, Selene. I cannot sense a room beyond this wall. Are you sure that it is here and not elsewhere along this corridor?"

"The carvings say it is here, Shayell. Are you sure you feel nothing?" Selene lowered her head with a sigh.

"Err... Shayell..." Lana tapped the arm of the noam. "Is this something important?" Lana had been clearing rubble that had built up against the wall and stood pointing to a deeply carved section that looked like a lightning cloud. The noam crouched to examine the carving. Placing his hand upon it as he had to the wall just a moment before. In a second he pulled his hand away, sharply wincing and gasping for air.

"What is it, Shayell?" Selene put her hand to his shoulder and steadied him.

"It may be your answer, Selene. It is a lock, perhaps to your door, perhaps not. But I cannot open it, no noam could. Only thighearna-stoirm might open this lock."

Selene's jaw dropped, her face blanched. "But... That cannot be... Shayell. That cannot be. thighearna-stoirm do not exist."

"Then it cannot be opened, Selene. For it must be struck with... Forgive me, Lana, I do not know this word in your language... It must be struck with dealanach."

"Lightning." Selene's voice was low and sad.

The noam nodded. "The stone still holds the bite of the power. I cannot attempt to unlock it or trace its path without pain."

Selene sighed, her head dropped. "Then we will leave it, for now. Perhaps we will find another way."

Rubble blocked the far end of the corridor. Columns had tumbled and stones as large as Lana had fallen away from the ceiling. The soil and dirt of many thousands of years pressed against the walls. Shayell and Selene examined the rubble, carefully pulling those sections that were part of the temple away and scraping dirt from features.

"There is no doubt that this was done deliberately, Selene." Shayell was holding a circular piece of stone that had come from one column that had fallen. "This part of the building was blocked off long before the temple became unused."

"You are certain, Shayell?" Selene had found another inscribed piece of stone, a small section of a larger carving, and was trying to decipher its message.

"I am, Selene. Whoever did this allowed the temple room to stand and remain in use. It suggests that they were trying to hide, or prevent something from happening in the area beyond this corridor."

"Is there a way through, Shayell?"

The noam shook his head. "Not without help, Selene. If we attempt to clear this area, it will simply result in more of the earth above it falling in. We could, perhaps, dig from above, or try to access the space below the blockage and hope that leads us where you wish to be. But it would be dangerous to dig through this rubble. It is too loose to make stable."

"What is below us?"

"I cannot be certain. There is space, and I believe it to be another corridor. There will certainly be access to it somewhere along here and if we were to dig down into it, there would, no doubt, be a point at which we could ascend once more." The noam paused. "Unless this destruction has also been done there."

"There are so many searches that we are being forced to abandon here. I feel that there is something being hidden from us, deliberately hidden, something important. I do not want to give up on this. Can you access the space beneath us?"

Shayell nodded slowly. "I can, Selene, but I do not know if I should. I do not know how safe it is."

"Is there danger in removing some of these stones to look into that space?" The sylph seemed almost to plead in her question.

"There could be. Removing one stone could cause the rest to weaken and falter."

Selene slumped to the floor, her head bowed, her face hidden by her arms. Her shoulders shook. Lana sat beside her, putting her arm around the sylph's shoulder and pulling her friend gently toward her. They sat for a while in silence, simply holding each other as Shayell moved along the corridor, examining the floor stones carefully.

"There is a stone here which is a little loose." The noam called after some time. "I believe I can remove it without affecting those stones around it. If that is what you want, Selene." The sylph remained silent but nodded, wiping tears from her eyes with her sleeves.

"Do you need help, Shayell?" Lana's voice was soft but still seemed to echo through the silence of the temple corridor.

"No, Lana. I will manage this alone. I think, however, it would be safer for you both to wait in the temple while I work on it. In case I am wrong."

As day turned to night, Selene sat in the temple, piecing together the broken stones that held carvings. Lana sat close to her, working through the buckets of rubble they had gathered, checking for more stones for the sylphs puzzle.

"Selene… What's a chee-yurn-ah sto-irm?"

Selene smiled at her friend's elongated pronunciation of the word. "Thig-hearna-stoirm were only legends, at least, I thought they were. I'm beginning to re-think that with everything that is happening here. They were said to be the firstborn of Qura and Zeor, though some say they were actually the gods themselves. They held the ability to summon storms and create lightning from nothing but the air around them. Our legends say that they were dangerous, very dangerous. It is said that they were confined, their lines allowed to die out for fear that their power was causing them to grow mad."

Lana's nose wrinkled as she listened to her friend, her head to one side. "Do you think Qura might have locked them up here?"

Selene shook her head. "I do not think so, Lana. That lock seems to suggest that they locked something, or someone, up here rather than being confined themselves. I wonder what it is they might have wanted to hide away and if it was them that caused the eventual destruction."

"Do the carvings tell you anything?" Lana peered over her friend's stone puzzle.

"These stones? No. Not yet, there are too many missing or else I have not yet found the correct order. I am certain they will make sense if we can find more. We are doing well here, though it is disheartening. Every question that we are forced to ask is a step forward and each should, in time, be answerable."

"Are you feeling a little better, then?"

Selene nodded with a smile. "I am, Lana. It feels that with each step forward, we must take three back, and that overwhelmed me for a moment. But I am alright, thank you. You were a great comfort."

The friends shared a comforting embrace and a smile for a moment that was broken by the heavy footsteps of the noam running back into the temple room.

"It is done." Shayell came through the empty doorway of the corridor carrying a large floor stone, a wide grin across his face. "And there were no collapses, at least not so far. The space below appears to be a room, a high room too, the floor is lost to the darkness."

The torch burned five metres below them, throwing a small circle of light into the darkness of the room. Selene wrapped the rope around her waist, checking and double checking the knot, before squeezing through the hole in the floor.

"If there is anything that makes you uncomfortable, Selene, simply call and I will pull you up." Shayell tied the other end of the rope around his waist and coiled it around his arm.

"Are you sure about this? It might not be safe. I can go instead. I've got my staff if there are any beasties down there."

Selene shook her head. "I am, Lana. Shayell doesn't fit, and I'd rather not put you at risk. I will have a brief look around, see if I can find a way up and then come back. If everything is safe, we can all go down later."

"I am ready when you are, Selene." Shayell gave a little tug on the rope to make sure he had a good grip. The sylph nodded and stepped into the hole.

Lighting a second torch from the sack she carried, she walked into the darkness, looking for a wall sconce to hang it from.

The room was smaller than she had expected, a little bigger than her room at the library, but not by much. She found places for a torch on each wall and looked around, her eyes wide. Every wall held a carving as ornate and detailed as the ones in the corridor above were. The remains of a bed lay in one corner and several scrolls, flaking and turned to dust, were scattered around the floor. Following the line of the space above, there was an archway into a passage. A wooden door had fallen away, splintered and crumbling with age. Selene untied the rope around her and wandered out of the room.

"May I talk with you, Lana?" Shayell sat on the passage floor, the rope loose around his arm. He spoke in a whisper and titled his head close to hers.

"Of course, Shayell. Is it about you and Selene? I think you'd make a wonderful couple." Lana grinned.

The noam spluttered and blushed, his face near glowing red.

"Selene? Well, no... I mean, she is very nice and all, but no... It is not about her. Not really. It is more complicated than that."

Lana nodded with a smile. "Well, if it isn't about Selene and I already know about your gold." She giggled. "What is it, Shayell? You can tell me anything."

"You have met the queen of the dryad. Is she a good person, Lana?"

"Oh yes! At least she seems to be. She was very nice to me and all the dryad love her. And she got on well with Queen Rhiannon... Why?"

"Do you know what happens when we die, Lana?"

"Yes... At least, I know what people say happens. I don't think anyone could possibly know for sure, though. Some say when humans die, our spirits spread across the world and feed all the plants and turn to rain and all kinds of things.

Other people, usually people that fight a lot, say that they go to a place where they drink and eat lots with other warriors."

Shayell nodded. "And fae? Do you know what happens to fae?"

"Well, if you deliberately make a promise you know you won't keep, the same thing happens to you. That's what Queen Olerivia told me. But if you never do that, then your spirit gets born again as someone else."

"That is... Yes... That is close enough." Shayell gave a half smile. "When sylph die, they become sylph again because their people never split. When nymph die, they become nymph again because they never leave fresh waters, and mer become mer because they never leave the seas. Dryad have always become dryad and noam become noam. But... I feel that, perhaps, that is not always the way."

Lana took a deep breath and opened her mouth to speak, then paused and exhaled, slumping a little with a confused look.

"Our spirits, noam and dryad, they merge with the earth, Lana, and then we stay within the earth until we are reborn. I believe my spirit somehow became tied to stone but also to tree. Though I do not know how. I know it sounds unbelievable but I feel, every day, that I am, at least in some way, dryad. I cannot connect with the trees as they do, but... I feel an affinity that other noam do not feel. I know that I do not look dryad. I know that I do not have the ability of the dryad, and I look as a noam looks. But I have memories, I have feelings. It is... I feel... I cannot explain it clearly, but I feel not entirely noam."

"But you can talk to stone, and shape them and find metals and gems. Those are noam things." Lana reached a hand out to Shayell. She didn't know what he was going through, but she could see by his face that it was difficult for him and she wanted to comfort him.

Shayell nodded slowly. "I can. I do not truly know how to put it into words. It is a feeling that I have. I can do all those things, that is true, but I do not feel truly comfortable with stone. I know it makes little sense, that it sounds a strange thing."

Lana squeezed his hand gently and put her head gently to his shoulder.

"I don't know lots of things, Shayell. I can do things I shouldn't be able to and I see things that are strange all the time. I see the goddesses and sometimes I see the war and the battle at the castle on the lake. And... Well, I haven't died but I feel like I have a different life than I used to. I was s'posed to be a milkmaid and live my whole life in a small stead. And now I'm living in the Queen's palace and learning about history and diplomacy and court life. I remember playing in the pastures and looking up at the clouds making up stories from their shapes. But sometimes I feel like my old life is dead and gone and now I have a new one that is so different. I feel like that Lana doesn't really exist anymore. So I do understand, a bit. At least, I know what it's like to be different. So... If you tell me you feel like you're part dryad, I believe you. But... What can I do to help you? Would you like me to talk to Queen Olerivia for you and see if she understands better? Would you like to see if she can help you?"

"I do not know that I can be helped, Lana. Except into death, so that I can be reborn. But I do not wish to die yet. There is much for me to do in this life." Shayell paused. "I just wanted to say it, I think. To have somebody know my mind and my heart. I do not expect help. I hope for understanding, and I believe that of all people, you are more capable of that than any other."

Lana gave Shayell a warm smile and threw her arms around their neck, hugging them tightly.

"Of course... But, Shayell... Being part dryad wouldn't stop you from liking Selene..."

The red of Shayell's cheeks flared again, and they gave Lana a gentle, playful shove.

"Do you want me to call you something other than noam, Shayell? Or... Or do you want me not to call you Shayell and call you something else? It's a very noamy name."

Shayell shook their head slowly. "I think, at least for the moment, I would rather no one else knew of this, Lana. I just needed to say it out loud, to tell somebody I can trust. Thank you."

Chapter Twenty-Two

Kingsmead

"You had best get up on the deck, Cat. Your captain is about to flog one of his crew and he won't listen to me. He's in a proper rage."

It had been two weeks, but Cat was still struggling with the pitching and rocking of the ship. Her mood was sour, and she scared all but Laywyn and Adney with her quick tongue lashings and flashing blades. And so it was her old guardian that had come to her room to give the bad news.

"My captain? What happened to 'me love'? Are you two having a tiff?"

"Why'd you have to be so mean about it, Cat? Anyway, even Laywyn can't make him listen. You need to get up there."

Cat grabbed her knives, sliding them into place on her belt and made her way up to the deck with a growl.

"What in the void is going on here?" A crewman was stripped to the waist and lashed face first to the mainmast. Laywyn had his sword in his hand, casually resting it against his shoulder, but ready to use it in an instant. He was standing between Xentan and the bound sailor. The pirate captain had a whip unfurled in his hand.

"Tell yer man to be getting out of my way, Cat. This is ship's business and none of his."

"I've told you before, Xen, this ship is mine 'til we're home. If there's ship's business, it's my business. Now what's going on?"

The pirate scowled. "Aye, an if the ship wasn't yours, you'd be tied up there with 'im. It's as much your fault as his."

"What is, Xen? What are you growling about?"

"This idiot! When you tellt him to be getting rid of all me booze, he didn't stop at taking me rum and ale off the ship. He took half our water off an' all"

"We're surrounded by water, Xen, Get over it."

"Aye, an' it'll kill ya if ya try to drink it. You know nothing of the ocean do ya? It's full of salt is all that, if you drink it you'll be thirstier than ya were before you put it to ya lips and if ya keeps drinking it you'll drown afore ya thirst is quenched. We aint got enough water to last another week and we'll need to be stopping before we was supposed to. It'll cost ya time and coin, too."

Cat rolled her eyes, her face twisted. "Cut him down, Xen. He can work the crow's nest and clean out the privy for the rest of the voyage. If he does anything, this stupid again. You can have your way."

They rationed the water strictly over the following days, and his companions shunned the sailor responsible for their shortage. They kicked out at him as he passed and threw the spoils from their meals at him, forcing him to clean up.

Cat stayed in her cabin as the seas became rougher, her stomach mirroring the wild, harsh, waves. The ship climbed and fell over mountains of water that threatened to topple it and wash away all those on board. Sea water poured over the deck, dripping through the boards onto her bed and her table. She wished she had allowed the alcohol to stay aboard the ship at these times. At least she could drink herself into sleep and ignore what was going on around her if she had.

She locked her cabin door and yelled at any knockers to leave her alone over those days, not even allowing Laywyn in to talk. She had lost track of time completely when the banging started.

"Cat! Cat, are you still alive in there? We're pulling into port today. Xen reckons we'll get supplies, water and the likes and we'll be here a couple of days. I thought you'd want to go ashore. Get off the ship a bit." Laywyn shouted through the door.

There was a clatter and some scraping and the door opened a little, revealing a green-looking Cat, dark circles around her eyes and a vomit stained tunic.

"We could get a room at an inn, Cat. Get you a bath and err... Some new clothes..." Laywyn looked her up and down with an upturned nose.

The door slammed shut.

"Cat?"

Laywyn called out a few times and then put his ear to the door to hear the sound of his young friend retching.

Kingsmead was a military post that had grown into a city. They had built the harbour and the city on solid grey walls, narrow streets lined by buildings with narrow windows and heavy, reinforced doors.

The parade ground of the fortress was now an open air market, selling local foods, fruits that Cat had never seen before, as well as food brought in by ship from the mainland. Xentan, Adney and most of his crew elected to stay aboard the ship. He had many years behind him as a pirate and was well known on the islands of the southern seas. He was not someone that could hide his appearance and would undoubtedly be a target for the soldiers that remained in the city fort.

Adney was working her, admittedly rough and failing, charms on the gruff man. Knowing that he was her best chance now to return to the kind of lifestyle she had had as Keikon's wife. Her false giggles at his jokes and clinging to his side had made Cat as sick as the rough ocean crossing and the ex thief was pleased that her old nemesis wasn't joining them.

So she went ashore and, with Laywyn, headed straight from the ship to the Portland Inn. There they arranged rooms and baths and an enormous meal with enough cider and ale to drown a grown man twice over.

"I hate it Laywyn. It's gonna kill me, I swear. I really don't want to be going anywhere from here unless it's home." Cat mumbled through a half eaten chunk of bread, thick with cheese.

"I get it, Cat. You're having a rough journey, but you've a job to do. You gave your word to the Tay and I know you won't go against it just because it's not fun." Laywyn took a swig of his ale and sat back against the wall. "Besides. You aint leaving me to deal with that dirty pirate and his new wife."

Cat chuckled. "They probably will be married before this is all done, huh? She's determined, if nothing else. I'll be happy to leave her behind once and for all when this is all done, though. I keep expecting a knife in my back when she's around. She hated me before I threw her to the guard and I know her smiles is all for show now."

Laywyn nodded, a sausage hanging from his mouth. "I can't blame you for your suspicions, Cat. I don't trust her or Xentan for a minute and I don't much like our lives being so dependent on the pirate. He could be readying the ship to sail right now and we'd be stranded here."

Cat shook her head gently. "I trust him a lot more than I trust her, Laywyn. I've known him for years. He's gruff, but when he gives his word, he usually keeps it. It's her whispering in his ear that I worry about."

Cat poured herself another cup of cider and crammed the rest of her bread in her mouth, chewing through a contented smile.

The door to the inn burst open as Cat and Laywyn were finishing up their pitchers, both full, relaxed and sitting back in their chairs with their hands on their stomachs.

Xentan, his face red and a cudgel ready in his hand, stormed into the inn, pausing to look around for a moment before shouting. "Where is she? Where is the bitch?" Seeing Cat, he turned his attention to her. "Where is she, Cat? Where are you hiding her? I'll skin her when I get my hands on her and I'll skin you and all if you're in on it."

"In on what, Xentan? What are you going on about?" Cat was on her feet, her fingers resting lightly on the hilts of her blades.

The pirate snorted, in the way only a big man and a bull can. "That snake, Adney, Cat. Are you telling me you've nothing to with it?"

"You know I ain't no friend to Adney, Xentan but you aint telling me what she's done to get you mad enough to come ashore."

The pirate spluttered. "What she's done? What she... She took ma purse and ma safe box and she's run is what she's done. She's a snake, Cat. Made me think we was getting close and now she's gone with everything you paid me and everything I had set aside."

Cat slumped back down in her seat with a sigh. "I told you to watch her, Xen. I said she was trouble. But we need her. Damn. We need what she knows, Xen. How in the void did she get away from you?"

The pirate coughed, shifting his feet and trying to hide his face. "No need to go into that now, Cat. She's gone, and we needs to find her."

"You need to get back to the ship, Xentan. We'll start a look for her. We're on an island, one she doesn't know. She won't get far." Laywyn stepped towards the pirate, shuffling him out of the door before turning and nodding to the patrons of the inn.

Xentan organised those sailors that were not worried about being recognised and jailed and sent them out around the island to hunt down the missing woman. A task made difficult by the dark alleys full of drunken sailors and traders. They gave up the search late into the night, heading back to the ship with nothing but a few bruises and scrapes to show for their search and their questioning of the locals.

Cat fumed. She had never wanted to have Adney with them. She had thought she could trust Xentan to keep her safely bound on the ship and she was as angry at herself for trusting the pirate as she was at the matriarch of her old gang for running off.

"Ships'll be leaving the harbour on the morning tide and she might be on any of 'em. Can ye not be using some of yer new found influences to get the guard involved, Cat?" Xentan's face was still red through his beard and he was pacing the floor of his cabin, striking his cudgel against his own outstretched palm.

"I don't know that I have that kind of influence, Xen. And if we get the guard involved, what's to say they won't come and lock you up?" Cat sat on his desk, her feet up on the chair. "Can you not send word to the captains? Let them know that we're looking for her? Maybe offer a reward?"

"I aint got no money for a reward, Cat. She took everything I've got." The red of his cheeks grew deeper and Cat wondered if it was anger or embarrassment that afflicted him.

"I think Xentan's right, Cat. We aught to go to the guard and see if they can help. But you should get word out to the other ships too, Xentan. Put your name to work. It's your fault she's missing after all, and you've more to lose in the short term than we do." Laywyn was sitting on the pirate's bunk, his jaw set tight and his tone stern.

"Alright. Alright. I'll send word out. I just hope she hasn't gone and spent all me money already." The pirate scowled as he spoke.

"Cat?" Laywyn checked the young woman had heard him.

"Yeah. You're right Laywyn, though I'd rather you talked to the guard. You're a soldier and know how to speak with men like that... I have a way of winding 'em up, it aint meant, but it happens." Cat jumped down from the desk and walked toward the door. "Coming?" Laywyn nodded and stood to follow her.

"Well, you might just be in luck, Ser. To an extent, anyway. We've got yer woman and the lock box she was carrying with her, and yer fine to have that back. Can't let you have the woman though... Captain wouldn't allow that, not after what she done." The guard sat at a desk covered in papers, a large ring of keys at his belt.

"She's important to the journey we're on. We need her free if we're to succeed. What did she do to get arrested?" Laywyn called on his many years as a captain to show authority and calm as he talked to the guard. Something Cat was struggling with at his side.

"She... errrr... well, I errr, I probably shouldn't say, Ser. 'Cept that she and the captain had a, errr, a bit of a run in, Ser." The guard smirked as he spoke and gave Laywyn a wink that suggested everything he couldn't say.

Cat rolled her eyes with a sigh. "Can we talk to the captain?"

"Course you can, when he's back on shift. He comes back in around mid morning, m'lady. I can leave a note. Let him know you're coming. If you'd like?"

"That would be good, thank you. About the box..."

The guard stood and wandered over to a large locker on the far wall. It took him a few attempts to get the right key, but once he had it, he opened the locker up and handed Laywyn the small lockbox that Adney had stolen from Xentan.

"Thank you. We'll head back to our ship now. If there's any news during the night we'd appreciate hearing it..." Laywyn smiled.

"Aye, Ser. No bother." The guard saluted with the smile of a man that knows he has done his job well.

Chapter Twenty-Three

CHAINT

The river ran fast and white, roaring across rocks with a thunder that hid the noise of the approaching army. Thousands of warriors, men and women alike, warily climbing the steep path to the top of the rise. Guarded against ambush from above, shields and weapons in hands, ready.

Chaint rode a black mare, sleek and fast, it longed for the plains of Sindale and the chance to run free. The horse snorted in disgust at the mountainous climb it was being forced to undertake and Chaint dug in her heels.

In front of her rode MacKenna and MacStorey, two clan chiefs and gesiths of the tuath tribes. Two men easily manipulated into war, but stubborn in their approach to it. In time she would have both killed, once Northfort was hers and the tuath had succumbed to her control, but for now she needed them, for now she had to play the role of servant turned intermediate.

They had watched the town of Shadowatch for a moon before deciding upon their plan, her old body weakening, drawing closer to death, with every day. The human female they had chosen was young. She worked within the tower and was close to the Gesith through the day, returning to a small home she shared with her elderly mother late each evening. It had been easy for them to break into the wooden shack and perform the rite. Transferring Chaint's essence into the human body. The older woman had made little trouble for them as they cut her open, draining her blood to feed the new body of the goddess.

It had been easy from there for Chaint to whisper her stories of power and rebellion to the Gesith, and he loved every moment. His desire for the servant's body clear in his eyes and the dreams of power she sold him digging deep into his soul. He quickly set aside his reluctance and hesitations when she promised him an alliance with warriors that could guarantee him the north. When she introduced the man to her trusted daughter Nydoalin, he had almost passed out. The Tuath had been allied against the sgàil as long as they had existed, but he was under her spell, the lust that she had filled him with overpowered his reason and the history of his people.

She had thought then that it would be a simple task to march on the fortress and take the north, but one man had stood where others fell into line. One clan chief amongst them that chose to fight. That had cost them. It cost them men in that first meeting at the tower, men that would have led their clans into an alliance with her. And that had cost them time. For instead of having a banner holder to call his warriors, they had to march to each hold and convince the elders of the tales that the dead had already accepted.

And then there was MacKenna's insistence on taking Lochmead. The home of his enemy. An unnecessary step that Chaint had petitioned against.

She had almost killed him then. When he refused to listen to her, when he treated her like nothing more than a servant. Nydoalin had pleaded with her to let her bear the knife, to let her flay and hang the gesith's body in the centre of the camp so that all could see and all would fear the goddess. But that was too heavy a risk. She needed the tuath... She still needed the Tuath to give her the victory she seeks.

But soon, soon she would have Northfort, and then she would reveal herself. And once revealed, she would let Nydoalin do as she pleased with the Gesith.

A smile grew on her lips and she pushed her reluctant mare on.

Arrows greeted them as they arrived on the western shore, all but a few falling harmlessly into the raging torrent and swept off the cliff to the ravine below. Those that did reach their target were brushed aside by shields causing even less damage than the irritating biting insects that plagued the army in the warming weather of late earrach.

The destruction of the bridge, however, was a serious issue that threatened long delays and those problems that come with it. They needed to cross the river and reach the town beyond. They needed the supplies they would find there and the food that was growing on the plains below. Without those things, they would struggle. Without a bridge, the crossing seemed impossible.

MacKenna and MacStorey grew apoplectic, forcing a small group of the warriors on into the river, a rope tying them together to keep them secure.

A small island of rock lay in the centre of the river, previously housing the large support for the bridge and the warriors pushed to reach it. Before the front man reached the halfway point of the first stretch, though, the slick rocks and fast flowing water caused him to lose his footing. The rope pulled taut as he fell, bringing the man behind him down, and they pulled the two behind them into the waters and closer to the precipice. The third and fourth in line struggled, fighting against the current and their flailing friends. As the front two drew closer to the waterfall's edge, the third toppled and fell, instantly pulling the last section of the rope tight. The foremost warrior toppled over the edge.

Desperate and terrified, the last warrior in line drew his blade and hacked away at the rope, cutting through in four strikes and sending his clansmen to their deaths.

Chaint shook her head at the attempted crossing and the tantrum of the clan chiefs. She called to her children and took them aside, setting up camp below the rocks to the south.

"How much longer must we suffer this fool, goddess?" Nydoalin's voice was soft, but the scowl on her face gave away her contempt for the Tuath Gesith.

"Be patient, Nydoalin. I am still weak and we do not have the numbers to wage this war alone. Once we have Northfort, once we are secure, then I will reveal myself and take my rightful place. You can do as you want with him then. For now the tuath follow him and we need *them*, so we must suffer him."

"They would follow you out of fear if you would allow me to remove him."

"It is not their fear I need now, Nydoalin. I must have their love in order to grow my strength. These warriors, they at least must love me, desire to serve me. Fear is for the masses."

The sgàil warrior's face twisted. "Then I hope that day comes soon. These are not the tuath of old. Few are worthy of the title warrior, none are worthy of a place in your hall."

Chaint smiled. Her eyes, for a second, glazed and her mind in went to the past. "You would have despised the Tuath of old too, Nydoalin."

"Despised them? Yes, they stood in your way. But I would have respected them. They were fierce warriors. Or so the tales would make it seem."

"They were, Nydoalin. They fought with strength, skill and... Though I hate to admit it, honour. Misplaced but honour nevertheless."

The dark fae paused a moment, her face twisting once more. "We should have aligned with those we fought in the tower. That clan, at least, have some skill and fire within them."

"That clan would never stand at my side, child. You will have to be content that they will provide you with a challenge in the fight ahead."

A smile broke out on the warrior's face. "The clan chief's daughter will be a worthy opponent, that is certain, if she has survived her flight to the fortress."

As night fell and the clan chiefs huddled together, trying to solve the problem of the river crossing, a new threat appeared. A bright, burning barrel of pitch flew through the skies from the eastern bank, standing bright against the dark skies. Men and women scattered, shouting in panicked tones at their clans, trying to clear the area before the flaming projectile struck.

The barrel hit the rocks with a loud crack and an explosion of burning, sticky tar, causing fires to spring up around them. The warriors stumbled and scattered, abandoning their camp and their equipment to the flames. In no time at all, a second flame lit the skies in the east.

Six flaming barrels in all crashed down upon the camp of the rebel tuath warriors, causing frantic confusion and chaos, burning supplies and equipment and causing the army to fall back.

To the south of the camp, on a rocky outcrop at the river bank, Nydoalin stood with five other sgàil warriors, their dark leather armour seeming to soak up the light of the stars and the flames in the camp.

Rope in hand, Nydoalin leapt into the rushing water, allowing herself to float on her back, her feet pointing toward the drop, she used her legs to cushion her collision with rocks and push herself deeper into the centre of the river until her feet hit the rocks of the island at the centre of the rapids.

There she scrambled up onto the rocks, bruised and battered by the journey, and tied the rope to the remains of the bridge support. The first stretch of the crossing had been conquered. In the morning, the rope would provide the means to recreate the bridge.

Aside from a barrage of rocks, flung from the trebuchet in the morning, the tuath clans faced no more opposition from the town. Two more warriors died during the construction of the rope bridge, but the waytown on the eastern bank of the river was taken by mid day.

The occupants had fled, taking as much of their belongings with them as they could carry and burning what they could of the rest.

The army salvaged some objects of use and some supplies, enough to see them down the cliffs of the rise and onto the plains below at least.

Chaint looked out across the land to the north of them. In less than a week they would camp at the base of the mountain on which Northfort stood. Laying siege to the ancient fortress that had been built to hold against her. And there they would wait until the Tay and his army grew desperate and hungry enough to emerge and be killed in battle.

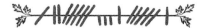

Caoimhe opened her eyes. She felt the sensations of her waking body through the fuzzy haze of her mind. She felt she had slept too long and the harsh light of the midday sun over head confirmed that.

She was not in her bed; she was not in the home that she shared with her mother; nor was she even indoors. As her mind recognised these things, she panicked. Where was she? She had been in her bed when she fell into sleep. What had happened to her?

She was sitting with her back against a hard leather saddle. To her right sat a woman, dressed in black leather armour, a baldric across her body that held a dozen knives and a belt from which two swords hung. To her left was a man. He wore dark robes and seemed to be a man of religion. A long staff lay on the grass at his side, and a small knife hung from his belt. Both people wore dark cowls covering their heads and casting dark shadows over their faces.

Caoimhe recognised neither of them.

A little further away, there were other warriors, all dressed in dark leather, all wearing the same deep cowls. Beyond them were a great number of men, dressed in the traditional armours of the tuath. Round shields and spears lay beside them as they sat in groups, eating.

Her stomach tightened as she looked around. Her breathing became quick and shallow. She felt her body shake.

"Where am I? Who are you?"

Her words caught those beside her off guard, and the man to her left jumped slightly. In a moment, his hand was on her face, holding her chin tight as he turned her to face him.

His face was pale, almost blue, his features were sharp. There was no colour in his eyes, no discernible pupils. They were jet black orbs that seemed to pierce her soul. He was fae. But he was not like any fae she had ever seen before, not a nymph nor a mer and certainly not a noam.

"What is happening, Senath?" The woman on her right spoke. Her voice was powerful, commanding, but there was a hint of concern in her question.

"It is the human soul, I do not know how." His movements were sharp and his grip on her face tightened. His finger tips dug into her cheeks.

"How are you still there? I wonder. The ritual was completed, the sacrifice made. You should be gone, banished into the oblivion of a human death."

She grabbed at his wrist and tried to pull herself free of his grip, her own hands shaking wildly now, her stomach convulsing.

"Let me go!" She tried to shout, but his hand around her chin prevented her from opening her mouth enough. Even so, her words concerned him, and he slapped his other hand over her mouth.

"The human is still there? You have failed, Senath. What has happened to Chaint if this human is talking?" The woman's tone was higher now, faster. She spoke in a harsh whisper and looked around as she asked her question, her right hand on the hilt of a sword at her side.

"The goddess is still there, I feel her, but she is... Asleep. We need to get her out of the light."

"And how do you suggest we do that, priest?" The woman spat that last word. "We are in the middle of a plain. There is no cover to be found for at least a day, and we are hours away from night. Knock her out."

"What?" The man looked concerned.

"We cannot risk the others finding out. We cannot allow the humans to discover the truth. Put her to sleep. I will ride with her on my horse when we move on, and you can sort out your mess when night falls."

"Fine, hold her. I'll..."

She did not see it coming, but she felt it. The woman's fist striking the side of her head, her eyes rolled up and backward and she fell into darkness.

Chapter Twenty-Four

A Small Moment of Joy

Tinnion woke, took a deep breath and stretched her body, the ferns beneath her soft and warm. Her cloak draped over her naked body, Cinerea's arm keeping it in place. She felt the heat of the dryad behind her, soft flesh against her back, and she smiled. Turning, she placed a gentle kiss on the dryad's cheek and sighed happily, wrapping herself around her sleeping lover.

Chapter Twenty-Five

Muguwar

The night was long and difficult. The three companions tossed and turned, getting very little rest as the sound of horns filled the air. Echoing through the forest from east to west. A sorrowful sound that spoke of death.

When morning came, Shayell and Selene lowered themselves through the floor into the rooms below the corridor. Selene had been extremely excited to recover what she could of the scrolls and books down in the rooms there, and Shayell was determined to find a way around the blockage that forced them through the hole in the flooring.

They had asked Lana to join them, and she had been excited to see what was down there, too. But as her mouth opened to say she would go, she stopped. "Actually... I think I'd like to look at the carvings up here a bit more. I'm sure there's an answer in them. There must be. You two go... I'll be fine." She smiled at Shayell as the noam lowered themself through the floor after Selene.

When her friends had safely landed on the floor below, Lana wandered over to the carvings they had been puzzling over and, yawning, traced her fingers across them.

The man paced back and forth in the thunderous cell like a panther caged. Streams of lightning flooded the walls and held him in the seamless, windowless room. The deep black of his skin absorbed the crackling, violent light. A crack appeared in one wall, slowly expanding to form a crude door that passed through the lightning as it opened. A sylph, aged and bent, stood in the opening holding a tray of food.

"Come, Muguwar. Take your food and eat. Tomorrow your mother will arrive and you will answer for your crimes."

The man stretched himself outward, standing straight and tall. His muscled frame rippling, his black eyes unreadable, fixed on the sylph. He drifted forward, as a dancer moves, to the opening and placed a hand upon the tray.

"Enjoy this meal, Muguwar. For it may be your last. The goddess has little patience for one that kills her children as you do." The old sylph's lips curled in a grin as he taunted the prisoner, who turned his face away.

In an instant, the prisoner's hand was tight around the wrist of the sylph. His grip like the coils of a python, squeezing relentlessly, crushing the bones of his jailor. The old man's face skewed into a grimace and he cursed. Clenching his teeth, he set his other hand to the chest of the prisoner and called upon the power at his command.

The earth shook around them and the prisoner's skin burned as the lightning surrounded him, but his grip held firm and he pulled the sylph toward him. As the old man passed through the streaming energy that kept his prisoner confined, he threw his head back with a cry of pain. The lightning danced around him, consuming him. His blue eyes turned to black, his skin burned. His teeth cracked and shattered with the clenching force of his jaw and his flesh fell away from his bone. The lightning flowing through his body, overpowering him. Too much for him to hold. With an anguished scream, the old man dropped to the floor, his bones and what remained of his flesh smoking in the now darkened room.

The prisoner stepped over the remains of the sylph into the corridor and placed his hand against the bare stone column that stood to his right. In a moment, the column shifted, sending dust to the floor. Muguwar pushed, his muscled body shaking, and the column collapsed. A crack as loud as thunder filled the corridor, and the roof fell.

Lana fell to her knees, her body shaking, retching in the corridor's darkness. Every torch had been extinguished. The smell of burning flesh lingered in her throat as though she had been there, as though she were actually present at the death of the sylph. The cold stone beneath comforted her as her stomach rid itself of her breakfast and she lay for a while, tears streaming down her cheek, trembling and whimpering in the dark.

Selene was the first to reach her and wrapped her in her arms, holding her, whispering to her in warm, comforting tones. They sat together as Shayell relit the torches and then together they moved to the temple and the fire, where Shayell prepared some food.

"It was horrible, Selene. It felt so real, as if I was actually there. It's never been like that before. It's never been so real. I could feel the heat, I could smell it... I... I never want that to happen again, Selene. I never want to feel like that again."

The sylph wiped sweat soaked hair from Lana's face then held her hand. "I wish I knew how I might stop it, Lana. But you seem touched by the gods and I do not know a way to deny them. Though I will do what I can to comfort you, always."

Lana placed her head to Selene's shoulder without a word.

Soon she was asleep, wrapped in a blanket in front of the fire. Snoring gently as her companions examined the things that they had found in the rooms below.

The horns blew again as night fell, but Lana didn't hear them. She was deep in sleep. The restlessness of the previous night and the events of the morning had drained her. The vision she had experienced was unlike those that had come before. There was no goddess in that vision, no calming presence. The vision hadn't come from the stone of the circlet she wore as many had. Nor had it come from the stone of Lochheart. Though it felt more akin to the vision she had experienced there.

This vision had been overbearing, visceral, full of fear and hate. It had held her tightly in its grasp; it had caused her pain. It had pulled at her soul.

And so she slept through the day and through the night, not soundly, but deeply. The sleep of one that has no energy to wake.

"You say that you recognise the man, Lana. That you have seen him on the Queen's Isle. But that cannot be. The destruction of the corridor; if that is indeed what you saw in your vision, and I have no reason to doubt that, happened thousands of years ago. Long before the war between human and fae. What you saw could not have been the same man." Shayell's voice was calm and reassuring, but they played nervously with the hem of their clothing as they spoke.

"No, it's him. I know it. He *felt* the same. I don't know what he is, or how it could be him, but it is. I'm sure of it. He moved the same way and his stare... It's like... It's like looking into the darkest pit you can imagine. As if it's never ever even seen the sun or a fire. He scares me, Shayell. Really scares me." Lana drew her blanket around her, more for its comfort than its warmth.

"And you saw him first beside some rocks?"

Lana nodded. "Yes. The rocks are as black as he is, and sharp, and nothing will grow near them. Even the trees are scared of them."

"In your vision, he placed his hand on the column before it fell?"

"Yes."

Shayell stood and walked through the corridor, their hand against the wall, until they came to the rubble that blocked their path. There they bent and brushed aside some of the fallen earth to reveal the curved stone of a column. They closed their eyes as they placed their hand upon it, taking a deep breath, which they held. Selene and Lana watched on, holding their breaths as if to help their friend. Before Lana felt the need to breathe out, Shayell had pulled their hand away from the stone so sharply that they toppled backward and sat on the stone floor, sweat dripping from their brow.

"I do not know what did this. It is like noam and yet, not noam. The stone recoils even now from its touch. The memory of that moment is darkness itself."

"The lock of the Thighearna-stoirm. It must have opened that cell which you saw, Lana. A cell made from a storm. This thing, whatever it is, can be held in lightning. This proves that the Thighearna-stoirm existed." Selene sighed. "And yet, they exist no more and we cannot recreate that cell. If this creature is on the Queen's Isle, as you believe, we have no way to contain it. Still, we must advise the queen of what we have found."

"What are you doing here? Did yo not hear the horns?" Three hunters stood in the doorway, their leathers torn and bloody, their faces drained of colour. "You must leave. All of you. We have to get to the city wall. We have to get to safety."

"What is it you fear, huntsman?" Shayell stepped forward, putting themself between the hunters and Selene.

"A creature of the night. Black as the void. It's an animal at times and at times it's a man. It's clawed its way through our camps these last two nights, tearing at anyone that gets in its way. I dunno what it is, but no one's been able to stand against it. We need to get to the city guard or the army. We need to get to safety."

"We're safe here... I think. He won't come in here. He hates it here." Lana's voice trembled as she spoke and she moved close to the fire.

Selene slid her arm through Lana's, linking them and gently holding her. "You cannot be certain of that, Lana. You cannot be certain that it is the same man. We should gather our things and return to the city."

"If he can shape stone and he feels a bit like a noam, the city walls won't stop him. But, maybe the dryad can catch him? I know he can't enter the trees, so maybe they can make a cage that'll hold him? At least for a short time, until we figure out a better way." Lana gently pulled away from Selene and pulled on her belt as she spoke, checking her staff and her knife were in place.

Shayell nodded. "It is a possibility, Lana. Do you think you can convince the dryad to come?"

Selene sat herself by the fire, her legs held in her arms at her chest. She looked up to Lana, her eyes wide. "I do not like this, Lana. It is too dangerous. This man has attacked you twice, if it is him. We should stay together, we should stay together and leave here."

"I have to try, Selene. And I'll be safe. I just need to get to the nearest tree and I'll be gone... If I can find Daowiel... We... I'll... I'll come back as soon as I can." Lana faltered over her thoughts. The image of the sylph burning, invading her mind.

Selene shook her head frantically, her face white. "Please, Lana. We should go."

Shayell took Selene's hand and gently pulled her close. "No, Selene. I believe Lana is right. It is him. It must be, there is nothing else on this isle that could be described this way. And being the one Lana has seen, I believe we are safer here than taking the journey to Southport. There is no doubt that he... Whatever he is... holds a hatred for this place, perhaps even a fear of it. If Lana can bring the dryad, then we will be as safe here than we could be in the city."

Lana emerged from the oak close to a circle of dryad and quickly approached Daowiel, recounting what had happened in the temple.

"Whatever this thing is, Ògan, we should kill it. It is too dangerous to leave alive. I will bring a half dozen of my laoch. And we will end this man, whatever he may be."

Lana shook her head. "No, Daowiel. Even if we can, I don't think we should. We need to know who he is, what he is. I think we need to capture him and stop him from killing people, but I don't think we should kill him to do it."

"He has attacked you twice now, Ògan. Why do you believe he deserves to live?"

"I... I don't know, Daowiel. I think if he meant to kill me, really meant to do it, I would have died." Lana bit her lip and looked to the ground at her admission.

Daowiel looked at her friend for some time before speaking again, and then addressed her sisters. "Lothalilia, you will come with us. And six others. Which of you will join me in this hunt?" A dozen hands rose into the air and the princess smiled. "As much as I would have you all at my side, some of you must stay here. There will be other hunts, I am sure."

A forest's trees rarely pay attention to the death of humans. They see humans as invaders, often invaders that intend harm to the woodland. There are exceptions to that. Some people live in harmony with the woods and over time the trees come to accept and respect those people. They will mourn the death of those rare humans. But for the most part, the trees pay no attention when a human dies.

Today the trees of the Northcity Woodlands were screaming bloody murder. The manner of the killings haunted them and the creature that killed filled them with fear. A creature whose touch repulsed them, a creature that felt like death. Cold, dark, death stalking through the woodlands. Tearing human flesh from bone.

Daowiel placed her hand against the elm and shuddered.

"He was here recently. He moves without purpose, has no direction. I believe he is still close." She motioned to three of her laoch. "Go east a little. The man was heading north when he left here, but may have turned. Be careful, sisters." The dryad nodded in turn and headed east of the tree.

"I do not like this, Ògan. I know you do not wish to kill, and if it is safe to capture this man, I will. I gave you my word on that. But I believe, still, that we should end his life. There is no good in this man, only darkness and death. And if it proves unsafe to capture him, I will give the order to kill. I am sorry."

Lana looked at the remains of the hunter that lay at the base of the tree. His throat had been torn from his neck, not cut, but torn by powerful hands and sharp nails that ripped the surrounding flesh. His stomach lay open, his entrails spread around the tree's base. Lana had emptied her stomach and continued to retch. She looked up at her friend, a warrior, a princess, and one of the most confident people she had ever met. She saw the dryad shaking, and she nodded.

"I understand. I... I didn't know that he could do something like this."

The princess placed her hand softly on Lana's shoulder. "Perhaps you should return to your friends at the temple, Ògan. I do not want to put you in danger. You are good at our games and hold well in a fight, but I feel this is beyond you. You are not laoch." She gave her friend a smile. "Go, my sisters and I will do what can be done."

Lana had her hand to the tree as the scream rang through the woods. Daowiel and Lothalilia were first to react, running toward the sound, three other dryad close behind. Lana caught up with them quickly, her staff extended in her hand.

Lana ran quicker than the dryad could, weaving through the branches, leaping over stones and roots, and she reached the source of the scream some moments ahead of the others.

Those dryad warriors that had gone east, all three, lay at the feet of the dark man. Blood soaking the earth around their still forms. Lana cried out, pain and anger filling her shout, and launched herself at the man, her staff swinging above her head.

Her first blow struck the man's shoulder as he turned, and the scowl on his face showed she had hurt him. His reaction was faster than Lana had expected and his hand struck her cheek, his palm leaving a mark that stung in an instant. The force of his slap sent her off balance and she tumbled to the ground beside a motionless warrior whose neck he had broken. Scrambling away, she pushed herself to her feet a few metres from the man and shook her head, clearing the stinging pain and her thoughts. She brought her staff up in a defensive position, ready to knock aside any attempt to reach her.

The man smiled. The same dark staff he had fought her with before, growing in his hand.

"Piuthardia, dannsa."

He sprung forward, his staff raised. Lana blocked and countered a flurry of blows, each faster and stronger than the one that came before. The man moved like the head of a snake moves, his body low to the ground, a smile upon his face as he struck out at her.

Daowiel burst into the clearing, her staff raised and ran to the side of her friend, bringing her weapon down to meet the strike of her enemy. As the other dryad joined them, the man moved away, swinging his staff at each in turn as he stepped backward. In a moment he was running, heading east. At the edge of the clearing, he turned, his now empty hand pointing to Lana.

"Piuthardia. Teampall." He moved his hand to point east and then ran through the trees.

"The temple, Lana. Where is it?" Daowiel's voice was high and rushed. She held Lana's arm as she spoke, shaking her slightly.

"There." She pointed east, as the man had done. Through the woodland that way, perhaps a half day away?"

"Then we have to move. Aerea, see to our sister's death rites. Then return to the palace. Tell the queen what we have seen. This is no man, neither is it fae."

A dryad nodded and made her way to her fallen sisters as the others pushed their way into the trees and onto the bridge.

The dryad and Lana joined Selene, Shayell and the hunters around the fire in the temple. They ate slowly, their eyes glazed, their thoughts distant.

"This creature is not fae. It is neither noam nor sgàil, though it has the feel of both. It cannot shape wood and could, in theory, be trapped by it. Though it is strong and might break through a cage of branches. I do not know that we can contain it and I do not know that we can kill it. It is death, and I do not know that death can die." Daowiel addressed Shayell directly as she spoke.

"You are certain it is coming this way?" Selene's voice shook as she asked her question.

"Yes, it said as much. It wanted us to know. Or..." The princess looked at Lana, frowning. "It wanted Lana to know. It named you Piuthardia. Do you understand that?"

Lana shook her head, her eyes wide. "No. I don't know what it means. But it said the same thing at the lake."

Daowiel looked to Selene and Shayell. The fae's mouths were open, their brows raised, almost a mirror of each other. "I think we should talk, us three alone. Is there some place we can go apart?"

Shayell nodded. "None would hear our voices if we spoke at the end of the passage."

"Then let us go." Daowiel stood and ambled away from the fire.

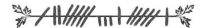

They set a watch for the night. Two people at one time would remain awake, sat either side of a hastily created alarm, and watch the entrance of the temple. Though the others slept only lightly, weapons drawn at their sides, ready for the moment the dark man appeared. That moment came before the moon had passed a half night in the sky. The alarm sounded and the occupants of the temple scrambled to their feet, weapons in hand.

The man paced back and forth at the temple entrance, barely seen against the ink black sky. A shadow moving in the night. His head tilted and moved, taking in the sight of those that faced him. He raised his hands and dark shadows grew from them, forming blades from the night, as easily as he had formed a staff previously.

A hunter loosed an arrow, well aimed but wasted, as the man easily cut it from the air with a blade.

"Teampall." The man spat the word and stared at the ground that marked the entrance. Raising his foot to step over the threshold, he hesitated and lashed out with his blade at the ancient empty doorway.

"Piuthardia..." The man pointed once more at Lana, his eyes wide. Then he gestured to the others. A snarl grew once more on his face. "Noam. Dryad. Sylph. Beathach duine. Marbhadh!" His voice was guttural, grating, filled with venom.

Shayell grabbed Lana by the arm and pulled her back, standing in front of her, holding an axe high. Daowiel stepped beside them, blocking Lana's path.

"What? What did he say? Selene? What did he say?"

"Kill. He said kill, noam, dryad, sylph and... I think he meant human. He's going to kill us all." Selene shook as she spoke, her eyes filled with tears.

"He won't, Selene, he won't. We'll capture him. He won't kill us all." Lana reached for her staff, but Selene held her wrist.

"No, Lana. Stay back. Let the laoch and hunters fight."

"I can fight him, Selene. I've fought him three times. I need to help."

"He has not fought you, Lana. Listen to me. I do not know why, I do not know what he means by it, but this man calls you sister. He was not fighting you, not to hurt you, not to kill you. He wants something from you and he will kill us all to get you."

"Then I have to fight. I have to stop him. If he won't hurt me, he can't fight." Lana pulled her hand free of Selene's.

"That was before he saw you sided with those he would kill. If you fight him to save us, he may not be so gentle. Lana, please. Stay back with me."

Lana shook her head and opened her staff, then pushed her way between her friends and ran at the dark man with a cry. "NO!"

Chapter Twenty-Six

A Cage of Wood

Selene had been right. The man had every intent to kill those gathered and Lana's decision to fight at their side did not dissuade him. He was strong, fast and deadly with the blades he held, and his hatred of the temple only seemed to motivate him to speed.

The hunters were the first to fall. They were strong with their bows but had little experience of fighting outside of an occasional street brawl with drunken peers. They were weaker than the fae and more scared than the laoch, which made them prone to mistakes.

The laoch fared a little better. Working together, they surrounded him, each stepping in and striking as he engaged another. And then there was Lana. She leaped toward the dark man, bringing her staff down to meet his blade.

"NO! These are my friends. You will not hurt my friends!" She struck out at the man, blow after blow, targeting his legs, staying clear of his blades and with each strike she yelled at the man "NO!" She moved fast and struck hard and some of her blows landed but mostly the man was more than her equal. He landed one blow, not with his blade but with a fist, a fist as hard as a rock. Her eyes rolled back in her head and her legs gave way. She crumpled to the floor as a dropped cloak might crumple.

When Lana came round One of the dryad lay dead the other, along with Lothalilia, was beside her, blood seeping through their armour, breathing, but lightly. Lana pulled herself up, reaching out for her staff as she staggered to her feet, then turned to see the battle. Daowiel was holding the dark man at length with her staff, and Shayell was bent double, leaning against a wall, their axe out of reach on the floor. Daowiel was tiring. Her breathing was heavy, her arms lowering with each blow. Selene was in a corner, a knife in her shaking hand.

She had to do something. She had to make this end.

The dark man had shaped a staff when he saw Lana do that. When he stood in the doorway, he formed blades. If he could do that. If he could form blades where a staff had been... Lana closed her eyes and reached out to the wood in her hand. She formed in her mind a staff tipped with a blade and she pushed that image into the wood.

She opened her eyes to see Daowiel stumble; the princess escaping the dark mans blades only by falling under them. With the dryad on the floor, the man turned back to Shayell. He raised his blade and swung it at their exposed neck.

The blade met the newly formed edge of Lana's staff and rolled aside. Then Lana brought her staff round, away from her friend and across the dark mans stomach, cutting a line into his flesh.

The man scowled at her and moved away, but Lana pushed forward, her newly formed weapon whirling around her.

"I won't let you hurt anyone else. Do you hear? I won't." The dark man dodged her blade, but she was ready for that. She kicked out at his knee and he stumbled, then she brought her weapon back round and cut his thigh. She pressed and pushed the man back, making him falter, making him fall. Then she struck out again with the butt of her staff and knocked the dark man unconscious.

"What is this you have done to your staff, Ògan?" The princess held Lana's staff, examining the blade at its end. Hard, dark wood, as long as a short sword and as sharp as any blade she had seen.

"I'm not sure, Daowiel. I guessed that if he could make a blade, then I could too. So I imagined it and asked my staff to be it. It really surprised me when it happened. I know I could have shaped a blade from another piece of wood, at least I could have made the shape. But I thought the staff would always be a staff and... Well I never imagined it could be this sharp."

They sat by the fire, wrapped in blankets. Lana still shook from the fight and Daowiel looked ill, her face pale, her eyes ringed in circles of darkness. Selene and Shayell sat with them, holding one another close. Another dozen dryad had come as the fight ended and helped to secure the dark man. A shaper worked with Daowiel to wrap him tight in tree root. His hands bound in the thick trunk of a tree stump. Once he was secure, they helped those that had fallen back through the trees to their homeland to be treated.

"I will stay with you and help watch him, then travel with you to the city. You will need me should he break the wood. It will be good for me to see how your people live in a city, too. I hear it differs greatly from the stead folk. For now, you must eat, then try to sleep. We will set a watch to keep him guarded." Daowiel spoke with authority and took a bowl of the porridge that bubbled over the fire.

The city guard met them as they rode from the woods and they bound the dark man to their wagon for further security and ease on their journey. Lana felt safer with the guard as their escort and grew excited when they offered to take the company and their prisoner to the queen.

"The Queen? She's here?" Lana's voice was joyful and bright, her eyes sparkled at the news.

"She is, m'lady. Arrived two days ago for the feast of the solstice. When she heard, this morning, of the problems in the woods, she sent us out to fetch you. You saved us a journey, m'Lady. And a hunt for the killer an all it seems. A difficult hunt, from what I hear too."

"It was, captain. A dangerous one that came at significant cost." Shayell spoke, their eyes downcast and their voice low.

"Then we're all the more grateful." The captain bowed his head.

"What is the creature, Selene? Is it a man or a beast? Is it sgàil, or a fae we do not know?" The queen sat on a throne in the great hall of the Tay's palace, Tay Gathwyn at her side.

"I can not say for certain your majesty, there are many documents from the temple yet to study. But we have pieced together some, with Lana's help and Shayell's, too." Selene paused, waiting for the sign to continue. The queen nodded, and she took a deep breath. "It seems, your majesty, that he is many thousands of years old. He was at one time held a prisoner at the temple of Qura, imprisoned in a cell of lightning by Thighearna-stoirm. He escaped that cell, killing the fae and destroying the temple. That we know from Lana's vision, your majesty. The records show his name is Muguwar and that they imprisoned him for killing, as he has killed in the woods. He appears to hold a hatred of life, your majesty. Both human and fae."

"If I may, your majesty?" Shayell interrupted.

"You may, of course, Shayell."

"There is a stone, your majesty. A stone as black as night with the appearance of glass. A volcano's fire creates it. It is called Obsidian, your majesty. I believe you have a sample in your crown. This Muguwar appears to resemble that stone. He has power over earth as some noam do, though he appears to be more than noam. Much more. I have never known nor heard of such a man until this moon. He does not feature in our legends. I do not believe he is fae, your majesty. I do not know what he might be, but he is not fae."

"Is he secure?" Gathwyn was leaning forward, stroking his beard.

Daowiel nodded. “Yes. He cannot shape wood, though he may in time break through it. He is strong. I believe if you hold him in wood, away from stone, it would be possible to keep him that way. Though I believe he should be executed. He is a danger to all life, your majesty.”

“I prefer not to kill, where killing can be avoided.” The queen rubbed her temples as she spoke. Her voice soft and uncertain.

“I don’t think we should kill him, your majesty.” Lana spoke. “Sorry Daowiel, I don’t. I think we need to find out what he is, who he is. He talks, your majesty, at least, he says some words. So he’s not some mindless monster. He must have a reason for what he does, even if we don’t agree with what it is. And... It’s not that I agree with him killing, and I think he should be punished for it... But we might be better for it, if we knew what his reason was.”

“I will have my men put him in a wooden cage and hang him from a gibbet over the cliffs, Your Majesty. He will not want to break free of that cage nor struggle too hard.” The Tay spoke with authority.

“So be it, Gathwyn. Have it done, and set a scribe from the library to question him each day. We will discover what he is and what he wants.” The queen sat back on the throne, her jaw set.

“Your Majesty, forgive me.” The heavy wooden doors at the back of the hall opened with a clatter and a soldier, dressed in chain and leather, half stumbled toward the throne. “This man insisted, your majesty. When he heard you were here.” The doorman’s voice trembled as he spoke.

“It is fine, Gillan. Close the doors again.” The Tay motioned to his aide to leave them.

The companions moved aside as the man walked toward the queen, giving him space to approach.

“How can we help you, warrior?” The queen’s voice was gentle.

“Your Majesty, I bring news frae the north.” The man looked around the room at the companions and stopped speaking.

“It is okay, you may speak. These people are friends to the crown.”

The warrior nodded and took a deep breath.

“It is war, your majesty. Many tuath have betrayed their vows. And all but clan MacFaern now march against the Tay.”

The queen's jaw dropped, her hand moved to her mouth. "It cannot be. The Tuath are loyal. How could this happen?"

"It... It is shadows, your majesty. They've whispered their poison in the ears of MacKenna and he leads the other lords tae war."

"The sgàil?" Selene gasped, then hid her face in her hands.

"The shadows are dead. They have long been dead." The queen exclaimed.

"They've returned, your majesty, two dozen or more, and they ride tae Northfort with the rebels. I fear they'll be there even now. Lord Cohade, himself sent me to you. I carry his letter, sealed."

The warrior took a note from his tunic and held it up to be taken. As the queen broke the seal and read the message, Lana spoke to the soldier.

"Clan MacFaern is Brighid's clan. She had ridden north. Was she with you?"

"Aye, she was. Though she was lucky tae be. She fought the shadows in the tower o' Shadowatch and barely escaped with her life. There was a sylph with her an all. Said she wis a thegn."

"Wren!" The voice came from a guard on the door and Lana looked back to see Yorane. She had not recognised the sylph in his uniform, his face covered by his silver helm.

"Your majesty, if Brighid is there I have to go. If she's in danger, I have to help." Lana moved closer to the podium and the queen's throne.

"No, Lana. It is not safe for you there. Not in war. We will send an army and Aelwynne will go as my voice. If there is any chance at peace, she will find it. If there is not, our army will end the uprising. There is nothing you could do in war that our army could not do."

"Please, your majesty. I can't leave her to fight alone. I have to go, I have to try. She's like my sister, your majesty. I can't let her fight alone." Tears fell from Lana's eyes as she pleaded.

"It is not safe, Lana. I forbid it. Do you hear me?" The queen's voice hardened as she spoke her command.

"Your majesty." Shayell cleared their throat before they spoke. "I owe Lana my life and I will protect her in the north. I will speak to my lord and call his banner men, and we will march as her guard. Three dozen noam will keep her safe."

Daowiel looked to the noam with a smile. "I too will go north with her. A score of dryad will, and I."

"And I will call my clan, your majesty. If I may. Wren is my sister. If she is to fight sgàil, then I must go north too. I will call a dozen sylph or more."

Gathwyn chuckled and sat back in his seat. "It seems there is mutiny right here, your majesty. Three score and ten fae is a small army and all as the young ladies' guard."

The queen sighed and slumped on the throne. "If I tried to stop you, Lana, what would you do?"

Lana shook her head but stayed silent.

"Lana. I would have your answer."

"I'm sorry, your majesty. I really am. I don't want to disobey you."

"But you feel you must." The queen sighed. "Seventy fae. And they would all march for you. I could not call upon seventy fae." The queen paused, her head in her hand. "You will do as Aelwynne tells you to do, Lana. You will follow her command without question."

Lana nodded in silence.

"I will speak with you further in the side chamber, Lana. We will speak alone. Can I leave you to deal with this little fae uprising, Gathwyn? I imagine food and drink will calm it while I talk with their leader." The queen smiled as her Tay nodded and she lead Lana from the hall.

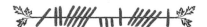

"Are you still loyal to me, Lana? Even now, with an army of fae at your back, are you still loyal to me?" The queen's voice was soft, her eyes warm, but her words were full of worry.

"Of course I am, your majesty. I didn't ask for an army. I just want to help my friends."

"And you will, Lana. I know I can't stop you from leaving. You would slip out of my palace and into the trees without a hope of me catching you. So I'm asking you, Lana, as one who cares for you. Please, don't rush into this. I know you will go, but you have to rest first. You and your friends. It will take one or two days to ready the army to march and your friends will need time to call on their own. You must take this time and think."

Lana nodded. "I will."

"Your friend, the one I made Gesith of Butterholt. Tinnion?" Lana nodded at the name. "I imagine she will want to know of this, and you should visit your family before you march off to war. So I want you to do this for me. Stay here and rest tonight. Tomorrow, those that have pledged themselves to you can call on their banners and gather their warriors. While they do that, go back to Butterholt and visit your kin. Spend some days there. Then you can meet the army heading north at Freybridge. That should give you a few days at home."

"Yes, your majesty, I will. Thank you."

"If you are to go, then I will use you, Lana. If there are truly shadows in the north, then Aelwynne will need your help. She is my closest advisor and my friend, and she is more than capable of making deals with humans. But I have to admit she will need you. You understand the fae better than anyone in my court. If there's peace to be had with shadows, it will be through you both. I will speak with her before the army marches. She will know my mind and my instruction to you." The queen fell into silence, looking Lana deep in the eyes.

"I'm very proud of you, Lana. I want you to know that before you leave. So proud of everything you've done here, the treaty with the dryad and everything that happened at the temple. I want you to know that I'm proud, because I feel you are growing beyond the role that I had hoped for you. I don't think you will ever be my advisor, or my voice. It saddens me, but there's something else in your future. I can feel it, even if I can't see what it is."

Tears fell from Lana's eyes and she wiped her nose with her sleeve, before realising what she was doing and mouthing a silent apology to the queen.

"Please, Lana. Be safe. You may never be what I thought you might be, but you are important to me and to my country. I don't want to lose you, especially not to a war you should never have seen."

Chapter Twenty-Seven

The Siege of Northfort

The fortress city was overly full. More than half of the families that had lived on the plains had travelled east, betting that they could make it to the safety of the liath cities without the rebel tuath hunting them down. But Northfort was never meant to be home to the people of the plains. It was designed to house the lord and his army, and it was uncomfortable when crowded.

There were small rain water wells in the fortress, but the people were struggling without the constant supply of river water from the valley below. Water that was, in peacetime, brought up in barrel laden wagons was lost to them because of the siege. The plains folk brought food from their farms before the siege began and piled it up in the stores beneath the fort, but what little remained of that now was spoiling.

The rationing was strict and hard on the people and tempers were fraying in every corner of the city. Fighting frequently broke out amongst the plains folk, forcing soldiers and warriors to intervene.

Trebuchet had been built and lined up on the southern walls of the fortress, but the rebel army camped too far away for them to be used and the walls were too high for the bowmen to be of use against those rebels that guarded the road.

"This is ridiculous. Our food is so low we're shooting birds from the sky. The brawls in the streets are daily now and there's barely enough water for a cup twice a day. We need tae do something before we starve tae death." Brighid was pacing the floor, her voice raised in frustration.

"What is it you suggest we do, Brighid? We are desperately outnumbered. They will slaughter us before we reach the eastern road." The Tay sat on his throne, dishevelled and pale. He had not slept since the siege began and looked ready to fall in a stiff breeze.

"We head down the hill, line up, and make these traitors pay. We break the siege or we die trying, taking as many of them with us as we can. There's nae one else coming, none that'll get here in time and we've nothing tae eat and no water. We don't have a choice, not anymore. We either make a stand now, or surrender in three days' time."

"We'll never win a battle, Brighid. We just don't have the warriors." The Tay's voice was low and his head bowed. "I never thought I would face a war. Never thought that this fortress would become my jail. Yet it has. It was built to defend to the east, to defend against shadows alone. Not to the west. Not from the tuath, for god's sake. We cannot win. With tuath against us, we could never win."

"We move at first light, Brighid." Cohade stood at the Tay's side. He had known the man for many years. Almost their entire lives. They had stood together in tournaments and clan talks, and he was deeply loyal to the man. Taking this decision was hard, and it showed on his face. "If it's just clan MacFaern, we will make our stand. Get a message tae our men and ask MacAllister if he'll stand his clan with ours. If we can get tae MacKenna hi'self and engage him directly, we may just turn things in our favour."

They sent word through the fortress that clan MacFaern were making their stand and any warrior that wanted to stand with them should ready themselves and say their goodbyes.

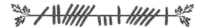

As the moon came close to the end of her arc, the warriors moved down the road to the plains below.

Four hundred warriors and two hundred stead folk that joined them lined up at the base of the mountain. The fortress towering above them. Across the plain, four thousand or more tuath moved into formation.

The front line of the defending formation consisted entirely of the Tay's soldiers. They had trained for tight unit combat and would be better prepared to meet the brunt of the rebel force. Once the lines opened up, the warriors of clan MacFaern and those that remained of clan MacTiern would have more room to fight their natural fight.

Brighid, Wren, Anndra and MacAllister flanked Cohade as he rode along the front line and gave the warriors a speech, a speech he hoped would build their energy and their focus.

"You will have heard that we have no chance to break this siege. You will have heard that we have marched down here to die. You will have heard your loved ones say goodbye, you will have seen their tears. In mere moments you will hear the battle cry of tuath clans. A cry that has sent fear into the hearts of many thousands over many thousands of years. You will have heard that we have no hope. What you have heard til this day is wrong!

The men and women we face here are not tuath! They gave up the right to that name when they marched here. They are not the men and women whose war cry has spread fear. They are not the warriors that are renowned frae coast to coast. They are rebels; they are cowards; they are without honour and they are living a lie. It is *they* have come here tae die!

For we are tuath, it is our cry that spreads fear; it is our blades that stand renowned and it is our spirit that gives us hope. We stand against thousands, but only one man needs tae fall. One man that might fall by any blade here. And when that one man falls, the siege fails. We are not here tae die; we are not here to destroy; we are here tae kill one man. One man and we win. One man and our families are saved. One man and we can all go back tae our homes in peace.

Bring me the head of MacKenna!"

The battle began before dawn, the rebel force of eight hundred men taking the initiative and marching toward the fortress. The clash of the lines was hard, sending a visible shock through the ranks as they staggered and braced. Shields smashing into shield, axes and swords swinging wildly through gaps no wider than half a man's hand.

Soldiers and rebel warriors fell; some were struck by flailing weapons, their cries filling the air, their blood soaking the earth. Others were pushed, forced off their balance and trampled in the crush. The injured lay side by side with the dead as the two armies stepped and retreated, one way then the next, always moving, going nowhere.

And then the lines opened. There was no warning, no sign of it happening. No horns sounded, no shouts were given. One man fell, and the line opened up. The attackers broke formation, and the defenders found themselves on the front foot.

"It's time." Brighid turned to her brother and her friends. Hugging her brother tight, she whispered goodbye and kissed his forehead. Then she did the same with Wren before turning to MacAllister. The warriors clasped arms. "Tae the death, Brighid. Ours or theirs."

"Tae the death." Brighid nodded. They turned to the front line and drew their weapons.

"By ma side!" Anndra called to a small group of warriors and moved toward the east of the line. MacAllister followed, calling his banner.

Wren turned to Brighid. "Together to the west?" Brighid nodded with a smile.

Side by side they pushed forward, weapons a blur, and carved out a space on the newly formed front. Blades and staff whirling, they fought in a dance around one another, striking and parrying blows. Acting as one, they defended each other and struck as a team. Deadly and relentless, they put fear into the hearts of those that stood against them and the surrounding space grew.

Sunlight glistened on Brighid's blade as it cut through the stomach of a rebel, sending him screaming to the ground.

Sunlight. Brighid grinned.

The skies erupted in the sounding of horns.

Two hundred of the more of the Tay's army crossed the plain, shields and spears in hand, blades at their sides. Their armour gleaming and strong.

The eastern flank of the rebel army faltered and fell beneath the unexpected troop and their use of the spear. Another blast of horns blew, this time from the south, and the rebels withdrew. Retreating toward the bulk of their forces.

Wren and Brighid stood, taking a moment of rest and calming themselves with deep breaths.

Those rebels who reacted too slowly were chased a short way and cut down. The battle had turned as was planned, the surprise of even a few more troops costing the rebels dearly. But the retreat had not been expected, and the momentum was lost. The two sides had separated, and the rebels were forming a new line, their naivety had cost them but it was gone now. They would fight with their full force.

MacKenna's banner was raised and the rebel lord rode forward, three hundred mounted warriors at his back. Behind him, a score of shadows joined the foot soldiers in their lines, their faces painted with blood.

As the two groups of warriors faced off across the plain, Clan MacFaern and the soldiers of Northfort reformed. Less than two hundred remained and of those, only a score of the Tay's men could be counted, while all the non-warrior stead folk lay dead.

Behind them, surrounded by six of his personal guard, Tay Jendawyn rode forward to meet with Cohade. His banner catching the wind and sending cheers through ranks of the devastated army. The Tay and the Gesith rode close to their army. Deasin and Tuath lords, as one, pushed their mounts and lead the final charge.

Tay Jendawyn fell in that meeting of horses. MacKennna's long sword cutting him from his saddle and sending him to the earth, turned and bloodied by the battle and the rebels rode on diminished but buoyed into the ranks of defenders beyond.

Overwhelmed by the force of the rebels, the defence of the fortress was beaten and broken, the plains sodden with blood and littered with bodies. Six horses, tired and battered, fled east, their riders low in the saddles, bloodied, bruised and exhausted. They barely stayed on their horses as they crossed the plains and when the horses failed, they lay on the ground beside them. Unable to run, too tired even to walk.

Twelve days from the battle twelve long, hard days, the six warriors staggered and stumbled over the hills of the plains, climbing above them with each painful step.

Finally, they reached the curve of the river Alawe as it flowed from the eastern rise. Slow and wide here, a calm flow of deep water, not the raging torrent of the mountains and ravines around the fort. The six warriors made camp, drinking deeply from the waters.

They had gathered some little food, vegetables grown in deserted steads and a handful of rabbits that hadn't led them a chase. A fire was lit and food roasted and for the first time in their flight, the six could relax. They set a watch, though there had been no sign of pursuit, and the warriors slept soundly between their turn.

As morning broke, Brighid bathed close to the river's bank, her belongings in the grass little more than an arm's reach away. Something stirred in the water a little upstream, disturbing her calmness and sending rings through the waters. Brighid waded closer. A fish, perhaps an otter, if she could catch it, it would give them some breakfast and a little energy for the morning's walk.

Bubbles broke the surface and the nymph healer from Northfort appeared, her long black hair covering her lightly dressed form. Her jaw dropped as she realised she wasn't alone and she turned to dive back into deep waters.

"Neve! It's me, Brighid! Neve! Don't fear."

The fae turned back and looked the warrior over.

"I had feared you dead, Brighid MacFaern. You, along with all others. I cannot tell you how glad I am to see you are not. Are there others?"

"My father and brother, Wren, MacAllister and my brother's friend Micheil. We fought the shadows and the tuath until we were alone. Then we took horses whose riders were dead, and we fled. We're heading east, Neve. Tae call on the Liath lords, and call on them tae march west if they aren't already. Our hope is tae take a force that can meet the queens. Gods willing, she sent an army too. But what happened at the fort?"

Neve's head dropped and her voice was quiet, her words reluctant. "The fortress was theirs by the middle of the day. The sgàil came first, their blades proving too quick for the old guard left behind. I have never seen destruction like that which followed, Brighid. They revelled in death, killing when there was no need, painting themselves in the blood of their victims, eating their flesh. I dived into a storm drain and hid. As night fell, I left the city and took to the river."

Brighid's eyes filled with tears, and she lowered her head. Her voice faltered as she spoke. "Was everyone killed?"

The nymph shook her head. "Not everyone, Brighid. Some were chained, those that did not fight. They were chained and herded like cattle. They are most likely enslaved now. I do not know which is worse, Brighid, enslaved by the sgàil or dead. I suppose, if they live, there is a chance they will be freed when the queen's army comes."

Brighid nodded slowly and wiped the tears from her face. "Come, we have a fire and a little food. Have you eaten?"

The fae smiled. "There I can help you perhaps, Brighid." She reached into a net like bag at her waist and pulled out three fish by their tails.

Chapter Twenty-Eight

BUTTERHOLT

"Lana! Look at you. You look like a proper lady in your fancy frock." Lana blushed at her mother's greeting as she walked toward the manor grounds.

"Well, I was made a lady of the court by the queen, mam. I can't be wandering around in my old clothes when I'm representing the crown." She smiled.

"So, are you too much of a lady to come give your mam a hug?" Ellie teased her daughter with a grin.

"Course not!" Lana ran to her mother and threw her arms around her, hugging her tight.

"Are you here for lady Tinnion's big day then, Lana?"

Lana turned her head, her brow furrowed. "Her big day? What's she doing?"

"You don't know? I didn't think you could have gotten the news already, but we weren't expecting you here this moon so..."

"I Know, mam. There're things happening, and I needed to speak with you and dad and Tinnion too. But you haven't told me what Tinnion's big day is."

"Well, maybe she'd want to tell you herself, Lana. I wouldn't want to take that away from her. You should head into the manor to see her instead of standing out here."

"I was going there, mam. Will you come with me?"

Ellie nodded and linked Lana's arm, walking with her to the Manor House, filling her in on the stead gossip as they walked.

A table was set in the manor's grand hall, Tinnion sat at one end Cinerea at her left hand Hayal and Sera to her right. When Ellie walked through the door with Lana, the room fell silent and everybody stood, their faces wide with grins.

"Lana! You got my message? I was sure that it would arrive too late, but I had to try. I really wanted you here. I'm so pleased you could come." Tinnion moved around the table to greet her friend.

Lana shook her head. "Sorry, Tinnion. I didn't get any message. My mam's just told me that something big was happening but she wouldn't tell me what. Said you'd want to tell me yourself. You look really happy, so it must be something good."

"I am, Lana. I really am. You met Cinerea at Southport?"

"I did." Lana smiled past her friend to the dryad hunter. "We danced together with the princesses. It was such a fun evening. But..." Lana paused, biting her lip and tilting her head to get a better view of the dryad. "You asked me to talk that evening, but you never said anything. Not anything that would need you to ask permission for, anyway." Lana moved her head back to look at her friend and she smiled wickedly, sending a blush into Tinnion's cheeks.

"So..."

"So, we're to be bound, Lana. Cinerea and I. We're to be bound in the morning."

Lana hugged her friend tightly with a smile so wide it threatened to divide her head in two.

"Well, I think there's something you should know about your betrothed, Tinnion."

"Oh?" Tinnion's brow furrowed.

"Yes... I think it's important, Tin. Your wife to be, she dances better, much, much better after two cups of wine!"

Tinnion chuckled and playfully shoved her friend aside. "We're making some arrangements for a feast right now... Will you join us?"

"Of course I will, Tinnion! I wouldn't miss it for the world."

"I need to talk to you, dad. You and mam." Tinnion had called an end to the meeting and, though she expressed her hope to spend some time alone with Lana, she went for a walk with Cinerea instead so that Lana could spend time with her family.

"There's a problem in the north. It might be a war, and the queen's sending her army to try to sort it out. Lady Aelwynne is going and I'm going too. I came to tell you and to tell Tinnion, cos our friend Brighid is up there and she's in trouble. That's why I have to go. I need to go to help Brighid."

Hayal put his arm around Ellie as she began to cry and Lana moved to hug them both, putting her arm around her mother's waist and her head to her father's chest. "You understand, don't you? I have to go. I can't stay away when my friend needs help. I'll be safe, though, I promise. The queen's army will be there and... And there'll be dryad and noam and sylph going too and they're only going 'cos I'm going there. They won't let anyone hurt me."

"I'm not happy about it, Lana. I don't want you going if there's going to be war." Hayal choked back his tears as he spoke.

"I know, dad. And I wouldn't be going if I had any choice. But I don't. I really don't."

"You aren't to say anything to lady Tinnion 'til after her binding. Not a thing. You won't spoil her day."

"I wouldn't, dad! I never would. She should be happy. I hope that the queen or princess Erinia don't tell Cinerea, though. Daowiel is telling them now and Cinerea's acted as part of their guard recently."

"When will you be leaving?" Ellie's voice was shaking through her tears, and she sniffed after she spoke.

"I think it depends on Tinnion, mam. I have to meet up with the army in Freybridge in just under a moon from now. So I can stay a little while, ten days maybe."

Tinnion didn't sleep well at all. She was more nervous now than she had ever been in her life. She had never envisioned being married this young, let alone being bound. She wasn't even entirely sure what being bound with a dryad would be like.

Cinerea had spoken with her, tried to explain, but it was difficult to really understand. A bracelet would be made from living wood taken from Cinerea's birth tree. A slither of that would pierce her skin. It wouldn't hurt. Cinerea had promised her that. It would pierce her skin and join itself with her vein. Sap from the tree and blood from Tinnion would mix, and the two would be joined.

A dryad had never joined with a human, at least not that was known or recorded for thousands of years, so what would happen next was not entirely certain, but Cinerea explained what happened when two dryad were bound.

Over time, as sap and blood mixed, the two dryad would feel a link between them. Sensing one another, no matter the distance. Their link would grow and, in time, they would be able to feel each other's mood. Tinnion had panicked at Cinerea's description. It sounded very close to being the same as the curse of Khyione, that curse that robbed a human of her humanity when bound to a noam.

"No! Tinnion, it is not like that at all." Cinerea had exclaimed. "I would never do that to you. For the noam, their gods curse allows them to sense you. That is true and over time, you feel their feelings and hear their thoughts, but that is one way. The human hears the noam's thoughts, and they force the humans own out of her head. They control the human by replacing her thoughts with their own. This is not like that. I will feel your mood and you will feel mine. It is possible, in time, I suppose that we will hear each other's thoughts. But mine will never replace yours, just as yours will never replace mine. This is a joining of two beings, not a possession of one by the other."

It was the longest day of the year and it started in a field on the border between stead and forest. The field in which the heroic bull normally lived. They had moved the bull for the safety of those attending the joining, he really didn't understand the occasion and when he didn't understand things, he liked to stomp on them.

A willow arch had been covered with flowers and placed on the tree line, where fencing had been removed at the start of an animal track.

Tinnion waited in the field with her advisors and friends around her. Lana stood at her right side, the two friends linking arms. Around the eastern fence of the field stood the stead folk, all eager to witness their gesith's most happy day.

As the sun touched the top of the trees in the east, a horn blew. A horn that echoed around the forest, and an honour guard of dryad stepped out from the trees. With the guard in place, Queen Olerivia stepped from the forest through the willow arch, wearing a dress that seemed made from overlapping leaves, with hundreds of shades and hues of green and red. Behind her, Princess Erinia and Princess Daowiel walked arm in arm, Daowiel in a dress of golden leaves reminiscent of an t-fhoghar. It was the first time Lana had seen Daowiel in a dress and it made her smile. The princess was much more comfortable in her leathers, ready to hunt or fight at a moment's notice. But Lana thought she looked beautiful in that moment, wearing a dress with her hair loose and curled. Her sister, Erinia, wore a dress of silver green leaves and looked every bit as regal as her mother.

"Lady Tinnion, Gesith of Butterholt and ally to the dryad. You have come here today to be joined with the sealgair Cinerea. This joining will bind your souls together for eternity. You will be as one and will grow to know each other as well as you know your own self. Once bound, you cannot be unbound, not in life, nor in death. The dryad are taught these things and know them well, but I must ask you, Tinnion. Do you understand what I have said here?" Olerivia looked closely at Tinnion, her eyes sharp and alert.

"I understand, your Majesty. This is not a hand fasting, it is much more than that, I know. And I am ready to be joined with my love."

The queen turned her gaze to Lana. "Lana, you have been a friend to dryad and valued advisor. Tell me Lana. Is your friend ready?"

Lana's mouth opened in shock at the question. She had not expected to be asked her opinion and didn't think it was important. "Your majesty. I don't know that it's my place to say. Tinnion loves Cinerea, I know that. I've seen it in her eyes and in her smile. She never really smiled before..." She turned her head to her friend and gave her a smile, her nose crinkling and shoulders rising with it. "If she says that she's ready, then I believe her. She doesn't usually do anything 'til she's sure it's the right thing to do. And I think they're already pretty much joined in their hearts, anyway. Besides, Tinnion's as close as you can be to being a dryad without being a dryad. And they both hate to dance. I think they're perfect for each other."

The queen smiled. "Eloquent as ever, Lana. Then let it be known that I give my blessing to this joining and welcome Tinnion, lady of Butterholt, into my forest as my kin. Cinerea awaits you at her tree, Tinnion. You must enter the forest naked, for you must begin your new life as you began this one. You may choose one to accompany you as your witness and your guide. We will enter together when you are ready."

"Will you come, Lana?" Tinnion turned to her friend with hope in her eyes.

"Of course, if you want me to." Lana smiled.

The two made their way toward the arch and Tinnion removed her cloak, revealing her naked body, before stepping into the forest.

The ceremony itself was short and intimate. The queen and her daughters sat beside Lana to one side of Cinerea's tree and the lovers sat facing one another at its roots. Tinnion had plaited a lock of her hair and she wrapped it silently around the left wrist of Cinerea, biting her lip as she tied the knot that would keep it in place. Once the knot was tied she placed a soft kiss on Cinerea's lips and then held out her own, shaking wrist to the dryad.

She felt little more than a pinch as the wood pierced her skin, though it was a little uncomfortable and her wrist became stiff. She did not feel a sudden connection to Cinerea, there was no instant change in her feelings or her mind. She took a deep breath and lowered her eyes. Then she felt Cinerea's fingers under her chin, gently raising her head. The dryad placed a kiss on her lips.

Lana felt a tap on her shoulder and turned to see the others stood. Daowiel beckoned her to join them and the four slipped quietly into a tree as the lovers embraced, becoming one.

As the sun reached its zenith, Cinerea took Tinnion's hand and placed it flat, against the trunk of her tree. Kneeling behind her, the dryad wrapped her right arm wrapped around Tinnion's waist, holding her, supporting her. She felt a gentle pressure as the dryad lightly pushed her hand against the tree, and then the tree seemed to shift beneath her fingers and her hand gently sank into the bark as though pressing on soft butter. Tinnion gasped, her jaw dropping, and felt herself fall back, pressing her body to her lovers.

"So it is true. We are one, my love. In time, my tree will accept you and then all trees will, as long as you live as one with them as dryad do." Cinerea's voice was soft and warm. Her breath on Tinnion's neck made the huntress's heart skip.

They moved their hands from the tree and Tinnion turned, kissing her lover deeply.

It was late as the couple emerged from the forest and the stead folk were all happily preparing for a feast. They had dressed in hunting leathers that Cinerea had supplied and looked to all the world, like two dryad. Though Tinnion was a little shorter than her partner, you would need to be up close to see that she did not have the telltale point to her ears. Their eyes glistened and the smiles they wore were infectious.

The feast itself was a fun affair and ran deep into the night, with all the folk of the stead and many dryad in attendance. The happy couple even managed a graceful dance, drawing cheers from their guests and merry laughter from Lana.

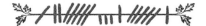

The hall was warm, even without a fire. The large oak table was laden with platters of fruit, breads and cheeses and three pitchers of cider had been poured from the barrel.

Tinnion sat at the head of the table, with Cinerea at her left. Lana sat at the side of the dryad and her family sat opposite. The smiles and laughter of the solstice and Tinnion's binding three days before replaced by stern looks and trepidation.

"Why didn't you tell me this when you arrived, Lana?" Tinnion dug the tip of her knife into the table, twisting it into the wood as her face twisted.

"It's not like I was keeping it secret, Tinnion. I just didn't want you to be worried on your special day. The army won't be anywhere near Freybridge yet so even if you knew then, we couldn't have done anything. It would just have made you sad when you were supposed to be happy."

Tinnion sighed. "You're right, I suppose. I just feel helpless sitting here when I know Brighid could be in danger. The journey we took to Southport made us close, and I swore I'd stand by her in trouble."

"I know." Lana stretched her arm across the table and Tinnion squeezed her hand in a moment of solidarity and support. "We're going to get her out of there, Tinnion. We'll march up to Northfort and we'll stop the rebellion and we'll throw the rebel lords into a cell so they can't do anymore harm."

Tinnion shook her head. "I hope that you're right, Lana. And perhaps, with an army big enough against them, they'll be happy to talk, but these things usually end badly. How many are marching?"

"The queens sending Lady Aelwynne and Commander Qilan with a thousand men, and then there's the fae that have promised to march with me. Daowiel said she would bring a score of the laoch and Shayell promised me three dozen noam. We'll meet them at Freybridge. Then we'll go to the coast and meet Yorane's sylph. He says he should be able to get a dozen friends and family to come, what with Wren being up there too."

Tinnion nodded slowly. "I will join you, of course. I don't have people to bring with me, but I will come."

"You have your sheriff's, m'Lady." Andel retorted, his voice firm.

"No, Andel. You will stay here with your father and keep the stead safe. Hubertus might decide he wants to try his luck again if I'm gone. And besides, you have more pressing commitments to take care of." Tinnion nodded to Ara with a smile.

Andel nodded, a proud look on his face, and held his wife's hand.

"I will come, as well. I would not let my love ride into battle without me." Cinerea took Tinnion's hand with a melancholy smile.

"I would not ask you." Tinnion shook her head slowly.

"You do not have to, my love. I will be at your side."

Chapter Twenty-Nine

A Bitter End to Rivalry

When morning came Cat and Laywyn took breakfast in the inn's main room and then made their way to the city jail. They hoped that Adney would repent and be freed, though Cat considered she could use some of the coin the Tay had given her and arrange the woman's release that way. She did not want to resort to that however, unless it was absolutely necessary.

As they arrived at the jail, they were greeted by the captain that had been Adney's victim the evening before. Three deep scratches, still red and angry looking, marked his cheek, and Cat let out a sigh. The old woman was more trouble than she was worth. If only they could get her to speak, she could be left behind then.

What happened next surprised them both. The captain was a burly man and clearly angry at what had occurred. He had developed a deep dislike of the woman that matched Cat's own in a very short period and had ordered she be hung in a cage from the walls of the harbour.

"You can't put a woman in a cage like that because she disagrees with you, captain. Rescind your order. Throw her in a cell, fine, but you can't cage her on the harbour wall. She'll likely drown if there's a swell."

"Aye, she should an' all. And right it'd be. Disagreement, indeed. Do you not see her mark? And that aint all she did neither. No, not by a long mark. If it had just been me purse she'd stolen or me face she'd marked I might have done as you say but she... That evil hag... She..." The captain put his hand over his face and turned away from them, his shoulders heaving.

"I know what she is, captain. I was the victim of her mood many's the time, but she's needed for something, something bigger than me and you. How much to set her free?" Cat's face was as soft as her voice and she reached to her purse.

"She killed my Sally! There aint no money makes up for what she did! Evil witch. I aught to strangle her myself, I aught to. But, I'm a captain of the guard and that wouldn't be right. So I'll cage her instead."

"Captain, I apologise, I didn't know she had murdered your... Wife?" Laywyn clasped his hand to the man's shoulder. "We need information from her, though. If we could speak to her before..."

"Wife? I ain't married, you damned fool. I wouldn't have been anywhere near the evil hag if I were, now would I? Dunno, what you takes me for."

"So, Sally isn't..." Laywyn started.

"Sally's my... she was my... Oh poor Sally. She was my bird."

Cat bit her cheek at the announcement, hoping that her face didn't give away the laughter that was building inside her. Clearly the captain and his pet had been close, but she never would have thought that Adney would get herself caged over the death of a bird.

"I'll let you both talk with her, but I ain't changing my mind." The captain announced stubbornly as he signalled his guard to open the door to the cells.

"Well, you've gone and done it this time Adney. That captain's going to see you dangled from the harbour wall and likely dead." Cat shook her head as she spoke.

"You can fix it though, Cat darling. You can get me free, like you did in the city. Small town like this, you can easily fix it."

"No, Adney. I can't. I had a bit of influence over the jailor in Southport. I ain't got nothing out here. These people don't know me or care much for who

I am. And the captain aint taking no bribe. You've gone and gotten yourself into something I can't fix."

"Nah, you're just being daft. Just winding me up, you are." Adney started to shake, her voice rising in pitch.

"I'm sorry, Adney. There's nothing I can do. The man's set his mind, and he's the law here. But I still need to know what you know. Talk to me Adney, tell me the names."

"Fat chance of that! Not if I'm going in that cage. Oh no, to damn with that, Cat. You'll get nothin' from me, not a peep."

Cat scowled. "Then you'll hang in a cage and most likely drown and I won't bat an eyelash, Adney. Why would I? You've been nothing but pain and misery all my life. Xen won't have you back on the ship and this captain wants to see you dead. Good riddance to you's what I say. Not a good bone in your body. Not one good deed, not even in the end."

She walked away from the bars of cell and called on the guard to open the door to the captain's office. Adney calling and screaming her name behind her.

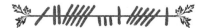

They lined up to watch her being put in the cage. Cat, Laywyn and Xentan, all stood with the captain of the guard. Sea spray blown in their faces as they glared at the prisoner. They watched her struggle in her chains as two guards forced her into the metal box, before they slammed the door shut and chained it up.

She begged and pleaded to be set free. But she never said sorry, not once. There was no contrition in her pleas, only anger and fear at what was to come. She cursed and swore and she spat at the guard, but she never said sorry, nor offered the names that Cat needed. And then the guards pushed the cage over the edge of the wall and it hung on its chain over the crashing waves and she screamed.

"Lower it!" The captain's order was sharp and harsh, his face set like stone. The guards nodded and started turning the wheel that would lower the cage down to the ocean. As the cage dropped out of sight, Cat turned and walked away.

"We really gonna leave her there then, Cat?" Xentan wiped the beer foam from his beard and smacked his lips together.

"I wouldn't think you would care, Xen. She robbed you blind before she ran."

"Aye, she did that. But drownin' aint no death I'd wish on anyone and when the wind lifts, she'll drown. Make no mistake o that. Might not be all at once, but them waves'll fill her up and she'll drown."

Cat slumped in her seat, her face screwed tight. "What am I to do then, Xen? What? Bribe the captain to free her? We tried that. Tell him she's needed for a mission? We tried that too. And even if we tried again, even if that worked, then what? You let her back on the ship, no harm. No matter. Everything hunky dory again? Then we just sit and wait 'til she betrays us again? She's gotten herself into this. Nothin' to do with me this time. And I ain't gonna feel guilty 'bout it, you hear?"

"I hear you say the words, Cat, but I see your eyes tellin' their own story an' all." The pirate sipped at his ale.

"Would it be safe to take the dinghy round the wall?" Laywyn stroked his chin as he asked.

"It'd be safe to go round that side of the wall with a crew o' men know's what they're doing. Ye'd not get close to the cage, though, not without breaking the boat up and drownin' yerselves."

"So what do we do then, Cat? We don't have the names we need to go much further and if she dies we never will. Do we just turn back and tell the Tay we failed?" Laywyn poured himself another cup of ale from the pitcher.

Cat shook her head, her face growing red and her voice rising. "Do you think she'd tell us? Even if we have her set free? She's shown no signs of it so far, and she ran from us first chance she got. If she hadn't riled up the wrong man, she'd have been on the first ship outta port and gone. I say we get what supplies we need and go on. It'll be harder to find what we need at the end, but we'll manage. We aint useless and there's always loose tongues if you know where to look."

"I don't like leaving folk to die, Cat." Laywyn stayed calm despite Cat's frustration.

"I don't much like it either, Laywyn. But it aint my fault and I'm done putting my neck on the line for her. She's had chance after chance and she's shown she'll not change. It was only your word and my own softness stopped her from dying in the tunnels. Not this time, though. This time she has to deal with the consequences of what she's done."

Cat stood on the deck of the ship and watched the waves strike the wall as they sailed out of the harbour. The cage was battered by the spray and tossed about upon the high waves, crashing against the stone. Adney's screams lost in the roar of the ocean.

Her stomach knotted, and her heart sank, leaving a feeling of emptiness in her chest. She had hated the woman and feared her. All her life Adney had hurt her and ordered her beaten, had watched in glee as she'd gone days without food. In the final days of Keikon's thieves, the woman had ordered Cat dead. She'd offered money and prizes for her head. And yet Cat felt a sorrow as she watched the woman now. If she could, in that moment, she would reach out and take away Adney's pain, take away her fear, make what must be her last moments of life, pass away in peace and calm. Cat felt her eyes fill and her throat tighten.

An enormous wave rose and smashed the cage against the wall, the white salty foam of the ocean spraying up and over the pathway atop it. The cage was lost for a moment within the water. Cat watched as the chain went slack and then tightened again as the wave subsided. She could see Adney's body, limp in the cage, still and silent. Another wave crashed, and another, and Cat vomited over the side of the ship. Her face red and stained with tears.

Chapter Thirty

A Cry in the Night

Ebon Bluff Tower was a liath stronghold nestled in the eastern rise. Bordered on three sides by the river and by mountains to the north, the stronghold was a highly defensible point. The survivors approached carefully, taking a day and a night to watch the surroundings, hiding in craggy outcrops of rock.

They saw no warriors in the day, no people coming or going at all, no traders, no farmers, no humans nor fae. As evening and darkness fell, they saw no lights were lit, no fires or candles. There were no signs of life there at all. And so the survivors of the siege climbed the last few hundred metres and opened the heavily reinforced door at the tower's base.

"I cannot believe it's deserted. What a waste. It's built as strong as Northfort. An easy place tae defend." Anndra wandered around the circular hall in awe at the build.

"Aye, dinnae get comfortable though, Anndra. We'll not be staying long either. We've tae get back round tae the north and the east and get us some help. We'll not find any here, it seems. Nor in many holds of Fearann an Liath I reckon. We can only hope MacHuran's still the man he was." Cohade pulled a chair from the table in the centre of the room and sat. "See whit ye can find by the way of food and equipment down here Brighid. Anndra take Micheil and head up the tower. See whit there is and make certain we've not missed anyone. Can ye sense a well, Neve?"

"Yes, lord. There is a well beneath us. There must be a way down to it. I will find it." The nymph nodded and headed into the corridor, looking for a way down.

The tower seemed to be only recently deserted; the building was strong and the furniture good, if in need of a clean. There were no signs of why it might be abandoned, no signs of struggle or problems. The water was fresh and plentiful; they found salted meat that was still good and there was a vegetable garden on the southern side.

They barred the door and lit a fire, then made a stew and ate before sleeping in rooms and beds for the first time in a moon.

The air took an icy chill despite the fire and the recent turning of seasons, and Brighid added her cloak to the blanket she had wrapped around her. A howl floated on the wind, a haunting cry that echoed around the tower and sent a shiver through Brighid as biting as the chill air had.

As morning came, the creeping sun warmed the air, and the survivors reheated the stew for their breakfast. They talked of their sleep through yawns and stretches, but none mentioned the howl that had disturbed Brighid's night.

"You must have heard it. It wis as loud as an entire pack o' wolves and as chilling as an ice bath. You'll no sit there and tell me in honesty that there's no one of you's heard it?" Brighid's face was red. She had been certain of the cry, but not one of her companions had heard it, at least not one that would admit to it, and she wondered if she had dreamt it. If it had been a dream, it had felt very real.

"It's ma feeling we should stay awhile." Cohade interrupted a playful tussle as Anndra teased his sister. "There's more food than we can carry here and it'd do us nae harm to rest and fatten up a wee bit afore we head off again. We've had a hard year and there's more tae come. A few days tae recover our senses a bit will do the world o good."

"Aye, it seems a fair plan, Cohade. I'm happy for tae be surrounded by walls and tae sleep in a bed. I'll gladly stop a few days and eat ma fill before heading out again." MacAllister had found a dozen barrels of ale and filled his tankard with a grin as he spoke.

The group split that morning to explore their surroundings. Neve declaring she'd head along the river to fish while Wren intended to explore the high ground. The sylph invited Brighid to join her but the tuath's dislike for heights saw her spend the day with the nymph and Anndra accompanied Wren. Micheil and MacAllister meanwhile kept Cohade and the barrels of ale company. By the time the others returned, the three were slurring their speech and beyond the point of needing their beds. Brighid and Neve had caught a dozen fish, more than enough to give them fresh meat for a few days, an alternate option to the salted goat meat they had found.

As Wren and Anndra returned, they reported that they had seen no signs of anyone following or of any wolves in the area. That last part was aimed specifically at Brighid, and Anndra laughed as he delivered the news.

"I'm just surprised ye saw anything, brother. Other than Wren's behind, anyway. You've barely been able tae drag yer eyes away from it since we left home. I've no idea how you survived the battle." Brighid chuckled and three drunken tuath almost fell off their seats as they laughed and mocked him relentlessly.

"Oh aye, laugh it up, Micheil, cos we'll be talking of where you're keeping your eyes next!" Anndra's childhood friend coughed and sat bolt upright, his face turning red as he tried to keep his laugh in.

"There's nae need fer that, Anndra! I thought ye were ma friend?"

"Oh, aye! We're friends now, is it?" Anndra chuckled. "How's about ye stop yer laughing and start setting us all a plate and a tankard? Or have ye drank all the ale?"

"We've tried, Anndra! Fer sure, we've tried, but yer fathers getting awa old and yer friend here drinks like a wee girl." MacAllister gave Micheil a shove, and the warrior fell off his chair.

The same haunting howls interrupted Brighid's sleep and, as she woke, she grabbed her belt and ran into Wren's room.

"You must hear that! Wren?" The blanketed shape on the bed shifted. "Come on, Wren. How're ye sleeping through this? Wake up!" Brighid went to her friend's side to shake her awake. As she reached out her hand, the blanket shifted, revealing the sylph's face bloodied and bruised, her nose and lips split. Her eyes, bloodshot, sunk into black pits. The fae opened her mouth, her teeth broken and smashed and let out a scream, then reached out a hand, cut and bloodied to the warriors, nails digging into Brighid's arm. The tuath grabbed her friend's wrist and pulled her own arm free, letting out a cry as the sylph's flesh crumbled away in her grip.

Brighid ran from the room and to her brothers. Calling his name through strained breaths. As she flung open his door, he hastily pulled his blanket over his naked form and yelled.

"What the void, Brighid! What're you screaming about?"

"It's Wren, something's wrong, Anndra."

"There's nothing wrong with Wren, Brighid." Anndra rolled his eyes and sighed. Then the second blanket beside him shifted and Brighid's jaw dropped as Anndra sat on the edge of his bed, revealing the sylph at his side.

"Wren? But... There's something in yer room, Wren. Something in yer bed. "

Anndra wrapped the blanket around him and stood, putting his hand gently on Brighid's arm and leading her from his room into the corridor. Together they went to Wren's room to check on what Brighid had seen, but they found it empty. The bed untouched, no sign at all of what had shaken Brighid's nerves.

"There wis something here, Anndra. I swear, and it looked just like Wren. Except... Like she would if she were dead. I'm not lying, Anndra, and I aint crazy either."

Anndra put his arm around Brighid's shoulder. "Go back tae yer room, Brighid. Lock the door, if it makes ye feel better, and rest. We'll talk in the morning."

Brighid nodded and walked away slowly, shaking her head, her eyes heavy with tears.

There was no teasing in the morning, only sharp breaths and concerned looks as Brighid described what had she had seen. Neve placed her hands on either side of the tuath's head, her fingers gently resting at the temples. She closed her eyes and took a deep breath. A few moments passed, the survivors all sat in silence, before the Nymph let her breath go and opened her eyes.

"There does not appear to be anything wrong with you, Brighid. Aside from a little anxiety at our situation, this is normal. It appears to be little more than a nightmare. Though it may seem very real in the moment. I will give you a draft tonight before we retire to our rooms. It will help you sleep sound." The nymph gave a warm smile.

"Thank you, Neve. I... Perhaps I am just tired. I didn't sleep well with all the noise the night before. Still, I'd feel a wee bit better if we could all take some time tae have another look around. It felt too real and you've said yerself there's nothing wrong with me."

They found nothing in their daytime searches, they saw no animal tracks that might explain the howling and there was nothing in the tower that could explain what Brighid had seen.

As night fell, Neve prepared a hot drink for Brighid and sent the warrior off to her bed.

The howling pierced the silence of night, sending a shiver through the warrior's soul. And as the howling stopped, the screaming started.

Brighid's eyes and her limbs were heavy. She could barely move and barely see. But she knew the screams came from the nymph's room, so she reached for her blade and staggered to her feet. Stumbling through her chamber door, she lost her footing and slid down the facing wall, her blade held limply in her hand. Unable to stand, she crawled along the stone floor to the fae's room and, kneeling, pulled at the handle that opened the door.

A figure stood over the nymph, its flesh as white as mountain snow, its skin marked with blood and dirt, long talons grew from its fingers. It clawed at the large wooden bowl the nymph was using as a shield, leaving deep gauges that would soon see it split.

"Anndra!" Brighid called out.

The creature, hearing her call, spun and lashed out. Its talons biting deep into her left arm, she yelped in pain and struck with the blade in her right, cutting at the flesh of the creature's leg. Howling, its mouth opened wide, bloody teeth as sharp as blades glistening against the darkness. Brighid struggled but raised her arm and swung her blade once more at the creature, sending a spray of blood from its thigh that splattered against her face. Dark and hot, she felt the blood cover her, dripping from her nose. Her eyes closed, as heavy as the night itself, and she fell to the floor.

When Wren heard the call of her friend, she leapt from her bed, grabbed her staff and ran from her room. The corridor was long and Neve's room was at the far end of it, but Wren saw the creature strike out at Brighid and watched as her friend fell to the floor. She closed the distance between them quickly, sprinting through the passage, determined and desperate to reach the room before the creature could strike again.

The tip of her staff struck the creature's chin as it bent to maul the drugged and sleeping Brighid. The creature staggered backward and hissed at the oncoming form of the Sylph before turning and leaping out of the tower window, sending glass and lead flying into the night.

Wren followed the creature, not slowing her run as she leapt across her friend and into the darkness.

Neve was kneeling over Brighid, wrapping her bloodied arm as Anndra arrived at the Nymph's door. He had his blade in hand and his blanket wrapped hastily around him.

"What happened here?" His words were clipped.

"Never mind this. She'll be fine. Get out there. Wren's alone against it."

Anndra nodded and ran back down the corridor toward the stairs, calling on MacAllister and Michiel as he went.

The three tuath warriors burst through the tower door and frantically searched for signs of the sylph and the creature.

"There!" Michiel called and pointed to an outcrop of rock some hundred metres away. He didn't wait before running toward it, drawing his sword as he went.

Anndra and MacAllister followed, not too far back and quickly making up ground.

Wren swung her staff as she landed, striking the trailing leg of the creature and causing it to stumble. It hit the ground and rolled, howling as it tumbled. A cry that was answered from the darkness surrounding them. The creature tried to stand but its left leg, bloody and limp, couldn't support it and it fell, hissing and spitting to the stone. Three others joined it from the darkness, each stalking through the night, wary and crouched, ready to attack. They stared at Wren and hissed before leaping at her, talons spread, sharp teeth bared.

Michiel ran into the fray, his blade swinging wildly. He managed to get a cut to one of the creature's arms and it left the fight with Wren to face him. It stepped to its left and drew the warrior's blade and then the creature leapt. Landing hard against the warrior's chest, it sent him to the ground, its talons tearing at his flesh and its teeth buried deep into his neck before it arched its back with a cry and fell atop the tuath. Anndra's sword severing its spine.

He didn't stop to check on his friend. There were still three creatures to fight off and Wren, though holding them so far, seemed to tire.

With MacAllister just behind him, and the sylph reinvigorated at the arrival of her friends, the creatures were soon beaten back and killed. Their haunting death screams filling the night and sending an ice chill through the veins of the warriors.

They carried Michiel back to the tower, his neck open and bloody, his chest gouged deeply. They had little hope that he would survive the night, but they had to try, and if there was a hope, it lay with the nymph healer.

"What were those things?" Anndra was still breathing heavily as he slumped by the fire.

"Baosith. Creatures that feed off the blood of their prey. Their song lulls their victims to sleep before they strike. We are fortunate that Brighid heard their howl behind the lullaby." Wren sat at the warrior's side, wrapping a wound on her forearm.

"Why is it Brighid was nae lulled by them?"

Wren sat for a moment, her head bowed and chewed on her lip. "It is said that their song cannot affect those marked by the gods."

"Is that some fancy way o' saying ma sisters dying?" Anndra's brow furrowed.

"No, Anndra. No more than any of us are. No, it is meant to say those that have been marked by the gods to a specific fate. A person whose doom is set. It is nothing more than folklore, but I know of no other explanation to give."

ACT THREE

THE STORM

Chapter Thirty-One

A Coming Together

Lana felt the familiar shape of the old oak as she touched the wall at the end of the bridge. A silent greeting was shared and she pushed through into the clearing that had been the sight of her first battle. Before she moved on or looked around she turned back to the tree and wrapped her arms around it. "It's good to see you again, Mr Oak." She heard the sound of familiar laughter from across the clearing.

"I'm sure 'Mr Oak' is happy to see you too Ògan." Daowiel chuckled. "It doesn't feel right calling you that now, Lana. You've grown a lot this past year. Perhaps..." She paused a moment and then smirked. "Darach beag. That seems to suit you more and speaks of your connection to your favourite tree there."

"Or, you could call me Lana..." Lana said with a smile, then she cleared her throat and stood as a soldier stands to attention. "Ciamar a tha thu, a charaid?" She spoke slowly, pronouncing each syllable carefully.

"You are learning, Lana! I am well, thank you. But I wasn't expecting you this soon. Are things well in the stead?"

"They are. Tinnion's made a lot of changes there but they all seem good. Her and Cinerea are very happy and they're going to come with us. I just wanted to see if everything was going well here. If you're still coming? I haven't seen you or heard from you since their binding."

The dryad princess smiled. "Of course I am, Lana. And I have two dozen laoch to come with us. My mother is as concerned for your safety as Queen Rhiannon and insists that we keep you safe."

"Is there any news of the queen's army?"

"They have reached the southern edge of the woodlands here. I believe they are four days from this camp. The noam march with them, two score of them. Your friend has been as busy at raising his lords banners as we have. I must confess, my laoch are a little nervous at so many noam heading this way. The thousand human soldiers were enough to make them worry, but we have a treaty with your queen and we trust her word. The noam though we have no agreement with, only millennia of mistrust."

"Shayell swore them to me, Daowiel. They wouldn't ever do anything against you. Besides, Shayell is..." Lana bit her cheek. "Shayell isn't like the Stonemount noam. If there could be a treaty between you both Shayell would be thrilled."

"We will see, Lana. Let us make sure the sgàil do not kill us all first and then we can talk with your friend. Will you be staying here until the army arrive?"

Lana shook her head. "No, I'm going straight back to the stead. I need to say goodbye to my family. Tinnion will need to ride here anyway so Cinerea and me will ride with her. We'll meet you all at Freybridge. You won't fight with Shayell, will you?"

"Of course not, Lana. He has sworn to protect you and if for nothing else I respect him for that."

Lana smiled and gave her friend a long hug. "I'll see you at the new moon, then."

The journey through the countryside was a relaxed and pleasant one. The weather was warm, and the sun kept their spirits as bright as it did the day. They shared the first eight days of their journey with another wagon, laden with goods from the stead to be traded with the people of Wildflower.

They would arrive in Freybridge ahead of the army despite their relaxed pace and so they made the most of their time. Stopping often to eat and talk and sometimes allowing Tinnion and Cinerea to hunt. It was during one of those breaks that Lana noticed the forest's trees reaction to Tinnion changing. Just a week earlier, before being joined with the dryad, the trees had seen Tinnion in a deep orange shade. A human hunter, that killed in the forest and may be dangerous to the dryad within. Now she appeared to them in a soft yellow hue, not fully trusted, not yet, but a lot closer to it. Lana thought that in time the hunter might even travel the bridge. On that day, she would surely be a match to any dryad hunter, perhaps even more deadly.

As they stopped at Wildflower, they were greeted happily by the stead folk and taken to the manor to spend the evening in the gesith's company. A cheerful man, round and red faced with a laugh that filled his hall. The gesith was happy to make a new friend in the 'great lady Tinnion, gesith of Butterholt.' He mused happily at the dairy products she had sent his way and expressed his hope that she had enjoyed his mead half as much many times during the evening. He had tried to show a nonchalant casualness at having a dryad in his hall, but was clearly just as amazed and nervous as his stead folk had been.

That evening ended in an agreement to create a road between the steads, a road that would pass through a small, new waypoint at which the folk of both stead could trade. They selected an area to the south of the beck as it looped between holds. Each promising resources and builders to man it.

With the honourable lady of Butterholt in his hall with her dryad wife, the lord of Wildflower paid little attention to Lana. Imagining her little more than a lady's maid. His jaw dropped when he asked the purpose of their journey and was told that they rode as Lana's guard. Realising he had someone of great standing in his presence, he offered his sheriff to ride with them, at least as far as the border with the north. Lana smiled sweetly and declined his kind offer, affecting a formal tone that was used in the queen's court. "Should we fail, lord, we will need your men to defend the queen's isle."

The lord feigned disappointment with a sigh and a nod. "Aye, that's true, m'lady. I'll take your wise counsel and be ready."

The army of Mortara was not one simple force. It was made up of four separate units, each with it's own specialisation. 'The Red', made up the bulk of the force. Men and women skilled in melee fighting. Some with sword or axe and shield, some with two handed spears. They dressed in heavy chain armour. Others in 'The Red' used war-bows to shower their enemies with arrows before joining the melee with large axes and hammers.

Then there was 'The Green'. A much smaller group than 'The Red', they often worked in small teams or alone, scouting and tracking. Skilled with sword and bow as well as reading the land. Others that marched with the army were not fighters. 'The Yellow' were engineers, able builders that were skilled in erecting defences and creating siege weapons. And 'The Blue', men and women that studied the art of healing. Each unit wore its own colours and had its own banner flying above their section of the camp.

The dryad stayed close to the tree line to the south of the bridge. While the Queen's army, a thousand men strong in total, separated them from the noam.

Though closer to Southport than to Northfort, the city of Freybridge was on the northern bank of the great river that marked the border between taydoms and fell under the administration of Tay Jendawyn. So it was that the commander of the queen's army, a large man named Qilan, had ridden into the city with his entourage to guard Lady Aelwynne. There they met with the gesith to gauge the man's loyalties and arrange passage through the growing city.

With the queen's voice and her commander in the city, Lana was free from duty and brought her friends together to make camp. Daowiel greeted Cinerea and Tinnion with a hug. "Have you been accepted now by the forest, Tinnion?"

The hunter shook her head. "I can feel the trees now and know they're still wary of me, but it feels like the day is getting closer."

The princess nodded with a smile. "I am certain that by the time we return, you will find yourself able to travel the bridge, with help, of course."

"Don't let Daowiel teach you... She'll just laugh at you when you stumble." Lana chuckled as she spoke.

Shayell smiled as they arrived at Lana's camp, a look of relief in their eyes.

"Have you two had separate camps the whole way from the woods?" Lana asked as she sat at the campfire and rolled her cloak to make a pillow.

"My laoch aren't quite ready to trust an army of noam yet, Lana." Daowiel shrugged.

"But you know each other, at least a little. You know we're all on the same side. Are you ready to trust each other?"

Shayell nodded. "For my part, Lana, it is certain."

Daowiel gave the noam a glance through narrowed eyes. "I am, Lana. Because you trust in him, and I trust you."

"Good!" Lana smiled broadly. "When the laoch and the noam see that the two of you can share a camp, they'll be less worried, I'm sure."

"Share?" Shayell tilted their head.

"Uh huh. Of course. You're my friends. You were going to camp with me, weren't you? Or..." Lana sighed. "Were you going to camp with your warriors the whole way and leave me stuck in the middle on my own?"

"I had not truly thought of it that way, Lana. Of course I had hoped that we would share a camp..." Shayell stopped, their mouth open as if to speak, but nothing else came out.

"You didn't think my other friends would?" Lana sighed as she spoke.

"No, it is not... I..." The noam's cheeks flushed. "I had hoped that they might. I did not think of the broader implication of that, is all. It will seem odd to my men. And now it is upon us I feel a little... nervous."

"Pfft. What's odd is thinking my friends wouldn't all be together." Lana smiled warmly. "I understand your nerves, Shayell. Have you thought about... sharing what we talked about?"

The noam's head shook frantically, their eyes wide. "No! No... I... I do not think I could. Not yet."

Lana nodded and offered her hand to the noam. "You don't have to... You never have to, if you don't want. If you're not ready. But if you do, I'll help."

The noam lowered their head and whispered a "Thank you."

"Let's have lunch! Everything always feels a little bit better once you've eaten with each other." Lana smiled and disappeared into her tent, reappearing with a platter of fruit.

"Can I ask you something, Tinnion?" The evening was drawing on and the companions sat around their fire with a small meal of bread and cheese. They had cider and a small casque of strong mead from Wildflower.

The hunter nodded. "Of course you can."

"I just... I wondered what it's like? Not you figuring out the tree thing, I know what that's like. But what's it like to be joined with someone?"

Tinnion paused for a moment, pulling her fingers across her chin, then she smiled. "It's a bit like the tree thing, Lana. When you're under the trees, you can sense them, right?" Lana nodded her agreement before the huntress continued. "Well, it's a bit like that. I can feel where Cinerea is. Not that I know exactly where she is, but that I can feel which direction she is in and how far away she is. It's getting stronger every day too. I think one day I will know exactly where she is. I think I'll be able to close my eyes and feel the things around her."

Lana nodded. "I can do that with the trees. I can send my mind to a tree I know and feel if there are people there or animals. I can feel how the tree feels about things. Mostly the weather. Can you feel what Cinerea feels?"

"Kind of. Not like I can tell you exactly how she feels, I think our emotions are a bit more difficult to figure out than a tree's. But I..." She paused for a moment, trying to find the words to explain. "I know when she's angry at something, I can feel that even when we're nowhere near each other. I think that'll grow too, that I'll be able to feel more when we're closer, when we know each other better. I suppose I can feel the things that I'd see if we were face to face. Not the little things perhaps, but the big ones."

Daowiel gave the huntress a smile. "When two dryad join, they begin to feel even those small things. I do not know that it will be the same with you, Tinnion. I hope it will be. You understand our forest and you respect our ways. I am happy that you have joined us."

"Does the Ògan have thoughts of binding with a special person?" Cinerea smiled, her eyes twinkled in the firelight.

"Oh... No... I... No I'm not ready for that, I haven't even met anyone I could... No. I'm just curious. It's so different from being hand fast and I couldn't imagine what it would be like." Lana's cheeks reddened.

"Oh." Cinerea sighed. "I hoped we might have another ceremony to keep our spirits high before the war starts."

"I hope there won't be a war. I hope we just go there and talk and they see sense and we can all go home peacefully." Lana chewed on her cheek.

"I hope that too, Ògan. I hope." The sealgair nodded. "I am not laoch and fighting is not something I am very good at, though I shoot well enough."

"We'll be fine." Lana said determinedly. "Once they see all the people we have with us, they'll not want to fight."

Chapter Thirty-Two

THE ROAD TO TRAISBEN

Five days north of Freybridge, at a small waypoint where the army took some supplies, the road split. One path heading straight north, the other toward the northwest and the coast.

"I told Yorane that we'd meet him in a place called Traisben on the coast, Aelwynne. He'll be expecting us there."

"We'll send a messenger, Lana. It will take us too far out of our way. That village is on the cliffs of the western shore. We don't have the supplies to see us take that kind of detour and we can't guarantee them on that road. Besides, we cannot march an army through the small holds of the north. We have to stay on the Northern Road. "

"So I'll go without the army. Just me and the fae. We can meet again in that city you talked about yesterday, Glamithren. We can go a little faster than you can with a thousand men, so we should still get there at the same time as you, even if it's a little longer going our way. I can't just send a messenger, Aelwynne. It's too important."

"The queen wanted you to stay close."

"She wanted me to stay safe... I've sixty four warriors and four wonderful friends with me to protect me. No one in a stead or farm is going to make trouble for us. And, even though there's a lot of us, we don't quite look like an army either, so we won't scare everyone to death."

The Queen's Voice thought for a while, sighing and shaking her head. "Fine." She nodded reluctantly. "I know the princess will do her best to keep you out of trouble. Make your way to Glamithren as soon as you can, but don't enter the city. We don't know how they stand. There are lakes to the south of it. Camp between them and we'll meet you there."

"Alright!" Lana grinned and turned to go before looking back at her mentor with a giggle. "Will you be okay alone with all these rugged men?"

Aelwynne shook her head with a laugh. "Stay out of trouble, Lana. I don't want to have to go back to Queens Isle and explain why you aren't with me."

"I will! I promise."

The road was a busy one with traders and workmen travelling to and from Freybridge so the company travelled in groups to fit in, no more than ten fae in each. On occasion they took to the countryside along the path rather than walk upon it. Progress, in spite of their meandering, was a lot faster without the needs of an army to meet. The fae could cover more ground in a day than a group of humans could; often leading, in the early days of the journey, to Tinnion and Lana tiring out long before their friends. As the journey progressed, however, they became used to the pace, and the distances covered.

Within four days, they came to the village of Dornberg. A small settlement that seemed to have grown from a joining of farmsteads. As they approached the village, a half dozen sheriffs met them, their hands on their weapons and a nervous look in their eyes.

"What're you wanting here? There's nothing here for stealing, nowhere fer fae to be sleeping neither. We've enough trouble without inviting more." The man's voice shook a little as he spoke, and his fingers played nervously with the hilt of his sword.

"I am Lana, lady of Queen Rhiannon's court. These are my friends, Lady Tinnion, gesith of Butterholt; Princess Daowiel and Cinerea of the Heartwood and Shayell of Southport. We're travelling north, to Traisben. We just need a few supplies, that we'll buy and we'll be on our way. We aren't coming to cause trouble for you." Lana gave the man a smile.

"You'll find nothing in Traisben, sides rubble and burnt wood. Best turn back now, get yourself back in the south where the queen's name still protects you."

Lana's eyes narrowed a little as she looked at the group of sheriffs. They wore the uniform of the men that protected steads across Mortara, but the queen's badge had been removed. Replaced by a patch depicting a tower. "We're meeting friends in Traisben. What happened there?"

"They refused to pay what Lord Siosal set in taxes, so he took it from them. If yer friend was there, they're dead or taken prisoner. Like I says, nothing there for you. Nothing here neither." The man's fingers tightened around the leather grip of his sword.

"You don't want to draw that." Tinnion's voice was steel. Her hand had settled on her bow. The man looked nervously between the huntress and the friends that surrounded her.

"Siosal, was that his name? He'll not cause you trouble either, we'll see to it you're safe from him." Lana stepped toward the man, her eyes set on his. The man laughed a nervous laugh.

"You aint capable of protecting no one from him. I told ye the Queen's name don't mean nothing here no more. There's been a change in the north and Lord Siosal is the new King's man."

"And you?" Lana tilted her head slightly. "Who's man are you? The queens or the lord that kills his own folk?"

"I'm Siosal's man. We're all Siosal's men, the whole town here. He made us swear. Took our families and made us kneel to him."

"I'm going to give you a choice, then. You're sheriffs, so you swore an oath to the queen at some time. Swear it again, renounce this Siosal and protect this town in the queen's name like you used to..." She paused a moment and glanced back at her friends. Each stood still, composed and ready to act if needed. "Or... Or you can go back to your lord and tell him we're coming. I promise you though, if you take the second choice, you'll be punished with him and a man that kills his own folk won't get off lightly. Are there still people to trade with here?"

"What?" The man looked surprised at Lana's question.

"Are there people to trade with or has he killed them and taken them prisoner too?"

"They're gone." He shook his head, his brow furrowed.

"Then we'll take what we need and give you time to swear your oaths or run."

"There's two score men in the town." The man looked at the men at his side. "There's five of you."

"We're not alone. There are more of us, close, that you can't see. Whatever you want to do, you don't want to fight us. You wouldn't win. You six wouldn't even get back into the town to warn your friends. Swear your swords to the queen through me. I'll take your oath and hold you to it, and we'll make sure Siosal pays for what he's done."

The man looked to his friends and each in turn nodded, then took to his knees, laying his sword before him the hilt toward Lana.

The road from Dornberg to Traisben was deserted, to its west the beaches and cliffs of the western shore. To the east scorched fields and burnt out farm buildings littered the landscape. There was a ghostly feeling of death as they made their way north. No villagers, no traders, no livestock on the plains. They marched in silence, their thoughts on the destruction and hints of death around them, their moods low. By the time they set camp, Lana's face showed her sadness.

"Are you alright, Lana?" Tinnion's voice was soft as she sat down beside her friend.

"I will be, I guess. I've never seen anything like this, Tin. So much waste and death. I didn't think that people could be this evil. Not even Heriloth went this far. It's like Muguwar 'cept he isn't like us. He didn't seem to understand life. The man that's done this doesn't have that excuse." She felt Tinnion's arm around her, pulling her close and rested her head against her friend's shoulder.

"There are many more good people in the world than evil. Sometimes, though, the bad ones do things so bad they make it seem like the whole world is wrong. We have to do what we can to balance that out."

"I dunno how to balance it out." Lana lifted her head to look up at her friend. "I can't make things right for everyone that's lost their homes or their families. I can't bring back dead people."

Tinnion's eyes were heavy and her voice soft. "You don't have to, Lana. That isn't for you to even try. What you did in Dornberg, giving those men a chance, showing them they didn't have to kill or die. That made a difference. That made them think and hopefully they'll remember when they face others. Things like that help make the world right."

"Why do I feel like I want to kill Siosal, then? Why do I feel like that would make it feel better?" Lana chewed on her lip, her eyes welling with tears.

"Sometimes there are people so bad you can't let them go. If you do, they keep killing. This Siosal seems to be one of them. He either needs to be locked in a cell forever or killed to protect the rest of the world. Sometimes it can't be avoided. You do what you have to do to save others."

The friends sat a while in silence, holding one another and watched the flames of the campfire dance.

"Where are Daowiel, Cinerea and Shayell? Have they gone to check the warriors?" Lana sat upright, wiping her eyes and putting her hand on Tinnion's.

Tinnion shook her head. "They went off together a few moments ago, over toward the beach. They seemed to need some privacy for something they were discussing."

"Oh... How are you and Cinerea now? Can you feel more?"

Tinnion smiled. "I can. I know that she's relaxed and with friends and I could point to her in the dark without difficulty. It's not how I thought it would be, not the way you hear them talk about the curse of Khyione. It doesn't interfere with my own feelings at all. I just feel her there, in a small part of my mind, like I'm carrying a mini Cinerea, in a pouch in my head."

"It sounds kind of nice." Lana smiled.

Tinnion tilted her head to see Lana's face. "You're thinking about it often, aren't you? Are you sure you aren't thinking of someone special? The Princess?"

"Daowiel?" Lana chuckled. "No... Oh, no... I like Daowiel, I love her even. Same as I love you and Brighid, but not like that."

"Shayell then?" Tinnion's voice was almost a whisper, and Lana shook her head.

"No. Shayell's... I... No. Shayell and Selene might join one day. I know Shayell likes her and I'm pretty sure she likes Shayell. I don't think I love anyone in that way, not yet. I just think it's nice."

Tinnion nodded. "It's probably best it's not Shayell. You don't want to bind with a noam, you don't want the curse."

"I don't want the curse, I know... But do you think everyone gets the curse the way they say? Daowiel says she's not sure how strong your bond will be with Cinerea. Maybe the bond with noam's depends on the person too?"

"I'm not sure I'd want to see you risk finding out, Lana. I want you to find love, of course. I'd hate to watch you lose your thoughts to a noam, though. You wouldn't be the same and I love who you are." Tinnion put her arm back around Lana's shoulder. "There're lots of humans and dryad and other fae."

"I know... It's just, I never dream of lying curled up in a woman's arms. That's alright, isn't it?"

"Of course!" Tinnion laughed gently. "Just because I do, and the dryad do doesn't mean that's the only way to be. I enjoyed curling up with men before I met Cinerea. And no one in your family shares themselves with someone the same as them. People love who they love. Sometimes it's a forever love, sometimes it's just for a night." She winked with a wide grin. "If you like men more, then you find yourself a man. Just be careful. Men can get you into all kinds of trouble beyond the curse!"

The deep red light of the setting sun reflected on the ocean waves as the three fae companions talked on the dune. "We will need to come together and figure a way to stand against the sgàil. Their speed and their viciousness in battle makes them a formidable opponent and we will need to be at our best to defeat them." Shayell sat with the dryad pair on the water's edge.

"That is true, Shayell." Daowiel nodded slowly. "We will need the sylph and their speed too. They have a chance of taking the fight to the sgàil as we concentrate on defending Lana."

Cinerea's brow furrowed as Daowiel spoke. "But, surely, it is the Ògan that will defeat the shadows, your highness?" Daowiel opened her mouth to reply, but was interrupted by Shayell.

"I am confused. I have often heard the princess call Lana, Ògan, and took it as a term of endearment. Yet you, and other dryad, refer to her as 'The Ògan'. Is there something more important to the name that I am missing?"

Cinerea smiled. "The Ògan will lead the dryad to our freedom and restore to us our ancient homelands across Mortara. All trees will be ours once more and we will rule alongside the humans."

"You believe Lana carries a doom?" Shayell leant toward Cinerea, their head tilted slightly.

"The gods touch her, Shayell. That is clear for all to see. There is no doubt that she will cause the dryad's rise. In fact, it has already started. Our new accord with the humans is just the beginning and without the Ògan that would not be."

"It is superstition, Shayell, nothing more." The princess shook her head. "I watched Lana grow. I saw how she tried to talk to the trees. It made me laugh and made me curious, so I watched over her and see how she progressed. Some considered my curiosity a sign that she was part dryad, others thought she carried this doom. Lana is what she is, a young woman that has the unique ability to touch the lives of those she meets. We do not need to create prophecy and dooms to burden her with."

"But Cinerea's words would make sense of the obsidian ma..." Shayell began.

"That is something we will not discuss, Shayell. Not here. There will come a time to speak about it, but that time is not now." Daowiel's tone was commanding and caused Shayell to close their mouth fast.

Chapter Thirty-Three

TOLLS, THEFT AND TROUBLED MINDS

Brighid worried for her brother. Anndra had known Michiel throughout his life and trusted the man more than he trusted any other, even his own family. They had fought side by side in tournaments across Fearann a Tuath from the time they could hold their blades; he thought them invincible. And for good reason, only Brighid had ever defeated them in a tourney. The warrior's death at the claws of the baosith had left her brother shaken, both at the loss of his friend and the sudden realisation that death was real and could take him at any moment. He walked in silence, his face ashen, his eyes set in dark rings. She had tried to talk with him, to comfort him, but his grief made him lash out at her and her father had taken her aside. "Leave him be, Brighid. He needs time is all, give him that and he'll be right."

So she walked at his side, in silence, there to give support if he chose to accept it.

For two days they walked the highland road, cautious and quiet, Wren scouting ahead along the ridges above them. And then the path crossed the river. A wooden bridge spanning the gap between rises. Barriers had been erected along the bridge, spiked fences that narrowed the path, forcing them to walk in single file and in a zig zagging manner that left them vulnerable to attack.

On the far side of the bridge a half-dozen men, their clothes ragged and dirty, sat around a campfire cooking a meal in a large pot that hung over the flames. They reached for their weapons when they saw the survivors approach and formed a line at their end of the bridge.

"Hold there! There be a toll on this here bridge. Send the small one there with yer purses and ye can pass once we're clear." The larger of the men pointed a well beaten blade toward Neve.

MacAllister took the axe from his back and moved to the front of the group, a determined look on his face.

"Clear out! The lot of ye. Ye'll no be getting yer hands on anything we've got."

"Shoot the big oaf." The brigand signalled to the man on his left who obliged by sending an arrow through the air.

The shot was on target but weak, the man clearly lacking the strength to draw the bow fully, and MacAllister knocked the arrow from the air with ease. "Yer mine!" He broke into a run, Brighid close on his heels. Wren leapt to the bridges rail and ran at the brigands, beating two men down before MacAllister reached them and took the arm of the bowman with one swing of his axe.

The fight was over in no time; the bandits lying dead on the ground where they had stood.

A stew bubbled in the pot over the fire, spitting thick, hot water onto the flames with a hiss.

They came across a small stead two days later, a small Liath village with a few fields growing crops and a couple of barns. Taking to the hills, they waited for nightfall, keeping themselves out of sight; and as the moon rose, they crept into the stead, filling two packs with vegetables and fruit.

In another four days they came to the town of Dunhaever, a walled town as large as Freybridge and the seat of the holds gesith. The Liath lord, Tregaskis, had always been a man of honour but was not a warrior and had no banner men to call, only a few score sheriff. Sheriffs that had abandoned the hold to rebellion and locked the town's gates in fear.

"Tregaskis wis always the Tay's man. He'll no have sided wi the rebels, he'd die first. If I can get tae see him I ken he'll give us shelter and food." Cohade stood on the hilltop overlooking the town. His voice soft, almost weak and his shoulders hunched. Brighid could see her father's age for the first time weighing heavily upon him. She placed her hand on his shoulder and stood at his side.

"Then we'll get you in faither. We'll get you in tae see him."

They walked toward the town gate holding a holly branch aloft.

"Hold! Who approaches?" A sheriff appeared on the wall above the gate.

"Cohade MacFaern, lord of Lochmead and friend to Lord Tregaskis. I'd speak wi your gesith."

The sheriff disappeared without a word, leaving them stood on the road with no knowledge of what would happen next. In time they sat at the roadside, taking a drink in the shade of some trees. When a voice was heard again, Cohade smiled and stood.

"Cohade MacFaern? Is that you?"

"Aye, Tregaskis. It's myself and ma family. We're seeking shelter for the night and supplies. Will we find it here, old friend?"

"For the night only?" The gesith looked around the road, his eyes darting over the trees and rocks that might hide a person.

"Aye. One night only. We're heading tae the northern road and would nae be bothering ye fer more than ye can comfortably give."

"How many are you?"

"There's six of us. My bairns, MacAllister of Sindale, Neve, a healer frae Northfort and the lady Wren frae Iaswiytan."

"You all fought at Northfort? You fought against MacKenna?"

Cohade pulled his shoulders back, standing straight and strong. "Aye, we did that. We fought at Jendawyn's side and still stand wi the Queen and the oaths we all swore."

Tregaskis nodded, his jaw clenched. "Open the gate. Let them pass." He ordered the sheriffs below him.

The gesith's hall was bare, the food he served basic but his company was warm. He was a man suffering under the early days of the new regime, his outspoken support for the old Tay and his refusal to pander to oath breakers made him and his people a target for the self-proclaimed king. Though no force had been sent to his hold as yet, he believed it would only be a matter of time.

"We sent word tae the queen afore the siege began. We're hopeful she'll have sent an army north. We'll be takin' the road northeast ourselves, tae MacHuran in the hopes that he'll ride and we've a chance of meeting them. I'll no rest 'til MacKenna pays fer his crimes." Cohade took a drink of the warm ale that had been offered. "We'll not have oath breakers claiming position. Not If I can dae something tae stop it."

Tregaskis sighed. "I wish you the best Cohade, the death of Jendawyn was a blow and the death of honour in the north disgusts me. But I have no warriors I can send to help, no supplies I can gift to an army. I'll give you this advice. Some lords still stand against MacKenna. MacHuran, of course, up in Norhill and Devlin to the west in Glamithren. That might make a firm base from which to fight."

"Aye. That seems another potential move. Devlin's a good man right enough. Has MacKenna's force moved south o the rise at all?"

"No, not that my people have reported. Though he sent out a call to arms. He's strengthening his position, old friend. Removing him won't be a simple task."

Cohade slumped in his chair. "He has support?"

"He has fear, Cohade. Many Liath lords have heard the shadows have returned and stand with the Tuath. Our enemy and our protector stood as one. They'll do as they're ordered through fear. It was that kept them from answering your call."

"You'll not join him?"

"I'd die first, Cohade. I might not be a help in the war, but I won't break my oath. I'd never serve MacKenna."

They left Dunhaever with Tregaskis' best wishes and a promise to send word should MacKenna move through the pass and south of the rise. He provided packs full of food, bread, cheese, and a few vegetables. They were given new cloaks and bows and had their melee weapons sharpened. Then they joined the road northeast, more certain of their path and less worried of bumping into an army of MacKenna's men.

They left the road after three more days and walked due north across the wide glens to the hills around the sgàil mountains. Eight days after leaving Dunhaever, they climbed the first hills to the south of Norhill and looked out over the plains to the west. Smoke billowed into the skies from several directions, and their hearts felt heavy.

"The war is spreading." Anndra had barely spoken since the tower of Ebon Bluff. His voice was flat and listless.

"Then the queen'll have no choice, but tae send an army north. She'll not stand for this, I'm certain of that." Brighid sat on a rock by her brother. Her cloak wrapped tight around her to guard her from the wind.

"If he's burning the steads here, a few liath lords must have fallen or joined. We've nae hope here. We'd be best going south now and joining the road further on in hopes of meeting her army." The young warrior slumped to the grassy ground.

"No, we'll keep our path. We've a day 'til we reach the city and there's plenty of cover. We'll be safe, but we'll be able tae watch the road and be sure of what's happening. Fer all we ken, that's the queen's men fighting there already." Cohade's tone was final. He had made a decision and would brook no dissent.

Chapter Thirty-Four

A Sleepless Night

Progress slowed a little as the road began its gentle climb, leaving the beaches below them. The land to the east rose and fell in hills that seemed to echo the waves to the west. The ocean winds were cold and strong and brought with them rain that seemed to bite Lana's skin with its icy touch. She pulled the hood of her cloak further forward, restricting her view but giving her a little protection from the weather. Puddles grew along the road and a small stream flowed down the centre of their path as the rain fell without restraint.

As the sun, hidden from sight by thick grey clouds, began its descent and the world darkened, a noam from the scouting group approached.

"There are caves ahead, Shayell. They will provide a dry place to rest for the night and are easily accessible along a narrow path down the face of the cliff." The noam turned his face from Shayell to gaze at Lana.

"Will they shelter us all, Grant?" Shayell's voice was not as enthusiastic as the young noam's.

"They will, lord." The noam's gaze did not shift for a moment, his eyes set on Lana. Then he grinned and turned back to Shayell. "The closest entrance is narrow, but it opens out into chambers that would house double our numbers."

"Lana, Princess, would you take this opportunity or would you rather continue and hope to find other shelter?" Shayell turned to the companions, their face reddened by the icy winds.

Daowiel's face twisted. "I would rather not spend the night in a cave. There are trees on the hills and my laoch would be more comfortable within those. Perhaps we should find our own comforts tonight and regroup in the morning?"

Shayell nodded their agreement. "It would seem wise. We cannot stay in the open and the dryad would not find the same comfort in caves as my men do. Lana?"

Lana nodded. "I think you're right. We'll split tonight and come back together in the morning."

"Will you stay with us tonight, Lana? It would be good for my men to know that you will not always favour the dryad when our people split." Shayell's brows were raised, their tone suggesting that they felt it important. Lana nodded.

"I will, Shayell. If we need it. Shall we make our way? Tinnion..." She looked at the huntress with a smile.

"Actually..." Tinnion looked between her friend and her wife. "I may be able to stay with the dryad... I've been close recently."

"Oh." Lana's eyes widened in surprise. "I didn't know. That's wonderful!" She smiled and gave her friend a quick hug. "You'll be so comfy, Tin. I think you'll like it..." She looked between the dryad and Shayell for a moment, chewing her lip. "I'd join you normally, you know. I enjoy being within the trees. It's nice. But I should show the noam that I appreciate them too. They've come because of me, and I spend most of my time with you and the laoch."

Daowiel nodded at her. "You are our leader, Lana. You cannot be seen to favour one group over another. I understand that. I am sure that the noam will see that you are comfortable. Though we will miss your company."

"Next time we split, I'll stay with you. That's the best way I think."

The caves were dry and gave shelter from the wind. The noam got small fires going near fissures in the rock that channelled the smoke out of the cavern and Lana sat with Shayell beside one, her blanket wrapped around her as her cloak dried out on a rock.

"You and Daowiel have spoken a few times. I'm happy that you are getting along. Maybe there's a chance you'll be able to bring everyone together a bit more." Lana smiled at her friend.

"She is a good person, Lana. And we share a common friend. That helps when we talk. We are both here for you, and it gives us something to fall back on when we disagree on other things." Shayell nodded.

"Have you mentioned your..." Lana lowered her voice. "Your feelings?"

Shayell shook their head quickly. "No, not yet. I have thought to do that a few times now but could not when the moment comes. I will, in time, but most of our talks are on a different topic. Something I must keep private, for now. I am sorry."

Lana nodded her head slowly. "I understand. You all have things to do besides the things I'm involved in. I hope you know I'll help if I can though... Whatever it is."

"We both know this, Lana. Thank you." Shayell smiled, pulling food from their pack and offering some to their friend.

The cave was cold despite the fire and the stone was uncomfortable to lie on. Neither of these things seemed to bother Shayell or the other noam, and they slept happily, filling the cavern with their echoing snores. Lana, though, struggled to find sleep.

She lay by the fire, her blanket wrapped tight around her, and stared out into the darkness. Then she saw three noam stand and make their way together, deeper into the caves. Curious and frustrated with her inability to sleep, she stood and followed the men to see what they were doing. As she grew closer, she saw they had entered a chamber of the cave and had placed a small figurine in a hollow of the wall. They knelt before the figure and prayed.

Lana stepped back, and sat at the opening, her back against the stone and listened. She didn't understand the words spoken for a while, most were words spoken in the fae's language, but she realised after some time that the noam had stopped speaking in unison and were now speaking separately. Their voices were low and hard to hear, but they had switched to the common language of Mortara.

"We pray that our campaign in the north be successful, that our brothers be protected from death." Lana recognised the man that spoke as the noam that had reported the existence of the caves. A younger noam, taller than most and well muscled, he had the presence of a well-trained warrior which stood out as most of noam with them were men that could fight but had other occupations.

"By Khyione's will." The other two noam joined their voices to the prayer.

"We pray that our brothers in Southport continue to spread the word in our absence." Another of the noam spoke alone before the unison call of "By Khyione's will."

And so they spoke, each in turn, before finishing their prayer in unison. Several wishes were spoken. That their families be safe, that their god's strength and influence grow, that they would find honour and victory in battle, that they would live long and healthy lives filled with wealth. Prayers you might hear in any temple, wishes common to fae and human alike. And then she heard a prayer that made her stomach knot and jump.

"We pray that the females in our company find their place within our collars and homes." It was the large noam that spoke, the one named Grant. "By Khyione's will." The others chanted.

Lana stood, intending to move away from the makeshift temple and back to the fire. As she moved, a small pile of stone shifted and fell. She felt herself freeze and held her breath.

"Show yourself, spy." The voice was hard as iron.

Lana turned into the opening. "I'm not a spy. I was… I was just curious, is all. I'm going to go back to the fire now and get warm. Sorry if I disturbed you."

"And what will you say to Shayell when you get there?" A bulky noam to the right of Grant spoke, his voice full of gravel.

"Nothing. Why would I? You're just praying." Lana tried to push the last thing she heard from her mind. '*Khyione is gone anyway. The prayers don't make any difference when he's not here to hear them.*' She thought to herself. Then she caught the glint in Grant's eye and pulled her blanket around herself, trying to hide herself from his gaze.

"There is no need to worry, Okrem. She has nothing to say to the lord's mouthpiece. We have done nothing wrong in our prayers." Grant spoke to the noam on his right, but his eyes never left Lana's.

"I'm going now." Lana turned and made her way back to the spot where Shayell slept. Hoping the presence of her friend would be enough to comfort her and let her sleep despite the words that echoed in her mind. "That the females in our company find their place within our collars and our homes."

"Do the Southport noam still pray to Khyione?" Lana asked Shayell as she packed away her blanket.

"No, none of those outside Stonemount believe he can help them now that he is gone from our world. Why do you ask?" Shayell was too busy packing their belongings to see the surprise at his answer.

Lana shook her head. "No reason, I just wondered. I guess it's just seeing how comfortable you all are in the caves. Made me wonder if you still worshipped him." She felt no need to tell Shayell what she had seen. She knew her friend would just worry about the things that she had heard and would confront the three that had been praying. That would cause unrest, and Lana wanted to avoid that. Besides, she thought, it was all just wishes really and everyone wishes for something.

In no time at all, the noam had packed away their belongings and were heading back up the narrow path to the main road. The Wind still blew strong, but the sky was clear and the sun was drying the earth.

Lana watched from the road as the dryad emerged from the trees on the hills. Her aching back and heavy eyes made her wish that she had joined them and she promised herself that, given the choice, she would sleep in the trees next time.

Chapter Thirty-Five

A Gesith Falls

Five camp fires burned on the golden sands of the beach and the dinghies that carried the sylph to shore rowed back into the deep waters where their ship had anchored.

Lana sat around a fire with Shayell, Daowiel, Tinnion and Cinerea. A sylph lord, Liayol, sat with them, his face twisted with concern. "There was nobody living when we arrived. We buried those that were left in the streets and waited here. We did not want to camp near the village. Yorane was supposed to be here two nights ago. We were about to give up hope."

Lana frowned. "He was supposed to meet us here too and left days before us. I can't believe he would go somewhere else."

"His body was not with those we buried. If he was here, he was among those that have been taken. My sword is promised to you, lady, but I would see our brother freed or avenged."

Lana looked into the fire, the anger she had felt when she heard of the village's fate bubbled up in her again, threatening to boil over.

"We'll go straight to Glamithren and meet with Aelwynne and the army, then we'll make Siosal free the people he took and we'll make him pay for what he's done. Aelwynne will put him in a cell forever. I'm sure. We'll get Yorane free and we'll make Siosal pay. He'll never hurt anyone ever again, not ever. I won't let him."

They were two days from Glamithren. Lana and her close friends walking a few hours ahead of the fae army. Smoke and the sounds of panic filled the air, and they pushed themselves into a run. In moments, they came upon a farmstead being cleared and burned by soldiers. The occupants, mostly older people and children, were struggling against the armed men and losing their fight for survival. The sight horrified Lana. She had never seen something so callous, so inhumane. These people were innocent. They weren't warriors or criminals; they were guilty of nothing but the inability to pay a greedy lord what he insisted on having.

No one spoke, nothing needed to be said. The companions moved forward as one, drawing their weapons as they went.

Tinnion took out two of the soldiers before they knew they needed to defend themselves. Cinerea hit another with her arrow, and the man fell to the ground, the feathers protruding from his chest. As they grew closer, Lana, Daowiel and Shayell ran into a line of soldiers, sending the men to the muddy ground with ease. These soldiers were not the well-trained tuath that Lana had heard of. They didn't appear to be much more than thugs, fighting with the skill of men outside a tavern. Tinnion and Cinerea stood a little way back from the melee, sending arrows into the fray with precision.

The battle was over almost as quickly as it had started and the stead folk that remained bent over their fallen, desperately trying to revive them.

"What was happening here?" Lana asked an elderly lady that had cowered against a stone boundary wall.

"They said we was to burn all our homes to the ground, m'lady. Said there's an army coming, and they had to get rid of everything what they could use. We've got nothing else but our homes though, lady. So we was trying to protect them. Then they killed Tam, and it all went bad from there." The woman broke down into tears. "He was all mouth was Tam, but he was a good man. There was no need to be killing him for standing up to 'em. Look at 'em. Soldiers? Pah. Soldiers wouldn't be killing no bairns or older folk like me. What chance'd we ever have against men with swords?"

"I'm so sorry we didn't arrive sooner. There is an army coming, but they're coming to help, not to hurt people. They'd never have hurt you." She reached out a hand to the woman and helped her to stand. "Come on, I've some food and water in my pack and a cloak you can have. You need it more than me now." Lana turned to Shayell and shouted over to the noam. "Shayell! See if there's a building still good for these people to shelter in. And give them our food. We'll be fine without for one day, but these folks are desperate now."

"Lana!" Tinnion stood over an injured soldier and seemed angry. "They say the Gesith has Yorane. He's holed up in his castle with everything his people have grown or made all season and killed all those that are too old to serve him, or left them to starve to death."

Lana felt her anger build. She had been careful not to kill any of the soldiers. She'd beaten them instead, until they submitted or couldn't fight on. But the anger she felt toward Siosal was clouding her mind.

"It's time we went to see Siosal. Tell the warriors to be ready. I'm not letting him do this again."

"What of our meeting with Aelwynne and the army?" Daowiel placed her hand on Lana's shoulder.

Lana turned back to the villager. "That army is coming by here. The Queen's Voice is leading it. She's my friend and I'm supposed to meet her between the lakes. But I have to stop Siosal. I can't leave him another day. Not when he's doing this. We'll make sure you've got food and somewhere to sleep so's you're safe. When they come, can you tell them what has happened and that we've gone straight to Glamithren?"

The old lady nodded. "We'll tell yer friends where you're at, m'lady. Soon as they come by, we'll tell 'em, no fear. And we'll tell 'em how gracious ye've been too, m'lady. We'll not forget what you've done here."

The force Lana unleashed on the city gate sent a deafening crack across the plains. Heavy wood doors splintered into a million tiny pieces, flying into the courtyard beyond. The iron bars that had reinforced them fell with a loud clatter to the floor and a hundred nails flew through the air, killing the guards that had been behind them in the square in an instant of agony. The force of the exploding doors caused the wall above to crack with a deafening boom, sending the soldiers that had tried to prevent their entry into the city tumbling down its face and the hill below them.

Soldiers rushed into the city streets from buildings set against the walls, most unarmed, coming out into the night to investigate the deafening destruction that had disturbed their sleep. Those that were armed ran at Lana, but found only the butt of her staff and a quick slip into unconsciousness.

Rain pounded the stone slabs of the square, mixing with the blood of those that opposed her. A small river of rainwater and blood soon flowed to the gates.

Daowiel, Shayell and Tinnion drew their weapons and followed Lana as she walked over the debris into the city square. Tinnion unleashed arrows, and Daowiel moved ahead, her staff swirling and flashing in the light of the fading sun. Shayell, using their strength and their axe, sent men crashing to the floor in agony. Lana walked on, determined. She took the legs from under one man with a swing of her staff, sending him tumbling to the ground, then leant down and grabbed his tunic, growling at him through clenched teeth.

"Where are they? Where are the Gesith and his men?"

The man whimpered and spluttered, pointing up the hill toward the keep.

"The keep... They're up there in the keep."

She stood straight again and brought her staff down onto the man's forehead. Sending him to a darkness as deep as any night.

"Lana." Shayell called and Lana looked up from the unconscious soldier. They were surrounded. The chaos that had followed the destruction of the gate had subdued and been replaced by organised soldiers, all ready to take them captive or kill them. "Now!" Lana let out a cry that could be heard over the din of battle, and the air filled with arrows. Dozens, whizzing past their heads and into the soldiers that faced them. Chaos broke out as the fae army entered the city square and in moments, the defending soldiers fell or surrendered.

The sun was low in the cloud filled sky when they climbed the hill to the wall of the inner castle. The darkness and crashing thunder gave the companions cover as they made their way toward the gates.

Cinerea walked the perimeter with Tinnion looking for a place to enter that would not involve destroying the walls. They had left the army below in favour of stealth and surprise and hoped to get into the keep without too much destruction. Daowiel, Shayell and Lana stayed close to the large wooden doors of the entrance. It didn't take long before Lana heard the scrape of metal as the doors were unbolted and they readied themselves, prepared to attack whoever opened them. They smiled in relief as they realised it was Cinerea and Tinnion that stood on the other side. The couple had found a spot where the wall had crumbled and entered the courtyard, dispatching the two men guarding it quickly and silently. The five companions, now inside the walls, looked to the keep itself. A large stone building with narrow windows. Lanterns burned in every room, casting their faint light out into the courtyard. It sounded as though those within were feasting. Raucous laughter filled the square, and the companions moved toward the windows, peering through to see what they could see.

The room was long, with a heavy double door at one end, the only way in or out. Twenty-three soldiers, by Tinnion's count, were sitting around a long table with the Gesith at its head. They were drinking and eating and looked to be celebrating. The sight of them enjoying the spoils of their looting and destruction made Lana's anger rise again.

"If we get ourselves into the corridor on the other side of those doors, these men will be trapped. They'll have to answer to us." Tinnion spoke in a low whisper, one hand on Lana's shoulder.

"Why don't we just break through the windows here and shoot them all?" Cinerea asked. "Tinnion and I could have half of them dead before they knew what was happening."

Lana shook her head. "No, we should give them a chance to surrender themselves. We've killed too many already. I don't want to become what they are."

They moved to the main entrance, and Tinnion tried the door. It opened without a problem or a sound, and they entered the building cautiously. When they got to the double doors of the hall, Shayell threw them open with a clatter and stood with Lana in the opening.

Men shifted in their seats, reaching out for their weapons and stood.

"Sit down and leave your blades!" Lana commanded. "I am Lana Ni Hayal. Queen's lady, and I demand your surrender. You will pay for the deaths and anguish you have caused."

"We're no the queen's men, no more, lassie. There's a king in Northfort now and we're his men. Get yerself back tae the south and tell yer queen there's a new order in the North." The gesith spat his words through a half eaten leg of chicken and threw half a cup of ale into his mouth once he had finished.

"Your words are treason and your actions around your hold are evil. Surrender yourself and face trial."

"Or what? Lass, eh? What're you and yer wee friends there gonna do if I decide not tae?"

"We've taken the city. The prisoners and slaves you took are being released and I've an army behind me. You've lost, Siosal. All that's left to decide is how you'll pay. Surrender and you'll live."

"I'll no surrender, lass. You might think ye can come here and kill me, but I'll see you die afore I do."

Lana didn't have a chance to respond. An arrow, wrapped in cloth and set aflame, whizzed past her ear and embedded itself into the tapestry behind the gesith's chair. In a moment, the wall was ablaze and the soldiers in the room were moving toward them with swords in hand. Two more arrows buzzed past Lana's ears. One dug into the shoulder of the Gesith the other into the hand of the closest soldier. He dropped his sword and held his bloodied hand up to his face, now a mask of pain.

"There's no need for you to die here. Put your swords down and surrender yourselves." Lana's tone was commanding and confident. The gesith, though, screamed orders to attack, and the men pushed forward. Shayell stepped in front of Lana, their axe gripped tightly in both hands and raised, ready to strike. It was their boot that met the chest of the first onrushing soldier though, and he staggered backward with the force of the kick, falling into the man behind him.

Two more arrows flew into the room, this time aimed to kill.

With the fire taking hold of the walls and the arrows flying, the soldiers quickly turned their energies from wanting to fight to trying to scramble to safety. A chair was thrown through one window, smashing the lead glass to the courtyard stone below. With the rush of air, the flames grew and the gesith's robes caught fire. One soldier threw himself through the hole in the stone wall, only to be met with the end of Daowiel's staff to his forehead.

The gesith screamed. "Alright, alright, we're done. Let us out, we'll no fight ye." He was ripping the tunic from his body as he spoke, trying desperately to escape the flames. There was a clatter of swords hitting the flagstone floor, and the soldiers all placed their hands to their heads. Shayell and Lana stepped aside, and the soldiers walked in single file out into the courtyard, where Daowiel and Cinerea waited for them.

The gesith was on the floor, crying and rolling, half naked and red from the flames. Lana grabbed a pitcher from the table and threw its contents over him, then grabbed his ear and dragged him, sobbing, from the room. Once outside, he was tied and bound to a thick wooden post and left to cry himself to a peaceful state.

With the fighting over, they moved back down the hill with their prisoners, now bound, and joined the fae army in the city. The keep burned behind them, filling the air with smoke and flame.

Chapter Thirty-Six

A Gesith Revived

The fae army had been busy in the city while Lana and her friends took the keep. The Sylph had found out where the prisoners were being held and freed those that had been taken from steads across the hold. Yorane had been amongst them and was now with Liayol and an elderly man at a table in the main square. A platter of food had been served and a pitcher of ale, and he was eating as though he hadn't had the chance for days.

As Lana approached with Siosal, bound in tow, the old man struggled to his feet.

"That's him! Guard! Take that bastard to the cells!" Two of the towns guard stood near the man and jumped to attention and made their way toward Lana.

She let go of Siosal's ear, letting him drop to the cobblestone, and drew her staff. "Hold your place. There's no one going to the cells until I say so."

"Take him! Do it now! This child is not your gesith." Lana looked to Shayell, and the noam stepped over their prisoner, guarding him from the soldiers.

"I am the queen's lady, Lana Ni Hayal, and the gesith is my prisoner. I'm going to see him pay for his crimes and I'm going to see this city put back to normal, but I'll be doing it in my time."

"Lana." Yorane stood. He was dirty and looked tired. His voice was strained and low. "Lana, this is Lord Devlin, the true gesith of Glamithren. That man was the head of his guard. He rebelled and took the city in MacKenna's name when the rebel named himself king of the northern lands. He was never Gesith, except in MacKenna's court."

Lana bowed her head. "I'm sorry, Lord. I wasn't told these things, only that Siosal was gesith. The queen's voice is on her way, at the head of an army, she will be here soon. I'd like to help you put things right where I can, if you'll let me, me and my friends."

"Your friends?" The old man raised his brow. "A human girl at the head of a fae army. As I live and breathe, I never thought I'd see the like." The man sat back down, his legs too weak to hold him. "Well, Lana Ni Hayal. You've destroyed my gates and my wall and by the looks of it, you've raised my keep in flame. Is this the kind of help you usually give?"

Lana narrowed her eyes and bit her cheek. "When it's needed, Lord. And it *was* needed. We did what we had to. If we'd waited for the queen's army and taken the city with catapults and siege towers, it would have been a lot worse."

"She's fiery, your friend." The gesith turned to Yorane.

"Yes, Lord. Full of fire, but deeply earnest and filled with caring as well. She would see no harm done to any that did not force her hand, nor damage done that could be avoided." Yorane's face was as serious as the guards that stood before her.

"Come and join us then, Lana Ni Hayal, and tell me why you took it upon yourself to burn down my home." The old man gestured to a seat beside Yorane. "Bring more food and drink!"

The fae worked hard the following day to patch what they could and by sunset, the gatehouse and wall were defendable once more. The keep would take time to repair and rebuild, but the noam and dryad did what they could. In the meantime, the true gesith was housed at the inn, along with Lana and her closest friends.

Siosal had been imprisoned, along with his cohorts, and word was sent around the hold's steads that those whose homes were burned out by the traitor would be welcomed in the city.

Lord Devlin, it turned out, had been a good man and an honourable gesith. He had always cared for those in his hold, and his outrage at the actions of Siosal was clear. He wanted the pretender dead and Lana knew that once she was gone, he would most likely have his way.

"I wanted him dead too, Lord. I wanted to kill him, to make him suffer like he made all those people suffer. But I can't be like him. I can't kill someone that isn't fighting or able to hurt anyone. Put him to work, make him rebuild the things he destroyed. Make him work in the fields to feed the families he broke. Killing him won't help anyone, not now." Lana stood before the gesith's seat in his makeshift court at the inn. "Making him do some good is probably the worst punishment as you can give him. He'll hate every moment of it." She took a deep breath and watched the elderly gesith as he considered her advice. His face thin and drawn. Then he chuckled, a merry little laugh cut short by coughing and a few moments of wheezing before he spoke again.

"I like this one, Yorane. If I were half the age I am, I'd be making her my wife." He smiled at the sylph warrior that had become his closest friend.

"There would be a line to join, Lord. If she showed any signs of taking a husband." Yorane nodded.

"Well, I'm not young enough now, anyway. Still, I like her. She'd make a good gesith, I'll wager, too. Perhaps she'll let me make her my heir, if not my wife?"

"I'm not really wanting to be a gesith, lord, or anyone's wife. I just want to go north and make sure my friends are alright." Lana played with the hem of her tunic as she spoke. Her cheeks turning a soft shade of red.

"And let's say they are, lass, and let's say you win this war and save the north for the queen. What then?"

"Then we all get to go home and be happy. And you'll be safe again in your city, with your people." Lana smiled.

The gesith shook his head, his hand to his mouth as he coughed. "No, lass. That's not the way it'll be for me or my people. I'll be dead afore you turn tae your home again. I'm an old man and my jail has made me ill. Ach, maybe the queen's voice'll have a say when she gets here. But I've no line tae hand my seat to now and I'll be wanting tae know the one that takes my place is as good as yerself." He stopped to take a drink from his cup. "Anyway. Aye, I like your plan. I'll have Siosal work the fields with a chain on his ankles and wrists. He'll no run nor cause trouble, and he'll feed a few before he dies." He nodded as he spoke, then sat back in his seat and closed his eyes for a moment. "I think I'll take tae ma bed a while."

Yorane called over a maid, and between them they helped the gesith to his room.

The sun was at its height on their third day at Glamithren when the horns sounded. Lana rushed to the gate with Shayell and watched as the queen's army marched up the road to the city.

The streets quickly filled with city folk and fae, and a cheer rang through the crowds as Aelwynne and Crurith rode to the main square. Lana and the Noam guiding them to the inn.

"I told you to stay out of trouble, Lana."

"I know, Aelwynne, and I'm sorry. I really am. But I had to do something. I couldn't stand by and watch as he kept killing." Lana sat at the crowded table opposite her mentor. The cities gesith at its head.

"Now, now, Aelwynne. Don't be harsh on the lass. She saved my city and my life, much as it is now. I've nothing but gratitude tae her." Lord Devlin spoke to Aelwynne like he'd known her throughout her life, and the queen's voice lowered her head.

"I'll have my medics help you, Devlin. There's plenty of life in you yet." Aelwynne placed her hand lightly on top of the mans. "And I won't be too hard on Lana. I worry for her, that's all. She's proven herself dear to a great number of people, and the queen would never forgive me if anything happened to her."

The old man nodded. "Aye, I was ready tae tear a strip off her myself when I saw she'd set my keep a hold. But the lass is a treasure, right enough. She'd melt any old man's heart, sure as she did mine." He turned to Lana with a smile. "Though she's cunning too, she'll be a danger tae any daft enough tae stand against her. I don't think ye've tae worry too much on her safety, Aelwynne."

"But I do, Devlin. I do. She's still young enough to be naïve, and we're heading into a war. If half of what I've heard is true, there's no chance of the peace we hoped to secure."

The old man looked around the table to the people gathered there. Daowiel sat to Lana's right, Cinerea and Tinnion to hers. Beyond them sat Shayell and Grant, completing that side of the table. To his left sat Aelwynne and Yorane, with Liayol beside him. Then Qilan, the army's commander and Crurith, who Tay Gathwyn had insisted guard his daughter. There was political power and strength of arms around the table, and the old man smiled.

"You've grown up a great woman, Aelwynne. Yer father and the queen must be so proud. And you'll win this war, nae doubt, with this army at yer back you'll win." He put his hand to his mouth and coughed, a dry cough that made Lana's throat tingle. "Aye, but at what cost, lass? At what cost? You'll need tae look out for yourself as much as ye do for the bairn here. These aint no honourable people yer heading toward. Ye cannot trust them tae behave as you would." The man patted her hand lightly and sighed. "I've known ye since before ye could talk, Aelwynne. And I've known yer father thrice as long as that. So you'll forgive me for what I'm going tae say." He wheezed as he spoke, his chest rising and falling as he struggled to fill his lungs. "Let yer men go North, let them lead the army and pull Northfort tae the ground. Have them kill all those within. But get yerself home, lass. You and yer wee friend. Or stay here where it's safe. You've no place in a battle neither one of you. There's no talks tae be had, not with MacKenna. The lass could take my seat when I'm gone. She'd do well here when there's peace."

They sat for a moment in silence, Aelwynne's hand between the lords.

"You aren't going anywhere, old man. I forbid it and I'm the Queen's Voice. You have to do as I say." A tear fell across Aelwynne's cheek. "And we'll be just fine, both of us. All of us. We'll come and eat a celebration meal with you on our way home. When we've won the day. So you'd better have plenty of wine and food ready!"

They stayed another night in the city of Glamithren. Aelwynne spent a large portion of it alone with the gesith, discussing old times and future plans. Amongst other things, she arranged for a healer to stay behind and care for the man when they departed. Though not nymph, the army healers were among the best in Mortara and the old lord needed that if he was to live, despite Aelwynne's order to do just that.

Shayell, Daowiel, Cinerea, Tinnion, Yorane and Liayol spent the evening locked in a room, deep in discussion, leaving Lana feeling alone and at a loss.

"I am sorry, Lana. You know I do not mean to exclude you. Sadly, there are things that I must discuss with my fellow fae that cannot yet be shared." Daowiel's hand was on Lana's arm as she spoke, a gentle touch that highlighted the princesses genuine sadness at excluding her friend.

"Well, if it's between fae, can I at least spend time with Tin?"

The dryad shook her head. "With Tinnion bound to Cinerea, she will have a sense of what is being said. It is better she hears all than is left guessing and making more of it than it is."

Lana sighed. "I'll just go explore a little then. There were some old-looking ruins on one of the hills close by that seemed interesting. I'll go see if there's anything to find there." Lana smiled, thinking back to the colourful stones she found at the ruins of Lochheart.

"You shouldn't be leaving the city alone, Lana." Tinnion gave her friend a concerned look.

"I'll be alright. It isn't far and there were plenty trees nearby. If there's anything bad around, I can hide away or come back here to the inn's gardens."

"It pleases me, Lord Liayol, that the council chose to send one of their own alongside your warriors. That makes what we have to discuss a little easier." Princess Daowiel sat at the head of the table and took early control of the proceedings.

"When we heard of the alliance that was forming here, we decided that this was too important an event to leave solely to our warriors. This meeting, you have called, makes me think it may be even more important than we considered." The sylph spoke evenly and calmly.

Daowiel nodded. "What we speak of here cannot leave this room. In time, it may become necessary, but as things are, we must not share anything that is said. Are we in agreement?"

The fae nodded slowly as one, each looking around the table to check they weren't alone in their agreement.

"As we fought the creature, we now call the 'obsidian man'. He said one thing that disturbed us. Up to now, only Shayell, Selene and I have been aware of this, but I believe it is important enough that I make the leaders of our forces here aware. It will no doubt affect our preparation and tactics for the battle that we face."

"You have us intrigued, princess. What ramblings of a murderous creature could be so important?" Yorane sat back in his chair, his arms crossed across his chest.

"One word, Yorane, one word that might change all we know. Piuthardia."

"I don't understand, your highness, what does it mean?" Tinnion's head tilted, her brow furrowed.

"In your tongue? Perhaps divine sister, perhaps sister god? But to whom was it said?" Liayol's eyes were wide at hearing the word.

"To Lana."

"The young woman that leads us?" The sylph lord's brow furrowed. "But she is little more than a child, one that has excelled with your teaching, princess, for sure but nevertheless, little more than a child."

"No, she is The Ògan, lord." Cinerea interjected.

"But then what is this creature and what does it mean by the word? The gods have departed or they are dead. There were eight, and eight alone." Liayol placed a finger to his chin.

"In truth, we do not know." Daowiel's voice became soft. "But this creature is not human nor fae. We have no records of anything like it, neither us dryad nor the noam or indeed the library in Southport. It is possible that it is related to the gods. His naming of Lana as sister, though, is what concerns me most. We know she has shown herself capable of feats only the firstborn dryad have ever achieved. And she has shown signs she is capable of things only sylph can do."

The princess looked around the table at those gathered and smiled. "Whatever he meant by it, she will always be Lana, always the child that touched our hearts. We came here because our love for her meant we felt a need to protect her. But she is, undoubtedly, more than we know. We must not fail to protect her. No matter the cost. We must all be prepared to give our lives for hers."

"Should we not then involve the humans in this? The queen's voice, at least."

"I don't think they are ready to hear it, Yorane. I know Aelwynne well enough to know that she will do all she can to see Lana safe without this knowledge. And I feel we should try to understand it more ourselves before confusing the humans with talk of new gods."

"New gods?" Tinnion's jaw dropped. "Are you really saying Lana is a god?"

"No, Tinnion. At least, I do not believe that she is. Only that we must ask ourselves the question. Why would this creature call her that?"

Chapter Thirty-Seven

REVELATIONS

It was late when Lana returned to the inn, and her friends had already eaten. She slumped on the bench next to Tinnion and took a piece of bread from the platter on the table centre before pouring herself a cup of wine. "All these hills make walking so tiring." She huffed as she spoke. "Is there any flat land between here and Northfort?" Tinnion laughed and pulled her friend toward her, wrapping her arm around her shoulder. "Now you know how your horse feels, Lana... And worse, it has to carry you as it climbs!" Lana pushed the huntress away playfully and pouted. "Well, my horse is better off than some..." She chuckled and threw Shayell a glance, sticking her tongue out at the noam.

"Well, I have never been so insulted!" The noam laughed. "This must be why the Stonemount noam forbid their women to speak."

"And that's why the Stonemount noam are all stuck down in dingy caves. If they let the women rule, they'd be living in lovely houses with cosy beds and sofas. I'm sure they'd be a lot happier for it, too."

"You are right, Lana." Shayell smiled. "I cannot disagree with you. I find my house and bed so much more comforting than a cave."

"So, how was your secret meeting? Have you planned on how to take over the world?" Lana screwed her lips to the side.

"Oh, no, Lana. You will not catch us out so easy!" Daowiel grinned. "We were just making sure we had enough honeyed buns to keep you going through the rest of the journey. The planning that task takes is far too difficult for one person alone."

Lana rolled her eyes. "Well, I don't need to know your secrets, anyway. I know lots of things too... But... Are there any honeyed buns?" She looked around the table hungrily.

The corridor on which her room was located was narrow and dimly lit. Her legs felt heavy, and she stumbled as she walked. The late night, the hill walk and the wine she had gulped down combining to make her unsteady.

"You should not drink so much."

She turned at the sound of the deep, gravelly voice.

"Oh... Grant? I'm fine. Just tired. I didn't drink that much." Lana leant against the wall as the momentum of her turning almost toppled her to the floor. The noam took her elbow, his grip gentle but strong, and helped her stand upright.

"Then you should not drink at all. You clearly struggle to deal with the effects of wine."

Lana's eyes narrowed, and she scowled at the noam. "I'm fine! And I'm the queen's lady, so you need to be more m'lady-ish and less judgy." She staggered a little as she lifted her eyes to meet his, and he shifted his hand to her back to keep her upright.

"The title you have been given is of no importance. You are drunk and need to be in your bed. If you were mine, I would ensure that you did not become so helpless on wine."

"I'm not a child for you to put to bed and I'm not yours!" She balled her fist and weakly hit the noam's chest. Grant snorted.

"Khyione will see that you become what you are destined to be. You cannot escape the fate our father created for you. Come, I will take you to your bed before you injure yourself." The noam moved around her and half carried her to her room. Lifting her as they entered and placing her on the bed with ease. "When you have enough of your senses back, you should take a cup of water. That will help keep you from suffering too much in the morning."

Lana looked up at the noam. His grey eyes looked soft and warm in the dim light of the room. She sighed and hit his chest again.

"Stoppit. Stop talking to me like that. I'm a woman, not a child, and definitely not a thing you can own."

Grant gently moved her hand from his chest and pulled her blanket over her legs. "Listen to me, Lana Ni Hayal. The accord prevents me from simply taking you now as mine, and perhaps that is a good thing. But I believe that my god created you and your kind for a purpose and I believe he will see you bound. In time you will wear a collar, Lana, you will be bound to a noam and when you are, you will learn the lore of Khyione. Then you will understand why I talk to you so, and you will feel pride at being bound." Grant stroked a finger across her cheek, then poured a cup of water from the pitcher by her bed and held it to her lips. "Drink."

Lana took the cup from the noam and gulped down its content. "Thank you. But I'm still not your possession." She gave the noam a stare before lying down and turning on her side, her back to him.

"In time, that may change, Lana. By Khyione's will."

When Lana woke, she still felt tired. Her head was a little foggy but not so bad that she felt ill. She poured herself a cup of water and gulped it down as though she hadn't had a drink in a week. She saw the figurine as she put the cup back on her nightstand. A small figure of Khyione, shaped in jade. She felt her stomach knot and her hand went to her shoulder as Grant's words came back to her. Why did men keep insisting on trying to own her? Why couldn't they just love her like Andel does with Ara?

Her friends had eaten and left the inn when Lana came down for her breakfast. Only Aelwynne was still in the hall. "Your friends have taken a walk, Lana. They seem to get on well, a good sign for the future, I hope. Would you join me for breakfast?" Lana smiled and sat next to her mentor. "Yeah, they seem to be setting their differences aside. It makes me happy to see them getting on. Maybe we can get them to sign agreements with each other when all this over."

"That would be good, Lana. But I wouldn't put any pressure on them. It's surprising enough as it is that they haven't started fighting each other. Are you well enough to travel today? I heard you stumble in the corridor last night."

Lana lowered her head. "I'm fine. I didn't drink a lot... It's just that I got back too late to eat and the wine went straight to my head. I should have known better."

Aelwynne laughed. "Not to worry, it will be a brief ride today. The sun is already high and I don't want to push too hard. It's been nice having a proper bed to sleep on these last few nights, and it's good to see Lord Devlin again. He and my father have always been close."

"It was funny to see someone talking to you like he does. It's the way people talk to me too, like you're still little. Everyone else seems scared of you."

"Most people see my title instead of me. Sometimes it's nice to be with someone that doesn't." Aelwynne nodded with a smile.

"Do I do that? Treat you more like a title, I mean? I want to be respectful to you cos I really appreciate what you teach me, but I like you too. I'd like to be your friend..."

"You're fine, Lana. Sometimes it's best that you remember what I am and not think of me as a friend. When we're in talks or in meetings. Not that we can't be friends... That we aren't friends. But we have to be professional, especially when others can see us or hear us. You understand that, don't you?" Lana nodded quietly and then the server brought a platter of fruit and one of her sticky buns and Lana smiled, her eyes wide.

They stopped for the night in a valley and went about setting up camp. When their chores were done the fae leaders gathered to talk again, so Lana went for a walk.

She found the noam sat in a circle of stones on a hilltop to the west of the camp and threw the jade figurine to the grass at his feet.

"You left this behind."

The noam grinned. "I asked Khyione to watch over you as you slept."

Lana furrowed her brow and snorted. "I don't need you asking your god to look over me. It's not your place. You aren't even supposed to be praying to Khyione, anyway. Shayell said noam outside Stonemount don't do that."

Grant rolled his eyes. "Neither Shayell nor his lord know their people well. There are many New Khyionists in Southport, our numbers grow with each year. Shayell follows his father's rules. Dismissing the lore of Khyione to live in deference to humans. We do not. It is possible to live with humans, to follow those laws set out in the accord and still follow Khyione's Lores of living. In time you will understand that, you may even pray at my side." He picked up the figurine from the grass and held it out to her. "It is a gift, a token of my intentions, a reminder of the truth."

"Your prayers don't make what you're saying my 'truth'. No matter how much you pray, your god can't make me be what I'm not." Lana scowled at the fae.

The noam smiled. "I do not intend to make you what you are not. Khyione created you to serve. All humans were created for that purpose. You may be a lady and wear tokens of power and clothes that set you apart from those females in collars, but you're no different from those. You were created in the same way as the first female, and you will serve as that one served. That is Khyione's will." He looked at the figurine in his outstretched hand. "And Khyione's will has brought you to me here. Here, to one of his altars."

Lana looked around her at the standing stones. Tall and wide, they formed a circle that surrounded the hilltop. In the west stood an altar stone stood, inscribed in weather worn runes. The words of Khyione, his lore, passed on to his noam for tens of thousands of years. She felt her chest tighten, her stomach felt suddenly empty.

"Now you see the truth in my words, I think. You know the reason Khyione created women, gave them life. You know what you are."

"The last man that wanted to own me died when he tried to claim me." She crossed her arms in front of her chest, her hands on her shoulders.

"You killed him?" The noam cocked his head.

"No..." Lana lowered her head and her voice. "He was trampled by a bull."

Grant laughed, a deep laugh. "There are no bulls here. And I am not trying to claim you. If it is Khyione's will, you will kneel and take my collar. You will pray beside me and receive our god's blessing. I have asked it and believe that Khyione will make it so." He stood and stepped toward her, towering over her, his left hand reaching to a large leather pouch at his belt. "You feel Khyione's will even now. Our god has brought you to me once more at his shrine. You try to fight, but you know in time it will happen. It's in your heart. You know it to be true. You know you will be mine." His left hand moved from the pouch, a jade collar in his grip, the tight linked chain of the leash dangling from his fingers.

Lana tilted her head back to look him in the eye and pressed her hand flat to his chest. She felt his strength beneath her palm. He was as solid and unmovable as the stones that surrounded her and almost as large. She felt her mouth open to shout at him, to tell him he was wrong, but no sound came out and she shook. Her stomach knotted.

"You're silent, Lana. Does that mean you accept the truth?"

Lana shook her head quickly, unable to speak. Her breathing hastened, and she felt a heat building in her face. The noam lifted the collar, holding it to her face so that she could see it clearly. The rounded edge looked soft and she could see no join in the smooth stone band. She swallowed hard, pushing her hand against his chest, with little effect. She tried to step back, away from the noam, but her feet wouldn't move. Her hand went to his, and she shook her head again, slowly, her eyes wide and pleading.

"You feel it. I see that in your eyes. You feel Khyione's will, you want to be mine. Look at me." His right hand moved to her face, and he wiped a tear from her cheek. "Do you deny my words? Can you deny my will?"

Lana didn't answer. She looked into his eyes, grey but warm, as warm as his hand against her cheek. She had been drawn here as she walked through the valley, though she hadn't expected to find the noam. When she had seen him she had paused, watching him, her fingers playing and rubbing, absent-mindedly, against the figurine in her purse. He was large and strong, even for a noam. His dark grey hair, almost black, reached below his shoulders despite being plaited and tied. His voice was soft, yet commanding, and Lana found herself being drawn into his prayers as he sat before her. It had been the memory of his declaration and his desire to own her that had snapped her back into the moment and made her throw the jade figure at his feet. But now he was standing before her, his rich voice causing her stomach to flutter, his strong, warm hand caressing her cheek. His scent, like patchouli, filled her nostrils. She felt her knees weaken and swayed toward him, her hand leaving his to steady herself once more against his chest. Her forward movement brought her head closer to him and his hand moved to her back, his fingers moved gently up her spine. The collar opened with a soft click, the left side of it hanging against the noam's forearm.

Grant moved his right hand toward the open section of the collar and brought it around Lana's neck.

"Don't, please don't." Her words were weak, her voice quiet and shaking. "Please." The noam stopped and looked into her eyes.

"Do you deny Khyione's will? Do you deny that you are meant to be mine?"

She raised her hands back to his, holding his wrists but not attempting to pull them away from her. "Yes, I need to be free. I need to stand with my friends."

"That is not a denial of your feelings." The noam's voice was soft, almost a whisper.

Lana wanted to pull his hands away from her. She wanted to say that she had no feelings for him, wanted to tell him he was wrong, that she felt nothing but repulsion. She wanted to push him away and run back to the camp. She needed to be free; she needed to fight to make the world right again; she needed to be at her friends' sides, to laugh with them again, to be close to them again. Her eyes closed. She couldn't say the words or pull away.

Perhaps he was right? She had been drawn to him twice now, drawn to Khyione's sacred spaces. She felt a desire within her growing now that she was close to him. A desire to be held by him, a desire to feel his arms wrapped around her. His words in the cave had scared her, his certainty of her binding made her angry. But she saw the collar in his hand, she felt the warmth of his body; she felt his strength and his soft voice filling her mind and she felt calmed, lulled.

The wind picked up, and thunder crashed over the valley. Rain poured from grey clouds that had not been there when she climbed the hill and washed over Lana's head, clearing her mind. The feelings that were growing within her were gone, replaced by the cold, hard truth of the moment. If she did not move away, if she did not deny him and her feelings, he would close his collar around her neck, he would have her pray with him and he would bind her. The curse of Khyione would be on her and she would change. She would be his, her mind would be filled with his thoughts, his will would overcome hers. Lana pushed at the noam and the man, that a moment ago felt as immovable as a mountain, staggered backward.

"I am not yours. I will never be owned, not by you, not by any noam or any man. Not by Khyione himself. So you can pray, Grant. Pray every day to your god, but you'll never have what you want." She took a deep breath and turned, running down the hill and back towards the camp.

Chapter Thirty-Eight

Shadows in the Night

The hastily built bridge over the river Alawe was crude and unstable, uneven boards and logs barely held with rope moved in the rapids.

"It would be a miracle if this bridge held long enough for even a small part of the army to cross." Shayell groaned and shook their head. "It would be wise to secure the town and the path down to the plains with a small force, then my noam and I will create a new crossing. There is more than enough good stone here to work with. I doubt it would take too long."

"We can do it." Lana looked to Aelwynne. "Me and my friends can go over with the other dryad and sylph and start creating defences."

"I don't know that I want you over that side without the army, Lana." Aelwynne let out a sigh as she spoke, as though she knew her objection would be brushed aside.

"I'll be fine. We'll set a watch and we'll be able to see anyone coming for miles. Besides, it makes sense for the fae to start it. The dryad can build better defences than the army, and the sylph can keep watch and move around the rocks much better than any human could."

The queen's voice nodded. "Of course, it makes sense. You're not to go anywhere near the plains though, Lana. You're either in the town or in the camp here. Nowhere else. That is an order."

"Yes, Aelwynne." Lana nodded. "Just the town and here. I'll not go anywhere else unless it's really, really important."

Aelwynne shook her head. "No... If anything important comes up, you come and tell me before you do anything. This is really serious, Lana. Those people are warriors and killers. They're the best warriors in Mortara, and they're at war with us. Regardless of any peace we hope to achieve, right now we're at war."

"I understand, Aelwynne." Lana nodded.

The waytown was abandoned, wreckage strewn in the street, doors kicked off their hinges and furniture smashed. There had been a half-dozen men there recently, watching the crossing, no doubt, but they were gone before the fae crossed the river. Lana and her friends watched as they rode across the plains below, sending dust into the air as they pushed their horses to a gallop.

"They'll be in Northfort in two or three days if they keep that pace, a day for MacKenna to consider the news and four days to get his force here... We're on a schedule now." Tinnion's eye's never left the fleeing men.

"Do you think he will bring his army out of the fortress?" Yorane sounded surprised.

"I know nothing about the man, Yorane, but I'm sure he knows enough to know that the fortress is a cage when it's surrounded. They did not design it to stand a siege by a full army."

"Then we have the advantage. We hold the high ground and we have a supply line that he cannot reach to interrupt. If he comes to us, we will win this."

"He'll have been gathering more warriors. The liath lords and others will have turned or fallen the way Glamithren did. I imagine he'll have twice our number. There is even a chance he could have three or four men to each of ours." Tinnion stood between Lana and Cinerea, her arms linked with theirs.

"I will have stakes placed along the path down to the plains. They will not find the road up to the town easy." Daowiel's face was serious, with no hint of her usual playful smile.

"Can the laoch build catapults or trebuchet, Princess?" Liayol's eyes seemed fixed on something in the distance.

"I do not know these things, Liayol. But if you can show us how, my laoch can build whatever wooden defences and weapons we need."

"I can show you." Tinnion responded. "If we can do that, we can drop rocks on them while we're safe up here. They might just give up before we even meet."

"That would be a good thing." Daowiel nodded.

Being first to cross the river meant that the responsibility for cleaning up the town fell on Lana and those friends that were not involved in setting up the defences. It wasn't something that she did with much enthusiasm, but, with the help of those sylph not on patrol and Tinnion, it only took a couple of days. And being first did have its advantages. Once the inn was clear, Lana and her friends got first pick of the rooms. Lana convinced Daowiel to share with her, Cinerea and Tinnion shared a room, as did Liayol and Yorane. The other dryad all slept in a small woodland to the east of the town. A woodland filled mostly with pine trees, old and tall, and yet they had never known the company of the dryad. The sylph took over a couple of houses, though most of them spent their time outdoors around the cliff edges.

Six days passed, and the noam had created a new, sturdy stone bridge across the river. The bulk of the army camped at the foot of the rise within a wooden wall erected by the dryad. Further defences were set along the road and those parts of the cliff that were potentially climbable. A palisade was set around the town itself and the commander organised patrols. The waytown had become a small fortress and though it paled against the fortress city of Northfort, it felt secure; it felt safe, despite the army that they knew was marching toward them.

That army had been clearly visible on the plains for a day, their campfires had been visible two nights before. It had grown since the taking of Northfort and now numbered close to four thousand. A size advantage that had given MacKenna the confidence to leave his fortress and march toward his enemy.

The moon was high and full and the skies were clear. Lana's breath plumed before her and she pulled her cloak tight to keep off the chill. She stood on the cliff edge, looking out across the plain. Camp fires burned on the horizon a half day's march away.

Movement on the plains below caught her eye. It was too dark to make out what was causing it, but the long grass and the shrubbery was moving against the wind. Lana watched for a moment, trying to figure out what she was seeing.

"Yorane!" The sylph was walking through the town square with another sylph when Lana called and the two ran to her side. "There's someone moving down there. Look. Between the apple tree there and the rock." Lana pointed to the spot her eyes had not left in minutes.

"I do not see... wait! You are right, there is something, an animal perhaps?" Yorane stared out into the darkness for a moment. "No... That is not an animal, Lana. That is sgàil."

"A shadow assassin." His companion whispered. "Come." The sylph tugged at Yorane's arm and then leapt off the cliff edge. Yorane turned to Lana. "Stay here..." and then followed his friend to the plain below.

Lana watched as the warriors glided to the plains beneath them, as elegantly as geese in flight. Then another movement caught her eye. Off to her right, a second assassin moved through the long grass. She opened her mouth to shout to the warriors below but closed it as quick with a sigh. They couldn't hear her, not from this distance, and even if they could, the sgàil would be alerted and would run. Lana closed her eyes tight and took a deep breath, then, as steam plumed from her mouth, she opened her eyes and leapt.

She hadn't tried to glide from such a great height before, and the rush as she fell made her stomach leap into her throat. She spread her arms wide as she had seen the sylph do and glided silently to the area in which she had seen the sgàil. Having landed without a sound just a metre away from the source of the movement, Lana crept forward, the handle of her staff in hand.

A pair of shadow assassins picked their way across the base of the rise, ghosting through the darkness. Their pitch black leather armour making it difficult to keep them in sight. At their belts hung a pair of vicious looking black bladed knives. Each one, she imagined, set to be used in the assassination of one of her friends.

Lana's staff grew in silence as she crept toward the shadows, closing the gap between them. A strike to the base of the skull knocked the first fae to the ground, a powerful strike that was placed with perfection. The assassin's legs gave way, and he crumpled to the ground before he had even known she was there.

The second shadow turned, a knife in his hand, but Lana was ready. She spun her staff at his legs and caught his knee. It was enough of a blow to cause him pain and to limit his movement. He lunged forward, quicker than anything Lana had ever experienced, and slashed at her with his knife. The blow to his knee, however, had weakened his leg, and he stumbled, missing her face by a finger's width. She dropped close to the ground and kicked out at the shadows knee again, striking it with force. His leg gave way completely, and he dropped. As he hit the ground, Lana's staff struck the side of his head and he fell still.

Lana moved quickly. She called out to the sylph that had engaged the first assassin and started stripping the blades from the sgàil's armour. She bound their wrists behind them with their own belts and waited for help to arrive.

Beaten and bound, they dragged the three sgàil to the camp at the base of the rise and threw them in a cage, stripped of their weapons and armour. The soldiers gave them ragged clothing to keep their modesty and some warmth. As she had defeated them, Lana was given a set of their armour and a pair of the dark, sharp blades.

Lana. Daowiel and Tinnion sat on her bed looking at the armour. It was made of soft leather and seemed extremely light to wear, but deceptively hardy. As she turned it and moved it, she noticed it seemed to soak up the light from the candles around the room and made the surrounding space seem darker.

"In the age of the gods, Chaint would infuse her children's armour with shadow. That this armour behaves in that way is a concern. It would be good to know how they have recreated the effect." They kept their voices low as they talked in the room, but the worry in Daowiel's voice was clear. "I dislike the thought of fighting shadow assassins. The defences we set cannot protect against them and we will struggle to see them in this."

"Do you think they'll send more and come again?" Lana asked, her voice full of concern.

"No. Not tonight, at any rate. Who knows what tomorrow will bring? But we are safe enough for now." Daowiel reached out and took Lana's hand. "They will not know that the shadows failed until morning. By then, we will be close to starting the talks."

"Hold on. Just, go back a bit." Tinnion put a hand on Lana's. "You saw movement down on the plains, in the dark, from way up here on the watch point of the rise, while they were wearing this armour? Then you leapt off the cliff and floated two hundred metres down onto the plains?" Lana nodded at her friend and Tinnion went on. "I thought you were half dryad, not half sylph." Daowiel coughed and gave the huntress a look that made her pause. There was a barely noticeable shift in her tone as she continued. "So then you snuck up on two shadows and knocked them out cold, all by yourself?" Tinnion's eyes were wide, and she shook her head as she spoke.

Lana blushed. "You make it sound so… I don't know, so spectacular. I just did the same thing that Yorane and his friend did. You would do the same too."

"I would not be jumping off a mountain, nor picking a fight with sgàil. Lana, that's insane. And fighting two shadow assassins alone? One of those things could kill half a dozen trained men! Not to mention that Yorane and his friend are sylph and trained warriors and were looking at stopping just one shadow between them."

"She has been leaping from buildings since we arrived at the queen's palace, Tinnion. And you know, she rarely stops to think about the danger she is in before acting." Daowiel's smile was slight and her narrow eyes and flat tone suggested it hid her true feelings.

Lana shrugged and scrunched up her face. "You won't tell Aelwynne, will you? She'll have me locked up in here."

"I'll not say a word, Lana. But if you think she'll not hear about this, you're mad. It's the talk of the camp already." Tinnion's head was still shaking.

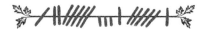

The following morning Lana and her friends sat down to a quick breakfast before preparations for the peace talks began.

"Have they said anything useful yet?" Lana hoped the shadows would tell their secrets and their plans in order to take the focus away from her and how they were captured.

"No, one was still out cold at sunrise. The others are refusing to say anything we can understand." Tinnion was sitting back in her chair, chewing on a piece of toasted bread.

Lana sighed. "Well, I got a couple of sharp knives that would make Cat really jealous. I s'pose that's something."

"You saved a couple of dozen lives, Lana. At least that many. You can be proud of that." Tinnion put her hand on Lana's shoulder and pulled her forward into a hug.

"Lady Lana." A soldier entered the room and stood at attention. "Lady Aelwynne calls for you."

Lana sighed and chewed on her lip. "Well, I guess I have to face the telling off sooner or later." She stood and brushed crumbs from her skirt before heading out of the small kitchen.

"Good luck, Lana!" Tinnion called after her.

Chapter Thirty-Nine

Negotiations

Each side chose six representatives to attend the talks, and the army erected a marquee with two tables and a dozen chairs to accommodate them. Aelwynne would be in charge of talks for the queen, Lana was there to observe and help where she could and Qilan provided a military perspective and a bit of muscle. Daowiel, Liayol and Shayell represented the fae. Facing them sat the rebel tuath lords, MacKenna and MacStorey and a liath lord named Balch. Beside them were two sgàil, one clearly a warrior, the other looked like a priest. A young tuath woman, a similar age to Lana, took the last seat. No other soldiers or warriors were allowed within three hundred metres of the marquis.

There was no talking as the representatives made themselves comfortable and poured cups of water from pitchers that both sides had placed in the centre of the tables.

Lana sat back in her seat and watched the people opposite her intently. She knew Aelwynne could not cede to their demand of an independent north with its own king. That was something Queen Rhiannon had insisted could never happen. Aside from that, and the imprisonment of MacKenna, they were free to negotiate whatever the queen's voice thought was needed to avoid further war. In order for the talks to be a success, Lana knew they would have to sow doubt in the minds of those they faced. Doubt that they could win a war and doubts about MacKenna's own intentions. They needed to divide the enemy, push them to turn on one another, and quit the war. This was not something Lana had ever had to do.

"Some of you I know, and you know me. MacKenna, MacStorey, Balch." Aelwynne nodded her head to the three men in turn. "Will you introduce your other friends, MacKenna?"

The rebel lord rolled his eyes and gestured to the sgàil. "This is Nydoalin, warrior of Ternbay and Senath, priest of Chaint."

"And the young lady? Your niece, perhaps?" Aelwynne gestured to the tuath girl.

"She's of no importance. A maid with a pretty face."

Lana noticed the sgàil warrior scowl at the rebel lord's words and she looked to the tuath maid with a smile. The maid didn't return the gesture.

"And who are these strangers ye've brought tae ma kingdom?" MacKenna sat back in his chair with a smirk at his own declaration of royalty.

"Commander Qilan of her majesty's army. I am certain you will remember him, MacKenna." She gestured to the commander and then to the fae. "Shayell, advisor to the lord of the Eastmarch Noam, Princess Daowiel of the Heartwood. Liayol, Lord of House Iaswiytan and Lana Ni Hayal, my charge."

The self-proclaimed king scowled at each one. "Well ye've all marched a long way tae surrender yerselves tae me. Are ye here tae swear yer fealty?"

"You would do well to take these talks seriously, MacKenna. They may be your only chance to live." Qilan barked at the tuath lord.

Aelwynne sat forward, gesturing for calm with her hands. "We're here to make and keep the peace, to negotiate an end to this uprising and to see that those who are innocent are unharmed. I hope that there will be no more need for violence. We are not here to surrender, however, and you might want to consider that as we continue." The Queen's Voice took a sip of her water and continued. "Setting aside your jokes and bravado, MacKenna, what is it you hope to achieve with your actions?"

"What do I hope tae achieve? Well, lass, I've achieved what I set out to. I am set up, quite happy, in Northfort and the lords o' the northern Taydom are swearing their allegiances tae me. I am King here now. The north is no more part o' Mortara and your queen's domain. Rhiannon can accept that or not. I'm not bothered either way. But I'll not have her army sat on ma doorstep. So I'm here tae tell you tae pack up your camp and get gone."

Lana leaned forward in her seat, gently touching Aelwynne's hand and glancing at her, asking for permission to speak. Her mentor gave her a slight nod.

"And the sgàil?" Lana looked to the fae opposite. "Mortara has changed a lot since you left. The fae and humans live together now. We're all equal and trying to make Mortara a better place for everyone. We would really like the opportunity to welcome you properly. Not like this. What is it you hope to do here?"

To everyone's surprise, it was the young tuath woman that answered. "We can talk about that once the North is truly free."

Lana looked at the young woman again. She was not much older than Lana and had the familiar features of a tuath. Red hair and pale, freckled skin. Her eyes were a grey blue but her pupils were larger than normal, almost engulfing the colour entirely. Lana felt her stomach tighten and the jewel in her circlet irritated her forehead. She closed her eyes tight for a moment, hoping to stave off the flashes of memory that often accompanied that sensation.

"I'm sorry, lady. I didn't know you spoke for the sgàil. Your lord seemed quite dismissive and didn't introduce you."

MacKenna slammed his cup down on the table. "Enough o' this. The girl is ma servant and a go between, nothing more. Yer here tae talk with me, so ye'll talk tae me or no one. Ye hear? Get on with it, Aelwynne, and keep yer pup silent or we're done."

Lana noticed again that it was the sgàil warrior that reacted to the rebel lord's words, not the young woman they described. The warrior moved in her seat but was calmed as the woman described as a maid placed her hand firmly upon her arm. Lana sat back in her seat, watching in silence, the itching sensation on her forehead growing by the second.

"Behave with respect, MacKenna. Or I'll take it upon myself to teach you some manners before we're done here." Qilan was impatient. He considered the talks a waste of time and, although he wasn't eager for war, he was keen to end MacKenna's self-proclaimed reign with a beating.

"You'll be wanting tae be quick then Qilan, I reckon our talks are about done. I'm not seeing any good come frae them."

"Don't be so eager for war, MacKenna. You might outnumber us, but all those with us are warriors, trained, disciplined, and skilled. Several hundred of yours are just farmers and brawlers."

"Aye farmers that have kept the north safe for hundreds of years, Qilan. Men that've fought in more battles than you with yer fancy armour and yer flimsy sword."

"Enough! I haven't come here to listen to two men bicker us into a war that we can avoid." Aelwynne's voice was sharp and Qilan sat back in his seat, his face red. "You know we can't accept your declaration of independence from Mortara, MacKenna. That will not happen, not now, not in a thousand years. It is nothing more than a power grab by a greedy man and not what the people of the north want."

"The people of my kingdom want whatever I say, Aelwynne. And I'm sick tae here of deasin rule." The rebel lifted his hand to his forehead.

"There is no deasin rule here, MacKenna. Jendawyn was chosen as tay by the king and the clan chiefs. He had no line, so on his death the clans would have gathered again with the queen to select a new tay. You have taken it upon yourself to start a war instead of making your case to your equals." Aelwynne stared directly at the rebel lord, and Lana noticed him wither a little. "The question now is. How do we end this without further death?"

"Ye want this tae end with no death? Pack up and go home. Tell Rhiannon we're done. Ye can live as ye like south o' Freybridge and east o' the sgàil mountains, but these lands are mine. I've no want for Mortara, I've no care for anything out o' the north, but I'll have ma country for my own."

"You've made your position clear and you are firm in it, so let me explain where we stand." Aelwynne spoke more forcefully and formally now. "Your people will return to your hold and we will take you to Southport, where you will face trial for treason. Should you choose instead to stand firm, you and your followers will be killed here in battle and your rebellion ended. There is room between these two outcomes for negotiation should you choose to engage in talks. I would highly recommend it."

"It would be wise to listen to the Lady, and to Lana." Daowiel spoke directly to the sgàil, ignoring the puffing of MacKenna. "They are here for peace, not war. The queen's lady Lana was instrumental in the treaty between my people and the humans. We too have come out of hiding this year, and that is because of Lana."

MacKenna spat to the ground at his feet. "Lady my arse. She's a whelp that can nae keep her eyes open long enough to even start talks." The rebel was red with fury.

Lana slammed her hand down on the table, shocking those around her into silence. "Stop it! You're bickering with everyone while good people are dying or scared that they'll die tomorrow. You've already killed hundreds of people because of your ego." She paused, taking a calming breath. "Why are you letting this happen?" Lana turned to the tuath girl opposite her. "You could end this, you could make him stop. You don't need to be starting wars, you don't need to be turning families against each other. You don't even need this lord. All this death and fighting it's all pointless."

MacKenna stood, his face now blotched in scarlet, his knuckles white as he squeezed his cup. "I told ye afore. Talk tae me, if you're going tae talk. This wench is nothing. Ye hear? Nothing."

Lana looked at the man and sighed, her eyes narrow and her brow furrowed. "I am sorry, MacKenna, but there isn't much point talking to you anymore. The truth is, you're already dead. You'll not see the end of the year whatever happens. You might die by the rope of a hangman in Southport, the blade of the commander here or... well, more likely, by whatever weapon your 'maid' prefers. Probably a black bladed knife." Lana gestured to the young woman across from her. "You're going to live whatever's left of your life the same as you have these last few months. As a puppet. Then, when you're not useful anymore, you'll die. I'd be surprised if you even lasted the night now. And if you call her a wench again, this lady..." She pointed to the silent but grimacing sgàil. "... is likely to see to it you don't say anything after it. If I was you I'd be shutting up, mebbes even packing up yourself and going south to beg for forgiveness and protection."

The rebel tuath lord launched his cup at Lana and Qilan leapt to his feet grabbing the man's sleeve, pulling him face down across the table. Aelwynne called on the commander to stop as the soldier raised his fist to strike. Nydoalin, the shadow warrior opposite, stood in the blink of an eye and launched herself diagonally across the table, a smirk on her face. MacStorey and Balch staggered out of their seats, grasping for swords that weren't on their belts. MacKenna, now free of the commander's grip, backed himself into the corner of the tent with the sgàil priest turning to face him.

Liayol, recognising the danger, lashed out at the shadow warrior as she slid past him, throwing a punch that skimmed her shoulder but did no harm.

Qilan stumbled backward, unbalanced by Nydoalin's speed and force, as she twisted and launched her knee into his stomach. He fell to the ground, the shadow warrior quickly on top of him.

Aelwynne, her faced white, retreated away from the scramble between the commander and the shadow. She instinctively put her arm around Lana and dragged her away, too. Putting the fae between them and the fight.

The rebel lords regained their composure and moved to attack the fae, MacStorey made his way around the side of the table and Balch slid his body across it. Shayell moved to cut off MacStorey a look of grim determination on their face. They picked up the large pitcher from the table and slammed it into the side of the rebel's head, sending the man to the floor.

Daowiel placed her hands on the table and pushed it to grow, sending spikes of wood deep into Balch's leg. The man's face turned white, and he opened his mouth to scream. The pain as his flesh tore, unbearable.

Nydoalin pulled a knife, black as night, from a hiding place, deep within her boot, and she slid it between Qilan's ribs, forcing it into his chest before Liayol aimed a kick at her, this time finding his mark and knocking the warrior clear of Qilan.

"Enough." The word was spoken with little effort but filled the air, felt as much as it was heard. Everyone froze in silence.

"How do you know me, child?" The 'maid' was staring directly at Lana.

"I... I could feel you were more than you seemed to be." Lana shrugged. "Besides, your warrior gave you away. You remained too calm while she wanted to tear out MacKenna's throat every time he spoke about you. And your eyes too, the shadow is taking over your eyes. But... Why are you here? How are you here? What have you done to the girl?"

"We each have questions, child. Perhaps in time we will both have answers, but your observation has cost me and I will need to press my claim earlier than I had hoped. Take these fools. They are no use to me now." The goddess gestured to MacStorey and Balch. "I'm afraid these talks are over, but I feel we have both learned much from them. Out of respect to you, I will give your commanders three days to have your camp packed and remove your army from this valley. Tell your Queen to stay clear of the north." The goddess scowled.

"No, we need to talk. This doesn't have to end this way. You're just going to make sure of war if we do it this way."

"It is too late for that, child." She turned as she spoke. "Come, Nydoalin. Leave them. And bring MacKenna, it is time to reveal ourselves to the other lords and take control of the army."

In a moment, the shadows and the goddess were gone, leaving two rebel lords behind.

Chapter Forty

DECISIONS

The rebel lords were bound and thrown into the holding cage alongside the shadow assassins. Neither group seemed pleased by the company they were being forced to keep, and a scuffle broke out within moments of them entering the enclosure. Qilan, pale and barely conscious, was rushed to the small building that the armies healers had set themselves up in. The medics assured Lana that he would live, though they looked concerned and couldn't say that he would fully recover. Cinerea and Tinnion, unaware of what had happened, caught up with Lana as she walked through the town.

"You did it, Lana. You captured the rebels, it's over." Tinnion threw her arms around her friend and hugged her in celebration.

Lana shook her head, her face red and hot. "No, Tinnion. The sgàil gave them to us. It's even worse than we thought. Worse even than we worried it might be."

Tinnion loosened the grip on her friend and moved her head back, looking the young lady in the eye. "What is it, Lana? What could be worse?"

"It's the sgàil, Tinnion... They're in control now and..."

"I'm sure we'll be fine, Lana." Tinnion pulled her close again. "This is a well-trained army, and the addition of the fae make us very strong. Besides, without their leaders, the Tuath won't be so keen on fighting. Right?"

"Lady Lana." A soldier interrupted the friends. "Lady Aelwynne has sent for you. Lady Tinnion and Cinerea as well."

The three friends walked arm in arm to the town's inn, where the leaders of the various groups making up the army met to discuss their options.

The tables in the inn's main hall had been gathered and placed together, the benches and chairs set around them. Aelwynne sat at the head. Beside her, in the chair usually occupied by Qilan, sat Crurith. Daowiel, Shayell and Liayol represented the fae and Ceowald, a captain of the southern army, sat in for Qilan. When the three friends arrived, the room fell silent and all eyes turned to them.

"I want the three of you to join us here for each meeting from now on. Your thoughts will be most useful. Besides, Lana seems to know much more than anyone else at the moment. A situation I'm growing used to, much to my discomfort." Aelwynne gestured to three empty seats across from her and the friends sat. Lana lowered her head and pulled her chair to the table without a word.

"What happened out there?" Crurith's expression was filled with concern.

"MacKenna was, as you thought he would be, doing his best to ensure we went to war. Throwing insults and naming himself king. Lana made an observation, one I'm yet to understand, then Qilan took offence when the self proclaimed king threw a cup at my ward. At that point, any hope of peace was lost, resulting in Qilan's injury and the handing over of the rebel gesiths." Aelwynne's voice was stern and matter of fact.

"It seems to me, we can do me that nothing more until we know what your ward saw out there then." The Tay's guard looked over at Lana, his voice was harsh. "Well, Lana. Can you explain?"

"Go easy on her, Crurith. Whatever happened isn't Lana's fault, and I was never in danger." Aelwynne placed her hand on her guard's shoulder as she spoke.

Crurith nodded with a gentle smile. "I'm sorry, Lana. Sometimes I'm too hard on folk. Especially when it comes to protecting Lady Aelwynne. Her father would skin me if she so much as caught a chill. Still, we need to understand what it is we're dealing with here. If you could explain, Lana."

Lana nodded. "It's Chaint." Her voice was little more than a whisper. "I don't know how, but it is her. She's in that tuath girl. I could feel her." There was a sharp intake of breath around the table and a clatter as Ceowald dropped his cup.

"Your ward has gone mad, Lady. Chaint is dead, the gods are all dead." The soldier interjected.

"No, they're gone, not dead. Most of them at least... Ulios is still in the oceans and now Chaint is back. She must have been hiding away somewhere. Solumus didn't leave either. Maybe he's dead, but the others aren't." Lana's voice remained low, her head bowed.

"Utter nonsense." The soldier shook his head and refilled his cup from a pitcher of ale.

"It's true. And she's given us three days to leave. I think we should go... For now... Go back south and tell the queen and raise a bigger army. Or... or something else. I don't know what. But I'm scared now. I wasn't scared when I thought it was rebel lords. That's just people and you can beat people, even if it's really hard. But how do you beat a god? Especially a god like Chaint."

"This is why we don't leave decisions to children." The captain rolled his eyes. "We've marched here to shut down this rebellion and we're going to do just that. If you can't talk them down, we'll beat them down. You, though..." He pointed a finger at Lana. "You need to keep your silly fantasies to yourself. We don't need stupid rumours spreading around the camp."

"You were not there, human." Daowiel spat the last word as an insult to the soldier. "You did not see what we saw nor hear what we heard. There is no doubt in my mind that the goddess has returned and possessed that tuath child. I saw her eyes, and I heard her speak. Commanding the sgàil, declaring her control."

"I too stand by Lana's word. Though I did not see what she saw. I heard the tuath girl and felt the power in her words once she revealed herself." Shayell agreed with the princess.

The captain slurped on his cup of ale noisily, his brow creased, but said nothing more.

"You're certain, Lana?" Aelwynne's voice was soft as she addressed her ward.

"Yes." Lana nodded, but didn't speak more than to give her answer.

"Our reports suggest that there were still only two dozen sgàil with the army, and we have three of them in a cage. Some of the clan will surely give up the fight now we have two of their lords caught an all. I reckon we can defeat them. God or not. It'll be hard, yes, but I believe it's possible." Crurith twisted his knife in the table as he spoke.

Liayol looked at the other fae in the room. "If we allow Chaint to take the north, it will not be long before she sets her eyes on the rest of Mortara. I believe we need to make a stand before she can solidify her hold here. If we can gain the support of some clans, we stand a chance. We fae can hold the sgàil, with our numbers as they are. If you humans can take care of those clans that still stand against us. I do not know how we defeat a goddess, but I am certain that without her shadows, she will not be so keen to face us." The sylph lord held the attention of his fellow fae as he spoke. "The question is, will you stand? Knowing what we know, will you stand?"

Daowiel sighed. "I believe you are right, Lord Liayol. We cannot, neither fae nor human, allow Chaint to return to Mortara. We would all suffer at her hands. I will not, though, leave Lana's side. If she stands or leaves, I will do as she does. That is why I am here. That is what I am sworn to do." The sylph nodded in recognition of the Dryad's words.

"I too am sworn to Lana's protection. If she stays, we will stand. If she chooses to go, I will go. Though I believe it is our duty to do what we can here." Shayell's face was as set as stone, impossible to read and hardened against whatever feelings they held.

"Then we are where we were in Southport." Aelwynne's voice was steady, but her fingers played with the cuff of her dress, giving away the nerves she felt.

"Lana must make her decision for her own stance and for the fae's. And I must give my decision for the queen's army. The advice, from all, appears to be to stand and fight. I am leaning toward that option, though I don't think it will be possible without the fae. What do you say, Lana?"

"I came here to help Brighid. I don't know what's happened to her and I'm scared she could be dead. I'd rather know, though, no matter how hard it is to hear. If you all think we should stay and fight, I'll stay with you. I'm not going to run away. But I don't want to say that's what we have to do either. You're all leaders; I'm just a farm girl. It's your choice, not mine. The fae followed me to keep me safe, not because I'm their leader. I'll not ask the people I love to go fighting a goddess if they want to leave."

Daowiel turned to her friend with a solemn look. "I am sorry, Lana. In this, you are our leader. We followed you because we each, in our way, love you. But in following you, we made you our leader in this matter and we will do, all of us, what you believe to be right."

Lana shook her head, and a tear fell from her eye. "I have to stay, Daowiel. I have to know what happened to Brighid, and if there's a hope she's alive, I have to help her. But I won't make you stay... I release you from the oath you swore. I release you all from your oaths."

"Then I will stay and fight at your side, Lana. And I swear a new oath to protect you." The princess pulled her friend close and wrapped her arm around Lana's shoulder.

Aelwynne, too, reached across the table and touched Lana's hand. "I think we should take the burden from you and make a more formal declaration. All those that think we aught to stand our ground say 'aye'."

The decision was unanimous, they would stay and they would stand against the goddess that threatened the north. The goddess that would, in time, threaten the whole of Mortara. Messengers were sent to the south and Queen Rhiannon, informing her of the danger and the decision. Daowiel sent a messenger to her mother and Liayol sent another to the High Council of the Sylph.

In three days, they might all be dead. They knew that; they accepted that as the risk of staying. But they knew, also, that if they did not stay, the entire country would, in time, be subject to the goddesses' sadistic desires. Their actions and their potential sacrifice might save countless thousands.

That knowledge did not make Lana feel any happier at the decision. Not that she wasn't ready to stand and fight or even that she wanted to leave. She was scared, certainly, but she had come this far, ready to die, in order to stand with her friends. What upset Lana was that she might live to watch her friends die; that was something she could not cope with. It was something that she feared was more of a possibility now than ever before.

She walked through the town, her mind a tangle of emotion, and found a path. Old and overgrown, the path lead further up the rise to the cliffs that shadowed and protected the town from the southern winds and the raging river. Rough, ancient steps were hewn from the stone and she climbed, pushing away the bushes and vines that clung to the bottom of the cliff.

As she climbed, the sun faded, and the sky became red, but Lana didn't notice, her mind was fixed solely on the events of the day. The talks that ended with Qilan almost dead, the discovery that it was Chaint herself that lead the sgàil and the meeting that followed. She played them over and over in her head, trying to see where it all went wrong, trying to see what they might have done to change the outcome. She saw again the hate in the sgàil warrior's face as MacKenna belittled her still disguised goddess and the darkness in the possessed tuath girl's eyes. And she saw the uncontrolled ego and rage of the rebel lord as he named himself king and railed at any questioning him.

Lana barely noticed she had reached the top of the path or her surroundings. She walked to the large grey standing stone, and she sat at its base, her back up against it. She watched the sun setting and thought that the deep red clouds in the sky resembled a pool of blood. Then she closed her eyes for a moment. Just a moment.

Chapter Forty-One

SHADOWS AND STONES

News of the coming danger and the war to be fought spread quickly around the camp and the town, and the leaders of the various groups started ordering their warriors to prepare. The noam began setting up workshops and forges. The dryad started working on arrows and adding to the defences of the camp at the bottom of the road to the town. Sylph and humans alike worked on their armour and weapons, ensuring they were ready and in good condition. And soldiers began training while the sun's light still lit the rise.

As the moon rose, they took to their tents or the buildings they had been assigned, sat around fires and opened barrels of ale. Drowning their thoughts in their cups and eating together. Their laughter and chatter belying the fear and worry they felt.

Tinnion and Cinerea sat around a small fire close to the centre of the town when the alarm rang. Down in the camp, those that had been guarding their prisoners had been found dead. One shadow had also been killed and lay in the cage alongside the two rebel lords whose throats had been torn from their necks, their spines snapped in two. The other two shadows were gone.

The huntresses joined those engaged in tracking the fleeing prisoners as they climbed up to the town. "The tracks are faint, but with enough light, I could follow. They're headed to the trees on the east of the town. Bring torches and be ready to fight. They have the guard's blades. I can't believe they got by us all. We need to set a better watch... By the gods, I can't believe they didn't attack us." Tinnion crouched over the grass at the top of the road, holding a burning torch close to the ground.

The going was slow, the light footsteps of the shadows barely marking the ground and the flickering torch light making tracking much harder. As they reached the trees and the moonlight disappeared, Cinerea reached out, searching through the branches and roots for the feel of the sgàil's passing. The whispers of the woodland that would point her to their hiding place.

The trees were still unused to the dryad and rejoiced at her touch. They filled her head with songs and tales. They told her of their lives, of the humans that lived in the nearby town, that cut them and burned them and hunted amongst them. They told her of the animals that lived in their shelter and the flowers that filled the air with their sweet scents.

They had no knowledge of what the sgàil were. They knew only that unknown fae were walking under their branches. They sensed the stolen steel the shadows carried and their readiness to use it. They sensed the tension within them and the darkness that seemed to surround them. They pulled themselves away from the dark fae they felt amongst them, fearing that the steel would be used to fell or to cut them. And they begged for Cinerea and her bound one to protect them.

Cinerea began to sink into the tree, seeking the bridge, looking to the area where the shadows sat, resting.

"No, Cinerea. Not that way." Tinnion's voice was soft, but the words echoed in the dryad's head as she spoke. "The shadows are dangerous. We need to hunt them together and our friends can't go that way."

"You're right, of course." The dryad smiled at the huntress. "They sit close to the eastern edge of the wooded land. We can reach them before the moon is at its height if we move now. It would be best to extinguish the torches, however. We will not need them and they cause the trees anxiety."

He stood within the circle of stones, his dark cowl covering his face in shadow. He raised his hands, and the land shifted, rising from the plains, rising high above the plains. Water rushed from between two rocks, threatening to flood this new plateau, so he raised his hands higher and the land on which he stood rose further, leaving the growing river below to the south. The stone circle sat like a crown on the rise and the God lowered his hands.

"Lana Ni Hayal. That is the name the humans gave you, is it not?"

Lana's mouth opened, but she did not respond. This was just a vision, like all those visions she had experienced before. It wasn't real, it couldn't be. She was watching the creation of the rise thousands of years before her time. She wasn't truly there. This couldn't truly be happening.

"This is a name that I have heard for many nights, a name that haunts the mind of my child, a name that is whispered in their prayers and devotions. This is how you are called?"

"Who are you? What's happening?"

"I am he that created the earth upon which you walk. I am he that created the noam, children of the earth. I am he that is known by the children as Khyione. I am your creator and I am your god."

"How can you see me? How can you be here? You left, you all left, I saw it."

"I did not leave this world with my brother and sisters. Instead, I became part of it. That is my strength, the power of the earth. I live in every rock and every stone. I am the dirt and the sand. I am all around you, Lana Ni Hayal. This is my temple, and you have come to me, as I called upon you to do."

Lana reached to the wooden handle hanging from her belt, her stomach so knotted she felt her insides might burst. "Why?"

The god laughed. "Be still. You cannot strike me, you cannot fight your god." She felt her arm stiffen at his words, her hand tight around the shaft of the dryad staff.

"The world turns, time draws on, destinies and dangers collide to threaten my children. We decided to leave the world, to allow our children to grow away from our influence, so that they may better protect themselves from you and your kind. A decision that was taken by all. But we were betrayed and not all travelled to Loch Heart, So I too stayed. Now the darkness threatens my children. The darkness that you have seen, that you have recognised, that you have brought my children to fight. You have put my children in danger."

"I didn't." Lana shook her head quickly. "I didn't bring them here to fight her. I didn't even bring them here. They came because Shayell called them, not me. Shayell wanted to protect me from the tuath, we didn't know that Chaint was here. I don't want anyone to be in danger."

"I have no interest in your wants. I have no interest in your thoughts or in your reasons. You will be silent, you will listen and you will obey." The god made a gesture with his hands as though swatting away a midge and the skies went black. Nothing existed outside of the circle and Lana swallowed hard, her heart beating fast, her body shaking.

"I Created your kind to serve my sons, to wear their collars and carry their seed. I created your kind to continue my children's line. That is your worth. That is your reason. There is one here, the great son of my first son, one who is destined to rule, one that will bring glory to the noam. One that will carry my essence. He will learn to channel my gifts as you have learnt the gifts off my sister. He will protect my children in the coming wars. That one has laid a claim to you."

Lana shook her head wildly. "You mean Grant don't you? Well, I don't care. I don't care who you are, I don't care that you're a god. I'll not wear his collar. I'll not be some puppet to do his bidding and carry his seed."

The god looked closely at the girl that sat at his temple. "You defy me, child? How can that be? I created your kind to serve. I created your kind to follow my will. You cannot defy me. No human can."

"Well, I can... and I am. I don't belong to Grant and I don't belong to you. And you can't change that, you can't make me. I know that now, because if you could,

you wouldn't be talking to me. You'd just change me. You'd take away my thoughts. But you can't."

The god approached Lana. Grabbing her face in his hand, he turned her toward him and stared deep into her eyes. Then he cursed.

"How is this possible? How could this be? I have been betrayed by my sisters. My sisters! They reach out from the void to deny me. You... They reach out through you. They live within you."

Tinnion took her position behind the tangled limbs of a hawthorn, an arrow nocked on her string, ready to draw. She knelt in silence and waited. A small troop of dryad were in the trees to the west, and Shayell stood with Yorane ready to pounce on the enemy at the given signal. She could feel Cinerea on the bridge, her strength and determination tinged with nerves. She sensed her bound one's worry of ambushing a trained assassin, the fear that the sgàil, faster than her and able to use the shadows, would be too quick, too well prepared and prove deadly. And then she felt the dryad's mind shift, reach out to the wall between the bridge and this world, and she drew the string of her bow back, taking aim at the chest of the shadow. It was time.

The sgàil didn't move as Cinerea's arm emerged from the tree and wrapped around its throat. It collapsed as the dryad pushed forward and the two fae bundled to the floor.

"He is dead! His throat gone." The dryad stood, picking grass and using it to wipe the dark, viscous blood from her arm.

The other dryad emerged from the cover of their trees, their weapons ready, their eyes darting side to side, watching for the second assassin. Tinnion remained where she was, letting the string of her bow relax but keeping the arrow nocked.

"It is clear, love. The other has fled. It is no longer beneath the trees." She heard Cinerea's thoughts as clear as her own and emerged from the tree scouring the floor for signs of the second escapee.

"Why would they have fought? Why kill him when they were so close to escape?" Shayell stepped into the clearing and crouched at the side of the body, checking its wound in the pale light of the moon.

"The other has fled out on the rocks. I can't track it across the hard stone, not in this light. We should head back, let the camp know there's still one on the loose, and come back in the morning. I'll be able to track it in the sun." Tinnion walked back to her friends, shaking her head.

"Yes, it will be weaker in the sun. A lot less dangerous than trying to catch it at night." Yorane sheathed his blade as he spoke.

"I agree, Yorane. What should be done with this one?" Cinerea looked up at her friends, her brow raised.

"Leave it, its flesh will feed those that need it. There's no benefit for us to drag it back to the town. It wouldn't serve any purpose now." Tinnion held out her hand to her wife, helping her to her feet.

The moon was high and the chill of the stone was seeping into Lana's back, making her feel stiff. She opened her eyes and brought her knees up to her chest as she saw him kneeling in front of her, only a metre away from her feet. Her stomach, still tight from the vision, turned and she wretched, her mouth filling with water.

"Again, you find yourself drawn to Khyione. And now you find peace at his altar?" His voice was soft, deep and almost hypnotic.

"I didn't know what it was when I came here... I just needed to get away from the noise of the camp, get some peace so I could think. I didn't know it was Khyione's temple. It's not like there's a sign. How was I to know he was worshipped up here?"

"We worship him in all mountains, large or small. In every cave, on every cliff. Every standing stone is his altar, every circle of stones his temple." The noam moved his hand toward her as he spoke, his soft voice filling her ears, sending all other sounds to the winds. "Three times now Khyione has called, and you have come. Three times now you have come to an altar, to pray with me, to receive our gods' blessing."

She pushed herself back against the stone as if to sink within it as she could with the trees. "I told you, I'm not yours. I'm not gonna be owned like some object. I don't care what you think your god is doing. I don't care what he says. And even if it was true, it wouldn't matter 'cos he isn't really here but Chaint is, and she's going to kill us, all of us, 'cos of me. 'Cos I couldn't make her listen." Tears filled her eyes. She raised her hands to her face, hiding behind them as she tried to sniff back a cry.

Grant placed a hand on her raised knee. "I have heard what passed at the talks. Shayell was quick to advise us of the coming battle and order our preparations. But I will not die in this war, and nor will you. Of that I am certain, for that is what Khyione has shown me."

"He isn't here, Grant. Not really, and I don't care what you say. He can't help you, he can't save you, and he can't make me do what I don't want to do. No matter what he says." Her voice broke as she cried behind her hands.

"His form may be gone from this world, but his spirit remains in the stone. His will continues to be felt, his words are passed from father to son and his blessings are strong, as strong as they ever were. You know this, you fight and you deny it, but you know it to be true. You feel his presence, you feel his call. Why else would you seek his temple with each camp we set? Why else would you sit at his altar?"

"I didn't seek it out." She tried to fill the words with certainty, with strength enough to end the noam's accusations, but her voice betrayed her, and her words were timid. "I was just looking for quiet. Nothing more than that."

"And each time you look for a quiet place, you arrive at a site held sacred to Khyione. At a place I come to pray. At a time I come to pray. And this time you have sat in his temple, you have placed your head to his altar, you have found the peace you seek in his touch. This time you cannot deny that you sense his presence, that you hear his call."

Lana shook her head gently. "I don't care what your god is telling you, Grant. He isn't here the way he was. But Chaint is, and she's given us three days to leave, and I know that Aelwynne and Qilan won't go. We're going to war against a goddess and her army. And I'm going to stand with my friends, it's why I came here. It's why you're here. Because Shayell swore to stand with me and called on you and the others to come. I know that hundreds of people are going to die. I know we can't escape that. That's what I know. That's the truth."

"No. I came here to place my collar around your neck and to take you to Khyione's sanctuary. If I must fight the sgàil on my way to Stonemount, then I will do so and I will kill all that seek to part me from you." She felt his thumb caress her knee, his large hand strong but gentle.

"Why?" She felt a hollow in her stomach as he spoke and her voice wavered again. "Why do you even want me?"

"Why does any noam want a female? To join your voice with mine in prayer. To walk at my side, to kneel at my feet, to serve my needs, to carry my seed and to give me my son."

"But why me? Why don't you go claim a tuath girl while we're here or a searen woman on your way to Stonemount? Why are you doing this to me?" She felt a hollowness spread through her body and she swallowed hard, wiping her nose on her sleeve as she sniffed.

Grant smiled. "It is you I desire, and it is Khyione's will."

She closed her eyes tight, holding back the scream she felt forming. There was no reason for his insistence. She saw that now, none beyond his faith in his god, at least.

"I need to go back down to the camp. It's late." Her tears were gone, though her eyes remained puffy and red, and her voice still broke as she spoke.

"Why do you still fight against Khyione's will? Why do you fight that which you feel?" She felt his words vibrating in her chest. His deep voice seeming to fill her.

The question echoed in her mind, and she felt her shoulders slump. She had no answer to give him. There had been times that she watched him and even some nights that she dreamt of him since they met. Though she didn't like to admit it, her dreams of being wrapped in some mans arms had changed and the man had taken his face. She had felt something grow within her every time she had been alone with him. A desire to be held by him, to feel his arms around her, to live her dream. Now she felt his hand upon her knee and it felt good, comforting, safe.

"I don't know." Her voice was a whisper. There was no strength in it, no argument. "I don't know why, except I don't want to be owned. I don't want to lose who I am."

"To be bound is why you exist, Lana. It is why our god created your kind. You know this to be true. Do you deny even this?"

"No." Lana shook her head. "But things have changed since Khyione did that. We've changed, humans were given will and thought, we have lives beyond Khyione's will... or yours. And you've changed too. There's an accord now. Your family signed it, you're supposed to live by it."

"The accord does not change the reason for your life. It does not prevent you from wearing my collar. Nor does it prevent you from being bound or blessed. It does not prevent me from taking you to Stonemount, nor from spreading the word of our god."

"It stops you from putting your collar on me though. You can't do that unless I let you, or you'd have done it already. And none of it means I have to accept your god's lore. I don't. I'm not yours, I'm not his. I am me, Grant. I'm Lana Ni Hayal. And if you ever felt more than dirty lust for me, you'd never want that to change."

"That is true, Lana. And, in truth, I would not want you to change. Though you challenge me, I enjoy your fire. But that is not my choice. It is the blessing of Khyione and I cannot prevent it."

"Then you'll have to learn to stop yourself, Grant. You'll have to learn control. 'Cos you'll not have me and if your god really speaks to you, he'll tell you the same. Find someone else for your lust, someone I don't know, 'cos you'll not have any of my friends any more than you can have me."

Chapter Forty-Two

Obsidian Dreams

"Lana!" Tinnion called out across the square. "Where have you been? The shadows escaped and there's still one loose. We went hunting for it but it grew too dark so we came back here. Then we got told no one had seen you since sunset. We were about to send out a hunt for you."

"I'm fine, Tinnion. I just went on up the hill there for some quiet and some time to think about stuff. There's an old hidden path leading up there, and I guessed if it was that old and overgrown, I'd get to be alone awhile."

"Alone, Lana?" Tinnion smirked. "Alone with that man mountain there, is it? Did you get much thinking done, then?" The huntress' smile spread across her face and she winked as she pointed at the noam striding down the mountain path.

Lana's face turned red, her cheeks burned. "Hey! That's not... It's not what you're thinking. Nothing happened at all. I..."

Tinnion put her hand on her friend's shoulder and laughed. "Of course, Lana. Why don't you come have a cup with us before we head to our beds and tell us all about what you were up to, all alone with your friend there?"

The fire in the common room of the inn they shared was burning well and kept them comfortable. Lana sat, a cup of soft cider warming in her hands. Her cheeks were as hot as the fire with the attention of her friends on her.

"Our young friend is growing, Tinnion. She has been blooming into a woman since we left her in the city and now she is looking to get herself a man to keep her warm at night." Daowiel laughed as she spoke and sipped mead from her cup as she gestured toward Lana.

"You're right, Princess." Tinnion smiled. "She's grown fast, and I can't fault her for seeking fun. I'm just worried a man that size might squish her if he rolled over in their bed."

"It is another potential danger that concerns me, my love. Have you not noticed the size of his boots? It does not bode well for the men that might follow." Cinerea's words brought tears of laughter to Tinnion's eyes. Daowiel, though, had stopped laughing and looked concerned.

"He is a noam. There will be no man to follow, for he will collar her. The noam cannot be trusted with a woman."

"You're worrying too much, Princess." Tinnion held her wife's hand as she spoke. "He is a Southport noam. They live by the accord, not like the noam that your people knew."

"Perhaps she is not planning to have more after? She is not a warrior or hunter like ourselves, she has not spent her life looking on to the next fight or hunt. Perhaps she wants a small house of her own and a child to raise?" Cinerea's laugh turned to a smile, warm and friendly. "Are you looking for a husband, Lana? Or fun before the battle?"

"I'm not looking for anything, Cinerea. I just went up there to get away from the noise and bustle. It's not my fault he followed, and I swear nothing happened. We talked is all, and he prayed up there; it's a stone circle at the top of the hill, that's why he was there, though I didn't know it when I went up."

"Your face is too red for there to be nothing, Lana. Your cheeks would not be burning if you had not had some thoughts of him. And he is a handsome enough man, if you like men. You could do worse. There is no shame in a bit of desire." Cinerea continued with her teasing, though her friends had stopped.

Lana raised her cup to her lips and drank in silence, hoping her hands would hide her from her friends' gazes. She couldn't tell them what had happened. That she had seen Khyione, and that Grant had wanted to bind her. She couldn't tell them he had prayed again for her to be his and that she had sat quietly at his side while he petitioned his god.

"But what happened in the town? What happened with the shadows?"

The escaped shadow ran, his rags catching on brambles, the fear on his face plain to see in the moonlight. Fear of his hunter. He ran, though his legs were weak, and kept giving way, making him stumble. Lana walked through the night, her stride steady, her heart calm. She walked as fast as the shadow ran and when she raised her hands, the brambles rose and tore into the fleeing fae's skin. With a gesture, she twisted the roots beneath his feet and he stumbled. She lifted her head to the skies with a scowl and lightning burnt the ground around him, caging him in blinding light.

"Save me, Goddess!" His cry echoed over the rise.

"Seilbhbean!" She felt the chain pulled tight as the word pushed into her mind. "To heel, seilbhbean. He is mine to kill." She turned her head to see her lord, and she felt her stomach shiver. She was his, Grant had bound her, Khyione had blessed her. And as she smiled at her lord, she felt his pain. The long black blade, darker than night, pierced his body and he fell to his knees.

"Save me, Khyione!" She heard her lord's words in the stones at her feet, in her mind and bouncing from the rocks of the surrounding hills.

The dark man that had haunted Queens Isle and the woods north of Southport stood behind her fallen lord, his obsidian blade disappearing back into his hands.

"Piuthardia." His voice was like the rasp of a snake. He tore the bracelet that held the end of her leash from Grant's heavy arm and placed it on his own. "Piuthardia." The word echoed in her mind.

"Save me! Please!" Her cry split the rocks, and thunder rolled through the skies.

"It is too late for that, child." The goddess Chaint placed a hand on the shoulder of the dark man, her eyes black and cold. "You should have left when I allowed it."

Lana woke with a start; cold sweat soaking through her nightdress; and she reached for the small jade figurine of the god that hung on a leather cord around her neck. A gift from Grant, an apology for his behaviour, a promise that he would end his chase.

The camp was awake and busy before the rising sun could be seen in the east. Lana and her friends gathered to breakfast before going their own ways and make preparations for the coming battle. Tinnion and Cinerea, Shayell and Yorane would take a couple of dryad and sylph warriors and hunt down the remaining escapee. Daowiel had plans to build three trebuchet along the cliff top palisade and had gathered several laoch to make it happen. Other dryad were sent to the foot of the rise to work with most of the noam. They were building a defensible trench around the area with stakes that would impale the bulk of the attacking army should they fall into the trap. Those sylph that were not out on patrol and the remaining dryad would make barrels full of arrows in workshops alongside the noam and human blacksmiths, creating and repairing the army's weapons and armour.

Aelwynne, Crurith, Ceowald and Liayol were already sitting around a table in one of the repurposed houses, discussing their plans for the war. A meeting Lana had been told would be remarkably tedious and full of tough choices she wasn't ready to make. She felt certain that meant they were discussing who they could afford to lose and she knew she wasn't able to consider that acceptable.

She didn't want anyone to die. She knew it was inevitable, but the thought that it could be planned upset her.

With all of her friends occupied and explaining, kindly, that she was unsuited to the tasks they were carrying out, Lana found herself alone and at a loss. So she sat on a rock and watched as the town filled up with noise and the army below moved itself around the camp, doing those things they needed to do. To the north, the fires of Chaint's army burned, filling the skies with black smoke. There appeared to be thousands more camped across the plain than were busy in the camps of the queen's army and Lana's fears grew. Chaint had warned that she would kill them all, that the north was hers and would never be re-taken. Lana didn't want to die, she didn't want her friends to die. Her stomach turned at the thought of seeing her friends struggling for life. And then a coldness filled her. There had been no sign of Brighid. She knew the warrior had been in Northfort, but the city was now Chaint's. The city would not have fallen without a fight and Brighid would not have sat by and let others fight for her. Lana looked up to the skies, hoping for distraction, something, anything, to remove the dark thoughts that were haunting her.

A large white cow moved slowly across the sky before turning to mist and floating away. Lana wished she were in the pastures of Butterholt again, picking berries along the tree line and watching her father chase the cows. Her friends would all be there too and they'd spend every evening together, eating and drinking and telling stories and jokes.

The hunters made their way slowly through the woods; the dryad checking now and then with the trees around them for signs of the shadow assassin, but none were present. Tinnion knew where she had to go and made her way there directly. She didn't share the thought that the sgàil might have come back to the woods. It made little sense for them to do that, but she was just as happy having the bulk of their party making a full search. It left her to hunt alone, the way she always had. She would find the escaped fae and then call on her love. Together they would deal with the threat.

The tracks were hard to follow, even in the light of day, sgàil it seems stepped lightly and the ground had turned to rock. But Tinnion had been hunting her entire life. She placed a hand to the stone, a fine dust clung to her fingers, leaving a barely noticeable mark on the hard grey rock. In a moment she had found what she needed, the feint, partial outline of a foot. The shadow was hers now. She closed her eyes and filled her thoughts with an image of her love. A smile touched her lips as she felt the touch of Cinerea. The image faded to one of the woodland and she felt the question. *Where*? She focused on her position at the edge of the woods and, in a moment, Cinerea was with her. "You have found a trail, my love?" The dryad put a hand on Tinnion's shoulder.

"Yes, here. Do you see?" The dryad knelt at Tinnion's side and examined the ground.

"This?" She pointed to a small dark patch on the rock. "Are you certain, Tinnion? This appears to be little more than morning dew drying on a stone."

"I'm sure, Cinerea, look here." She traced a small area with her finger. "This is the ball of his foot and this here... This is his big toe. He's injured. Look, you can see how his left leg has dragged across the stone here. But there's no blood. I think this is the one that Lana defeated. You remember she described how she focused her strikes on his knee?"

Cinerea gently turned Tinnion's face to her and placed a kiss on her mouth. "You will be formidable when you can travel the bridge, my love. None will match your ability to hunt." Tinnion turned back to the stone, her cheeks touched with red.

"We'll have him in no time..." she reached for Cinerea's hand and the pair slowly followed the trail.

The sgàil was sat against a rock, his chest open, his heart gone. There were no obvious signs of struggle, but it was clear that something had killed him here, so Tinnion insisted on taking a closer look. A tiny shard of glass like stone was lodged in the open rib cage of the corpse. A shard as black as night. Tinnion gently took from the body and placed it in her pouch. She had only heard of one weapon that could have left this shard behind and she could not believe that it was at all possible for that to be here in the north. She wanted to show Shayell and Daowiel the evidence and get their opinions on it.

"It cannot be, Tinnion. I understand your concern but the obsidian man in safe in Southport, caged above the harbour. The Tay ordered it himself." Shayell's wide eyes and blanched face belied the confidence in their words.

"Did you see it done, Shayell? I left the city with Lana in the morn. His bindings were tight then, but he was still in the city cells." Daowiel looked directly at the noam, her eyes fixed on theirs.

"I did not, Princess. Though I heard no news to say that there had been problems. I was too busy calling my lord's banners to take the time. I feel, now, that this was a mistake."

"Don't lay blame on yourself, Shayell. The creature was caught and we don't know for sure that he isn't still. All we have is a tiny shard of stone. It could be another weapon." Tinnion clasped her hand to the noam's shoulder.

"Tinnion is right, Shayell. We do not know for certain that this is the creature. Though the violence of the deaths certainly makes me think it is a possibility. Even so, there is no blame to be appropriated. If it is him, we could all have done more to prevent his being here." Daowiel sat back in her seat, playing with the handle of her staff. "We should tell Lana and Aelwynne of our suspicions. We need to ensure that the watch is not completely focussed on the army across the plains. If it is him, we are all in extreme danger."

Chapter Forty-Three

And So It Begins

Lana woke to the sound of horns being blown around the camp, the signal of movement on the plains. Soldiers were grabbing and donning their armour, preparing for the battle that was almost upon them. Lana ran to the watch point and joined the army's leaders to look down onto the still dark plain. Close to five hundred foot soldiers were marching from the Tuath camp, flanked by at least fifty horsemen. Behind them, lines of men were dragging three trebuchet.

"Damn them who march to battle in the middle of night! Those things'll destroy our base camp if we let them get near enough. I need to go below and organise this army to meet them. You should be safe enough up here, m'lady. You will stay up here?" That last part sounded more like a command than a question. A way of speaking that Ceowald had perfected around Aelwynne. The large man took his leave then, running to the descending pathway without waiting for an answer.

"He'll not get there in time to keep them finding their range." Crurith's face was grim, the shadows cast across it by the torch he held made him seem worse.

"Then we'll meet them. Me and the sylph. We'll do what we can to delay them. If you can make certain Ceowald get's his army out to help as soon as possible." Lana fastened her belt around the leather vest she had taken from the shadow as she spoke and then she ran to the cliff edge.

Yorane looked around at his fellow sylph and followed her. Gliding with them to the plains below.

Lana's mind raced as she glided to the plains, the thrill of the movement lost in her worry. *My friends would ride out to meet the threat. They'd put the good of the army ahead of their own, I'm sure of it. So I have to do the same. I have to be brave like them.* Their faces flashed through her mind. She loved them all, deeply. If this was it, if this was to the moment she would take her last stand and fight then she knew she was doing what they would do. She knew that they'd understand and they'd forgive her. She didn't want to fight; she was scared, more scared than she had ever been. So scared it was causing her pain, causing her breathing to feel laboured. This would not be a fight like the one in the thieves shop or on the ship in Southport harbour, it would not be like the fight in the clearing, when she first travelled the bridge alone. This was war, it was a fight against trained warriors, the best in Mortara, and sgàil, the most feared, most sadistic of the fae. And if they managed to best all of them, against a goddess. The chances of her surviving this were slim, she wasn't certain they existed at all. But her friends would have fought and she was fighting now.

Tinnion was strapping a quiver full of arrows to her back, she already had one on either side of her belt. Cinerea was dressed in her leathers and checking her bow string. Shayell and Daowiel were guiding horses from the stables, a grim look on their faces. They had sworn to protect Lana at all costs, and each of them now were prepared to die, to die in order that she would live. Shayell was dressed in chain and plates of steel, a mighty war axe slung across their back. They mounted a large shire horse, not a speedy mount but a sturdy one, itself decked in armour.

As they rode toward the path they heard the cry.

"Lana!" The shout had come from Aelwynne, it was loud and filled with anguish. "You weren't to go out there, Lana. By the gods, child. Why don't you listen?" The queen's voice broke down into tears, falling to her knees in the town's dust.

The companions passed Ceowald on the road down the face of the rise and galloped through the encampment, calling out for the gates to be opened as they went. Once on the plain, they rode directly toward the advancing troop at speed. As they came within bow range, Tinnion, Daowiel and Cinerea drew arrows on their bows and peeled away from the others, moving parallel to the enemy line, loosing arrow after arrow with speed and precision.

Those marching toward them had not been prepared for an attack as quickly as it came. They could not have prepared for an attack such as the one they now faced. A troop of sylph, faster and stronger than they were, followed by dryad, their arrows piercing their ranks; and behind the dryad now rode the noam. A formidable force that would crash through their lines in an instant. They did not have archers ready to respond to the threat they faced, and they were being driven on, relentlessly, from the rear. They could not stop, they could not slow and defend themselves properly, so they raised their shields and did what they could to survive on the march. One man fell after another as the hunter's arrows found their marks. Their bodies causing the men behind to slow their march and stumble. Soon the line lost its form, and a crush formed in places as the momentum of the marching force behind the front line pushed. They staggered and halted. Panic took root and chaos broke out in the ranks. Soldiers pushed against those falling and those slowing down, trying to clear their own path, trying to avoid the arrows that flew with deadly accuracy toward them.

Then the sylph engaged with them, their blades and staffs a blur as they fought to break the line and destroy the siege weapons. Lana fought beside Yorane and Liayol, her staff topped with the blade that she had learned to craft. She cut through the tuath that faced her, tears flooding from her eyes as she fought.

A horn sounded from the rear of the army, and the opposing horsemen kicked their mounts into action, riding forward to meet the fae, weapons drawn. They sounded a war cry as their horses reached full gallop. The moonlight made their blades look ghostly. And then another horn sounded, drifting in on the wind from the east. And with a thunderous roar that shook the earth, an army of horsemen appeared. One hundred strong, they crashed into the flank of tuath horsemen. Sending bodies falling to the ground.

Brighid lead the new army in the collision, one hand on her reins, her blade in the other. The sharp edges flashed in the moon's light, finding their mark with each cutting swing. She parried blows left and right as she pushed her horse through the failing lines of their foe. When there was no room to push her horse forward, she leapt from her saddle, drawing her second blade and she danced.

Her companions were close behind her, their weapons already in hand, cutting and striking their way through the crowd, even as more of the rebels fell to the arrows of the huntress and the dryad.

Brighid's arrival, with an army at her back, sent the already panicking rebel force into full meltdown. Those moving the trebuchet turned and ran, forgetting any honour or oath they had sworn. They fled the field to save their lives and left the great weapons behind. In a moment, Wren was at Brighid's side. Her staff, tipped with steel, crashed into the heads and bodies of those men around her, breaking noses and ribs with ease. The pair were formidable. Months of fighting and training together gave them an instinctive bond. Where one parried, one struck, where one leaned to her right, the other moved to the left. No man could stand against their onslaught and those that did not fall ran for their lives.

The battle was over when the noam arrived. Their armoured horses and heavy axes scattered those rebels that remained. Then they set about turning the trebuchet before launching the ammunition intended to destroy their camp toward the mainstay of the rebel army.

"Lana! By the eight, girl, what are you doing out here?"

Lana ran to Brighid, tears flowing over a wide smile. She threw her arms around her friend's neck and held her tight. "Brighid! I'm so happy to see you. I didn't know if you'd be here, where you'd be or... Oh, but you are here and you're okay. I'm so happy." She clung to the warrior, showing no signs of letting go.

"I'm a wee bit tired and sore, Lana. We all are. But we're fine, I think. But why're you here, lass? A battlefield is no a safe place tae be."

Lana let her friend go. "I'm here to help you. I couldn't let you be here alone... Not that you're alone." She looked around the bloodied plain at those checking the fallen there. "But... well I couldn't just stay in the palace while you were up here fighting. I had to come. Oh, and Tinnion's here and her... Oh..." She paused. "No, she'll want to tell you that... But we came with an army. Well two armies really, a fae army and the queen's army. And the queen's voice, she's here too."

"Woah, Lana... Slow down. The army camped out on the rise there. That's the queen's army?"

Lana nodded. "Uh-huh. A thousand soldiers. Commander Qilan is in charge of them, or he was, he's injured now, but he's a brave big man and he's strong, so I'm sure he'll be fine. And Captain Crurith is with them, too. He's one of the Tay's most trusted men, Tay Gathwyn that is, not Tay Jendawyn. But the Tay sent him to look after his daughter. That's Aelwynne... The queen's voice..." Lana raced on, trying to cram a thousand thoughts into her answer. Brighid reached out and took her hand, smiling.

"Take a breath, Lana." She chuckled.

Lana wiped tears from her cheeks and smiled. "Sorry, I'm just so pleased you're here. We should all go to the waytown, it's getting late, I mean... early." She looked to the east and the rising sun. "Come on, we'll go meet our friends and head back. The others can do what needs to be done here."

"Aye we'll do that." Brighid smiled. "Have ye seen aught of MacKenna, this rabbles leader?"

"Oh, him. Yeah, I think he's prolly dead now. If he's not he's more scared than he's ever been. We put two of the other rebel lords in a cell with three of his shadow friends, but they're all dead. Someone killed them in the night. Oh, but there's so much more to tell."

Chapter Forty-Four

CATCHING UP

"I seem tae have missed a lot of happenings down in the south. Why aren't ye back home in the stead with your family?"

Brighid sat at Lana's side in the inn's hall. Feeling relaxed for the first time in many moons and desperate to chat about simpler things than the war that was so present in their lives.

"Oh, there's so much to tell, Brighid." Lana took a deep breath. "You remember Caitlin? The thief? Well she heard about a plot against the queen and we tried to tell the guard but they didn't listen and you were gone so we didn't know anyone that they would trust. So we stopped it all ourselves and the queen made Tinnion a lady and they made laywyn and Yorane sers and then she had the lady Aelwynne come to Butterholt with me and she freed my family. Then Tinnion shot the gesith, cos he was going to try to kill me and the queen made *her* gesith! After that we made a deal with the dryad to get wood cos we needed to rebuild the stead and that went really well, so the dryad wanted to meet the queen and they asked me to go back to the palace and learn to be Aelwynne's apprentice. So I did that for a bit and we signed a new treaty with the dryad. Then I went to the temple we found with Selene and there was this strange man, like a fae, but not. And he killed a lot of hunters until we captured him. So we took him prisoner and took him back to the Tay and the Queen and that's when we found out that there was trouble in the north, so I said I wanted to come stand with you. The queen said it was too dangerous so Shayell... You'll meet them tonight. I think they're just getting changed. Shayell is a noam an advisor to a lord, and they said they'd call their banner men and protect me and then Daowiel said she'd do the same and Yorane too cos he wanted to come rescue Wren." Lana smiled at the sylph warrior. "So the queen said I could come cos I had an army of my own. There's eighty fae with me, Brighid! Who would have ever thought that would happen? Dryad and noam and sylph together with humans? I think it's wonderful. Oh, and I'm kind of a lady too, now. Not really a proper one like Tinnion and Aelwynne and you, but the queen made me one of hers when I went to live in the palace."

Lana stopped talking and took a breath, smiling at her friend, whose eyes were wide.

"Ye've been busy, Lana. And a kinda Lady too! I never imagined that would happen. I am pleased for ye and for yer family. You're helping tae change the world, it seems."

"But what about you, Brighid? Are you alright? It's been hard for you, I know. I can see it in your eyes. I couldn't imagine everything you've had to do since you left Southport." Lana linked her arm through the warriors and gave her a hug as they sat.

"Aye, it's been difficult, Lana. We've watched a lot of our friends and families die and we've had tae kill as many folk tae stay alive ourselves. We've lost our homes and maybe our taydom. But we'll not stop fighting. Not while we can stand. It is so good tae see you and tae know that I've more friends tae stand with me. It's great tae see an army come tae help, too. I may sleep sound for the first time tonight!"

The reunion of the friends was a tearful event that lasted well into the middle hours of the afternoon. Cohade sat with Aelwynne, Liayol, Ceowald and Crurith. Speaking at length of everything that had occurred and discussing potential ways to proceed and the best tactics for various situations.

The others though, spent the rest of their day in lighter conversation. Catching up on all that was missed and reminiscing on times gone by as well as getting to know those friends that they hadn't previously met. The food they ate somehow tasted like the best meal at the palace and the cider flowed like the Alawe, fast and refreshing.

Lana spent the day with a broad smile on her face, even as her eyes became heavy and sleep tugged at her. She watched Brighid's delight as Tinnion introduced Cinerea and listened happily to the huntress, explaining what it is like to be bound to the dryad. She found herself gleefully excited when Anndra, caught in the moment of romance, asked Wren for her hand and burst into tears again when the sylph said yes. She didn't really know Wren, nor Anndra much beyond their names, but she knew Brighid had a love for both and that Yorane was willing to risk his own life for his sister. That was enough for Lana. If her friends loved these people so much, then she was sure they were good people that she would also come to adore.

As news spread of the proposal, the hall of the inn became full of revelry and cheer. The horrors that had passed and those yet to come were put aside, out of mind, and the day turned to a celebration of love.

As the afternoon wore on, Lana noticed her friends were peeling off into pairs and small groups, talking in private and sharing their news. Brighid and Tinnion sat in a corner of the inn, shadows concealing their faces, so Lana could not guess at the topic of their conversation. Shayell, Daowiel and Cinerea excused themselves and ventured outside for "fresh air". Anndra, Wren and Yorane moved away from the group to talk of their futures and MacAllister joined the lords and leaders of the army.

Lana felt herself yawning, her head nodding to her chest, and she put her cup down and rested her head in her hands.

"Lana." Aelwynne's voice was soft and Lana lifted her head to greet her with a tired smile. "You look exhausted, Lana. You should go to your bed. It was a long and difficult night." Lana nodded gently, her eyes barely open. "Come, I'll help you."

If the sun had risen that morning, Lana couldn't tell. The skies had filled with angry black clouds and rain poured down in sheets that soaked the earth, turning it to mud. Wind swept the plains below and Lana felt that the world was trying to rid itself of the horrors that had happened there.

It wasn't long before a guard entered the inn's hall and called Lana away from her breakfast and her friends, to Aelwynne's lodgings.

"I guess I knew this was coming." Lana sighed. "I was... I was just trying to help us all."

"And you did, Lana. But you have to understand, what you did could have ended so much differently. We're not scrapping with a few half starved bandits or a couple of priests here. It's war, and when you leapt off that cliff, Aelwynne thought she had lost you forever. She'll be angry, but it's because she was terrified. Remember that..." Tinnion held her friend's hand as she spoke.

"I will." Lana nodded sombrely .

"How are you feeling this morning? Did you sleep well?" Aelwynne sat in a high-backed chair beside a fire. Lana sat opposite her on a stool.

"I'm okay, thank you. I kept having nightmares, but I slept on and off. Did you sleep okay?"

Aelwynne nodded. "I did, Lana, thank you for asking. There are so many things to think about and do here. I find it difficult to find time for my bed, but when I find it, I sleep."

Lana smiled at her mentor before lowering her eyes. "You're mad at me, aren't you? I understand why. I know I promised you I would stay safe... I just... I saw the army, and I saw the panic and heard how we were all going to be in danger and... I... I didn't think, Aelwynne. I'm so sorry."

Aelwynne slid from her seat and to her knees on the floor in front of Lana. She wrapped her hands around her ward and pulled her forward into an embrace.

"I thought I'd lost you, Lana. I thought you'd never come back. And it isn't all about the promise I made to the queen. You understand that, don't you? You're my ward, my apprentice. You're... You're the person I spend the most of my time with. You make me laugh and feel like a person instead of just the queen's voice. I grew up in stuffy rooms with dusty books and old men like Coccus teaching me and lecturing me. I didn't have friends and then I moved to the palace and I started working for the queen. And I love her, Lana. She's a wonderful person.

But she's the queen. She never stops being a queen. When you and the princess came to the palace... That was the first time I was spending time with people that weren't much, much older than me. It was the first time I swam in the lake and laughed in the woods. I know you won't be back there, not in the same way. I know you don't enjoy what we do and won't be my apprentice anymore. I know sometimes you think I'm just spoiling your fun and being too strict. But I'm just doing what I have to do to keep you safe and help you learn. I don't want to lose you as part of my life, Lana. Even if we're days away from one another. I don't want to see you hurt, or worse. I couldn't live with that, not when I should have been protecting you."

Lana buried her head into Aelwynne's shoulder and cried, unable to speak through her tears. The two sat there for hours, in silence, gently holding and trying to comfort each other.

Chapter Forty-Five

EXPLANATIONS

The rain and wind swept the plains without stopping for two more days. Turning the land between the rise and the City of Northport into an impassable marshland. The weather made the mood of the soldiers in the camp as dark as the skies. They were wet and miserable; they struggled to train in mud inches deep, draining their energy and strength far too quickly. They could not work on keeping their equipment in the state it needed to be, unable to keep forges alight or leathers and chain-mail dry. The horses struggled too, with some turning ankles as they stumbled across the hastily fenced off pasture in search of shelter and food.

Things were a little better up in the waytown, the permanent structures of the buildings there at least providing those stationed there with shelter that the tents below could not. A lot of the ground there was rock, rather than earth, and so those staying there found movement a lot easier. Though those not actively training spent as much time as possible in doors, around fires.

"I think it is time we spoke with the humans and with Lana about our discussions. We cannot hide our suspicions and fears forever and Lana has shown that she simply does not consider her own safety when faced with the dangers we will face. She needs to understand the importance of caution." Shayell sat with Daowiel and Liayol under the trees of the eastern woodland.

"I am inclined to agree, Shayell. Her behaviour during the initial attack was brave, but incredibly reckless. We could have lost her that day had the sgàil been amongst those attacking." The sylph lord was frowning deeply as he spoke and Daowiel felt the need to defend her friend.

"She is impulsive, Liayol. I know this. But if we are to do this, you must not be harsh on her. Remember, though not well considered, her actions saved the camp on the plains and the soldiers within. She is often led by her heart and, though not an appropriate thing in war, that is not a fault. You must remember, she is not a warrior and was never trained to think as one." Daowiel's face was hard. She had seen how her friend had become withdrawn and unlike herself after Aelwynne's heart felt talk. She knew Lana had been that way, not because she was upset at her mentor, but because she felt guilt at hurting her so. The princess would not let her friend be hurt by what they had to say, and she knew the conversation would be difficult.

"Your concern for the girl is touching, Princess. I will do what I can to temper my words."

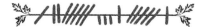

Brighid and Tinnion sat either side of Lana in the inn's hall, her other friends gathered around the rearranged tables and benches. Daowiel, Liayol and Shayell sat at the head of the tables with Aelwynne, Cohade, Anndra, MacAllister, MacHuran, Crurith and the happily recovered Qilan opposite the companions.

"Is this all of us?" Aelwynne looked to the dryad princess for an answer.

"It is, Aelwynne. Thank you all for coming. I know we all have things to be doing, preparations to make and training to be getting on with. I hope you all understand we would not have called you here unless we considered it important."

"Shall we get on with it then?" Cohade held a cup of ale in his hand that he had drained twice already. "Afore we can nae think clearly enough tae." He chuckled and raised his cup.

"Indeed." Liayol raised his brow. "May I, Princess?" Daowiel nodded her agreement.

"There are two issues we wish to address here. Perhaps it is best to start with the easiest. You may have noticed that I have increased the watch and guard significantly in the last few days. The reason for this goes back to those shadows who escaped from their cage." The sylph paused and took a drink of his wine. "As you know, Tinnion led a group of hunters in pursuit of those shadows. The news she returned with was... concerning. An unknown assailant had killed both. One that left no traces of its presence and killed in a manner that disturbed us all. The huntress's sharp eyes found our only clue as to the killer. A tiny shard of dark, glass like stone." The sylph held the shard up for those present to see.

The announcement was greeted with confusion by most, but Lana and Aelwynne both gasped.

"It can't be. We captured him... they put him in a cage, didn't they? Aelwynne?" Lana looked to her mentor, her eyes wide.

"They did, Lana." Aelwynne raised her hand to her mouth and took a deep breath. "They hung him over the cliff in a wooden cage, as we discussed." She paused, biting her lip. "Lore keepers were tasked to record any words he spoke and sat all day and night. They... I'm sorry, I should have told you all, but we thought it better for the army and for you to be unconcerned. On the second morning, the cage was empty. The city guard searched the land, but the cage was open at the bottom. They believed the creature must have fallen to his death in the ocean below."

"He's here... He's... He was in the camp. We have to find him, we have to catch him." Lana turned white and Brighid took her hand to comfort her.

"We thought him dead. We had no reason to believe he could have survived." Aelwynne's face mirrored Lana's now, and she looked at her apprentice her eyes pleading silently for forgiveness.

"There is no blame at your door, Aelwynne." Daowiel tried to calm the queen's voice. "We all thought that cage would hold him. Now that we know we need all be certain to keep our guard high. This creature is more dangerous than the army we face. Have no doubt about that."

"Now that we have confirmed that fear." Liayol began. "We must discuss the creatures words."

"What do you mean? He only said a few things... Said he wanted to kill us all and told us to go to the temple."

"He said one more thing, Lana. Do you remember it?"

Lana nodded at Daowiel. "Yes, he said Pewtahdeea." Liayol chuckled at Lana's drawn out pronunciation of the word.

"Piuthardia, Lana. And you know what that means?"

"Selene told me it means sister."

"It is more than that chi..."

"Lana." Daowiel interjected before the sylph lord could continue. "The word means more than that. It is two words really. Piuthar, meaning sister and Dia, meaning... God or divine."

"But that doesn't make sense, Daowiel. I mean, it didn't make any sense when he called me sister but that is even sillier." The princess smiled at her friend.

"Lana, you have visions sometimes, dreams of things past, correct?" Lana nodded confirmation to her friend. "Have you ever seen a meeting of the goddesses? Just the goddesses and some fae... Not the gods?"

Lana's brow furrowed, and she frowned. "Yes, one time I did. They were in... I think it was the temple in Southport. They were talking about their firstborn and watching a lady nurse her baby. They argued for a bit and said they were going to give the baby a gift."

The princess looked at the sylph lord. "It is true, then. I believe we have, at least, a partial answer."

"It seems so, Princess." The sylph nodded.

"Lana. You know what the firstborn are?"

"Of course, they're the fae that the gods made first. Like... You, you're great great great great grandma was the first dryad, and that's why you're a princess. That means you can shape wood when other dryad can't."

"That is right. Each of the firstborn had more ability than the others, and their lines are pure. We can trace them back for millennia. There are stories, little more than rumours now they are so old. They say that the goddesses gathered, in anger at the gods, and gifted a female baby those skills that their own firstborn possessed. That child lived in the temple of Qura and was taught to use those skills; and when she had a daughter, that daughter took her place. That ended when the humans took arms against the fae. But there is nothing to say that the line was broken."

"You think I'm related to that baby, don't you?" Lana slumped in her chair, her head lowered. "You think I'm like the firstborn cos of what the obsidian man said?"

"It is something we have to consider, Lana. Your abilities, the way you interact with trees and see things so clearly, they're stronger than all of my laoch, and your shaping. You know even I cannot shape the staff the way you have done. I cannot explain those things, except possibly, with this information." The room fell silent. No one dared look at the princess or at Lana and those two lowered their heads.

"I don't understand, Princess." Aelwynne broke the momentary silence. "This creature, the obsidian man, he was calling Lana divine sister?" Daowiel nodded slowly. "And you believe Lana's vision is proof that the goddesses gave the human child the gifts of the firstborn?" The princess continued to nod. "Now you believe that Lana is descended from that baby and that she holds the gifts of the gods?"

"I do." The princess raised her head once more. "But there is more. Though I have no proof and my friends here do not fully agree. It is my belief that when Lana entered the Heartwood, she encountered the stone over which the gods cast their final blessings. I believe that those blessings awakened that which lay dormant in Lana's line since their expulsion from the temple."

"What yer saying then is that this wee lass here is stronger than all the fae?" Cohade put his cup down and leant forward, his brow raised.

"No, Cohade. I believe she has great potential, but she is not, now, as strong as that."

"Ach, well what good is all this talking and thinking if she's no going tae be the answer tae our problems here?"

"Father! You've had a cup tae many. We're talking about the life of my friend here. A young lady. Not some kind of weapon tae be used. You should take tae te yer bed until yer thinking straight." Brighid's face was red as she scolded her father. "I'm sorry, Lana. He's not been the same since the battle. I think he's struggling tae come to terms with all we've lost."

Lana smiled at her friend and squeezed her hand. "It's Okay, Brighid. I understand. I think I'd like to go to my bed too, though."

"Ye can all go." Brighid looked up from her friend and took on a commanding tone. "All but Tinnion, Aelwynne and the princess." She looked about at the men around the table. "Go on! Get!" In one motion, all but those named stood, scraping benches and chairs across the floor. In a moment, the room was clear, only those closest to Lana left behind.

"Are you okay, Lana? It's a lot to take in." Tinnion turned to her friend her hand on her arm.

"I'm fine... I mean, I will be." Lana bit her cheek. "How long have you known? How long have you kept it secret from me?"

"I... I errrr." Tinnion looked around the room at her companions.

"I've seen you all talking, I know you all knew, 'cept Aelwynne." Lana stared at her feet.

"We did not intend to keep it from you, Lana. But we did not want to worry you, or put you under such pressure until we were more certain. I am sorry that it has hurt you." Daowiel looked shamed at her friends question.

"I've been hiding things too." Lana's face grew red.

"What do you mean, Lana?"

"It's not just visions anymore, not just the dreams. After that dream about the goddesses and the baby, I heard a voice. Well, it was in my head but it's like I heard it and it argued with me... Told me more or less the same things you're saying now. Said my mam could have done the same thing if they'd learnt. I don't know who it is though, it isn't one of the goddesses. I know their voices now. And then Khyione spoke to me once, too. That one was a bit like a vision, though. I saw him in the stone circle at the top of the rise. 'Cept it wasn't just a vision cos he spoke to me... Like directly to me. He told me that he didn't leave and that he still lives here but in the rocks and the earth and that the goddesses had become part of me. I don't know how but I think you're right, I think it was when I touched the stone in the old fortresses garden."

"By the eight, Lana! When did this happen?" Aelwynne had crossed the room to sit closer to Lana.

"The night the shadows escaped. That's when Khyione spoke to me."

"Wait... That was the night you were up on the rise with that noam. Are you... Are you sure about this, Lana?"

Lana blushed bright red. "He... Khyione didn't talk to me 'cos he wanted to tell me this stuff. He didn't even know 'til I refused to do what he wanted and then he got angry and grabbed me and looked into my soul and then he said he had been betrayed and the goddesses lived inside me."

"You refused an order from Khyione?" Daowiel laughed. "You are a wonder, Lana. I may be entirely wrong about all of this. I think you are truly my sister. You behave so much like a dryad!"

"I knew it! I kept checking the lassie's ears... I'll bet they're all pointy now." Brighid joined in with the princess's laughter and that caused everyone there to laugh.

"Doesn't anyone else want to know what our little sister here denied the god?" Tinnion looked around at her friends.

"It's not important." Lana tried to hide her face in her hands.

"I think if a god felt the need to appear to you and command you to do something, it must have been fairly important, Lana." Lana's friends all mumbled their agreement at Tinnion's statement and Lana sighed.

"He wanted me bound to someone... And I said there was no way that was ever going to happen. Then he got angry and after he shouted he... Well, he just kinda disappeared."

"And just who did he want you bound tae? Who does Khyione think is good enough for our little sister?"

"The noam warrior, Grant."

"I will kill him." Daowiel's hand went to her staff.

"No, Daowiel. He doesn't know anything about it, he wasn't there, he came after Khyione had gone."

"So it *was* that mountainous noam that tried to sneak down the rise after you?" Tinnion tilted her head and smirked. Lana nodded without a word.

Aelwynne coughed, redirecting the attention to her. "So, what are we going to do about all of this?"

"We have to protect her." Daowiel's tone was matter of fact. "We have to protect her, even if it means everyone of us dies. Because Lana is the only one of us that has a chance to defeat Chaint."

"But you said she wasn't strong enough to do that, Daowiel."

"She is not, yet. And I do not want those men to believe she is a weapon to be used. It may be that Lana is capable of standing against Chaint, with help, but I will not see her put in danger. I do not wish her near the battlefield unless she is ready. However, if we help her, if we do what we can to unlock that which is still within her, then she may be ready in time. If you want us to, Lana? I do not wish to place you under pressure. You are under no obligation. We may be capable of winning this war without killing Chaint if we destroy her army."

"I'll do it. I have to." Lana looked around at each of her friends. "If you all help me, perhaps I can face her. Maybe even win. I'm... I'm scared though. I don't think I'm what you all think I am. I don't feel any different to how I always felt. I don't really want to be what you think I am, either. But I want to help make things right."

Chapter Forty-Six

TRAINING

Lana spent the next two mornings with Daowiel, working on her abilities with the flora and wood shaping. Stretching her mind as far as she could within the network of trees, pushing out to include other plants. They didn't think the way trees thought, but Lana realised grasses had very similar connections with each other that the trees had and she explored beyond the borders of the woodland. She could sense the rebel army on the plains and the animals in the hills. She thought that with a lot of practice and a lot of concentration, she might even push herself and sense things as far away as Glamithren. Though she felt far from capable of that at the moment.

On the first afternoon Lana spent time with Yorane and Wren, the sylph taught her how the wind and the temperature could affect how air flows. They showed her how that could extend or shorten her gliding and showed her how to use her body to direct herself in the air on her longer glides.

On the second afternoon, Brighid and Tinnion joined them. The four friends carried training blades and attacked Lana, building the speed of their attacks as the afternoon wore on, pushing her to move faster and with more fluidity. She gained many bruises that afternoon and a nasty looking bump on her head. It did not impress Aelwynne.

"You were supposed to go at a pace she could manage and build slowly so she didn't get hurt."

Wren shrugged at the queen's voice. "She seemed to learn faster when she got a little knock."

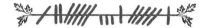

"Lana?" The healer, Neve stood at Lana's door.

"Uh-huh."

The nymph smiled at the response. "It is good to meet you at last, Lana. I heard much about you from the lady Brighid. She asked me to come by and check on your bruises. Oh my, That is a nasty lump you have on your head. May I come in?"

Lana opened up the door fully and gestured for the nymph the enter. The pair sat on her bed and Neve gently ran her fingers over the bump on Lana's head. "Now what were you doing to get in such a state, Lana?"

"My friends are helping me learn how to get better at sylph and dryad things. They were teaching me how to be faster in a battle. Sometimes they were too fast for me though." The nymph stifled a laugh at Lana's sulky last words.

"Well, this is strange indeed, a human trying to become more fae."

"I can do some fae things. Like I can shape wood and talk to trees and other things like the dryad and I can jump off things like a sylph and I'm getting faster too. But I was always quite fast at running. I always used to beat my dad in races. I'm just trying to get better and do more."

"And you think being beaten with sticks is the way to learn?"

Lana shrugged. "I don't really know how to learn. But Daowiel... err, I mean, Princess Daowiel and Yorane and Lady Wren, they all teach me using fighting."

"Of course, they are all warriors. But there are other ways. We nymph do not use fighting to teach our young."

"How do you teach them?" The sulking had passed from Lana's voice and was replaced by eager curiosity.

"I could show you if you would like? Though I am unsure how helpful it would be for you. I am skilled with water, not with trees nor jumping."

Lana smiled and touched the healer's forearm. "Could you? Please? Maybe how you teach things can help me get better with the things I know. I'd rather try that than get more bruises, for sure."

The nymph chuckled. "Very well, you bring over your water bowl and jug of water and we will try."

Lana jumped up and pulled her water stand toward the bed, then filled the bowl from the jug.

"Alright, Lana. Now, gently, put your hand flat in the water."

Lana looked at the bowl and flattened her hand, then gently lowered it into the chilly water with a small splash. The nymph bit her lip to hide a laugh.

"Hmmm. Yes, just like a child. When the dryad sleep they often do so in the trees. You say you are able to do some dryad things. Are you able to do that?"

Lana nodded, and the fae went on. "Good, tell me this. Were I to walk up to a tree and push my hand to it, what would happen?"

"If it was a small tree it'd bend, if it was a big tree, nothing would happen. 'Cept the tree would think you were odd."

"Yes, I imagine it would." The laughter was too hard to hold in, no matter how she tried. Once the laughter passed, the fae went on. "You can both push a tree like that and put your hand into the tree, can you not?"

"I can. It's different when you wanna go into the tree you have to... you have to push differently."

"Indeed. It is the same with water. Let me show you." The nymph placed her hand over the water and the gently lowered it within. As she did so, her hand became as clear as the water. Lana watched on with wide eyes and an open mouth.

"Now, if I were to 'enter the water' completely, as you do with the trees, I would be able to remain there, sleeping, or hiding. If I wished to explore a river or a lake, I could open my mind to the water and sense those things within, even sense the shape of the lake or the course of the river. Should I decide to move from one side of a lake to another, I would be able to 'push' myself to that place, provided I know it well enough."

Lana nodded with a wide smile. "Yes! I can do that with the trees too. If I wanted to, I could go all the way back down to Southport from here. I go across a kind of bridge and then when I come out the other side, I'm where I want to be. It's kinda the same when I shape wood too, 'cept instead of going in I explain to the wood what I want it to be and then kind of move it around until it is that. Sometimes you need to persuade the wood though 'cos some wood is stubborn."

The nymph smiled. "Like this?" She raised her hand from the bowl, cupping some of the water in her palm and then, with her other hand, drew the water upward into a small water tower, which she then twisted. Once she had the shape in her palm, she gave Lana a wink.

"Yes! So, you can do with water all the things that I can do with trees. Oh." Lana's eyes opened wide again. "You must be first born too! Only the first born dryad can shape."

The nymph nodded, her brow raised. "I am, Lana. You know some lore?"

"A little." Lana smiled. "Neve? Could I try again? Putting my hand in the water, I mean."

"Of course, Lana. If you think it would help you."

Lana straightened her fingers and placed her palm to the surface of the water, then she closed her eyes. She could feel a warmth in the water left over from the fae's hand and a tingling sensation where that warm water touched her skin. She imagined the water was the trunk of a tree and pushed gently with her fingers. The tingling sensation, the kind of tingle you feel as blood rushes back to your hand after sitting on it, spread.

"Lana!" Neve's voice was high pitched and breathy." Lana, how are you? How is that possible?"

Lana opened her eyes to see her fingers as translucent as the nymph's had been. She jerked her hand back from the bowl with a splash and held it up to her face. It was perfectly normal.

"You did it, Lana. You were entering the water. But that cannot be possible. You are not nymph, you have no nymph blood."

"I don't have dryad blood either." Lana shrugged.

"You do not? I thought... You are not...? You and the Princess?"

It was Lana's turn to laugh, and she did it loudly. "No! I mean, I love the princess, I do. But it's like I would love a sister, like I love my brother and my mam and dad. Same with Brighid and Tinnion too."

"I see, then... Then you are more complicated than I thought. Much more complicated. I think I would like to spend more time talking with you. If the circumstances allow. Could I join you and your friends when I am not working?"

"Of course, Neve! You'd be welcome anytime. Could you maybe help me with this bump, though?"

By morning, the bump was gone, and Lana's spirits were high. She wanted to tell all of her friends what had happened; she wanted to tell everyone, but with a little thought she realised it would be better if she didn't go shouting it around the camp.

She woke Daowiel early, shaking her gently from her sleep.

"What is it, Lana?" Daowiel's eye's were barely open and her voice was clipped.

"I put my hand in water, Daowiel! Last night when Neve was here."

"Uh huh. Very good." The princess groaned, closing her eyes and turning back onto her side.

"No." Lana sighed. "You don't understand. I put my fingers in the water the way the nymph do."

Daowiel sprang to a sitting position, her eyes wide open. "You did what?"

"Neve was showing me how the nymph teach their children and we talked a little about what they do and what we do and then I copied what she did in our water bowl 'cept I pretended it was a tree and my fingers entered the water like hers did!"

"You pretended it was a tree?"

Lana nodded with a wide smile. "Well, I realised. They do the same thing with the water as we do with trees, so they must do it the same way. So when I put my hand next to the water I closed my eyes, and I imagined I was next to a tree and then I pushed and then Neve sounded shocked and called my name and I opened my eyes and my fingers were gone... Well not gone, just, not there. Oh... Do you think?" Lana lifted her hand, spreading her fingers, and she closed her eyes. There was a slight draft from the window that she felt brushing past her fingers. She concentrated on the moving air and pushed.

Chapter Forty-Seven

THE MER

Giant bones stood like arched promenades along the beach, the sun bleached rib cages of giant creatures long dead. Scattered wooden planks, splintered barrels and other debris showed that passing ships had fared no better than the large, beached beasts.

"You're an idiot, Xen! There's nothing here. Not a thing worth picking up, never mind traipsing around and digging up rubble and piles of bloody sand for."

"Aye, ye keeps on sayin' it, Cat, and I keeps on tellin' ye, I've tokens hidden here, tokens we'll be needin' if we're gonna get any help in Dolphin Baye."

"What help are we goin' to get in Dolphin Baye, Xen? We need to get to Tanearam and stop wastin' time, stopping off at every island we pass. This aint s'posed to be a sight seein' trip. I just want to get the information I need and get myself back home."

"And how's ye gonna be doin' that then, Cat? Eh? Ye aint got no labos or loons or sols in yer purse to be payin' for the information and ye aint got none o the clothes they all wears. Ye'll stick out like a sore thumb and yer name 'n face'll be known across the whole island afore ye've gotten so much as directions to an inn." The pirate held his hand out in front of Cat and stopped walking. "There." He pointed to a grassy dune rising out of the sand a little ways north.

That's it, I'm certain of it, just on that there grassy dune. We'll dig up me chest and me tokens and we can go get back to the ship."

Cat sighed. "And you said that it was on that last bloody dune. I'm aching, wet and cut up from all that bloody grass. It'd be easier for me to take coins an' clothes from the circle priests themselves than it's been trudging around on some deserted, stinking beach looking fer something you lost years ago."

Cat threw down her spade and lay down on the pile of sand she had spent the afternoon shifting. "That's it Xen, I'm done. I can't dig anymore. We've been at this all day now and all I've got to show for it is blisters on my hands. I'm going back to the ship before it starts to get dark."

"Just give me a little while longer, Cat. I'm telling ye it's here. I swears it. One more hole, I promise, and we'll have it." The pirate looked up at the sun in the west and wiped his brow. "We've time."

"We've already moved so much of the sand the whole dune's shifted six foot to the north. There's nothing left up here, if there was ever anything up here to begin with."

Xentan opened his mouth to reply but snapped his lips closed as the sound of horns drifted from the south.

"Is that the ship, Xen? Tell me that aint the ship..." Cat sat up sharply, her eyes scanning the seas to the south for signs of problems.

"Aye. It could be naught to concern us, Cat. But per'aps we'd best be getting back like ye wanted just in case."

The young thief sprung to her feet, and started a run down the beach toward the small landing boat.

"Yer spade, Cat!" The pirate shouted after her.

"Dammit, Xen. Leave them and run, they'll still be here tomorrow... If we're able to use 'em."

The dinghy was surrounded by warriors, four of them in total, their long hair dripping wet, their blue skin glistening in the sun. Each of them carried barbed spears, vicious weapons that would tear the flesh as much on the way out as on the way in. At their sides hung blades, the likes of which Cat had never seen. Green and glass like, they looked as sharp as the best steel swords in Southport.

"Mer." Xentan hissed. "I'm sorry, Cat. I think we might be at the end of our journey."

"You're supposed to be a dreaded pirate, Xen. Draw your bloody sword and earn your purse."

"I'd rather run, Cat. They don't much like being out on the land too long. If we hide, we've a better chance to stay alive." The pirate looked back toward the dunes.

"Not likely, Xen. I didn't sail across that damnable ocean to be trapped on no bloody forsaken island. "

The battle was hard and long, Cat, already exhausted by a days digging felt heavy and slow as she ran toward the warriors. She drew a blade from her belt and threw it with deadly accuracy toward the closest mer. It struck the fae's chest and sank to the hilt in their flesh. The mer fell, his spear hitting the sand at his side. As she got closer, she dipped and rolled along the sand, narrowly avoiding a spear to her side. She grabbed the fallen mer's spear as she rose, slicing it across another warrior's stomach.

Xentan let out a roar as he ran toward the fae, his long, wide blade raised aloft. He struck the spear thrown toward him from the air and made the decision to target that warrior first. He ran straight at the mer, crashing into him and sending him to the ground. As the warrior hit the sand, the pirate straddled him and drew his sword across the man's throat.

The warrior facing Cat bared his teeth with a growl, one hand across his bleeding stomach, the other thrusting his spear randomly toward his opponent. Cat leapt backward, avoiding the point of the spear but lost her footing in the dusty sand and toppled to her back. The mer was on top of her in an instant, stabbing at her with his spear. She rolled to her right, and the spear dug into the sand by her ear. Her face blanched.

She swung her legs, catching the knee of the warrior as he was pulling his spear from the sand. His leg buckled and he let go of his weapon's shaft as he stumbled forward. Cat scrambled to pull the second knife from her belt as the mer fell across her, covering her tunic with his blood. She brought up her arm, stabbing at him wildly until she could no longer hear his breathing or feel him move. After struggling to push the heavy bodied mer from her, she lay back, exhausted. "Xen?"

The pirate screamed as a mer pulled their spear from his shoulder, pulling him backward from the dead warrior beneath him. Muscle and flesh pulled from the bone by the barbs on the weapon, his skin tore and his blood spilled to the sand. With his sword arm limp, Xentan grabbed his blade in his left hand and swung it wildly as he scrambled to his feet, deflecting a blow from the spear through sheer luck. Upright once more, the pirate used his size against the smaller mer, his sword slashing and thrusting at random. He growled at the warrior and leapt forward. The frenzied attack knocked the spear from the mer's hand and the pirate's momentum knocked him to the sand. As Xentan stumbled, his blade pierced the mer's stomach, driven deep into the sand beneath him by the pirate's weight. Dying, but not yet out of fight, the mer struck at Xentan's head with his fist. Pounding him repeatedly and causing him to black out.

The moon was high when Xentan and Cat climbed the rope ladder to the ship's deck. Greeted with panic and sailors running back and forth, they sought Laywyn and found him screaming at a sailor coming up from the stores.

"Get back down there and get the bleeding hole patched or we'll all be in the water."

"I'm telling you, ser. We're done. There's no way we can make the repairs while we're on the ocean." The sailor was soaked through and shaking.

"What the voids going on?" Xentan roared as he approached the men.

"Those bleeding mer have ripped a hole the size of a man's head in the hull. I've had men trying to get it patched, but they're struggling and the store's filling up. If we don't get ourselves out of here soon, they'll rip the ship apart."

The sound of banging and knocking came from below accompanied by the sounds of rushing water and sailors splashing around frantically and the ship began to creak.

"Right 'en. You." Xentan pointed at the sailor. "Get yourself below and get that hole patched. I want none of yer excuses. Get it done or I'll use yer own head to do it. Have those that aint helping ye drag anything heavy that isn't drinking water up here and throw it over. Cat, Laywyn, yer with me... We'll get this ship goin' and see if we can run far enough te get these damned fae off of us."

It wasn't difficult to motivate the sailors, and the ship was soon moving north, the main sail billowing full of wind. Men were running to and fro from the store, dumping whatever they could overboard.

"Throw that ballast harder, lads. Ye might hit one o' the buggers and keep 'em off us." Xentan wrestled with the ship's wheel as he shouted commands to the panicking sailors.

"Listen to me a minute, Cat." The pirate lowered his voice so only those beside him could hear. "I've somethin' to say and it's important. There's been times in the past I'd a happily seen ye dead, ye've been a thorn in me side more often than a friend. This isn't one o' those times, though. I wouldn't wish ye drowned or torn apart by them mer. If we're lucky, we'll get to the tail strait afore we go down. There's plenty ships and boats there to pick us out o' the ocean. When we start to go down, grab yersel something what floats and pull yersel up on it. Keep yersel out of the water much as ye can and hang on fer yer life." Cat frowned at the pirate's words.

"You've not been so annoying these last few moons yourself. We'll see this through together, Xen. You, me and Laywyn. We'll be fine, I know we will. I'll not die in the ocean, I refuse."

"Aye, lass. That's the spirit."

Chapter Forty-Eight

Memories

Lana sat on the rock alone. Her hair clung to her face, wet with the downpour of rain. She had been there since morning, trying, desperately, to join with the air as she could with the trees. She raised her hand and closed her eyes and as she felt the breeze brush against her fingers, she pushed.

What you are doing is not correct. Lana sighed. *I know that.* She shook her head as if to shake the words from her mind. In a moment more of concentration, she felt the breeze again and pushed.

What you are doing is not correct. Lana rolled her eyes. *I know it's not right.*

And yet you keep doing it. She paused for a moment and took a deep breath. *Because if I keep trying, I might be able to do it right.* Again she shook her head, again she raised her hand and pushed against the wind.

What you are doing is not correct. Lana brought her hand down in a fist to her knee and let out a grunt. *Why don't you leave me alone? Who are you anyway?*

I am memory. I cannot leave you alone. Lana paused. *Memories don't talk.*

I am not talking. The low growl that came from Lana startled the passing sylph that was out on patrol. She smiled to the warrior and shook her head. "Sorry, just, trying something..." She shrugged.

Well, if you're not talking, who is?

You are talking with yourself, or, rather, thinking against yourself. She squeezed her eyes tight, hoping that it might drive away the voice and its silly declarations. *If I'm talking to myself, then I want to stop so I can concentrate.* She had thought this last thought angrily and hoped it would work and the voice, her other voice? Would be silent. Then she closed her eyes and held up her hand and tried once more to join with the air.

What you are doing is not correct. *You aren't being helpful.* ***I am a memory, not a teacher. You know what you are doing is wrong. You hold that memory, yet you keep trying.*** *'Cos if I keep trying, I might get it right.* Lana's internal voice became high pitched and loud, irritated at repeating herself. ***You cannot get it right. You are not doing what you are doing badly. What you are doing is not correct.*** Lana took a deep breath and tried to calm herself. *This is silly, you can't be my memory 'cos I've never done it right so I couldn't remember that.*

Why would you think that I am your memory?

Lana stomped into the common room of the inn, causing a puddle to form where she stood.

"Where've ye been, Lana? You're soaking. Come over here by the fire and warm up before ye catch yer death of cold. Someone get her a cloth tae dry herself." Brighid put her arm around her friend, rubbing her arms as she walked her to the fire and sat her down.

"You look like there's more than rain making you miserable, Lana. What is it?" Tinnion handed her a cup of warm cider.

"I don't know what's wrong. I just can't seem to get it right no matter what I try, and..." She bit her lip, thinking better of talking about the argument she had with... Well, she still wasn't sure who or what she had argued with.

"And, what?" The huntress held her hand. "If there's something wrong you can tell us, perhaps we could help."

Lana looked around the room. Shayell sat in the corner snoring gently, but other than that they were alone.

"He came to see Daowiel, but the dryad are all in the woods. He's been snoring a good while now. Everyone else is doing their own thing, it's just us three and the sleeping noam."

Lana nodded and took a sip of her cider. "You remember when we all had that meeting, and you told me you thought I... Well, when you said I might not just be normal? I told you I heard a voice that I didn't know?" Her friends nodded. "I heard it again. Well, thought it. I think. It said it was a memory, and that I was just arguing with myself and I said it couldn't be cos it was telling me things I couldn't have remembered cos I haven't done them. And then it said it wasn't my memory. It's scaring me... and it's irritating. More irritating than Andel was when we were bairns. Am I going mad? Like the first born sylph did?"

"No, hen. Yer no going mad, I'm sure of that. We know yer circlet has given ye visions of things that have happened in the past. This must be part of that is all. There's nought tae worry on."

"Brighid's right, Lana. We all talk to ourselves from time to time. You're carrying around the memories of a god on your head. They're bound to seep through and confuse you from time to time." Tinnion smiled warmly at her friend, squeezing her hand gently.

"You're right." Lana's mouth dropped open, and a glint shone in her eyes. "I've got Qura's memories in the circlets stone. That's why she made it. And now I have them. I just need to work out how to remember them." She kissed both of her friends on the cheek. "You're so wonderful, both of you. Thank you!"

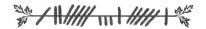

"Are you busy today, Tin?" Lana waved her sausage laden fork at her friend.

"Not in this rain, I'm not. Nobody is, except the poor sylph on patrol. Not that the rain seems to bother them. Why?"

"I was hoping you might come with me so I could show you something?" She covered her mouth as she spoke to stop from spreading bits of half chewed sausage across the table.

"Of course I will. Should we call on Brighid too?" Tinnion tore some bread from a bun and chewed on it.

"No, not today. I'd love for her to come, but she won't be able to. I'm sure she'll be fine having a drink with her family and maybe we can bring her something back as a present." Lana smiled and stabbed a piece of bacon with her fork.

Tinnion's eye's narrowed. "Just what have you got planned?"

"You'll see." She grinned.

"You've been sleeping in the trees, with Cinerea. Have you been inside by yourself yet?" The friends stood at the base of a young pine. Tinnion shook her head.

"Not yet, Lana. Cinerea's always been there with me. I'm not sure that I can yet. I know I can't use the bridge."

"You know how to talk to the trees, though? You know how to see through them and join their minds?"

"Yes. I've done that myself. Looking around the woods for prey... And for Cinerea."

Lana smiled widely. "Show me."

Tinnion raised her hand and placed it against the tree. Closing her eyes, she pushed her mind out to the tree and connected with the woodland. She jumped a little as she felt Lana's hand cover hers, but then smiled as she realised it was her friend.

"You're not talking, Tin. You're opening a door and walking in but you're not asking the tree or telling her who you are... Introduce yourself."

"Oh. I... I didn't realise. I'm sorry. Err hello, tree. I'm Tinnion... Is that right, Lana?" Tinnion's eye's remained closed but Lana could see the uncertainty in her face.

"Kind of, Tin. Yeah. It's how I did it when I was young, but the trees can't talk back that way. Try putting those words in your mind and gently, really softly, push them into the tree's mind."

Tinnion's brow furrowed, and Lana smiled. She could feel her friend's words echoing through the woods.

"You did it, Tin! Can you hear the trees now? Saying hello?" Tinnion nodded with a smile that filled her face.

"I can, Lana. I can! They're telling me all about themselves now."

Lana chuckled. "They'll talk to you forever if you let them, Tin. But there's more. Ask her if you can go inside." The huntresses brow furrowed again as she asked her question and her hand began to sink into the trunk of the pine.

They sat within the tree for a while, Tinnion smiling and chatting about her new experience, comparing their thoughts on the way she had come there.

"The more you talk to the trees, the easier it becomes. You get to know them, know what they think and how they feel. You learn how to greet each one properly too. They're just like us. Everyone has their own way. They like to say hello and talk. And you did ever so well. I'm so proud and so happy for you."

The huntress blushed. "Thank you, Lana... It feels strange, you teaching me. I've always thought of you like a little sister, someone to protect and to help. And here you are, being the teacher. Even Cinerea couldn't help me do this."

"I think sometimes, when you do something every day, when you grow up doing it and it's natural to you, you kinda forget what it is you're really doing. The trees feel a dryad and they just open up. They trust them. They feel it's natural. Even those that have never met a dryad figure it out quite quick. It means Daowiel and Cinerea never have to try to do these things, they just do them."

"Can I tell you something, Lana?" Tinnion's smile left her face for a moment and her voice went low. Lana nodded without a word.

"I know that you're scared. I mean, I know you fear the war and you're horrified by the death you've seen. That's normal. But I know that you're more scared by what we told you. I think you're scared that we think you're not Lana anymore. That you're scared you'll change and stop being the friend we all love." Lana nodded again, then lowered her eyes as they filled with tears. Tinnion took her hand in hers and smiled again.

"Well, you will change, Lana. You already have. But you're still our little sister and you always will be. Even when you're teaching us. You'll never lose that smile and that cheeky look when you're planning something. You'll never learn to breathe between your words when you're excited. And we'll always love you. You aren't going to lose us. I promise you that. Even when the worst thing happens, even when we're gone, we'll always be with you and you'll always be in our hearts."

The tears rolled down Lana's cheeks, and she put her head to Tinnion's. "Thank you." She managed to whisper through her sobs.

Chapter Forty-Nine

When Hope Dies Friends Rally

By morning, the skies had cleared and the sun's warmth touched the plains, causing a heavy mist to form. Lana used her newly strengthened ability and pushed her mind through the network of grasses and plants across the plain, checking on the opposing army and ensuring there were no assassins heading their way. She was happy to report to her group of friends that the rebels remained in place, though there were no signs at all of the sgàil or their goddess.

"Aye, they'll be up in the dry and comfort of Northfort, nae doubt. Nae reason for them tae have suffered the winds and rains now they've been unmasked and have full control of the army." The thought of shadows in the fortress built to protect the north against them made Brighid grimace.

"Do you think they'll move today?"

"I doubt it, Lana. The plains will take a few days tae dry out and they'll not be keen tae attack through the mud. I'd imagine Chaint will mak her way down frae the fortress to give the command an' all. I think we'll have a while tae shake the rust off and train, check our defences and ready ourselves."

"At least the rain's let us prepare a bit more then, and spend a bit more time together." Lana's smile was as bright as it had been since the rains started.

"Aye, it has that. Tinnion was well pleased with yer day together yesterday. She said ye made her cry though... I've not seen her do that before."

Lana smiled. "It was nice. I wish you could have been with us, but it was something I really wanted to help her with. You understand, don't you?"

Brighid chuckled. "Of course! I'd have loved it, of course. But I ken there are things I cannae dae with you. I'm thinking I'll move my things over and stay with you all in the inn, though. I love ma family, but I miss hearing yer tales after ye've had a cup or two o' wine."

"I made you something yesterday. I hope you like it." Lana reached into her bag and pulled a wooden circlet from it, at its centre a large piece of amber set into the stylised head of a white hart.

"Ye made this? It's beautiful! I'll treasure it as long as I live." The tuath warrior pulled her friend into an embrace with a smile. "Is it yer intent tae mak us all cry afore we fight?" Lana gripped the leathers of her friend tightly and refused to let go.

"I just want you all to know what you mean to me. Just in case. You and Tin and Daowiel and Selene. You're my best friends in the world. I don't think I'd have made it if I hadn't met the four of you. If friends could bind their souls like lovers can I'd be with you all forever and ever." Brighid hid her face in Lana's hair, but she felt the tuath's tears against her skin and her own ran down her cheek.

"Brighid? What will it be like, fighting in the final battle with so many warriors?" Brighid broke the embrace and turned to look at Lana, placing a hand on her shoulder, comforting and strong.

"It's hard Lana, it's physically exhausting and tears at yer heart. It's not like the small battle we had in the clearing. Or even the battle we won a few days back. There's little room tae move and no room tae dance as we do. When the lines meet, there will be a crash like thunder and then a crush. Warriors falling at your feet, their bodies stopping your movement. Weapons hacking and swinging wildly. Strength and luck are all you have in those moments. Your skill will nae help until the majority fall or the line breaks. And ye canna stop, there aint no stopping til it's over and by then ye've been ready tae fall yerself a half dozen times or more."

Lana looked up at her friend. The warrior that was always so sure, always confidently laughing at things that scared Lana, looked worn and weary. She looked scared. "If it's like that, if we're going to be outnumbered by so many, if it comes to fighting like that, can we win?"

There was a moment for quiet. "No." Brighid pulled Lana close and wrapped her arm around her. "But we'll try. We'll fight until we fall and then we'll haunt them. We've an advantage if they come tae us here, with our trebuchet and our walls. We may be able tae defeat them without a pitched battle. With any luck we'll take out MacKenna without one and his shadows will leave. If not, we'll make them pay dearly afore the end."

Lana looked down to the camp at the base of rise. Soldiers and servants bustling and busying themselves with their tasks. Noam swinging hammers and heating steel to keep weapons and armour in the best shape. Dryad inspecting the wooden walls for problems after the storm. A tear filled her eye, and she felt her heart drop.

"They're all going to die, aren't they?"

Tinnion moved behind them and joined the embrace. "Don't linger on it, Lana. What will be will be. We can only face what's in front of us, and for now, that's the chance to train and prepare as best we can."

The friends stood in silence, feeling the weight of the moment. They held one another close until the smell of bacon and fresh baked bread floated from the inn.

"We'll be fine Lana..." Brighid eventually broke the silence. "We've the best warriors in all of Mortara and we've an alliance with the fae the likes o which has never been seen. MacKenna and the goddess have nae got a chance." She laughed, a warm, gentle laugh, but her eyes showed her sorrow.

They walked back to the inn and the promise of breakfast.

With breakfast done Lana and her friends made their way out to the square, training weapons in hand.

"We'll start with Wren, Yorane and Lana in the middle, defending. The rest of us will attack. Have you your blunted arrows, Tin? I think it's time tae add them tae the mix."

"I've a couple dozen, Brighid. That should be enough." The huntress gave her friends a wink and a smile.

Without warning or further talk, Daowiel launched herself toward Lana, her staff aimed low in a swinging arc. Lana jumped, clearing the princesses height from a standing position and swung her own staff on her return the ground. The princess parried with a smile. "The sylph have you leaping like a frog, Ògan. I shall have to aim higher or keep you rooted to the ground." Lana chuckled and gave a 'ribbit' before taking the initiative and launching a whirlwind of strikes toward her friend. In a moment Brighid was at the princesses side, her blades joining the fray.

Cinerea, Shayell and Anndra circled the sylph siblings who stood back to back, ready to defend one another at the first sign of attack. It was Anndra that moved first, leading with his shield, his sword point close to its edge. He kept his frame small as he moved, protecting himself from his lovers' staff, but as he came close enough to strike, he opened up. Lunging forward, first with the shield to throw the sylph off balance, he deflected her defensive blow with the boss of the shield and thrust at her with his sword. The tip of his wooden sword was met by the edge of Yorane's as the staff of Wren struck out toward the unsuspecting Shayell. The sylph had fought together since childhood and knew how to turn defence into attack in a moment by switching position. Yorane's second sword struck Anndra's arm, and the tuath moved back. "I see." He smiled at his brother to be and shook his arm. "Care tae try again?" His eyes glistened as he leapt back into the fight, this time more prepared, this time more able.

Tinnion launched an arrow at Lana, just as the defender was ducking an attack from Brighid's swords. An arrow that flew at speed, toward her heart. Lana switched her staff to her left hand, swinging it without resistance toward Daowiel's side. Her right hand coming over her body to pluck the arrow from the air. An arrow she grew into a blade and thrust at Brighid's stomach.

The warriors moved away from their smiling friend and sat on close by benches.

"I have never seen that done. Not in battle, not so quickly. Our staffs are quick to form because they have only ever been staffs since they were taken from the tree. For thousands of years they have known their form and they assume it quickly. To grow wood in that way, to do it with that kind of speed. You have excelled, Ògan."

"I've never been beaten like that, Lana. Except by the shadow, and her blow was not as deadly. I think you might be even quicker than the sgàil and I ken you've a sharper mind." Brighid rubbed her hand across her side.

An arrow flew through the air toward Lana's head. An arrow that was swatted aside before it hit its mark. "How? Twice in one day." Tinnion walked toward her friends and slumped on the bench. "Either you have found some hidden well of ability and speed or we're all still drunk from last night's wine."

"I don't know about a well, Tin. But I've been trying really hard to connect with the air like the sylph. I haven't managed to join with it yet but I've learnt to be more sensitive to it. I could feel your arrows and Brighid's swords and Daowiel's staff moving the air in front of them before they were close enough to touch me, so I had a little more time to react. And Brighid has always taught me to move and strike where there's less resistance. Now I can feel the air move. It's almost like I can see where that is and I move into the space." Lana sat cross-legged on the stone in front of her friends.

"I think our little sister might be all grown up now." Tinnion smiled. "Doesn't it make you proud?"

"Aye, it does that." Brighid's frown turned to a smile, and she clapped her hands to her thighs.

"Change o' plans, everyone. It's us all against our wee sister here. First tae mark her gets first pick o the platter at dinner!" The tuath swung her sword before she stood. It swiped through the air where Lana's head had been just a second before.

The door to the inn's common room opened and Cohade stood in the frame, his beard and hair combed, his armour set aside in favour of a tunic.

"Have ye a moment, Lana? I'd like tae talk."

"Of course, lord." Lana looked to Brighid for a moment, her brows raised, the tuath returned the look with a shrug.

"Would you like to go somewhere private, lord?" She stood as the man approached.

"No, there's nae need fer that. What I've tae say I can say in front o yer friends." The tuath lord gave his daughter a glance. "That's a braw head piece yer wearing, hen."

Brighid smiled. "Thank ye, da. It was a gift from Lana."

The lord nodded and cleared his throat. "I came tae say I'm sorry, Lana. I was ill-behaved in the meeting with yer friends. I'd had more tae drink than I should and I was drowning in thoughts of my wife up in the fortress, held prisoner by those killers. I saw ye as a chance tae end this, tae take the fight tae them. I was nae seeing the girl you are." He coughed again. "Sorry, I mean, the woman ye are. I hope ye'll forgive me, lass. I wis nae right tae say what I said."

Lana smiled at the lord and reached out her hand to him. He took it in his and she felt him shake. "I didn't hold it against you, lord. You've lost so much, you've fought so hard. I'd give anything to end this so we could all go to our homes and our families and friends and be happy again. So I might have done the same thing. Besides..." She turned to Brighid and scrunched her nose into a smile that made her friend laugh. "You're Brighid's dad and I could never stay upset at one of my big sisters' family."

The man looked to his daughter, his head tilted. "We're all one big family, da. The princess, the huntress and our wee sister, Lana. We've plenty o cousins too." The warrior looked around the room at her friends. "And that makes you our daddy!" A laugh went round the table and the tuath lord smiled.

"Will you join us for a drink, lord... Da?" Lana giggled.

"Aye. I think I need one havin' just adopted three lassies!" He pulled a chair to the table and sat as Lana poured him a cup of wine.

"To Fearran a Tuath and Clan MacFaern. And going home to the ones we love." Lana raised her cup.

"Tae loved ones here, them we knew afore and those we're growing tae know now." Cohade raised his cup with a nod to Lana.

The lord drained his cup and looked to his daughter. "I'll be off tae my bed, if ye'll excuse me. I'm grateful I got tae share this moment. Good night tae ye all, may yer heads be clear in the morn. Oidhche mhath, princess." He nodded to Daowiel.

"Oidhche mhath, lord." The princess replied with a smile.

"I didn't know your father could speak fae, Brighid."

"Aye, he's a good man, Lana. And not badly educated for a Tuath. I only hope ye get tae see his true self one day. He's not been quite that since Shadowatch."

Chapter Fifty

The Dark of the Moon

Lana dressed in the armour she took from the shadow assassin and strapped her belt to her waist, then she checked on Daowiel, who was snoring in the bed on the other side of the room. The princess was out for the night. She drew the curtain to one side and opened the window before climbing out on to the narrow ledge. She gently pushed the window closed with her foot and then floated to the ground. The sky was clear and stars glistened in the dark purple skies, but the moon was dark and no light touched the earth.

She covered the ground toward the rebel camp in very little time and, as she reached that point where her voice could be heard within, she planted her makeshift banner of parlance and called out.

"I am here to talk with the goddess. I know she is with you. I feel her here."

The camp woke, and Lana could see men running from their tents toward the north. She sat cross-legged on the ground and waited, watching through the darkness of night.

"You have courage, child. To come here alone." The same warrior and priest that had accompanied her to the talks flanked the goddess. "I gave you time you leave here and yet I still see your army on the plains and on the rise."

"There was a vote and a decision to stand. The army is loyal to the queen and confident in their ability." Lana's voice was flat and emotionless as she talked the way Aelwynne had taught her.

"I see things differently, child. But I will put that aside for now. Why have you come here?"

"For peace."

Chaint shook her head. "There will be no peace. That chance is lost to you. But you might be allowed to live." The goddess seemed to float toward her and stood, now, close enough to reach out and touch her. Lana swallowed hard. "I sense your fear, child. It gives me strength. Kneel to me, name me your goddess and you can live."

Lana's brow furrowed, and she stared into the goddess's eyes. "When I was young, in the stead, we used to celebrate the god days. Eight times a year we'd get together and leave a meal for you all and sing songs and celebrate your names. We don't worship you the way the fae do, but we honoured you. And I always thought you must be wonderful. I thought you must be so wise and so loving. Even you, even after all the stories of what you did here. And then I saw your sisters and Zeor give up their homes to give their children a chance to live and I thought you must all be so noble." Lana turned up her nose. "Then I met Khyione." The goddess before her snarled at the mention of that name and Lana paused. "He is not noble or loving or wise. He's a man that hurts the people he's supposed to love, he enslaves them to feel powerful. And now I've met you, and I see you're just the same. Torturing and killing and making people fear you. You want power, that's all you want, and you think you can get it through being scary and evil. You're nothing like you're s'posed to be. Nothing like your sisters."

The goddess moved so quickly that Lana barely saw it. She grabbed her by throat and bared her teeth with a growl. "I am not Khyione! I am not that."

"You live through fear and cruelty, you're exactly like him." Lana whispered as she struggled for air, her neck held tight, the goddess's nails drawing blood.

With a cry, the goddess threw her to the ground. "Listen now, Child, and learn of the world." The goddess leant over her as she spoke. "I am a god and gods live through devotion. I have the love of my children and that feeds me. I have the fear of the humans and that fills me. I have the hate of those who would take my place and that fuels me. And you, child. You know this, you feel this. You feed on the love of your people. I know this, I see it. You and I are the same. But I am not as Khyione is."

"He hurt you, didn't he?" Lana's eyes never left the goddesses as they spoke and she knew. She knew she had found a weakness. Chaint's face turned to a grimace.

"What did he do?" The slap was hard and unexpected, and Lana's cheek bled into her mouth.

"You will be silent and listen. You say there was a vote, you say the army is loyal to the queen. But they are not. Not all. The fae do not care for the queen. They stand here for you. They put their enmity and their fears aside for you. They would die for you. And they will die for you, slow, painful deaths. But it isn't just the fae, is it, child?" Lana's mouth opened, blood coating her lips. "You see it now, child. And there is one more thing for you to learn. Through your heart, I will have their devotion. And I will have your heart, whether it beats still in your chest or I tear it from you. It will be mine."

"Piuthardia. Màthair." The words came from the darkness of the east and the goddess spun her head. "Who is there? Is this some kind of trick, child?"

Lana's face was white as a full moon and her eyes were wide, she shook as she spoke. "It's not a trick... It's him... The obsidian man. He'll kill us."

The goddess looked into her eyes. "You speak the truth and you fear this man, more even than you fear me." She raised her arm to the east and called on her companions. "Find him. Kill him, bring his head to me."

The sgàil moved to intercept the obsidian man, and the goddess stood, drawing a knife from her belt. With Chaint no longer above her, Lana scrambled to her feet and reached for her staff.

A scream came from the darkness and Senath, the priest, staggered toward them, his head rolling on the grass before him. A moment later and Nydoalin fell to the ground, her blades loose at her side. Her head was intact, though bloody.

And then the man came from the shadows, a blade in each hand. He raised his right to Lana. "Piuthardia." Chaint turned to stare at Lana.

"He sees what I did not. Who is this man?"

"I… I don't know."

As the goddess turned her eyes back to the man, he leapt at her, his blades raised high, a cry of "Màthair!" On his lips. As he brought his blades down on the unprepared Chaint, they struck the staff of Lana an inch from the goddess's face. With a grunt, Lana pushed the blades and the man away and stood between him and Chaint. "I don't want to hurt you. I don't want to fight." Her words had no effect on the man, who crouched low to the ground with a hiss, as a snake preparing to strike. "Fine."

She ran toward the obsidian man, her staff ready, a stern look on her face. As the man sprung forward, she parried his blades to one side and brought her staff around to strike his ribs. The man let out a cry and then attacked with a speed that pushed Lana to her best. She parried his blows and deflected, but his ferocious attack pushed her back. The clear skies clouded over and thunder echoed over the plain.

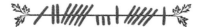

The growing storm disturbed the sleep of those in the waytown and the camp at the foot of the rise. Daowiel turned in her bed, her eye's opened to slits. "Close your mouth, Lana." She called into the darkness. With no answer, the princess turned back to the wall and closed her eyes again, pulling the blanket over her head. *That girl snores up a storm after a cup or two of wine, she thought.*

Lightening struck the ground at their feet as they fought, the goddess and Lana keeping the obsidian man at bay, though barely. Every time Lana pushed herself to go faster, to strike harder, her opponent matched her and then went further.

"The lightning, child. Use the lightning." Chaint called to Lana as she pushed the man away. "I am too weak in this body to bind him in the night."

"I can't. I don't know how." Lana called back, swinging her staff at the obsidian mans legs, trying to hamper his movement and slow him down. Lightning cracked the sky, stretching from fortress to rise.

"The tear of Qura, child. Open yourself to the tear."

Lana pushed herself once more, striking their opponent repeatedly, relentlessly, pushing him back to give herself space. Then she dropped to her knees and closed her eyes.

The tingling at the centre of Lana's forehead turned to an almost unbearable sensation of being repeatedly pricked with a thousand burning hot needles. She squeezed her eyes tight and clamped her jaw together, bringing her fingers to her temples in agony, but she continued to push her mind into the tear.

You have come, at last. The voice echoed through Lana's head.

Lana fell to the crystalline floor, exhausted and soaked in sweat. The pain was receding but her head still throbbed.

Which of our memories do you wish to share in?

She stood and looked around. Crystal walls that reminded her of honeycombs stretched from the floor and up, out of sight. Each one had a hazy, moving image within. The cool air within the vast hall helped to ease the pain and clear her head. *I need to learn how to control the lightning. Is there something you can do, or show me, that can help with that?*

I have told you, I am not a teacher. I cannot directly help you with that. I am only your guide to the memories. Do you wish to see the firstborn learning this ability?

Yes. Please.

The obsidian man stood over the fallen Chaint, his blades ready to strike as Lana pulled her mind from the tear. In that moment, she knew she had to act or see her chance of peace die.

She drew a deep breath and held it, drawing the energy from the surrounding storm into her body. Then she placed her palms in front of her mouth and exhaled. Lightning arced between her hands. Her body shook as she drew more energy to her, using her spark of lightning to attract more power, and when she felt she could handle no more, she threw her hands forward, sending a ball of sparkling, explosive light toward her attacker.

The blast hit the obsidian man in the chest, sending him backward to the ground with a cry that pierced her mind. The goddess scrambled to her feet, her head bloody, and walked over to the fallen man. Placing her hand to his head, she whispered to him. "Sleep now." The man's body went limp and his cries stopped. "You took your time, child." She turned to Lana, her lips drawn tight.

"It's not as if that was easy. I've never done it before and it hurt so much I thought I would die." Lana struggled to her feet as she spoke and picked up her staff, ready to defend herself.

"Hmm, you may yet. None of my sister's firstborn survive." The goddess smirked as she approached her saviour. "And what now, child? Now that you have found your true bite?"

Lana looked into the goddess's eyes and saw a sadness behind the hatred that had filled them before. "He's your son, isn't he?"

The goddess stared at her for a moment before responding. "You have saved my life twice this night. I would rip out your throat for daring to speak to me in this manner, had you not. But I owe you, so I will answer your questions. He is my son, though I thought him long dead."

"This... This is why you hate Khyione so much. He did something to you, to your son."

Chaint's eyes closed, and she took a deep breath. "He used me, and then, when my son was born, he took him and hid him away in the depths of Stonemount. I had no contact with him. I never saw him. I thought he must be long dead and yet here he is, and he tried to kill me."

"I'm… I'm sorry that you had to live with that… A man did that to my friend in the stead… Used her and left her with his child. He cut out her tongue. Then he tried to use me. He cut his initials into me as he lay on me." She placed her hand to her shoulder and rubbed at the scar.

"I have many regrets over the creation of the human male. Your story and mine are similar, and one I have heard and seen many times in my lifetime. You killed your attacker?" The goddess's voice was soft now, almost human.

"No, not me. He died on top of me. Before he could have me a bull ran at us and kicked his head." A tear ran down Lana's cheek as the memory took her.

A shadow caught Lana's eye and Nydoalin, now partially recovered, returned to the goddess's side as she spoke. "And so we come back to the question I asked when my son fell. What now?" Chaint caught Lana's gaze and held it, staring into her soul.

"I came for peace. What I want hasn't changed."

"I cannot give you the peace you want, you know this. I would lose the faith of my children, I would cease to exist."

Lana sighed. "I don't want to fight you. I don't want anyone to have to fight. But if I have to, to save my friends, I will. If we have to kill each other for peace, then that's what I'll do."

The goddess smirked. "No, I cannot fight you. I do not have the power, not in this body, at this time, to stand against you. Nor do you, my daughter!" The goddess turned to Nydoalin. "Put your blades down lest she kill you." The shadow warrior dropped her swords, a look of pained relief on her face.

"But I will make you an offer. Stand with me, child. Together, we will rule. You and I."

"No." Lana took a step back from the goddess. "I don't want to rule and I'd never let you cause so much pain as you have."

The goddess sneered. "You are naïve and allow your heart to lead you, but you have power and the love of your people. With my sisters gifts you have too much power. You will understand my hatred in time, as you see humanity's truth. Your eyes will be opened." Chaint reached out with great speed and placed her fingers to Lana's head with a smile. "You are not one of them now. No, Lana Ni Hayal. You are no longer a simple, dull human. So I will not fight, for I cannot win, and if you will not stand at my side, we will each swear an oath. I will leave this world with my son. I will return to the void and to my sisters. In return, you will allow my children to live. They will return to our island to live in peace and they will be allowed to worship me. Will you swear to this?"

Lana nodded. "I swear to you, if you do that, I will tell Aelwynne and everyone else that your children should be allowed to live in peace for as long as they leave us in peace."

"You understand, Lana, that your soul has been changed by my sisters. You can no more break an oath than my own children. I want you to understand this before I accept your word." The goddess placed her hand on Lana's chin and held it.

"I wasn't certain, but I thought that might be true. It doesn't change my answer." There was no fear in her voice, or her eyes. Chaint wouldn't try to hurt her, she wouldn't lie to her. She could see the fear in the goddess' eye.

"Then I accept your word, Lana. And I give you mine. I will leave before dawn and take my son with me."

"I will lead my sisters and brothers back to the island, Goddess." The shadow warrior knelt at her mother's feet. "I will have them build a new temple to you and we will feed you without fail as the sun sets on every day." Nydoalin's eyes were heavy with tears at her goddess's oath.

"No, Nydoalin. I said that we would each swear an oath. You must swear too. You are my daughter, my most trusted and beloved. You will swear an oath to protect and obey this child. For she carries all that remains on this world of my sisters and she will need you for what is to come."

"You wish me to serve this human, Goddess?" A scowl flashed across the sgàil's face.

"As though she were me, Nydoalin." The goddess's face was stern, a warning to her child.

"Then I swear to you. My goddess, that I will protect and obey this child."

"Then offer her your sword and your life, my daughter. While I still remain."

The warrior knelt before Lana, drawing her sword and offering the handle to Lana. "Will you accept my service?"

Lana took the sword and examined it. It was similar in construction to the blades she took from the shadow assassins and appeared as sharp as any blade she had seen. It reminded her, in some ways, of Brighid's own swords. Having examined the blade, she offered the hilt back to the sgàil, placing and holding the point to her own stomach. "I accept your service, Nydoalin. If it is offered in good faith."

The goddess laughed loudly. "Your mistress tests your honour at the first, my child. A brave move."

"If I were to kill you now, my goddess could stay and Mortara would be ours." The shadow fixed her dark eyes on Lana's.

"That's true. And you would have broken your vow and the promise your goddess has given." Lana nodded, returning the sgàil's gaze.

The warrior slowly took her blade and placed it back into its scabbard. "I have sworn my oath."

Lana smiled.

"There is one last thing to be done. You carry my sisters' gifts, you have been changed by them and you will grow to be more than you are, even now. I would give of myself what you have been given by them. Will you accept it?"

"I won't be possessed by you." Lana shook her head, but the goddess laughed.

"Child. I could not possess you if I wished to. No, my sisters' presence within you would not allow it. I offer you only what you have of them. A connection, a strength, an ability to use those gifts I gave to your ancestor."

"Then I accept." Lana nodded.

"You will sleep when my gift is passed to you. Nydoalin will return you to your people and see that you are safe." The goddess placed her fingers to Lana's temples and smiled. "When you wake, we will be joined, as you are joined with my sisters and we will all be whole once more."

Chapter Fifty-One

A Reckoning

"Lady Brighid. There is a shadow at the gate. They insist on speaking with the dryad princess. They have your friend with them." The guard stood breathless in the doorway of the inn.

"What do ye mean, they have my friend? Which friend?" Brighid was still half asleep, she had been woken by the banging on the door and was cursing as she opened it.

"The young lady that leads the fae, my lady. They have her."

"We'll be there." She slammed the door and ran to the top of the stairs and the room Lana shared with Daowiel. The door hit the wooden wall with a bang as she burst through it and pulled the blankets from Lana's bed. Daowiel, wakened by the noise, turned over.

"What are you doing, Brighid? Did she keep you awake with her drunken snoring too?"

"Damnit, Daowiel, open your eyes. She's not here. The shadows have her below. Get dressed. They insist on talking tae ye."

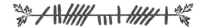

Daowiel walked through the gates, flanked by Brighid and Tinnion. Cinerea and Shayell followed close behind. Each bore their weapons, ready to attack the warrior that stood over Lana's body.

"You bring a flag of peace, yet you stand over our friend. Return her or die." The princess had a face as dark as the previous night's storm.

"We have a peace, though you do not know it. My lady will explain when she wakes. For now, I will surrender myself to you, and you alone, princess." Nydoalin's voice was flat and emotionless, though a smile touched her lips as her words caused confusion in those that approached her.

"Explain yourself, shadow." Brighid's voice bellowed in a way that would bring fear into any man's heart.

"My lady and my mother spoke late into the night. They agreed a peace between the sgàil and Mortara. I cannot speak for the humans you face. Perhaps they will continue this war, but my sisters and brothers have returned to our hideaway and my mother has joined her sisters in the void."

"You keep mentioning your lady. To whom are you referring?" Daowiel stepped forward, her staff resting across her shoulder.

"To my lady, here." Nydoalin gestured to Lana with a smile. "She accepted my sword and my service. I, like you all, have sworn my life to protect her. You might say that I am your sister." The shadow's smile widened as she taunted those she faced.

Brighid stepped forward, her blades glistening in the rising sun, but Daowiel brought her staff down to block the Tuath's path. "You say you are sworn to Lana. You say you will surrender to me until she confirms your tale? Then remove your armour and weapons and kneel before me. You will be held in our cell until Lana awakes."

The smile disappeared from Nydoalin's face, but she did as Daowiel asked and Lana was carried back to her room.

"Good morning, Lana. How do you feel?" Neve sat at the bedside, a seemingly ever-present smile on her face.

"I... I'm fine, I think, Neve. A few bruises and scratches is all. How... How did I get back here?"

"A shadow brought you to the gate below. Your friends carried you to your bed. I need to check on you, Lana. May I place my hands to your head?" Lana rubbed sleep from her eyes and nodded.

The nymph placed her fingers to Lana's temple and closed her eyes, gently probing the edges of Lana's mind with her own. She smiled as she removed her fingers and opened her eyes.

"We were worried that Chaint may have done something to you. But you are fine." She ran her thumb gently across Lana's cheek. "Your friends and the commanders await you in the common room. Apparently you have information they say is vitally important."

Lana sighed. "If I sneak out of the window again, could you just pretend I'm still sleeping? I don't think I'm ready for all the shouting and wagging fingers."

Neve gave a gentle laugh. "Yes, I believe you are right. There will be some shouting and pointing. But they are friends, Lana, and they care about you. They are worried and worried people shout. You know this already."

"Yeah." Lana nodded sullenly. "I'd best put some clean clothes on."

The common room was set as it had been for the meeting earlier in the moon and was full. Platters of bread and cheese were on the table with pitchers of soft cider and fresh water from the Alawe. There was a space between Brighid and Daowiel, and Lana clambered over it, relieved that her friends would be at her side. She smiled timidly at the people around the table and took some bread and cheese before pouring a cup of water. She pulled some bread from her roll and popped it in her mouth. "I guess I slept through the sausages, huh?" Brighid squeezed Lana's knee under the table, a friendly warning not to make too many jokes.

"You have news for us, it seems." Aelwynne sat at the head of the table today, signalling her intent to take control.

"Yes." Lana lowered her head, her smile gone. "Chaint is gone and the sgàil won't fight us. I swore we would let them leave Mortara and live in peace, too."

"You gave promises to the goddess and sgàil without my consent, nor the queen's authorisation. By what authority did you do this?"

Lana looked at her mentor and then to each of the soldiers at her side. She looked at Shayell and Liayol across the table and she shifted in her seat. Sitting straight and clearing her throat. She looked back to Aelwynne, her gaze firm. When she spoke, she did so with the authoritative tone she had used outside Dornberg when confronting the sheriffs. "By my own, lady Aelwynne. The only authority the goddess was willing to accept." Brighid squeezed her knee again and Lana glanced at her, giving her a smile. "I know that this is not normal, my lady. I know that many of you will believe that I have overstepped and that I have done wrong. But you taught me that we must know the person we sit opposite. You told me that we must use our knowledge and our good sense to achieve our goals, to get those things we want or need. You told me that I could not do things as you do and that I must find my way. I am still learning, my lady. But my mentor is the best in Mortara, and I believe this peace I have claimed with your teachings serves Mortara and our queen well." Brighid's squeezing became a gentle tapping.

Aelwynne nodded, her face showing no emotion. "There is a sgàil warrior in our cell. She claims to serve you."

"Yes, my lady. She is sworn to me. I do not like it, nor do I like her too much, but she gave her oath to both myself and her goddess. She can be trusted."

The voice of the queen turned to the leaders of the army. "We have a choice to make, gentlemen. Meet me in my quarters." The heads of each force, other than the dryad, nodded and left the inn, leaving only Aelwynne, Lana, and her friends.

"You wouldn't have let me go if I had talked to you. None of you would have. And you all swore to die protecting me. I couldn't let that happen. I couldn't let you die or get hurt, even. I can't live without you all. You're my family and you all know what I'll do to protect my family. I'm sorry that I hurt you. I'm sorry I let you down, but I'm not sorry that I did it. I had to." Lana had shifted again, her confident tone and straight back gone, her eyes lowered.

"I cannot say that I am not hurt, Ògan. I am hurt that you chose not to trust me. But I cannot be angry with you without being doubly so with myself. I know you. I should have known what you would do." Daowiel turned to face her friend as she spoke.

"It's not that I don't trust you, Daowiel. Any of you." Lana looked around the table at her friends. "In fact, it's the opposite. I do trust you, I trust you to do what you say and I know you will do it very well, because you always do. That's why I couldn't tell you. I knew what I had to do, and I trusted that you would do what you felt you needed to do, too. I wouldn't have blamed you. I wouldn't have been mad, because I know that you would have been doing it to protect me."

"And you did what you did to protect us." Tinnion reached her hand across the table to her friend. Lana stretched her hand out too and the two friends touched fingers with a smile. "I understand, and I'll get over the hurt."

"Aye, me too, Lana. Though I'm not keen on the idea o' that shadow being 'round." Brighid's hand joined her friends across the table and was joined by Daowiel and Cinerea. Lana looked to Aelwynne, but her mentor only stood. "I have important matters to take care of." And with those words, Aelwynne left the inn.

"Dinnae worry, Lana. She'll come 'round." Brighid smiled.

Chapter Fifty-Two

A Rebellion Failed

In the end the battle for Northfort was little more than a scuffle. When the rebel army saw the army of humans and fae approaching and realised that the sgàil were no longer with them, most of them dropped their arms and fell to their knees to surrender. MacKenna alone pushed his clansmen to fight while all others ran. The noam, Grant, gained the gratitude of Clan MacFaern when he placed himself between the lord Cohade and the charging horse of a desperate MacKenna. But it was Brighid that took the rebel lord's head and ended the uprising once and for all. Those few too slow or too stubborn to give up once their lord had fallen died quickly and the army of the queen marched toward Northfort with little more than a few scratches.

With the fortress liberated and secured, the sylph, most of the noam and the dryad returned to their homes and Tinnion, excited by the new relationship she had with the trees since her day with Lana, took the bridge home to Butterholt. Lana made promises to visit her and Daowiel before the samhradh passed and then travelled north, to the fortress, with the staff and small guard that hadn't marched on the rebel army.

They gave Lana her own room in the keep, less glamorous than the one she had in the queen's palace but comfortable all the same. Nydoalin had been housed in a smaller servant's room beside her. Her friends were roomed along the same corridor while Cohade, Aelwynne, Anndra, MacHuran and MacAllister were one floor above them in those suites previously occupied by the Tay and his closest men.

Aelwynne had avoided or ignored Lana's presence and her petitions to talk about what had happened since the morning in the inn, and that had badly affected Lana's mood. In the last three days Lana had locked herself in her room, ignoring calls to the dining hall and the knocks at her door. She insisted, with each knock from her friends, that she was alright, that she would be back in good spirits and amongst them the following day. But when the following day came, her door was still locked.

On the fourth day, a knocking woke her from her sleep. She turned over, set to ignore it, but the voice that came through the wood wasn't one that would be ignored. "Open this door, Lana Ni Hayal. I am done with this petulance. You are a guest in the home of a Tay and you are behaving like a sullen child."

Lana climbed from her bed and unlocked the door to let her mentor in. Then she returned to her bed and sat on its edge. Her hair, wild and knotted, her bloodshot eyes surrounded by dark circles and her nose and top lip encrusted with snot.

"You look a state and you stink. When was the last time you washed?" Lana shifted back on her bed and leaned against the wall, crossing her legs and pulling her nightdress down to her feet.

"Why does it matter?" Her voice was hoarse and barely reached a whisper.

Aelwynne turned back to the door and closed it gently, locking it behind her. She moved to the bed and sat on it at the foot. "Your friends are worried about you. I'm worried about you. This isn't like you at all, Lana. When you're upset or angry, you tend to show it and have done with it. So what is this all about?"

"I'm usually angry at people that have done horrible things. I'm usually upset at people that hurt my friends. This time I'm angry and upset at you and I can't just shout at you or turn your ship into planks or burn your keep down." Lana wiped her nose on her sleeve, though it made little difference to her appearance. Aelwynne sighed.

"You explained why you did what you did, and I listened. Will you listen if I explain why I was so distant from you?"

Lana nodded without speaking and Aelwynne shifted on the bed to sit as Lana was, against the wall and by her apprentice's side.

"There was concern before we left Southport, concern that in a matter of moments, you were able to call upon an army of fae that would follow you into battle. Concern that after thousands of years of enmity, the dryad and noam would put their differences aside and stand together. Not because there was a war in the north that threatened the queen's reign, but for you. For a milkmaid from a small stead in the middle of nowhere, for an apprentice with no formal title or standing in Mortara. But the queen and I both spoke against the concerns. We said that you were as loyal a person as I. We said that no matter the stories about your abilities and the army that marched for you, you would never act outside the queen's wishes. You would never defy my orders nor undermine my position as queen's voice. We assured all those that worried that despite the loyalty shown to you, all those that marched north with us were entirely loyal to the queen. That there were no divided loyalties, that thoughts of such a thing were nonsensical. That, in fact, all of those agreeing to join you were simply your friends, people that had known you and loved you for some time.

And then you took Glamithren. You. Almost single-handedly, took a tuath fortress. Stories of your power grew, as did the nature and strength of your powers within those stories. But, that was okay because you rescued the gesith and he could take back control of his city within moments of being free. We could quell any other stories or worries. But then Devlin tried to name you his heir, and the concerns that followed your acquisition of an army resurfaced.

Devlin wasn't a long-term friend of yours. He is an elder of the tuath, a lord of great standing and some renown, and he offered you power. The very thing those with doubts were concerned you would grab."

"But I turned that down. I don't want to be gesith or anything else." Lana brought her knees up to her chest and wrapped her arms around them.

"I know. And I was able to stop the talking because you did. And I had to do the same again after the failed peace talks, where you saw what I could not. But when you went to Chaint and made a peace without my knowledge, I couldn't stop the talking. I couldn't stop the rumours. Half the men think you're a god reborn. Some fear you and some love you. You saved their lives, but you also forced Chaint to leave the world. In their minds, you must be extremely powerful and the gods themselves must fear you."

"That's silly. I'm not a god and I don't want any power. I'm just me. I just want my friends and family to be safe. I don't care about money or titles or land or anything else like that."

Aelwynne touched her fingers to Lana's and smiled, a bittersweet smile. "I know, Lana. And if that was the only problem..."

"What? What is it?" Lana opened her hand a little, moving it into Aelwynne's.

"If I tell it doesn't leave this room, not one word of it. Not to Brighid or the princess or anyone. Do you swear?" Aelwynne lowered her voice and Lana nodded her response.

"The Princess, Shayell, Yorane. They all love you. They'd do anything for you and everyone knows it. But we were able to pass that off. They're fae, and they're your friends. Like I said, no divided loyalties. But Brighid and Tinnion and then Devlin. They're people with titles, with status. Brighid and Tinnion were the queen's own choices and we all see that they would give their lives in your defence. That's divided loyalty, Lana. What if... What if, for some reason, you stood against the queen? Whose side would they stand at? They serve the queen, but they love you. I would bet they would stand with you. And that's a problem. Not that anyone thinks it would ever happen. But for Qilan it's a problem because he has to think about these things. And for the people that think you're already too influential? It's something they'll use against you and the queen." She paused and took a deep breath, lacing her fingers between Lana's.

"And then there's me, Lana. I'm the queen's voice. I can't have any loyalty other than to the queen. She must always be first in my mind. But you've changed that. That's why I avoided you. That's why I couldn't speak to you. Because I can't be the queen's voice when I'm thinking of you and how important you've become to me. I see you with Brighid, Tinnion and the Princess and I become envious. I even feel myself being jealous of them and I realise how badly I want to have that same friendship with you, because I feel that love for you. But I have to stay distanced, no matter how I feel, and that's difficult with you."

"I'm sorry, Aelwynne. I didn't know. I thought... I thought you hated me after what I did. You looked so angry." Lana squeezed her hand gently in Aelwynne's and then, without warning, jumped up off the bed and ran to the window.

"What's wrong, Lana. Have I said too much?" Aelwynne bit her lip.

"No. I just realised what you said when you came in. I haven't left my bed or washed for four days. I must smell really bad and there's you sitting so close to me and... I feel stupid. I've been stupid."

Aelwynne let out a little laugh and then closed her lips tight to stop laughing more. "You do smell quite bad." She wrinkled her nose and Lana laughed, the tension between them gone for a moment. "I've things I have to do. Now we've talked. Will you join us for dinner tonight? Brighid misses you and Cohade's been wanting to talk with you."

Lana nodded. "I'll come. If I can find enough water to get clean again."

Aelwynne walked over to her apprentice and brushed some of the hair from her face with her finger. "You'll need to find a good strong brush, too." She gave her a warm smile. "You forgive me?"

"Of course." Lana tried to look sweet, but her wild hair and bloodshot eyes made her look more crazy.

"Perhaps you could go to the waytown and stand under the waterfall..." Aelwynne laughed and made her way to the door, unlocking it. She paused as she opened it and turned back to Lana. "When I taught you to use what you know of the person opposite you to your advantage, I didn't mean for you to use it against me... Though you made me very proud in that meeting, you had the commanders eating out of your palm."

"I had the best teacher." Lana smiled.

Chapter Fifty-Three

Recreating the North

When Lana entered the dining hall, a hush spread across the tables. She had taken Aelwynne's joking advice and travelled the bridge to the waytown, spending an age in the cold, fresh waters of the waterfall. It had washed away her gloom as well as her smell and so the young woman that stepped into the room was bright, well groomed and wearing her favourite blue dress. Her eyes sparkled as much as the stone at her forehead and the jewels around her neck. She looked every bit a high lady, perhaps even a princess. The jaws of the men fell open when she smiled across the room at her friends. They had all seen her in the camp and on the journey north, but she had always worn her leathers and had the dirt of the day on her and she always tied up her hair. Her transformation had them transfixed.

"Ah, Lana hen. Come on, lass, take a seat here at ma table." Cohade stood and gestured for her to join them at the lord's table.

Supplies were still low and dinner was a small fare but there was ale and wine a plenty in the cellars and it didn't take long for the hall to be filled with songs and tales, as the warriors and soldiers drank the stress of the war and the day away.

"So, Lass. What's with the fancy clothes and touched up hair? Are ye looking for a man tae bring ye back hame tae Fearann a Tuath and give ye a family?" Cohade poured Lana another cup of wine as he spoke.

"No!" Lana's cheeks flushed. "I just like wearing nice dresses. I grew up on a farm and dreamt of having nice clothes. Now I have them, I like to make the most of it." She paused. "What do you mean, bring me back home?"

"Well, look at ye, hen. If yer no tuath I'm a dryad! We joked about adopting ye but in truth ye could pass for ma daughter in any company and I'd be glad of it an all."

"Knowing your daughter, I take that as a great compliment, lord. She is a beautiful person and the strongest I know." She turned to Brighid and gave her a smile.

"Aye, she is that. She left a trail of men as long as the southern road behind her when she left Lochmead. All heartbroken, thinking they had missed a chance of her hand."

"She left a few in Southport too, lord. Especially..." Brighid pulled her friend toward her and playfully covered her mouth.

"Wheesht, Lana. Ma father does nae need tae hear yer stories about me. He's wanting tae know more about you." Brighid laughed as she let her friend go.

"It seems that I'm sworn to secrecy on that thought, lord." Lana chuckled. "Perhaps another time." She gave Cohade an exaggerated wink and bumped her shoulder to Brighid's.

"Lord Cohade's thought is interesting, Lana. What do you know of your families history?" Aelwynne sat back in her chair, her half-filled cup on her lap.

"Not a lot. I know my dad grew up in the stead and his dad too. I think my mam's mam came from somewhere else, though. I never knew her. But I know my mam wasn't born on the stead. I figured they were just from a different farm in the hold, though. Why would they go to Butterholt if they were from a different hold? There's nothing there, 'cept cows and trees."

"Who knows, Lana? Perhaps 'nothing' is what they were looking for. There are plenty of people in the world that have reason to want to be in a quiet place out of the way." Aelwynne smiled.

"Aye, that's why I like tae go tae Eastmarch. Not, a sign of civilisation." Brighid laughed and the tuath around the table all joined in, raising their cups and spilling as much ale as they drank. Aelwynne shook her head with a smirk.

"So you see, Lana. Ye could be one of us! Perhaps I even knew your gran in ma youth." Cohade stood and raised his cup. "Tae Lana, o' the Tuath!" A cheer went up around the room and the lord sat down with a grin. "There, it's settled! They all agree you're one o' us."

"You're drunk again, da. Have a cup o' water next round." Brighid laughed.

The following morning saw many of the same people sat around a table in the library. Aelwynne sat at one end, Qilan and Lana at her side. Cohade, MacAllister and MacHuran sat at the opposite end of the table with Brighid, Anndra, Wren and Grant beside them. Nydoalin sat at the edge of the room, seemingly asleep.

"I have spent much time considering the possible solutions and problems of rebuilding the northern taydom and believe I have a temporary solution that will suit all. At least until the Queen can examine the issue and effect more permanent and official change." Aelwynne had adopted her formal tone and sat straight in her chair, a pile of papers before her. "As you know, I am able to name stewards, temporary custodians of lands and those things that lie within. It is for the Queen, though, to decide on titles and permanent placements. I have permission, on this occasion, to name a steward for each hold vacated by the war and for the taydom itself. As you can imagine, this has been no easy task."

Those present nodded their agreement.

"Still, I think you will be pleased." Aelwynne spread a map of the northern taydom across the table. "First, let us deal with the southern holds. They were, in fact, the easiest as there is little change. Only Lord Devlin's neighbouring holds fell to the rebels' attack or their promises, thanks to Lana and her friends. So I have simply named Lord Devlin as steward of those holds. All else remains the same."

"Aye, that seems fair. Devlin is as good a man as ye get in the southern holds. I couldn't see a better choice." Cohade nodded his agreement.

"In Fearann a Liath, only one lord rode in the Queen's name and though few fell to the army, one or two pledged themselves to the rebel cause. Lord MacHuran. You answered lord Cohade's call to arms and rode into battle where your fellows would not. I name you steward of those holds vacated in Fearann a Liath."

"I'm honoured, Lady." MacHuran bowed his head.

"Now to the west. Fearann a Tuath was by far the worst effected by the war. Those holds that did not swear to the rebels have been destroyed. That leaves a lot of land and very few lords or clan chiefs. So I have made decisions that may cause brows to raise, but they are my decisions and will stand until the Queen reviews them." Aelwynne looked around the room for any signs of dissent.

"Aye, we'd not argue with you, lady Aelwynne. You're the Queen's Voice and you've shown yourself considerate and fair in this." Cohade spoke authoritatively.

"Good. Then in the west, from Shadowatch to the southern shore, Lady Wren will stand Steward." That news did raise brows amongst the older lords, but they all nodded their acceptance.

"The central holds, those that include Lochmead, will be watched over by your heir, Lord Cohade. Anndra will be steward there. The Northern plains will be held by Lady Brighid and the southern plains by MacAllister."

"I've no title nor standing in any clan, lady. Perhaps the plains should all be held by the Lady Brighid." MacAllister shook his head.

"You have standing with those lords around you and with me, MacAllister. And you hold the title Steward as of today."

The warrior's cheeks flushed a little, and he bowed his head. "Thank you, m'lady." Aelwynne and Lana both smiled at the newly named steward.

"If anything, I'd rather it the other way round, MacAllister. I've no real desire to be gesith." Brighid lowered her head as she spoke.

"You wish to refuse position, Brighid?" Aelwynne frowned.

"No, Aelwynne. I'll not refuse, as you need a steward. But I'd ask you tae advise the queen of better choices when it comes tae naming a permanent gesith."

Aelwynne nodded with a sigh. "Lastly, then the lands around Northfort and the stewardship of the Taydom fall to the man that stood strong against the enemy. Lord Cohade." Aelwynne bowed her head to the clan chief opposite her.

"Thank you, Aelwynne. I'll dae what I can." Cohade bowed his head in return.

"I take it then that there is no objection to my decisions?" A smile flashed across the ladies face.

"None from me, Lady Aelwynne. Though I've a request tae make. You cannae make gesiths or a tay, and that's right enough but this noam here saved my skin at the last, and I'd see him named ser. I could dae that my own self and he'd hold title in Lochmead that'd be honoured across the north, but I'd rather he be recognised throughout Mortara."

Aelwynne paused for a moment before nodding her consent. "Very well, there's no land for me to offer and no purse I can give but I'll happily do as you wish and recognise his title. With that all done, I will be leaving in the morning. I must talk with the queen and my father and I miss my home. I offer you the use of the army that marched north with me, Lord Cohade. To assist you in your work and aid in keeping the peace while you rebuild. I will take only my personal guard with me, a half-dozen men and commanders Crurith and Qilan. Those left here will be under your command, lord."

"That's kind and very helpful, lady." Cohade nodded.

"Can I speak to you, Aelwynne?" Lana paused at her mentor's door.

"Of course, Lana."

"Go on to my room and start packing things, Nydoalin. Thank you." Lana nodded to the fae who had almost literally become her shadow, following her every step.

They sat on Aelwynne's bed, facing one another, Lana's head lowered.

"Are you alright, Lana? You look upset."

"I'm just... I've been thinking about everything that's happened since we left Southport and about what you said in my room. And before that, even when you said you didn't think I'd be your apprentice anymore when we got back to the palace."

"I didn't think you enjoyed it, Lana, and I didn't really think it was working for you. You proved me wrong on that last part, though, with what you did." Aelwynne leaned forward, trying to catch Lana's eye.

"Maybe, but I think you're right. I don't think it's good for you or for me to stay as your apprentice. It's making you doubt yourself and that's making you very sad. And there's something I feel that I need to do. When I attacked Glamithren, I was angry, very angry, and I did things I didn't need to do. Things I shouldn't have done. I broke the walls and burnt down the keep and the things I did killed people that didn't deserve to die. I feel horrible about that, Aelwynne. I think I should go back there and help Lord Devlin and his people rebuild. Properly rebuild, not just patching things up. I'd like to try to make up a little for what I did there. I don't want to be his heir or anything. I just want to help."

Aelwynne reached a hand out to Lana, which she took with a sorrowful smile. "You don't have to leave the palace because of me, Lana. I don't want you to leave. This difficulty I have is mine. It's for me to resolve."

"But I think I need to, Aelwynne. I need to make up for my behaviour. And I can visit you any time. I can come to the ash in the palace garden and we can sit and talk 'til the sun goes down."

Aelwynne smiled. "I'd like that. The garden is beautiful in samhradh, so many flowers, so many colours and scents."

Lana leant forward, placing her forehead gently to Aelwynne's, and the two sat in silence.

EPILOGUE

Cat awoke, cold and soaked to the skin. She lay across a broken door surrounded by flotsam. There were no signs of Laywyn or Xentan, the ship was gone. Sunk to the depths of the ocean. There were boats in the distance, or maybe ships. She couldn't tell this far away. She grabbed at a piece of wood, part of the hull perhaps, and began to paddle with it toward the north, hoping one of the boats would pick her up and take her back to land.

THANKS

Writing a book is never something you do alone. Not really. And as such there are people I'd like to thank for this book.

Firstly, my best friend Allan. He's my brother in the same way that Brighid, Tinnion, Daowiel, Selene and Aelwynne are Lana's sisters. He encourages me and, on those moments that I have real belief in what I do it's because of him.

Then there are those that have had a more direct involvement in the creation of this book. As with the Elemental Stone before this, I was very lucky to have people willing to read through my earlier drafts and give me their thoughts. Hilary Taylor and Michael Ferry both did the work this time and their feedback helped me take my ramblings and create what you have just read.

A special mention to the members of Blyth Book Club, particularly Lynn Pattinson whose reading of The Elemental Stone led to a slightly hidden appearance in this book (did you see it, Lynn?). And to Loz Pattinson who's new found enthusiasm for fantasy makes me smile. Lastly, in this section, there is Stephanie Jones. Who, probably without realising it, made me open up the book that has been sitting in my cloud for more than a year and get it done! She also jumped in with a last minute proof read for which I am very grateful. Thank you!

And then to other people. People I don't know but without whom I couldn't have finished what I started. The wonderful people at Literature and Latte for Scrivener. By far my favourite writing software.

The good folks at Pro Writing Aid, for the software that caught so many of my mistakes (though I've no doubt there are still a few!).

The people at Procreate and Affinity Design who's software I used for all of the doodles.

And the people at Atticus.io I hated formatting and, what's more, I sucked at it until I found your software and let that do all the hard work for me!

So there you go. Though I wrote every word and drew every doodle, I was never alone in it and could never have completed it without all of these people. Now you know who to blame!

Printed in Great Britain
by Amazon

24407158R00229